New
Writing
4

edited by

A. S. BYATT
and
ALAN HOLLINGHURST

V

V I N T A G E
in association with
The British Council

Published by Vintage 1995

2 4 6 8 10 9 7 5 3

Selection, Introduction and Editorial Matter
© The British Council 1995
edited by A. S. Byatt and Alan Hollinghurst
For copyright of contributors see page x

The rights of the editors and the contributors to be identified as the
authors of these works have been asserted by them in accordance
with the Copyright, Designs and Patents Act, 1988

Vintage
Random House, 20 Vauxhall Bridge Road, London SW1V 2SA

Random House Australia (Pty) Limited
20 Alfred Street, Milsons Point, Sydney
New South Wales 2061, Australia

Random House New Zealand Limited
18 Poland Road, Glenfield,
Auckland 10, New Zealand

Random House, South Africa (Pty) Limited
PO Box 337, Bergvlei, South Africa

Random House UK Limited Reg. No. 954009

A CIP catalogue record for this book
is available from the British Library

ISBN 0 09 953231 X

Printed and bound in Great Britain by
The Guernsey Press Co. Ltd., Guernsey, Channel Islands

New Writing 4 is the fourth volume of an annual anthology, which has promoted the best in contemporary literature. It brings together some of our most formidable talent, placing new names alongside more established ones, and includes poetry, essays, short stories and previews of novels in progress. Distinctive, innovative and entertaining, it is essential for all those interested in British writing today. *New Writing 4* is published by Vintage in association with the British Council.

A. S. Byatt studied at Cambridge and taught at the Central School of Art and Design before moving to University College London to teach English and American literature. She is now a full-time writer. Her first novel, *The Shadow of the Sun*, appeared in 1964, and was followed by *The Game* (1967), *The Virgin in the Garden* (1978), *Still Life* (1985), *Possession* (1990), which won the Booker Prize for Fiction, and *Angels and Insects* (1992). Her collection of short stories, *Sugar and Other Stories*, appeared in 1987 and a volume of critical essays, *Passions of the Mind*, in 1991. In 1990 she was chairman of judges of the European Literary Prize. Her most recent books are *The Matisse Stories* (1994) and *The Djinn in the Nightingale's Eye* (also in 1994), both collections of stories.

Alan Hollinghurst was born in 1954. He is the author of two novels, *The Swimming-Pool Library* (1988), which won a Somerset Maugham Award and the E. M. Forster Award of the American Academy of Arts and Letters, and *The Folding Star* (1994), which was shortlisted for the Booker Prize. His translation of Racine's *Bajazet* was published in 1991. He has been on the staff of *The Times Literary Supplement* for thirteen years, and is the editor of the annual literary competition, *Nemo's Almanac*.

PREFACE

New Writing 4 is the fourth volume of an annual anthology founded in 1992 to provide a much-needed outlet for new short stories, work in progress, poetry and essays by established and new writers working in Britain or in the English language. Although *New Writing* is designed primarily as a forum for British writers, the object is to present a multi-faceted picture of modern Britain, and contributions from English-language writers of non-British nationality will occasionally be accepted if they contribute to this aim. It was initiated by the British Council's Literature Department, with the intention of responding to the strong interest in the newest British writing not only within Britain but overseas, where access to fresh developments is often difficult. Thus *New Writing* is not only a literary annual of important new work, but also an international shop window. Like all shop windows, it can only display a selection of the wealth of goods available within, a sampling of the literature which is being produced in Britain today. The aim is that, over the years, and through changing editorships, it will provide a stimulating, variegated, useful and reasonably reliable guide to the cultural and especially the literary scene in Britain during the 1990s: a period when, to quote Malcolm Bradbury in the first issue, walls are crumbling, connections fracturing, and bridges being precariously crossed.

The first volume, which appeared in 1992, was edited by Malcolm Bradbury and Judy Cooke, the second, *New Writing 2*, by Malcolm Bradbury and Andrew Motion and the third, *New Writing 3*, by Andrew Motion and Candice Rodd.

New Writing 5, edited by Christopher Hope and Peter Porter, will appear in March 1996. Though work is commissioned, submissions of unpublished material for consideration (stories, poetry, essays, literary interviews and sections from forthcoming works of fiction) are welcome. Two copies of submissions should be sent: they should be double-spaced, with page numbers, and accompanied by a stamped addressed envelope for the return of the material, if it cannot be used. They should be sent to

New Writing
Literature Department
The British Council
10 Spring Gardens
London SW1A 2BN

The annual deadline is 31 March.

CONTENTS

CONTENTS

CONTENTS

INTRODUCTION

BOOKS OF THIS kind are almost wholly unpredictable. They are brought into being by an invitation, or series of invitations: to the editors to edit, to a small list of writers the editors hope will contribute, and to British writers in general to send in prose and poetry of all kinds. Unlike most anthologies, whose editors range over a more or less defined field of work that already exists, *New Writing* is an occasion, an opportunity, for a body of unknown work to assemble itself. It can't be planned. Many of the authors A. S. Byatt and I invited to contribute did so, though often in unexpected ways: a poet would send a novel extract, a novelist an essay or a poem; they saw the opportunity themselves to experiment or break the mould in our pages. Others promised work which never materialised; others didn't bother to reply to our letter. The overall picture of activity was significant – the book was to be a sampler of its moment, and one that grew richer and more surprising as we read and read through the hundreds of submissions from authors old and young, well-known and (in many cases) quite unknown to us. We are delighted to include a high proportion of work by 'new' writers – those who have only published one book or who have yet to do so. But we have all along been careful not to equate the *New* in our title exclusively with youth. The past couple of years have seen high-profile promotions of Young British Novelists (discussed by A. S. Byatt in the closing essay of this book), and 'New Generation' poets, both commendable exercises, both well represented here, but both tending to imply that new life is only to be found in the work of the under-forties or under-thirties. Writing, of course, is not less new for being mature, and it is a strength of this collection that the ages of its youngest and most senior contributors differ by half a century. I believe the whole book to be original, catholic, undogmatic. Our criteria for inclusion (though never so baldly formulated by us) have been vision and voice: the ability to surprise and reveal and move, coupled with a love of language and a relish for form, however experimental. It is new writing, and it will last.

Alan Hollinghurst

Lawrence Norfolk

THE POPE'S RHINOCEROS
*Extract from a novel to be published by Sinclair-Stevenson,
1995*

THIS SEA WAS once a lake of ice. High mountains overlooked a glacial plain frosted with snow and scoured by the
freezing wind. Granite basins curved up from under the ice-
tonnage to rim it with irregular coasts. In ages still to come,
boulder waste and till will speak of the icepack's tortuous
inching over buried rock and sandstone; moraines and drumlins of advances and recessions which gouge out trenches and
shunt forward ridges. The sea-floor here was prepared long
before there was a sea to cover it, and in the interim came
the singular governance of ice.

Fault-lines and fractures healed and welded, grew invisible
until the Gulfs of Bothnia and Finland, of Riga and Gdansk
were indistinguishable from the central basin which joined
them. Northerly blizzards left their drifts of snow which
compacted down and thickened until the earth's very crust
tilted under the weight. Veins of frozen oil ran like the haw-
sers of a ruined fleet, looping and meeting in the dark far
below the surface. Grit speckled the icepack as though
blasted out of the earth and suspended in mid-air, boulders
shattered and hung immobile in the dark of this catastrophic
freeze. Nothing breathed here. This must once have been the
deadest place on earth.

This surface interruption: a pale disc of light germinating
in the snow-flecked sky suggests a radical tilt to the axis
below, gales cede to gusts and vicious whirlwinds, ice giants
shout in the night. An inch of silt marks a thousand years,
an aeon means a single degree of arc and by this scale a thaw
is under way. There will be a century of centuries of snarling

1

ice, an age of glacial strain until the first crystal's glistening melt to liquid spreads and seeps and creeps north across the frozen surface to make of it a mirror wherein the sun might see its face. Light slaps and dazzles the ice, sends thick fronts of heated air against the polar cold. Melt-waters dribble between ice and rock, refreeze and melt again. The nights are cold enough to strip the lungs of any beast foolish enough to venture on this wasted acreage, the wind which blasts across the vista turns hide and flesh to stone. An iceblink sky glares down at the nights' reverses which are boulder waste, scree and brine cells locked in rime. There are shelves where the sun never reaches and salts forced by the pressure lie as powder on the surface.

But the days grow longer, water-sheets spread, mean temperatures rise and vent mists which boil off the blazing ice. Secret cables of water are trickling down and prising the frigid bole from its case of rock, meeting and joining on the stony floors which the sun cannot find. A thousand miles of ice floats in an inch of water. Different orders are coming down the line. Crevasses and canyons rive the surface and snake forward cutting loose immense crystals which shatter and collapse. Water runs at the bottom of ravines a thousand metres deep, eating out the lowest levels of the icepack and rising until the whole is cut with rivers fed by their own corrosive increase. The landscape resounds with the crash of ice-columns and ice-arches, the unheard thunder of a million wrecks. Glassy ridges sink and settle in pools which lengthen and rise, become fissures until this territory of waste is neither solid nor liquid but an archipelago of drifting icebergs dwindling in a sea of their own dissolved bodies and a fog so thick with damp it is neither air nor water. Unhinged mountains collide in the green subsurface light and send up rafts to the surface where the sun can melt them. Small floes bob and rock in the water's cradle while sunbeams draw them into the sky as clouds which spread in filaments, snap, and shrink to nothing. Where there was ice, is water.

Still, this is an empty expanse. More temperate, more fluid, but the gulfs sprawl north and east, the central body curls south then west much as they did before. The change is local, confined to the westernmost strait, or most perceptible there. Are the northern mountains less towering, the Åland islands less numerous? Is the Landsort Deep sunk lower than before? The rise in water level is a matter of feet in a landscape of leagues, the product of differing coefficients – water expands, ice contracts – and yet this alone is not enough to drown islands and creep up cliffs. The movement runs deeper, reaches back further. A compacted weight has lifted, an oppressed floor is rising, tilting back and tipping water south and west towards the Belts and Sound of Zealand. Low rocky sills seem to shrink before the slow surge of the lake waters, are overrun as the thaw reaches the northernmost coves. The breach is made and water races west to join the seething grey of an ocean which has waited some million years for the arrival of this, the last of its tributaries. Rocky lowlands offer little resistance to the forward flood; these shelving plains were always meant to be seabeds. Faster now, welling up and spilling over the scarps, forced on by the tilting basin at its back, the flood follows the lowest contours to meet the greater ocean. The battered coast is outflanked and overrun in one extraordinary moment as the first tongue of water trickles out of the dunes and runs down the shore, laps at the lapping waves and tastes the ocean's unfamiliar salt for the first time. An hour old and raw from the breach, it is the youngest sea on earth.

The thousand-mile ridge of rock which bars the northern gulfs from the ocean collects snow all through the dark of winter. Spring brings melt-waters tumbling down the mountainsides to boil in the ravines. A water-table of distant plateaux and barren fells feeds great rivers to the north and east. Showers are frequent, though rarely sustained for long. Short hot summers give way to drizzly autumns. The first men to gaze on these waters would have found a placid, temperate sea, thick with reed-beds. About its southernmost coast – for they came from the south – the waters meandered haphazardly, prising intricate spits and bodden out of the coast, baring reddish sandstone to the blast of the odd winter gale. Healing drifts of clay covered the ice-scarred granite of the seabed, purple heather shaded the long humps of eskers and drumlins back into a boggy foreshore. They were easy waters, and the thick forests of oak and beech through which they must have travelled might have supplied the timbers for a vessel. But something deterred them and sent them east along the shore rather than north across the sea. Some journeys are irresistible, some no more than the thudding of feet. They set their sunburned faces towards the interior mysteries and left behind them vague currents, placid convections and stirrings. Drift.

This strange and gentle sea, reed-fringed and resting in a granite cradle still rocking in the aftermath of ice, dotted with islands and bounded with stony northern coasts, fed by melted snow and rainwater, almost enclosed behind the jut of the peninsula, yet appears somehow lacustrine, an outbreak of water arrested at the edge of the ocean, frozen in the moment of joining. The bulk and heave of brine calls from beyond the strait, but its newest dominion still clings to an earlier being, of a freezing and preservative stillness. Weak inflows through Skagerrak and Kattegat signal distant oceanic storms, but mostly the sluggish currents roll under the impetus of debouching rainfall and snow. These yeasty yellow waters are almost saltless, almost tideless, almost stagnant in the deeps of Arkona or Landsort. The northern gulfs still freeze over five winters in ten. This sea will always keep something of the character of ice.

The first men never returned. Peat bogs, beech scrub and moorland lay undisturbed for centuries while fish entered by the Belts, spawned in the brackish waters, grew fat on sea snails, brown shrimps, bristle worms and soft-shelled crabs. Atlantic salmon sped east with the sea trout and grayling to spawn in the great rivers whose mouths in summer would choke with the bodies of spent lampreys until shrieking gulls and goosanders plucked them from the water. Flounder, dab, sand-eels and lumpsuckers grazed the saline bottom waters while gudgeon, pike and dace hovered about the freshwater outflows. Cod spawned in Arkona Deep, grew huge, ate each other. The spring and autumn herring founded their colonies in the nearby shallows off the islands of Rügen and Usedom. A million undisturbed existences floated, swam, spawned and died before the first keel cut the waves above and the nets descended to haul the sea's fat harvest ashore. Invasions, battles and slaughter were a vague clangour, dim thuds in the deathly air; the pale bodies sank quietly watched by lidless, curious eyes. Spars and planks drifted off the exploded coast. Dim shapes sank amidst the skerries.

Herring-lives circled such interruptions; supple cycles of eating and breeding stretched to allow their passage. Storms had brought no more than the puny challenge of barrel staves and broken oars in the past. As the rising wind churned the surface they would sink, whole shoals diving for shelter in the lee of the cliff until the swell died down and they could rise to feed. This storm was different, its course bending away from them, its first shudders familiar enough, but then exceeding all they had known before. They dived and waited, but the storm only roiled and thudded overhead, a bludgeoning throb reaching deeper than ever before. In the deep off Usedom, they shook as the tempest tore loose sea grass and kelp, sent fogs of clay billowing out of the trenches, buried its violence in the depths. They never suspected the transaction taking place above, so stubbornly held by the spit running off the line of the coast, so violent a wresting as the waves clawed this gift for them from the land. The thrashing surface-creatures above were yielding up a surpassing tribute to the waiting shoals, greater and more intricate, different in kind as well as scale, and more enduring.

The herring knew the coastal cities as compacted secrets, the ends of tunnels emerging at night under a moonless sky. Looping wakes converged there, linking each to each, one confirming the next as the vessels passed overhead with their dim shouts and the pressure of the hulls fumbling dully in the depths like minor showers on their way to somewhere else. The herring tracked them home to port, suffered grey death in the nets which were hauled aboard with the full-grown fish strung about the middle, trying to jack-knife free and drowning as the threads tightened over their gills. A foaming cloak of scum protected these places from prying herring eyes, thickening about the piers, breaking up in the wash beyond the headlands. Such a traffic, such a thickening of these solitary creatures. Hungry places, these cities. But beyond the vague maw, the strange tightening and deadening of currents, where were the teeth, the gullet, the stomach?

This: felt first as a distant disturbance in the storm's fury, a vast crumbling or drawn-out collapse. Out of the battered cliff, great shards of clay were coming loose. Slabs of sandstone tumbled free, crashing down the sheer edge and dropping into the deep. The sea took great swings at the spit, cutting away until the weight above drove down its own foundation and followed it into the waters. A massive submergence, a vast pulse of pressure, clay misting and clogging their eyes and gills, clearing and revealing to them the scale of the displacement. Greater than the greatest vessel, this awaited mystery still locked in the aftermath of its deliverance, too strange and exceeding them all as it lowered itself to the seabed. There it was, laid out below the shoal, with all its people, buildings, carts and livestock stretching further than they could see with the reek they had tasted before only from a distance. Here it was thick and strong, all the tantalising stenches blended together and curling thickly through the water. They waited and felt the surface grow calm. They saw each other's fat silver bodies turn this way and that before the yielded gift. And then the first few flipped their tails and descended. The thrashing creatures above had delivered as tribute a city.

The older herring swam with its citizens, circled their temples and overlooked their marts. Paddling in and out the doors and windows, they sought out the clumsy giants in flowing robes who promenaded through the drowned streets. Lurching in the waters' flow, they were more like plants than men. The herring rose, and sank, and rose again. Other shoals gathered about them. The upper waters glittered with fry. They would never forget the pact forged in the storm. The city would grow familiar to them as the sea-floor itself, and in time indistinguishable.

Gifts and years: bladderwrack creeps closer to the shore, loamy soils flocculate and wash away. Near-tidelessness means the survival of low landscapes and improbable islands. Sharks' teeth and whalejaws are the oldest bones in the sea.

Weed rafts drift and are blown by northerly gusts into estuaries and lagoons. Sinking canvas wheels down into the darkness, goblets and bracelets glitter and are eclipsed. Spear shafts, scabbards, rope-ends and corn sacks take their own trajectories through the fathoms. Smashed hulls lurch while mastheads dive, but all are voided and deposited on the seabed. Surface-creatures drown. If the ice was a barrier no object could breach, then the sea which took its place will accept all; a subtler poison, for everything sinks in the end. The herring understand. Not since the city – and that was a hundred generations before – have they clustered so thickly and so curiously as now. The tribute from above is always puzzling and clumsy, always awkward and misshapen; this is no exception. And yet it neither floats nor sinks, seeming to hover in the water like themselves. They move closer, and it begins to shake. They feel the waters agitate around it. A booming sound resonates with their otoliths and their fins begin to twitch. It is almost invisible in the murk of these depths; something hangs beneath it. What? Is this finally the key to the mystery of the city? Something snakes away above, tautens as they circle slowly, comes loose and disappears. The larger fish butt against the intruder. These are herring waters and this is the coldest water-layer. But perhaps they were mistaken, for it seems to be sinking now, tumbling down out of sight. Some turn away as deep-water currents take the intruder, weird tribute from above, drifting in the saltless tideless waters fed by melt-water springs, racked by memories of ice, scourged by serrated coasts, darker and deeper and further down towards the city. Lost? No, not quite. Blunt herring noses butt against its sides. Their curiosity sustains it; its own weirdness buoys it up. But what? In this sea a barrel is sinking, and in this barrel is a man.

Alasdair Gray

MONEY

ONLY SNOBS, PERVERTS and desperate folk want to be friends with folk richer or poorer than them. Maybe in Iceland or Holland or Canada factory-owners and labourers, fishermen and high court judges eat in each other's houses and go holidays together. If they do they must look and feel as good as each other, so the thing is impossible in Scotland or England. Mackay disagrees. He says the Scots have a tradition which lets them forget social differences. He says his father was gardener to a big house in the north and the owner was his dad's best friend. On rainy days they sat in the gardener's shed and drank a bottle of whisky together. But equal wages and savings allow steadier friendship than equal drunkenness. I did not want to borrow money from Mackay because it proved I was poorer. He insisted on lending, which ruined more than our friendship.

I needed a thousand pounds cash to complete a piece of business and phoned my bank to arrange a loan. They said I could have it at an interest of eleven per cent plus a £40 arrangement fee. I told them I would repay in five days but they said that made no difference – for £1,000 now I must repay £1,150, even if I did so tomorrow. I groaned and said I would call for the money in half an hour, and put down the phone, and saw Mackay was in the room. He had strolled in from his office next door. We did the same sort of work in those days, but were not competitors. When I got more business than I could handle I passed it to him, and vice versa.

He said, 'What have you to groan about?'

I told him and added, 'I can easily pay eleven per cent et cetera but I hate it. I belong to the financial past – all interest above five per cent strikes me as extortion.'

'I'll lend you a thousand, interest free,' said Mackay, pulling out his cheque book. While I explained why I never borrow money from friends he filled in a cheque, tore it off and held it out saying, 'Stop raving about equality and take this to my bank. I'll phone them and they'll cash it at once. We're still equals – in an emergency you would do the same for me.'

I blushed because he was almost certainly wrong. Then I shrugged, took the cheque and said, 'If this is what you want, Mackay, all right. Fine. I'll return it within five days, or within a fortnight at most.'

'Harry, I know that. Don't worry,' said Mackay soothingly and started talking about something else. I felt grateful but angry because I hate feeling grateful. I also hated his easy assumption that his money was perfectly safe. Had I lent *him* a thousand pounds I would have worried myself sick until I got it back. If being aristocratic means preferring good manners to money then Mackay was definitely posher than me. Did he think his dad's boozing sessions with Lord Glenbannock had ennobled the Mackays? The loan was already spoiling our friendship.

Five days later my business was triumphantly concluded and I added a cheque for over ten thousand pounds to my bank account. I was strongly tempted not to repay Mackay at once, just to show him I was something more dangerous than decent, honest, dependable old Harry. I stayed honest a little longer by remembering that if I repaid promptly I would be able to borrow from him again on the same convenient terms. Handing him a cheque would have been as embarrassing as taking one so I decided to put the cash straight back into his bank since my bank would have taken days to transfer the money, despite computerisation. I collected ten crisp new hundred-pound notes in a smooth envelope, placed envelope in inner jacket pocket and walked the half mile towards Mackay's bank. The morning air was mild but fresh, the sky one sheet of high grey cloud which threatened rain but might hold off till nightfall.

Mackay's bank is at the end of a road where I lived when I was married, but I seldom go there now. The buildings on one side have been demolished and replaced by a cutting holding a six-lane motorway. Tenements and shops on the remaining side no longer have a thriving look. I was walking carefully along the cracked and pitted pavement when I heard a woman say, 'Harry, what are *you* doing here?' She was thin, sprightly, short-haired and (like most attractive women nowadays) struck me as any age between sixteen and forty. I said I was going to a bank to repay money I owed. She looked like someone I knew so I said, 'How are your folk up at Ardnamurchan, Liz?'

She laughed and said, 'I'm Mish, you idiot! Come inside – Wee Dougie and Davenport and Roy and Roberta are there and we haven't seen you for ages.'

I remembered none of these names but never say no to women who want me – it does not often happen. I followed her into The Whangie, though it was not a pub I liked. The best pubs had all been on the demolished side of the street, and while The Whangie's customers may not have been prone to violence I had always suspected they were, so the pleasure I felt at the sight of the drab brown dusty interior was unexpected. It was exactly as it had been twenty or thirty years before, exactly like most Scottish pubs before the big breweries used extravagant tax reliefs to buy and remake them like Old English taverns or Spanish bistros. This was still a dour Scottish drinking-den which kept the prices down by spending nothing on appearances. The only wall decorations were solidly framed mirrors frosted with the names and emblems of defunct whisky blends. And the place was nearly empty, for it was soon after opening-time.

Crying, 'Look who's here!' Mish led me to some people round a corner table, one of whom I recognised.

'Let me get you a drink, Harry,' he said, starting to stand, but, 'No no no, sit down, sit down,' I said, hurrying to the bar. Outside the envelope in my inner jacket pocket I had just enough cash to buy a half pint of lager. I carried this back to the people in the corner. They made room for me.

A fashion note. None of us looked smart. The others wore jeans with shapeless denim or leather jackets, I wore my old tweed jacket and crumpled corduroys. Only my age marked me off from the rest, I thought, and not much. We had all been to university in the seventies or eighties. The only man I knew well, a musician called Roy, was almost my age. The one oddity among us was the hair of the not-Mish woman, Roberta. It was the colour of dry straw and stood straight upright on top of her skull, being clipped or shaved to thin stubble at the back and sides. The wing of her right nostril was pierced by several fine little silver rings, her lipstick was dull purple. She affected me like someone with a facial deformity so to avoid staring hard I ignored her completely. This was easy as she never said a word the whole time I was in The Whangie. She seemed depressed about something: when others spoke to her she answered by sighing or grunting or shrugging her shoulders.

First they asked how I was getting on and I answered, 'Not bad – not good.' The truth was that like many professional folk nowadays I am doing extremely well, even though I have to borrow money sometimes, but it would have been unkind to say how much better off I was than them. They were obviously unemployed. Why else did they drink, and drink very slowly, at half past eleven on Thursday morning? I avoided distressing topics by talking to Roy, the musician. We had met at a party where he sang and played the fiddle really well. Since then I had seen him busking in the shopping precincts, and had passed quickly on the opposite side of the street to avoid embarrassing him, for he was too good a musician to be living that way. I asked him about the people who had held the party, not having seen them since. Neither had Roy so we discussed the party.

Ten minutes later we had nothing more to say about it and I had drunk my half pint. I stood up and said, 'Have to go now, folks.' They fell silent and looked at me. I sensed, maybe mistakenly, that they expected something, and blushed, and spoke carefully to avoid stammering: 'You see,

I would like to buy a round before I go but I've no cash on me. I mean, I've plenty of money in my bank – and I have my cheque book here – could one of you cash a cheque for five pounds? – I promise it won't stott.'

Nobody answered. I realised nobody there had five pounds on them, or the means of turning my cheque back into cash if they had.

'Cash it at the bar, Harry,' suggested Mish.

'I would like to – but do you think the barman will do it without a cheque card?'

'No cheque card?' said Mish on a shrill note.

'None! I've never had a cheque card. If I had I would lose it. I'm always losing things. But the barmen in Tennent's cash my cheques without one . . .'

'Jimmy!' cried Davenport, who had a black beard and a firm manner and had waved to the barman, 'Jimmy, this pal of ours wants to cash a cheque. He's Harry Haines, a well-known character in the west end with a good going business – '

'In fact he's loaded,' said Mish –

' – and he would like you to cash a cheque for him. He's left his cheque card at home.'

'Sorry,' said the barman, 'there's nothing I can do about that,' and turned his back on us.

'I'm sorry too,' I told them helplessly.

'You,' Mish told me, 'are a mean old fart. You are not only mean, you are totally uninteresting.'

At these words my embarrassment vanished and I cheered up. I no longer minded being superior. With an air of mock sadness I said, 'True! So I must leave you. Goodbye, folks.'

I think the three men were also amused by the turn things had taken. They said cheerio to me quite pleasantly.

I left The Whangie and went towards Mackay's bank, carefully remembering the previous twelve minutes to see if I might have done better with them. I did not regret entering The Whangie with Mish. She had pleasantly excited me and I had not known she only saw me as a source of free drink. True, I had talked boringly – had bored myself as well as them – but interesting topics would have emphasised the social gulf between us. I might have amused them with queer stories about celebrities whose private lives are more open to me than to popular journalism (that was probably how the duke entertained Mackay's father between drams in the tool shed) but it strikes me as an unpleasant way to cadge favour with unequals. I was pleased to think I had been no worse than a ten-minute bore. I had made a fool of myself by appearing to want credit for a round of drinks I could not buy, but that kind of foolery hurts nobody. If Mish and her pals despised me for it, good luck to them. I did not despise myself for it, or only slightly. In the unexpected circumstances I was sure I could not have behaved better.

The idea of taking a hundred-pound note from Mackay's money, handing it to Mish, saying 'Share this with the others,' and leaving fast before she could reply only came to me later. So did a better idea: I could have laid five hundred-pound notes on the table, said 'Conscience money, a hundred each,' and hurried off to put the rest in Mackay's account. Later I could have told him, 'I paid back half what I owe today, but you'll have to wait till next week for the rest. I've done something stupid with it.' As he heard the details his mouth would open wider and wider or his frown grow sterner and sterner. At last he would say, 'That's the last interest-free loan you get from me' – or something else. But he would have been as astonished as the five in the pub. I would have proved I was not predictable. Behaving like that would have changed my character for the better. But I could not imagine doing such things then. I can only imagine them since my character changed for the worse.

I left The Whangie and went towards Mackay's bank, brooding on my recent adventure. No doubt there was a smug little smile on my lips. Then I noticed someone was walking beside me and heard a low voice say, 'Wait a minute.'

I stopped.

My companion was Roberta who stood staring at me. She was breathing hard, perhaps with the effort of overtaking me, and her mouth was set in something like a sneer. I could not help looking straight at her now. Everything I saw – weird hair and sneering face, shapeless leather jacket with hands thrust into flaps below her breasts, baggy grey jeans turned up at the bottoms to show clumsy thick-soled boots laced high up the ankles – all this insulted my notion of what was attractive and female. But her alert stillness as the breathing calmed made me feel very strange, as if I had seen her years ago, and often.

To break the strangeness I said sharply, 'Well?'

Awkwardly and huskily she said, 'I don't think you're mean or uninteresting. I like older men.'

Her eyes were so wide open that I saw the whole circle of the pupils, one brown, one blue. There was a kind of buzzing in my blood and the nearby traffic sounded fainter. I felt stronger and more alive than I had felt for years – alive in a way that I had never expected to feel again after my marriage went wrong. Her sneer was now less definite, perhaps because I felt it on my own lips. Yes, I was leering at her like a gangster confronting his moll in a 1940 cinema poster and she was staring back as if terrified to look anywhere else.

I was fascinated by the thin stubble at the sides of her head above the ears. It must feel exactly like my chin before I shaved in the morning. I wanted to rub it hard with the palms of my hands. I heard myself say, 'You want money I suppose. How and when?'

She murmured that I could visit my bank before we went to her place – or afterwards, if I preferred. My leer became a wide grin. I patted my inner pocket and said, 'No need for a bank, honey. I got everything you want right here. And we'll take a taxi to my place, not yours.'

I spoke with an American accent, and the day turned into one of the worst in my life.

Candia McWilliam

SEVEN MAGPIES

THE TRAIN WAS passing between still, high fields of standing corn. The light over the fields had a talcy glow that lightened and ceased to shimmer a yard or so into the sky. From time to time a small area of field flicked under a switch of wind, the specific unanimated flick of a creature's pelt. Rangy wild oats over the wide crop and flimsy poppies at its edges were the only intimations of natural disorder. Nothing much was moving but the train through this thinly chivalric part of England.

'Girls are like people, I realised it late on,' said the younger man to the older, who resembled him too much not to be linked to him by blood.

'It will have been my fault you did not see that before. Though I can't see the good it will do you to know it now.'

'Why do you say *now*?'

'You've already done your harm and it is late to begin any undoing.'

'You know more than most that there is no undoing. At least I need do no more harm now.' The young man spoke as though harm were something simple, like hammering.

The older man stood to open a window, with such urgency that he seemed in want of new air. The air that entered the train brought nothing new with it but dust more rural than the dust within.

'You dramatise yourself, Findlay, a pointless thing to do in your profession and very tiring in hot weather.' Sitting down, the older man pinched his trousers and flung his right leg over his left as though this gave depth to his paternal but unfatherly dictum.

'Gum?' rejoined his son, loosening a white tooth of chewing gum from its packet with his thumb and offering it gingerly to his father. It might have been the elegant old man in his old cream linen who had been uncouth. But the reprimand was lost on Robert Meldrum who sat now looking at his son over his own, just touching, fingertips.

Knowing that his father was waiting for him to offend, Findlay shot five bits of gum into his own mouth and began to champ until his throat was flooded with minty saliva and his jaw was aching. Would it be the professional or the private life that was coming into the old man's sights, he wondered, with the same dishonourable curiosity that led him to encourage people to repeat themselves indefinitely and to tell him stories he already knew.

'I followed a trade all my life and I fear you are too good for that.' The word 'good' carried none of its customary decent replete weight. Nor did it imply its opposite, merely something lightweight, skittering, inconsiderable.

'Father, your life is not over,' said Findlay, hoping to divert attention from his own life, still, he felt, hardly begun. He almost forgot himself and began to flatter the hard old man, as he might have someone he loved less and trusted more, enticing him into discussion of the past with some welcome slipway down into memory, 'And what a life it has been, eh . . .'

'No, you can't catch me like that. Are you hungry at the stomach or is it the chewing you favour? If so, how odd. How unnatural indeed. You are like that.' Findlay knew his father meant 'you' the young. He himself was seventy-two; Findlay forty years younger. 'You are all appetite and no hunger. All temper and no rage.'

Only a man as stagy-looking as his father, black-browed, blue-eyed, white-haired, elongated but without idle languor, could speak in this public manner in a private place without self-consciousness. The natural dignity of his appearance had throughout his life lent authority to the actions and sayings of Robert Meldrum. Replacing the words in the mouth of a notional short man with clumps of hair, a man whom Findlay had begun to keep about him as a companion in subversion as a boy, was the way to subtract the awe inspired by his father's stern Scots glamour. Although he would have denied the word, the older man exploited the quality, as a preacher might have, in mixed vanity and good faith.

Findlay was slighter than his father, but like him tall and blue-eyed, the eyes seemingly set in the sockets by sooty fingers. His hair was black as his father's had been, but with needles of white at the back and sides. He was less dapper than his father, and as evidently clean to the pitch that actually repels dirt, rather than the holiday smartness that draws it and is ruined. Neither man wore a colour much beyond the neutral, although there was in Findlay's inner jacket pocket, when it flapped open, a row of pencils, crocus yellow, each with a small pink eraser bound to its top with a band of gold metal. Once or twice his right hand went up to these pencils and rolled them like a toy or an instrument. Their small geared hexagons made a noise only Findlay heard.

None the less he failed to notice when his father, in a train, in summer, in England, leant his fine head against the rough blue nap of his seat, drowsed, slept, and, sometime before arrival at their undesired destination, died.

'It's unfortunate you married a man so far superior to yourself,' said her husband.

There was a choice of replies to be made, but since it was breakfast time and their two children were watching Morag to see how she took Daddy's joke, she said, 'That is so, I'm afraid.'

Edward's comment had been made in front of the children before, but never before, as now, stripped of the pretence of levity. It was clear that today would continue the bleak barracking of the night before, until he was out of the house. On his return it would, as clearly, resume. She began to attend to his wants with an assiduity that was part of the ugly bargain she had some months ago made with fate: she would tend to him scrupulously if one day she might be delivered from him. She squeezed oranges down on to the juice extractor as though they were the breasts of the martyred St Agatha.

The table had no place, indeed no room, for her, and it was her pleasure to wait on her family. The thought of eating with them confused her; who would fetch things if she sat down? If she did sit down, she would surely have to rise, so it was easier not to. She thought these small acts of abnegation would attune her children at an early age to the deceits of family life and, even more importantly, the real place of women: these inoculations she, being ironic, took as salutary, and they, being innocent, took for example.

When told she was inferior, it came naturally to scrutinise the superior object. Morag was inferior to a large man nearing forty who sat like a stranger among his possessions and children and whose umbrella, had this been a normal day, he would later forget, causing him to return and feel obliged to kiss her.

In the garden below their first-floor kitchen window a cat moved with rumpy stealth towards a fit-looking magpie that had settled under the denuded roses, among petals lying profuse over the sodden grass. The cat kept its belly from touching the ground, as it would not have on a dry day. Its dark tail and ears cast their shadow in the fresh wet sunlight, its creamy body appearing too blurred and soft to be stockinged and tipped in so sharp a mode. All through the grass were spiders' webs still, though where the cat had been there was a bright trail through the webs' slick silver.

When the Siamese laid low the maggot-pie the squawks and cawings came from both. The cat batted the smart but loutish bird, deriding it to death, then crunching at it with a besotted look as if to say, 'Doesn't it suit me?' The big bird, now without its life, looked frivolous as a hat, but for the dainty giblets and bladders the cat was discarding from its feast. All the while wet petals fell with no sound and up in the kitchen the children, silenced by this pleasant domestic diversion as they had not been by their parent's contained wretchedness, watched, staying their eating only to exchange old saws:

'One for sorrow, two for joy,
Three for a girl, four for a boy,
Five for silver, six for gold,
Seven for a secret that's never been told.'

Morag caught the boiling milk as it reached its height and poured it for her husband on to the freshly brewed decaffeinated coffee. On noticing that there was a drop of coffee on the saucer, she fetched a clean cloth and wiped it, making sure that she took the cloth from the pile that was composed of cloths that touched clean surfaces only; not floors, the sink, the table or anything that had not already been washed at least once – a system instituted by Edward.

So as to prepare Edward's breakfast without distressing him, for he had washed his hair this morning as usual, she lit a candle, and set it in the sink to consume the frying smells from the children's breakfast. No one could say she had not colluded in her own demotion from love object to servant. The extravagant acts of obedience and enslavement had, she thought, been a conduit of intimacy between them. Now these actions had set into resented habits and their certainly fetishistic significance had fallen away. Sometimes, when Edward was far from home and she was able to think about him with the balance bestowed by distance, she suspected that she had invented some of his more demanding stipulations in order at first to have more ways of pleasing him, and at length to have more things to blame him for.

She extracted the unsalted butter that only he was permitted, and cut off a small nut or knob, as the books told one a small piece of butter was dubbed. It was not to her especially lubricious stuff.

The butter went into its own brick-shaped, lidded pot, to avoid taking on the smells of other substances. The openness of butter to corruption is extreme, Edward had taught her; only let it see garlic, or melon.

In the early days of their marriage the serene freedom from confusion that her husband had represented, with his distaste for muddle or inappropriateness and his almost mystical sense of what was proper, had been a relief to her: like entering clean sheets for good. A man who knew where things should be put was a man to honour in untidy times.

Now, though, Morag had come to think of mess as having an energy if not sublime at any rate fully human. She had begun to cultivate people who lived in a manner abhorrent to Edward, so that she might sit at their sticky kitchen tables to hear them unpick their troubles as they cleaned their children's faces with their own spit and a paper handkerchief and shook out cat litter, birdseed, flour and currants with impartial, unwashed hands. She fancied she saw a nobility and vigour she did not find in her own house in whose kitchen she never entertained.

'What are these?' Edward asked one evening after his bicycle ride home, his first bath and their wary kiss, during which he smelt her carefully and could guess almost her entire day from what he smelled.

Morag had once made an ebullient – the word occurred to her as she pitied herself for living with a man who did not love fun – an ebullient flower arrangement that included beautiful, fat, complicated globe artichokes. She had thrust their thick architectural stems deep into a vase and starred them about with blue cornflowers and asters the colour of plain chocolate.

Edward flinched when he saw it, at the whimsy as much as at the waste.

She set today's egg before him, and ten toast soldiers. He had never stipulated that he liked ten, but in complaining to a friend one day of her husband's ways, she had invented this one, and found herself complying.

'A man so attentive to detail must be attentive in other ways,' her friend had said, not wrongly, but displeasing Morag who was attached to her hobby of resentment. Her friend was anyway not to be trusted in the matter of men, changing her walk and lifting her tail and walking round the room only to stop, and softly pick things up to hold them against her cheek in the manner of a girl in an advertisement.

'You two go and clean your teeth,' Morag said to her children. She had retained enough tact not yet to enjoy displaying the faults in her marriage to its children, a stage that comes as a rule when the children can least begin to bear it.

Hearing her voice change, she said to Edward, while she took the crusts off his second piece of toast, placed it on a clean plate, and took away the used things before setting down a fresh knife, 'Would you like a second egg?'

He had never said 'Yes' in answer to this question and did not do so now. He did not take more than three eggs in the week, making sure to include in this tally units of egg that might have been incorporated into other things he ingested, for example cakes. Morag's question about the second egg therefore had to his ears something of the murderous in it.

'If you want to kill me', he said, 'continue to behave precisely as you have done for the past three months. You will find no one as good as me . . .'

She left before she heard this sentence end with the words, 'for you.'

She left the house with her raincoat, her handbag and a pair of painful silver shoes she had worn to annoy Edward that morning, but which by the end of a day that included the plane south, a journey on the tube that had been almost alarmingly smooth, as though she would never have human feelings again, a hot train journey through a part of England that made her homesick already for Scotland, and a promising period of eavesdropping that ended with one of its participants' disappointingly quiet death, annoyed her much more and burned her too, by virtue of their metallic finish.

Hard along the house's dusty yellow length the scaffolding was set, carrying all the blows taken to fix it tight together up to Jean's open window in the form of longitudinal shudderings and breathy irregular chimes. She was resting in a position that she had taught herself during the years of living in other people's houses. Braced everywhere but the neck, her body was arranged in the least comfortable chair in the room. This choice might not have been understood by people unashamed of their own ease. Her wrists and hands curled, ready at any moment to push her up, over the chair's splintlike arms. The plumbing of the house clanked and hissed without cease. In the sash window-frame of Jean's thin high room lay flakes of paint like peeled bark. A tentative persistent lichen grew in on the sill. The scaffolding seemed bold, an expression of someone's intention to hold things up against time.

Fresh yet heavy with the summer that sleeps low around an English river, the air brought into Jean's light sleep noises that came always at this time of day. She did not know she heard them but her closed eyes told her pictures as each noise came. The pictures were clear as illustrations in a first alphabet. She saw a cow, yeast-coloured, on a green field. Pigeons arrived in pairs behind her eyes as their cooing took her back to other houses of which she had become a part, and then fallen away at the given time when another job at the heart of a family withered.

Behind her warm lids, a train came, complete with funnel, condenser, signalman, smuts. She awoke with a start and a taste in her mouth like sucked coin. Morag was coming to stay here. She was arriving this afternoon, in the train.

Jean woke, remembering that Morag had left behind Edward, and, more deplorably, Ishbel and Geordie. She wiped the sleep from her face with a rough flannel as you clean the bloom from a plum, and prepared herself to see her daughter and look her straight in the eye. Morag would no doubt make free of a taxi from the station. Edward would already be beginning to pay for whatever his sin had been. Jean was made unsteady by the reasons Morag gave for leaving, as if there could be reasons for an unreasonable thing. The confusion of love with marriage was no help. Jean held love, in Morag's sense, to be what you felt before you knew a person well enough to know when they were lying. What came after that knowledge might have less fire but it was warmer also, she on principle imagined.

She filled her kettle from the wash basin and made a half cup of instant custard, watching the glowing pink flour melt to a suffused yellow, breathing in the smell of vanilla, sugar and starch. Quickly the custard set, with the spoon upright, as though in a cup of plaster of Paris. She powdered her face in a sketchy way, looking at the mirror's flecks and motes and not at her own, which did not interest her. Before leaving the room, she spooned and smoothed a layer of cooling thick custard into the half coconut that hung at her window for the birds. She could not bear to give the birds nothing, and had not the facilities or way of life that produced bacon rinds. It was a vegetarian household, had been so for eighty years.

'Mother, come down, I'm arrived. Or we are.'

The voice came from under the window. Jean looked down through the scaffolding.

'Do you want me to climb down to you?' asked Jean, in an admonitory whisper that subtracted the intended irony. In the heat the creeping plants that embraced the house were reaching tendrils towards the scaffolding, pitting their minute continual subversion against the clumsy man-made optimism of its structure. Should it remain too long, the plants would wind it about and bring it down.

'Shall I actually come in this way?' said a male Scots voice, perhaps drunk. Jean looked along the house. Just to the side of her own bathroom window, over the workroom of Ludovina her employer, was a man over thirty standing rather crouched in the hot box of air between the first-floor scaffolding bars. His colour was bad. It was hard to believe that here was a romantic motive for Morag's morning dash from Edinburgh, but it was Jean's duty to ask.

'Had you intended sharing a room? Ludo would not mind but I am not for haste in these things,' she said to the starling-coloured head of her daughter below. Morag was standing thigh-deep among blue agapanthus and the long belts of their leaves.

'Mother, I left my husband under twelve hours ago, and not because I don't love him. I may.' Morag began to look for a cigarette. She had taken up smoking in the last two hours. It had seemed impolite not to smoke in all the dejected rooms she and Findlay Meldrum had been put into after the finding of his father's body. There had been so little all these strangers could offer, it would have been unkind not to take their cigarettes.

'Have one of mine. You light the end that you don't put in your mouth,' said the man in the scaffolding, dropping a cigarette that fell some feet wide of Morag, and seeing the ineptitude of his throw, he burst into tears for the first time that afternoon, and fell limp out of the rungs down on to the deep lawn of moss where he lay on his back weeping at the English sky in gasps for his father as Jean and Morag looked down at him from their two heights, and, from her workroom in this house where she had been born, Ludovina heard what she had not for more than twenty years, the intractable grief of a man.

The obvious thing, to gather him up in comfort, was evidently up to Morag; but she only knew more about him, she did not *know* him any more than did her mother or Ludovina. Shy of any first touch, she wanted him and his misery, and the way it might bind them for even these hours, to be gone.

She had chosen this as her own day for drama, and events had eclipsed her. Things do not know when to happen, she thought, they are ruthless like children. Cheated of a weeping declamatory scene with her mother, she did not at that point choose to consider why she had not minded becoming involved with Findlay Meldrum's long distressing afternoon with the railway authorities, the police, the hospital.

Curiosity had made her listen to Findlay's conversation with his father. But the sight of him had passed into her with a speed and heat she had forgotten through the years of discipline and some kind of peace with Edward. This made harder the thought of gathering him to her as he beat his head back on the ground – to put it out of its misery, it seemed – and poured tears for his loss of a man she did not know. If she had thought of holding him it was not to give ease, or not at once.

In the end it was Ludovina who dealt with Findlay. Her presumption of competence always endowed her with it. She was good at the extreme states of others since they offended her sense of the stable, measured, discreet and sober way a rational life should be led. She was a satisfied atheist, a type that will take swift decisions without later compunction; her greatest impatience was against timewasters and ditherers. The rock of her unbelief had never once let her down.

Letting herself out by the apple-house door, she moved over the lawn in her sandals and djellabah, her stout decisive form at once becoming the focus of the group; the other two women were distraught at the sight of a man unmanned. Ludovina took over. She was at her best in a crisis, her certainty and bossiness becoming buoyant and purposeful, not chilling.

She thought aloud in the drawling unembarrassed tones that had served her perfectly well through eighty years of privileged activism and rash adventurous travels: 'Jean, you make a bed and a drink for him, if you would. Somewhere he can shout and howl without disturbing us. What's your name? Ah interesting, you are a Scot too then, at any rate at the start of your history. I live here because this is the house of the parents of my mother, and the house where I was born, but I owe myself to Scotland.' Here she spoke of what she found best in herself, her toughness, her independence, her sentimental effective brusqueness.

Ludovina remembered the urgency and stopped, delighted to be at the heart of things that were happening, not to have to kill time with talk. 'Morag, this is sudden, but I am pleased to see you. Since he is not your lover, don't be so foolish and hold his head to stop him doing that.' Ludovina knew well that a mistress would hold a lover who wept. She had herself conducted passionate rational adulteries throughout her long successful marriage.

Findlay had rolled on to his stomach and was beating his head down on the edge of the grass where it met the path of gravel and cinders. His shiny hair was dimmed by black dust. He began to like the distracting pain of smashing down his head among the sharp small stones. Morag squatted, sank and caught him under the arms so that his head was held in her lap where he lay tense and resisting until the reminder of life that came with being held for no reason but humanity entered him, and restored to him the superficial social emotions of a man watched by a short, composed octogenarian woman as he breathes in a stranger through her skirt wet with his own tears. Ludovina nodded as Findlay calmed down. She took her time. Her hard but inky hands were on her thick waist.

She had the thread of a new story almost in her grip. She could not wait to return to her pen, with which she had a further three hours to spend that day, before she went out to dig the evening's potatoes.

'I'm sorry,' Findlay said, apologising also to his father who, he thought, would have deplored every one of the actions taken by his son since his death. 'I had not known it would be like this. You are kind.' It was not easy to say these things lying down and into the lap of a woman he did not know, who smelt of lemon soap, ironing, cheese and pickle, blood and, on the fingers of her right hand that was now stroking, not holding rigid, his left shoulder, the beautiful autumnal domestic dirty smell of extinguished candle.

A. L. Kennedy

TRUE

Eel-grass.

That's what he'd woken up with – eel-grass. When he sat forward into the morning, he had felt that one word spinning under his scalp, flipping and tickling from the curve of his forehead to the fastening for his spine and then nuzzling clear out between his jaws.

'Eel-grass.'

He couldn't recall he'd ever seen some. Was it, for instance, a food for eels, perhaps a shelter, or eel-like, eel-tasting, a remedy for eels that were unwanted? He didn't know. He didn't care.

'Eel-grass.'

Dearie, dearie, dear, but it felt good. Among all the meaningless, numb, dumb and superfluous words his thoughts were clogged with, eel-grass had real potential and maybe even charm. To say, it felt like alternately licking ice and sherbet, or teasing out the opening to a particular kiss he'd been fond of for a while.

Experience suggested he should pounce on this surge of enthusiasm and allow it to carry him out of bed. He never could tell when his heart might drop again and leave him unable to remember any need to do anything. Whole days had burned themselves in and out while he looked at nothing but one or other of his hands, or folded them together, closed his eyes and tried to puzzle his way through the rushing inside his head. It was a race in there, a screaming, turning, tightening drop. Sometimes he wanted to explain this, to point out that he was not inactive, only paralysed by a kind of internal pursuit.

The night races were the worst. If he tried to move while the chase was on, he simply developed vertigo and his condition was lousy enough without adding that. Best to keep still and hold tight. Even if all he was holding only amounted to one word.

Eel-grass. Good old thing. He could already smile about it, as if he were conjuring up the name of an old, firm friend. It was such a sexy little collection of syllables he actually could quite fancy having a grab at it, getting those day-dreaming fingers to work. In fact, maybe, possibly, perhaps he was about to welcome a genuinely horny – if rather odd, but who was counting – urge he could succumb to. Right at this minute, an urge, a testosterone-bristling, real live urge could be on its way.

He waited, thumbing through appropriate memories to catch his interest, but felt his pulse slacken and the encouraging twinges die.

Trouble was, he'd always found that kind of thing ridiculous, even at the rudest and healthiest of times. He'd always been stupidly conscious of how he must look, doing it. Very silly, because this was just the time when he wouldn't be observed. It was the solitary vice, after all.

Whole and hearty, he could pump smartly up to a pleasant head of steam, finish the deed and forget all about it again, but in his current state it seemed a dreadful effort for nothing more than a damp reminder of his solitariness.

Truthfully, he couldn't be bothered with himself. Or his bloody negative thinking.

An urge was an urge, though, even a small one, and it signalled a clear improvement on the usual utter absence of vital signs. Indeed, the eel-grass urge ushered in a startling morning. He shambled determinedly through washing and shaving and dressing and tying his shoes. Success, success, success, success.

So. Now then. All dressed up and nowhere to go. That was something to think of.

He folded back the window shutters, not allowing his

concentration to be drawn by the wickedly large spider that bobbed down fatly from a left-hand hinge. It lived there, that was fine, it didn't matter.

Heat sprang up in long waves from the whitewashed building opposite, prickly with the tang of hot woodwork and incendiary glass. This was the smell of being abroad, of standing above the Rue de Daumpierre at 10.55 a.m. (9.55 a.m. at home). All interested parties here may extend themselves uncomfortably over the windowsill and find a lopsided square of sky in a flawlessly boiling blue.

When he told his wife he was coming here, it was the sky he thought of. He remembered bicycling three abreast from the railway station into the broad green of the valley floor, aiming for the chateau that poked up ahead, stretching the crown of the hill into one huge confectionary yellow offence. Later he learned it had a soft-sounded, edible name, the Château de la Madeleine, and that parts of it had been extending themselves into the skyline like a mammoth canary-coloured dick for something like nine hundred years. When they built things back then, they built them big and butch.

Talking of butch. He'd been with the boys then, with their tent and their guddle of socks, and strings and mess tins. He'd sung obscenities with them, taken both feet off his pedals and acquired the habit of 'Bonjour'. For three weeks his impatience, invisible in Scotland, had been wonderfully ground away by the imposition of 'Bonjour' – no business, however pressing, could proceed without it. The principles of his life slipped over to reveal bursts of an unfair courtesy, a shameless enjoyment of eating and an overbearing sun. This sun changed his speed, his colour, left his temperament balanced on a needle point. There was nothing like this at home.

He never left home again, though, never came back here again, not until now. His wife had never heard of him chasing naked along a riverbed with two other red, nude, hot, wet, insect-bitten, roaring students whose names had been Andy and Michael, and whom he had loved, both of them equally but for different reasons. They had all returned to Scotland together and then failed to keep in touch.

Perhaps they hadn't wanted to break their memories, or to find themselves ambushed by sentiment. For himself, he hadn't wanted to let them down, to be anyone less than he had been here and with them. It was a shame they'd seen his best.

Shouldn't have been that way. If he could, he would have saved something back to give his wife – a pre-payment for those nights and nights when he'd lain beside her with his whole existence shearing down and through his skull. He'd kept her awake. A lot.

One morning he eased his head over to look at the one woman he had ever prayed on his knees to touch, to talk to and then to marry. They had spent and shared and hoarded large parts of a compromising but not unhappy life. There had been no one and nothing but her. He didn't have hobbies, resented the time their work kept them from each other. It had all been going really very well. Then he'd seen her that morning and been unable to reach any feeling for her.

She appeared a little interesting because of the way the light was falling on her, that was all. He had wasted his last experience of fear, sweating it into the pillow next to hers. Then, in a matter of days, everything went. By the time he realised that nothing could touch or be touched by him, he could not even manage to be concerned. He was an occasional observer of his life's impossible accidents – sick leave, redundancy, benefits assessed and denied, the shortening of his wife's temper, the decline of their furniture and fittings, not to mention household morale, the thanking of God for giving them no children – he'd been around for most of it.

For his recovery, it was hoped, he would be away – here. His good health was hiding out, somewhere along the valley, written in the grain of the hill. It must be. He considered how his wife could have brought herself to find the money that sent him here. That strength of purpose alone must mean he would get better now. If he thought about it, he did have faith in her purpose, which might help his strength.

She had also given him a plan, they had discussed it frequently. Working a few hundred yards at a time, he would leave the hotel and walk up the street. In a matter of days he would make it past the church and then – this would take a week or so – he would begin to climb the deep, unwieldy steps he remembered leading to the Château de la Madeleine. By this time he would have used up ten or eleven of his fourteen days. When he reached the top of the hill and stepped on to the chateau's battlements he would be better. That was the plan.

Before he arrived, this all seemed a good idea. He had imagined leaning back on a hot parapet wall, looking at the opened valley and its sky and feeling the big, flat peace it would bring. This view had even loomed through his short dreams, but today he couldn't focus on it properly. Now that his shoes were on and his mind had fixed intentions of walking, he could only think of going to sit by the river and writing a letter in the sun. He wanted to tell his wife about the eel-grass and the way she could look quite interesting in a certain light. He wanted to tell her he was true. Still true.

Sean O'Brien

AMOURS DE GRIMSBY

When the sway of the exotic overwhelmed
My lyric impulse, I returned
At length to indigence and Grimsby.
On the quay where the fish-train set me down
And pulled away for Trebizond and Cleethorpes
No gift-box of herrings awaited me this time.
After the exhaustion of my early promise
In mannered elaboration of the same few
Arid tropes, I did not find in Grimsby
Girls in states of half-undress awaiting me
When they had got their shopping from the Co-op,
Had their hair done, phoned their sisters,
Read a magazine and thought I was the one.
I was *homo Grimsby*, brought to bed on spec.
When one bar in Grimsby turned into another –
Shelf of scratchings, half-averted clock,
The glassy roar when time was done
And steam rose from the massive sinks
In which the stars of Grimsby might have bathed –
I got my companionable end away
In Grimsby, or I sat on their settees,
My arms outstretched to mothers winding wool.
Therefore I live in Grimsby, cradled
In a fishwife's scarlet arms from dusk
To hobnailed dawn, my tongue awash
With anchovies and Grimsby's bitter Brown.
Mighty Humber's middle passage shrinks
To flooded footprints on a sandbar, each in turn

R=U=B=R=I =C

Inspected by a half-attentive moon. We sit
In smoke-rooms looking out. We know
That Grimsby is the midst of life, the long
Just-opened hour with its cellophane removed,
The modest editorial in which the world
Might change but does not, when the cellars
Empty back their waters, when the tide that comes
Discreetly to the doors enquires for old sake's sake
If this could be the night to sail away. From Grimsby?

R=U=B=R=I =C

It will not feature streetlamps, gable-ends
Or someone's fence thrown down by recent gales.
It will not tell us in a sidelong way
About your family's escape from Europe
In a *wagon-lit* disguised as pierrots, through forests
Thick with gamekeepers-turned-Nazis. It will not
PIne for Bukovina or for Rochdale.
It will not be Eurocentric, but in general
Atlases will leave it quite unmoved.
It will not satirise the times
Or praise a different period in terms
Which challenge our conception of the Good.
It will ignore the claims to eccentricity alleged
Among its fellow travellers on the Metro.
The library's oilclothed tables will not grant it
Access to black pools of divination.
It will not sing of ordinary life –
Of football, vinegar, domestic violence –
Or state the claims of art by means
Of imagery drawn from books of reproductions
Where the hero in a black suit stands
Before a maze of ice, or – donning a monastic cowl –
Among the sullen precincts of a temple
Framed with cypresses, to which a black-sailed ship
Draws near. It will not be ironic.

It will not speak to you in person
In an upper room where twelve are gathered
At the taxpayer's expense to hear
An explanation of themselves before they go
For pizza and a row. You will not hear it
Hail you in the accents of broad comedy or Ras Ta Far I
As you sit and mind your own business on the bus
Or in a padded cell. You cannot make it
Speak to your condition, nor to those
With a different sexual orientation,
Nor to those who neither know nor care to know
A poem from a cabbage or *Nintendo*.
Ask it not here, it won't be saying.
It will not glozingly insinuate itself
Through broadcast media. Sunday tea-time's
Safe for washing up and dismal contemplation
Of the weather which it also does not deal with.
It will not come between you and your lover
With a sudden intimation on the stairs
That all is lost, or place its hand imploringly
Upon your knee. It does not want to sleep with you,
Still less to drink its Vimto from your slipper;
Could not give a flying fuck for Nature
In its purest form or when as reconceived
At court it turns to pastoral; while God
Has never captured its attention fully –
Likewise the plains of Hell, the void or any
Combination of the three. It will not bear
The mark of Satan or the Library of Congress.
It will not write abuse in lipstick
On the mirror. Neither will it urinate
Upon the carpet having nicked the video.
It leaves the bathroom as we found it, like the world.
It would not slide the bad news from its folder,
Come to pray with you or hold your hand
As you confess a life of misdemeanours.
Nor will it permit you to interpret
Any of its absent gestures so
As to suggest an ur-, a sub-, a meta-text,

R=U=B=R=I=C

Having neither faith nor doubt
Nor any inclination worth a name, except
To know that it's what neither you nor I
Nor any of the pronouns lives to write,
Although we serve its sentence. Now begin.

Helen Simpson

CAPUT APRI

IT WAS BOXING Day and I must say I was quite glad to get out of the house. Another batch of in-laws had arrived that morning, and after a couple of hours of being chirpy I was actually pleased to find I'd forgotten the cranberries.

'I won't be a moment,' I promised. 'I'll just shoot down to Cullen's.'

It was lovely outside, frosty and sparkling, white ducks swimming on the village pond and so on. This was all very nice and I started to feel more cheerful. Along past the church I looked up and saw red berries and dark green holly leaves against the blue sky.

'Like a child's painting, isn't it?' said a voice at my shoulder.

You can always trust Yvonne Maitland to come out with something like that. How would one describe her? She's not exactly eccentric but on the other hand she's what my son would call, slightly off-the-wall. A wee bit arty. I was relieved to see Patricia Baron coming towards us. Salt of the earth, Patricia. On the same wavelength.

We chatted for a while about trees shedding needles and that sort of thing. Patricia was planning a picnic for her husband to take to the races – a flask of game soup, a manly steak sandwich, she didn't seem overjoyed.

'Aren't you going?' I asked.

'Oh no,' she sniffed. 'Client entertainment. No *wives*.' Her husband's with Bonner Kelman and Witt so she hardly ever sees him.

'Tough cheddar,' I said sympathetically. My husband's with Parringdon Knebworthy so I know the score.

'These City gents,' said Yvonne unexpectedly. She'd been watching us with her head on one side like a beady little robin. 'Let's have a drink,' she suggested. 'They're doing mulled wine at The White Horse, there's a log fire, we'll only be ten minutes.'

I saw Patricia hesitate. I was about to say No, surprised myself by barking out a Yes, and then Patricia caved in too.

We managed to bag a table by the fire and Yvonne organised the wine, which went straight to our heads in a very Christmassy way.

'This is fun,' said Patricia. 'If Malcolm could see me now.'

'I sometimes think,' said Yvonne, and stopped. She looked at us with an odd sort of expression. 'Let me tell you a story,' she said. 'It's all true, though I don't expect you'll believe me.'

I was quite happy to sit back holding my warm glass, and I could see Patricia felt the same, more than happy to let her chat away while we relaxed.

She started to tell the story, and I must say she told it very well, all the voices and actions and so forth. It was actually quite riveting. We soon forgot about the time completely.

Everard Ravenscroft possessed that blend of physical energy and emotional ruthlessness which is often called charisma (said Yvonne, her eyes in the middle distance, her mouth stained with hot wine). He flashed his sarcastic phrases like scissors around his family's ears, keeping them cowed and resentful. A fit fat barrister, he felt the cruelty was warranted, even salutary, a father's way of keeping them up to scratch.

One Christmas day some years ago, Everard was sitting at the head of the dining-table carving a fine varnished turkey watched by his wife Marion, who had cooked the bird, his son Charlie (shaking slightly as a result of substances ingested at a party attended the previous night), his permanently sulky adolescent daughter Natasha, and his youngest child, five-year-old Lucy.

'Good old turkey. Year in year out,' said Everard, addressing his wife. 'Sometimes, though, my dear, I must say I long to escape its flavourless clutches. Those mounds of bland flesh languishing for days afterwards.'

'You didn't like the spiced beef the year I did it,' she said.

'No, no. No more I did. It was quite repellently salty,' said Everard amiably. 'But perhaps another year we might have, let's see, a goose stuffed with Gascon prunes? A fruited loin of pork? Or even – memento of college days, that special Saturday before Christmas – a boar's head with a sodding great lemon in its mouth?'

'How totally disgusting,' said vegetarian Natasha, whose plate held a cheerless congregation of sprouts and potatoes. 'That makes me want to vomit.'

Her father narrowed his eyes dangerously at her and smiled his long thin smile. He had fierce light little eyes of arctic blue. The smile showed his teeth, which were all sharp and ship-shape if rather yellow.

'*Caput apri defero*,' he boomed, '*reddens laudes Domino*. The boar's head in hand bring I with garlands gay and rosemary.'

Charlie closed his eyes involuntarily, as though caught in a high bitter wind.

'And do you know why students used to sing a carol to the boar?' Everard continued, loud and remorseless. 'Because a long time ago, a *very* long time ago, a Queen's man was walking in the woods at Hinksey when a wild boar rushed out at him. Savage brute. Tusks to rip a horse up. Unluckily for him our man was carrying a copy of Aristotle's *Nicomachean Ethics* (which I feel you might read with some profit Natasha and you too Charlie in the not too distant future), and this he stuffed down the boar's throat, shouting *GRAECUM EST*.'

The table shuddered at the thunder of his voice.

'Then he cut off his head. The student cut off the boar's head, that is. Took it back to the college kitchen. And ever since.'

He stopped and surveyed the silent dinner-table with satisfaction. Clubbing them into submission with some crashing
great anecdote was one of his favourite techniques. Natasha
stared at him, at the big short-necked head with its brutally
turfy haircut, and envisioned it borne aloft on a pewter dish
of herbs.

'That's what's wrong with modern life,' continued Everard.
'It's tame. It's bland. It's not done to mention that the secret
of success is a matter of attack, of combative flair, that the
law of the jungle is not just an empty expression.'

'Darling,' said Marion plaintively. 'It *is* Christmas.'

After the meal, they all trooped off to the sitting-room and
dropped pensively into various armchairs.

'Can we open our presents?' said Lucy. She had truffled
out every package with her name on it from the mound of
parcels beneath the tree.

'Wait,' said Marion. 'Just wait till I've poured the coffee,
and we'll all open them together.'

'I suppose I'd better fetch your present, hadn't I?' said
Everard. 'Where's the Sellotape, et cetera?'

'Cardboard box on the landing,' said Marion tonelessly.
Everard groaned and set off, mock-lugubrious.

In his absence, Natasha opened her present, purchased by
her mother, paid for by her father, a jar of precious Pompeian
massage oil as requested, and gloated over it in a gloomy
cloud of narcissism. She and Charlie had jointly bought their
mother a reversible velvet scarf and their father a silver
money clip.

'You didn't get me the Barbie disco set!' wailed Lucy. 'I
told you to get the Barbie disco set! I hate you!'

'I did,' said Marion hurriedly. 'I *did*, darling. *Look*, darling.
What's this?'

'That's the Barbie aerobic studio. I don't want that! I hate
that! Oh!'

Lucy gave a shriek of grief and ran screaming from the
room, remembering however, even in the extremity of emotion, to give a wide berth to her father as he re-entered with
a hastily wrapped package.

'Happy Christmas,' he smiled, and Marion took the proffered parcel with a look of sullen fright. 'That child.'

'It's her age,' she said stiffly. 'Here's yours.' And she wheeled out an elaborate glittering construct from behind the piano.

'My goodness,' said Everard smugly. 'I wonder what this can be.'

'It took her hours to wrap,' Natasha accused him. 'She was crackling away all through *Where Eagles Dare*.'

'My goodness,' said Everard again, knee-deep in shimmering wrappings, staring at a bag of top-notch golf-clubs.

'I can change them,' Marion said. 'They said if I brought them back within twenty-one days.'

'Just what I wanted,' he said, and she winced as he landed a display kiss on her jaw.

Then she turned to her own parcel with the air of a bomb disposal expert confronted with an unfamiliar landmine.

'I hope it fits,' said Everard pleasantly, as she shook out the huge shroud-white nightdress, with its elasticated sleeves and high-necked goffered frill.

'Very practical,' gasped Marion.

'That frill's a bit like the bits on lamb cutlets,' said Charlie. 'Isn't it.'

'Mutton dressed as lamb!' laughed Marion, and ran sobbing into the Christmas tree. There was a soft gradual tinkling and rustling crash as one fell on top of the other.

After she had disentangled herself and struggled from the room covered in lametta, there was an awkward silence.

Then, 'She might have electrocuted herself on those lights,' commented Everard. 'Ridiculous.'

'Oh, Dad,' said Natasha. 'You are beastly.'

'Oh, I'm such a villain,' said Everard. 'Such a wicked patriarch. It's hard, Charlie. You'll find it hard too with your excellent education. We're the current trendy target for attack, purely because we have the misfortune to be middle class and male. I'm afraid you'll find everyone hates you before you've even opened your mouth.'

'Too right,' muttered Natasha, and followed her mother upstairs.

'What a monstrous regiment, eh,' observed Everard, selecting a virgin niblick and slicing the air with relish.

Charlie scowled at his father's profile. He wished he could punch him on his aquiline nose. In fact he would quite like to kill him, he noticed, raising a mental eyebrow. He quivered with fatigue, hunched his shoulders up round his ears, thrust his hands into his pockets.

As his left hand closed involuntarily around the powdery matt tablet, he remembered the Discobiscuit. It had cost him fifteen pounds last night, cheap at the price if it was the real thing, though he strongly suspected it wasn't. Nobody seemed to have seen or heard of the dealer before, and when Charlie, mindful of stories about ground lightbulb glass, had tried questions about the provenance of what he was being offered, he had been told to take it or leave it, but less politely.

With a chilly trickle of excitement, he now slid the Discobiscuit, unseen, into his father's coffee, where it fizzed gently for a moment or two. Then, mumbling an excuse, he left the room.

Half an hour later, Lucy pattered downstairs to watch *Mary Poppins*. She stopped outside the sitting-room when she heard the noises – vigorous snufflings and gruntings mixed with explosive gutturals. When she peeped around the door, her nose almost touched a flaring fleshy rosette, the open-nostrilled end to the wedge-like snout fronting the boar.

Its little eyes, gleaming with irritability and ill will, stared at her consideringly.

How could this be? You may well ask. The last wild boar in Britain was hunted to oblivion late in the eighteenth century. But butchers now will pay starry sums for meat from the hybrid marcassins sired by ex-zoo boars, housed in secure buildings under the Dangerous Animals Act: so perhaps this one was an escapee.

Perhaps.

Lucy's mouth opened to let out a thin high scream. She turned to run towards the stairs, and the boar, shrieking just as loudly, gave chase. When the child tripped, the boar thundered past her, its cloven trotters clipping the polished parquet flooring; and it turned its head slightly, dipped it down *en passant*, to allow one eight-inch tusk to rip through a sleeve into her upper arm.

Suddenly silent, Lucy scrambled to her feet while the boar wheeled, cumbersome as a leather suitcase, at the end of the hall. Then she shot off back up to her mother's room, clutching her dripping arm, while it stood at the foot of the stairs squealing with frustration.

When Marion saw her bleeding child step towards her, she grew uncharacteristically fleet and efficient, calm as a lizard, while her heart beat a tattoo.

A cursory examination of the First Aid box showed only little strips of plaster, not the bandages needed to bind shut the flap of gashed flesh. She cast around for clean white linen, seized on the new nightdress as ideal, and tore off a long strip from central hem to yoke. This she bound tightly round Lucy's arm, and watched the white of the makeshift bandage turn seepingly to scarlet while she dialled for an ambulance.

Natasha appeared at the bedroom door, and Charlie beside her. They both looked terrified.

'There's some sort of enormous pig,' said Natasha. 'Standing at the bottom of the stairs. Mum. Covered in bristles like a doormat.'

'Ah,' said Marion with unnatural calm. 'So that's what happened to Lucy's arm.'

When they saw their little sister, white as the Ace of Diamonds, Natasha gave a moan of distress while Charlie burst into tears.

'For goodness' sake, Charlie,' said Marion fiercely. 'Don't frighten her. Don't make things worse. There, there. It's all right, darling.'

Lucy's eyelids were flickering and she looked ready to faint. Charlie gave a sob. They could hear the animal's screams rising up the stairwell.

Marion placed the child against a bank of pillows.

'Where's your father?' she enquired of Natasha and Charlie.

'Haven't seen him,' said Natasha.

'Last time I saw him he was, um, drinking coffee in the front room,' sniffed Charlie.

Marion's mouth folded into a lipless pleat and she set off for the stairs.

'Everard! Everard!' she yelled, then stopped abruptly, half-way down, as her eyes met those of the boar. They stared at each other in mutual recognition. Marion's jaw dropped open like a nutcracker. The boar, fixing her with its tiny murderous eye, started scrabbling and shrieking again, frantic to climb the stairs. Marion clutched at her neck and lurched back to the bedroom.

'Everard,' she said in a clothy voice. 'It's Everard.'

'Oh Mum,' said Natasha. 'Is he hurt?'

'No,' said Marion. 'You don't understand. It's Everard.'

'You said,' said Natasha gently. 'But is he *hurt*?'

Charlie cleared his throat and wiped his eyes.

'She means the hairy pig is Dad,' he said, adding, 'It's all my fault.'

'What are you talking about?' said Marion. 'Come on. Tell me.'

'I put something in his coffee,' said Charlie.

'Something? What something?' said Natasha. 'Some sort of drug?'

'Yes,' said Charlie.

'Drugs?' said Marion. 'You?'

'Let's leave that one till later,' said Natasha. 'Shall we, Mum?'

'It isn't supposed to do this,' said Charlie helplessly. 'I mean, when you hallucinate, you might think you've turned into a wild boar. But you don't actually do it.'

'So *he* took the drug but he's forcing *us* to do the halluci-nating,' said Natasha. 'I see. Typical.'

She went out of the room to look again.

'He's smashing up those chairs you restored, Mum. You know, those ones you did in upholstery class,' she called.

'We'll have to go downstairs,' said Marion, joining her at the banisters, 'if we're going to get Lucy to the ambulance when it arrives.'

Charlie slid in between them.

'She's gone to sleep,' he said. 'Or passed out. You sit with her, Mother. We'll deal with, er, the animal.'

'Be careful,' said Marion. 'I don't want another of you needing stitches.'

'We'll be careful,' said Charlie. 'But you must stay in the room with Lucy. Keep her safe.'

Once Marion was out of the way Charlie started taking his father's weightier law books down from their shelves on the landing.

'Come on, Tasha,' he said. 'Ammunition.'

When they had built a workmanlike wall of fifty-odd volumes on the half-landing, they paused to consider the boar.

It stood about three feet high, with a long ferocious wedge of a head on a hefty paving-slab of a body. Its savage-looking tusks, one now dark with blood, gave it the mythical look of a woodcut in a bestiary, and were obviously well suited to their traditional task of destroying farmland and rooting up vineyards.

'Right,' said Charlie, and hurled *Equity and the Law of Trusts* straight at its head. He hit it in the eye and was rewarded with a bellow of fury.

'That's for sending me back to school when I said I'd kill myself,' he hissed.

Natasha took fire from her brother.

'And that's for never showing any interest in anything I've ever done,' she snarled, heaving *Private International Law* down the stairs.

'That's for telling me I've got no guts,' yelled Charlie. 'No staying power. No attack. I'll give you attack!' He threw book after book in a heavy rain.

'And that's for sneering at everything I've ever said,' cried Natasha, quite transported, white hot. 'Making me look stupid in front of my friends. Ignoring us all!'

The boar turned for a moment, half stunned by a blow to the temple from *The Law of Tort*'s sharp spine, groaning, swinging its long head from side to side; and in that moment, Charlie danced past it to the end of the hall, where the spotless golf-trolley stood, and seized a No. 3 iron.

'Come on, then,' he said, baring his teeth. 'Let's see who's got guts now.'

'Charlie!' screamed Natasha as the boar, pawing the parquet, made ready to charge.

But Charlie was quick. He swung the club above his head as he ran, and brought it down with sickening accuracy so that the full force of the blow curled into the beast's throat.

They watched his strangulated coughing fit and cheered his gradual noisy keeling over.

'Knife,' hissed Natasha. 'I'll get the carving knife.'

She ran off to the kitchen, while Charlie watched him start to revive.

'Quick,' he shouted. 'Quick. Give it to me. The throat. It's the only soft bit, he's built like a tank everywhere else.'

Natasha walked back down the hall holding the knife in both hands, staring at the bristly space indicated by her brother. Then she blinked as Marion flew past them both, whitely wild as a madwoman by Fuseli, to cast herself upon the felled wild boar.

'You'll kill me first,' she declared to her children.

At this point the doorbell rang. In the ensuing confusion – nobody knew exactly when or how – the boar disappeared and there was Everard on the floor, groaning, a long cut running across his forehead. He was taken off to hospital in the same ambulance as his daughter Lucy, and like her was absolutely unable to tell the hospital staff how he had received his injuries. It was a mystery, was all he would say.

Since that strange Christmas day, Everard has treated his first two children with real respect; and they, in turn, rein in their sense of damage done. As for his youngest daughter Lucy, he dotes on her, he knows the name of her best friend at school and of her second-best friend, he can tell you exactly how many teeth are in her head from day to day and precisely where she has got to in the Storychest scheme of things: but all this tenderness is painfully spiked, of course. In summer, when Lucy goes sleeveless, he winces at the scar on her arm, even though, sitting on his lap, she will laugh as she counts with her finger the seventeen stitch-marks at the side of his face. Then, of course, he is newly devoted to

Marion, and the neighbours clack about the amount of time they spend together, about how often they are seen out walking, talking, dawdling around arm in arm for all the world as if Everard wasn't one of the top silks in the country.

Not any more, he isn't? No. Well. There you are.

Yvonne fell silent. A log shifted on the fire and I blinked at the little shower of sparks. It was dark outside. We'd been here for hours! Whatever would my mother-in-law say? She'd be phoning round the hospitals by now.

'Arm in arm,' said Patricia, a bit oddly I thought. 'Not much to ask, is it, you wouldn't have thought. Still.' She straightened her back, flashed me a cheery grin. 'Better be getting back to the ravening hordes!'

'They'll be baying for our blood by now,' I agreed.

Then I remembered something.

'Cranberries,' I said. 'Oh *sugar*.'

Fay Weldon

RED ON BLACK

'I WILL NOT be defeated by a funeral,' said Maria to her mother. 'I will not.'

But her mother just blinked and smiled and went on playing Patience, red on black, black on red, on the shiny mahogany table. Black the colour of death, red the colour of blood, that is to say life. Blood streamed monthly to prove your youth. Yellow sun shone on cream pile carpet; pink-papered walls were lively with bursts of pale refracted light, as ocean waves beat against rocks below. The other side of the french windows, double-glazed to keep out the weather, the lawn which stretched to meet the sea-cliff was acid Easter green.

My mother did not even hear me, thought Maria. Black on red. Red on black. The black Jack moved up to be on the red Queen. 'I need a King,' said Maria's mother. 'An empty space, and no King. Please, St Anthony, bring me a King!' And there the next card was, black King of Spades, St Anthony's doing. Up went the Queen, and a train of dependants of lesser moment after her.

Maria's mother wore a dress splodged deep purple and bright mauve. Expensive imagined flowers clung to a body once slim, now bony. She's nearly seventy-five, thought Maria. But even as the colours bleach out of this one life, see how they reassert themselves all around.

Maria pulled the chintzy curtains to dull the glare from outside. Maria's mother went on playing cards. Maria was silent, sulking. 'Who did you say had died?' asked Maria's mother, eventually, when it became evident that this particular game would remain unresolved, and she'd swept up the cards, swiftly and certainly, the sooner to shuffle, deal, and begin again.

She will live out the rest of her life like this, thought Maria, proving to herself over and over again that resolution of any kind is a rare event indeed, and there is nothing to any of it other than luck. And if there is only luck, there can be no blame. Black on red, red on black, in a beautiful room by the edge of the sea.

'I didn't say,' said Maria. 'And put the black four on the red five,' said Maria, but her mother's hand had already moved. 'It was Bernard's father who died. He was eighty-nine, and it was expected. It's not so bad in itself. I saw him just a week ago. We parted on good terms. All the same it's a shock, and I don't like funerals.'

Maria's mother studied the cards, to make sure she'd missed nothing. 'Little Maria!' she observed absently, not even looking up. 'Always trying to see the best in everything. Your father could never look a fact in the face either.'

'I'm forty-two,' said Maria. 'I think I have my own nature by now.'

'I expect so,' agreed Maria's mother, and found the three she'd hoped for. Red on black, black on red. And there's the Ace. Good luck, bad luck, which will it be? Three coins in a fountain. Which one will the waters bless? Mother, father, Maria? Mother, when it comes to it. The one who leaves, not the ones who are left.

Mother left Maria with her father when Maria was fifteen to run off with a rich, rich man so that, now widowed, she can play Patience for ever at the edge of a sea. Today the weather was wild and bright, which was why the walls were so lively with shifting patches of light. You could search for a pattern and not find one; the wind-whipped waves broke out of proper sequence against their cliffs. Maria's car had been drenched in spray as she took the sea road up to her mother's house. Maria hated driving. Maria's car was cheap and old; Maria's mother's car was new and expensive and properly garaged, though seldom used. Maria was always constrained by money, by necessity, by proper feeling. Maria had to argue with her boss in order to take a couple of days off work to visit her mother, to go to a funeral. She had to go to her mother; her mother never came to her.

Maria had been exultant when her mother left home. It was the first and last illicit emotion she could remember. Sorry that Father was upset but exultant all the same, able at last to look after him. Mother gone! Now I can stop father's ears for ever to the sound of bitchery and complaint; only nice things will sound through this house from now on; at last I am in charge. Why should the world be all discord, when it can be harmony? Mother gone, so what? If a man has a daughter who loves him, what can he need with a wife? All his wife did was deny and deride him. Now we, the proper people, father and daughter, can start again. This gentle, kindly man deserves no less.

Only within the year Maria's father invited into his bed a woman called Eleanor; so Maria began to hear her mother's voice in her own, mocking and dispirited, carping and mean, whenever she spoke to her father, and it was so disagreeable a sound that Maria married Bernard rather than stay home a second longer than she need.

Maria's mother came to Maria's wedding with her new husband, Victor. Maria's father came with his new wife, Eleanor. Eleanor had lent Maria a dress – Maria lived on a student grant, Maria's father had no money to spare: talk of money distressed him – and Eleanor had posted off the invitations. Maria's mother hadn't helped at all: she just said Maria was too young to get married; she'd have nothing to do with any of it, and hadn't. Eleanor had done everything, had been wonderful.

Except that at the wedding Maria's mother said, 'I left because of Eleanor. I found her suspender belt in the marital bed. And you, Maria, didn't have the guts to stop her coming today. You want everything to be nice. You can never see why everyone shouldn't just be happy. But they can't be.' Maria had said, 'You're spoiling my wedding, please go away, like you did before,' and Maria's mother had done just that. Walking away down the path through the bright green grass, in a beige shantung suit and a little blue hat, next to grey-suited, solid Victor. In those days Maria's mother had dressed quietly. 'Never mind,' said Eleanor. 'We did what we could. At least we invited her.' 'Good riddance,' said Maria's father.

When family angels turn to demons, when the worm in the apple is healthier than the apple, what's a girl to do? Except marry Bernard, forget the whole thing; quarrel with your mother, remember never to forgive her for abandoning you; make a friend of your stepmother, see her through a pregnancy more troubled than your own; gain a half-sister the day you gain a son. Watch Father wander through the house, in this marriage as in the last, but happier. Watch for and iron out the note in your own voice that reminds you of your mother; eradicate it. Make things good, as your mother made things bad. Get on with loving Bernard.

Red on black. Black on red. Maria's mother is stuck on a nine. Not an eight anywhere in sight. Maria's hungry. But not till a game comes out will Maria's mother ring the bell, call the maid, ask her to serve lunch. When it comes it will be frugal.

Eleanor's table was always extravagant. Stepmother came with a ready-made family: brothers, sisters, aunts, uncles, cousins; peopling a world, filling it with conversation and event. Maria's father gave up his job on a matter of principle. Eleanor's earnings eventually kept everyone: even subsidised Bernard, Maria and little Maurice. Superwoman Eleanor! Bernard was getting a PhD. Maria tried to repay Eleanor by looking after little Winnie, her half-sister, when Eleanor's child-care arrangements broke down.

Another game. Red on black, black on red. She's polite, but she never really speaks to me. Can she really not forgive me because Eleanor asked her to my wedding, because on that one day I spoke out of turn? Eleanor, whose suspender belt had induced Maria's mother to leave home. Except it wasn't like that. Maria's mother had been mercenary, after Victor's money. That was the only reason she'd left home, abandoned everyone. It was because Maria's mother had done such a dreadful thing that Maria's father had needed the consolation of Eleanor. Everyone knew that. Maria's mother was the villain of the piece.

Perhaps I can't forgive my mother, thought Maria, not because she abandoned me, but because in leaving us she let me think my father could be mine, gave credence to my illicit fantasies. Didn't I once hate Eleanor? I can hardly remember. Eleanor and my father, rising as one from the evening's television, hand in hand, going off into the bedroom together, where he'd been with my mother since the beginning of time, that is to say the beginning of my life? Leaving me shut out and excluded, to listen out for the sounds of gasps and moans, not the plaintive rise and fall of marital reproaches. When did I stop hating Eleanor? I can't remember that. Perhaps the day I married Bernard, and my mother saw Eleanor there, and I had to choose between Eleanor and her, and I chose Eleanor. Is not-hating Eleanor the price I pay for not-hating my father?

'All you women,' Bernard would say, 'squabbling over one poor man.' Such passions as we had, Bernard would reduce to nonsense.

'You shouldn't wear grey,' said Maria's mother, clearing away the cards. 'And shouldn't you do something about your hair?'

'Bernard's father is dead,' Maria wanted to say, 'and I am in a state of distress. I am not entitled to official mourning: I have been disinherited from grief by divorce, along with everything else. I like grey. I will wear my hair as I want.' The dancing patches of light on the wall stilled, as if the waves were holding their breath. Maria said nothing. The pounding began again. A trick of sea and wind, working in unison for once. The curve of the wave, held in suspense, foam whipped along the crest, as a gust of wind beat it back, before falling into its mêlée of navy and white. Lunch was served. A little thin soup. A mackerel, freshly caught.

* * *

51

'How is Bernard?' asked Maria's mother. 'Still living in half your house?'

'It works well,' said Maria. 'It's sensible. There's no reason after a divorce why you shouldn't be friends.'

'Careful of the bones,' said Maria's mother. 'I wouldn't want you to choke.'

'And Maurice can go between us as and when he wants,' said Maria, hearing the plaintive edge to her voice. Why do I have to suffer so others can be happy? I have to live beneath my ex-husband Bernard so Maurice can run upstairs to see his father when he wants: so I don't even have proper possession of my own child: so Bernard can criticise the way I bring him up: the clothes he buys, the pocket-money he has; can find fault with me if I have any kind of social life: all the while congratulating himself on his forbearance, on his self-control – living above a wife who so aggravated him when she was with him, was so frigid, so neurotic, he was obliged to have girlfriend after girlfriend just to stay sane. And how, having a child in common, and being noble, he now helps her out. She is of course a hopeless mother – absent-minded, over-emotional: Bernard can't leave Maria unprotected in the world, because of the damage she might do to Maurice. So to the detriment of his own life, his own artistic, poetic need to be free, he puts up with staying where he is, in the ex-marital home, halved by hardboard. The stairs are shared. Up the stairs go the succession of girlfriends. Turn up the music so as not to hear the moans and the groans, the creaking of the floor. What kind of example is that for a growing boy? Bernard changes the girls so often. The backs of their legs are oddly the same. Bernard seems to like girls with solid calf muscles. Maria's own legs are thin; straight up and down without much ankle. Mad legs, Bernard would call them.

'We couldn't afford to buy two houses,' said Maria to her mother. 'We had no choice but to do it the way we did.'

Maria's mother pushes away her plate: the half-eaten mackerel lies dull upon it. The maid poaches them with the heads on. White, white sightless eyes.

'Disgusting fish,' said Maria's mother. 'I can't think why she buys them.'

'Because they're cheap, I suppose,' said Maria, and Maria's mother raised her eyebrows, in surprise that this should be seen to be an adequate motive for doing anything.

'I don't think I ever met Bernard's father,' said Maria's mother, and Maria said, 'He came to our wedding,' and then realised it might be better not to have said it.

'The wedding,' said Maria's mother. 'Of course, you asked that bitch to it and didn't warn me. Do you like ginger ice-cream? I'll get the maid to bring some in if you like.'

It was easier to say no, but Maria made herself say yes. The ice-cream came, a small single scoop in the middle of a large white plate. The 'maid' was a broad local woman, with shoes trodden down at the back; local wages were low. Maria's mother spent money carefully. Maria's father spent everything there was to spend, as soon as possible, and always absently, and seemed surprised when he'd done it. He'd look at bills wonderingly; it was a family joke. Eleanor worked long hours, perforce – she was a graphic designer; she worked freelance – but her voice never hardened into reproach and complaint. Maria would listen, as Eleanor spoke, to confirm that it didn't, and would listen to her own voice likewise.

'It's a wild day,' said Maria's mother: foam flew up the cliff and swept over the lawn and gently patterned the french windows. If the tide rose any higher it would not be so gentle. 'The other side of the glass the wind will be howling. And it's a high tide. Sometimes we get the foam up here, not often. The garden's salty. Growing things is a problem.'

'Twenty-three years later and you still call her a bitch,' said Maria, boldly.

'She was,' said Maria's mother. 'And you should never have asked her to your wedding. You're my daughter, not hers.'

'I didn't ask her,' lied Maria. 'She just came. I'm sorry. I didn't think you'd turn up. You were so against poor Bernard.'

'One look at Bernard,' said Maria's mother, 'and you could tell what would happen next. You'd see him through college, you'd have his child, you'd take responsibility, provide all the money, and he'd wander off. Another child, like your father, not a grown person at all. I'm glad that bitch Eleanor got what she deserved. I could never understand why you were so thick with her.'

She rose, as if to say the audience had ended. Her cheeks were pink: she knew she had been unduly talkative; she blamed her daughter for it. The maid came in to take the ice-cream plate from under Maria's nose. Maria sat with her head lowered, as if she were a disgraced child.

Eleanor had developed breast cancer and taken four years to die: Maria's father now lived well on her life insurance money. Maria had asked him, at the time of her divorce, for the loan of enough money to buy a house at a distance from Bernard. She'd never asked her father before for money. It had been her habit to ask Eleanor.

'I don't think lending you money would be a good idea,' said Maria's father. 'I don't want to interfere between husband and wife, even when they're allegedly exes. You two get along well enough. A divorce by mutual assent. Very civilised. If anyone can make it work, you can, Maria. I only wish your mother had been like you.'

Eleanor would have understood, would have lent her the money. Maria had cried for a week when Eleanor died. Bernard said, 'Crocodile tears. No one loves a stepmother.' But then he was angry at the time. Bernard didn't see why Maria wanted a divorce; why she couldn't adjust to a husband's need for sexual variety, or take lovers herself to ease the emotional burden from his shoulders; Maria was rigid in her outlook, he complained; hopelessly jealous and possessive; she needed therapy rather than a divorce. And a divorce would upset Maurice. Maria had persisted. Now every time Maurice had flu, or was in trouble at school, or failed to satisfy Bernard's expectations of him, Bernard would raise his eyebrows and say, 'His parents are divorced. Of course he's unhappy and disturbed. What did you think would happen?'

Maria took in Bernard's mail when he was out, looked after his cat when he was away, let in his girlfriends when they'd lost their keys. They'd look at her curiously. She wondered what Bernard said to them about her. 'Isn't it time you found yourself a boyfriend?' Bernard had asked her once or twice, meeting her on the stairs. 'But I suppose, since there's such a glut on the market of unattached women, you have a real problem.' Maria knew better than to protest. Bernard was a journalist, a columnist: he was clever, moody, talented. He had the statistics of society at his fingertips. If she looked doubtful, he'd quote such figures as suited him to prove his point.

'I do seem to have a problem,' she'd say, hoping he'd leave it there. Sometimes he did, sometimes he didn't. 'Divorced women over forty,' he'd say, 'rarely re-marry.' If she said she didn't want to re-marry, wasn't interested in men, he'd raise his eyebrows as if she was protesting too much. Maria felt uglier and uglier. At the beginning she'd given a couple of dinner parties; Bernard had asked himself down to them, and hogged the conversation, and laughed at her cooking, which was indeed bad. She didn't try again. He'd grabbed her on the stairs and kissed her once, a couple of years into the upstairs-downstairs arrangement, and said he was free on Saturday night, why didn't she come up after Maurice was asleep? Not to make it a habit, he said. Just the once to show there was no ill-feeling: that she didn't hold grudges: that she wasn't like her mother, and a nag and a bore. And just the once she'd gone, to prove exactly those things, and he had been a wonderful lover, and she'd thought perhaps she could put up with all those girls after all, but he hadn't asked her up again. Maria felt worse. And the next girl, Angela, seemed a permanent fixture. Maria didn't want Bernard to marry again, she wasn't quite sure why. Especially not someone like Angela, a currant bun: tight little curls, lax mouth, stocky legs. Why would anyone want Angela when they could have

Maria? Amend. Could have had Maria. These days Maria told her friends she loathed Bernard, they'd laugh at his dreadful behaviour, the things he'd done, but when he was away, when she couldn't hear the footsteps overhead, she was uneasy and nervous, though relieved of the burden of thinking about Angela and Bernard together.

Maria's mother sat down at the round mahogany table and dealt the cards again. Face downwards, blank, all but the last card in each row, face upwards. The pink faded from her cheeks.

'Be all that as it may,' Maria said, 'it's the present that counts, not the past. I don't mean to be defeated by a funeral. I hate funerals, but I'll go to this one.'

Red on black, black on red. Life on death, death on life. Her mother said nothing.

'Bernard's father lived with us for four whole years,' said Maria. 'Of course I want to pay him my last respects. He was gentle and nice. While he was about, Bernard behaved. It was after he left that the women got out of control. Their suspender belts in our bed. Well, you know about that.'

Slap, slap, slap went the cards.

'But I take a lot of the responsibility,' said Maria. 'I was working full-time and Maurice was still small, and I expect I neglected Bernard. I went off sex. Well, he said I did. I didn't notice. It can be like that, I suppose. It was understandable Bernard looked elsewhere. I expect I should just have put up with it. In the light of death these little dramas seem so pitiful.'

Maria's mother gave a little cough.

'Well, forget all that,' said Maria. 'I shouldn't burden you with it. I'm grown up now. Bernard and I will go to the funeral. At least this is something we share – a particular grief: his father's dying. The end of something. There were really good times, some of the time, when I was first married to Bernard. That's why the marriage had to end: I didn't want it to get spoiled, in retrospect: unravel itself out, backwards, into nothing. The divorce was damage limitation. Do you see? In a marriage the past is forever piling into the present.'

Maria's mother's game resolved itself. Four rows of up-turned, revealed cards announced finality: the imposition of order upon chaos, design over happenstance. Maria's mother smiled.

'I need a breath of fresh air,' she said, and threw the french windows open, and the sounds of wild weather and pounding sea charged into the room, spray damped their hair, the curtains billowed almost to the ceiling, Maria's mother's dress swirled around her legs, and the cards were flung about the room and in profound disorder again, as if thoroughly shuf-fled. Both women laughed, exhilarated.

Maria leaned against the windows to close them against the gale. Enough was enough.

'What do you mean?' asked her mother. 'You won't be defeated by a funeral? Why should you be defeated?'

'It's the journey,' said Maria. 'The drive. You know how I hate driving. The funeral's at the Golders Green Crema-torium. I hate driving into London. And I get lost.' Maria had been late for Eleanor's funeral. She couldn't forgive herself for that. She'd kept missing the turning: finding herself back on the one-way circuit. When she did get it right, she lost more time trying to park in a space too small anyway, panicking.

'Get Bernard to drive you,' said Maria's mother. 'That man must be of some use for something.'

When Maria got home, Maurice was back from school: he'd made his own supper. He was lying on the floor watching football on TV and doing his homework at the same time.

'Why didn't you go up to your father?' she asked.

'Because he doesn't like me watching football,' said Maurice in his croaky adolescent voice. 'He thinks television rots the brain. And he can't stand me rotting my brain and doing my homework at the same time. And Angela's there again, and she gets on my nerves. You know they're getting married?'

'Why her?' asked Maria, after a little.

'Because he really only likes stupid women,' said Maurice. 'And Angela is really stupid. Will you come to the wedding?'

'I expect so,' said Maria, bleakly. 'There's no point in making things more difficult than they are already. We all have to get along together somehow. I wish he'd told me himself.'

'He probably meant to tell you at Grandad's funeral,' said Maurice. 'You know what he's like. This is a really boring football match. I'll make you a cup of tea.'

'What is he like?' asked Maria. 'What is your father like?'

'How do you expect me to know what he's like?' enquired Maurice. 'He's my father. But you're okay.'

She had to be satisfied with that. If there was a battle, and she had tried so hard for there not to be, she was winning. Maurice was on her side. Later Maria called Bernard and asked him if he could give her a lift down to the funeral: it seemed a waste for two cars to go from the same address. Bernard said there was no room in his vehicle: it was only a sports car, he was of course taking Maurice down, and he was surprised to hear Maria wanted to go at all. Maria had in all probability triggered off the events which had led to the death in the first place. He and she were, after all, divorced. Divorce meant that his family and her family were wholly separate. And he would hardly expect to go to Maria's mother's funeral, for example. Maria said briskly that she would make her own way to the Crematorium.

Maria intended to start early: to allow at least two hours for a journey which would take Bernard one and a bit. She put on a grey suit. Black at funerals always seemed self-conscious, primitive. Widow's gear: the renunciation of sex. That's it, that's gone: the delights of the flesh deliquescing into mud. That's you served right for enjoying yourself. Black on red. Maria put on a red scarf to cheer the suit up. The hem of its skirt was unstitched. She found needle and cotton to see to it. Maurice had to be persuaded not to wear an overlarge, cannabis-worship jacket; pink curling puffs of smoke on a yellow background, and words she failed to understand but Maurice said were acceptable, Grandad wouldn't have minded. It grew later and later. Maria seemed unable to accept the dictates of the clock. Her will and the material world were at odds. Something rebelled. In the end she and Bernard left at the same time.

Bernard went down the stairs in front of her; he was wearing a grey suit; he carried a portable phone. She remembered Victor long ago. Bernard seemed a stranger to her. There was a clattering behind her, and Angela pushed past. She was wearing a light shiny blue suit, and a lot of pearls, as if she were going to a wedding.

"Scuse me, Maria. I hope you've got Maurice ready. We're going to be so late if you haven't.'

'I didn't know *she* was coming,' said Maurice, but he got into the car with Bernard and Angela, folding himself into the small space at the back, leaving Maria to stand on the doorstep. Perhaps it would be better if she didn't go? All that way, to what end? To stand in a dingy room, listening to melancholy music, contemplating mortality and the death of hope, the death of love, the death of her body? What sort of 'respect' was it that she thought she could pay? She had failed Bernard's father in this life, she had failed to keep him alive, let alone healthy; she couldn't even stay married to his son, a failure which had distressed the old man. She could just turn back now, into her half of the matrimonial home, take the day off work, get accustomed to the idea of Bernard, married to Angela, living on top of her. Accept her role as murderer, not mourner.

But her feet walked her, almost of their own accord, towards her car. Maria wore black court shoes, worn out of shape, as she felt she was herself. Denatured: altered perforce to fit the circumstances.

The Golders Green Crematorium is sombre and leafy, concrete-pathed and well-signposted: it serves large areas of the city. Its memorial rose garden is denatured. The ashes of the dead are dug into the soil, but somehow fail to produce abundance. Little red-brick chapels are used for individual services, as little individual jars of breakfast jam serve these days instead of the whole jar. Hearses come and go, quietly: coffins are carried by experts, expertly. An almost agreeable hush descends upon the little clusters of friends and relatives: the air is hard to breathe, as if the place were indoors, not outdoors, or at any rate covered by some invisible bell-jar: you might as well be in an airport, or a hospital, so devital-ised the place has become, by virtue of so many human passions stultified, brought up short by the advent of death. Too late now. For who ever lived totally as they wanted to: who ever, if they have time to think about it, dies wholly satisfied? And those who remain know it.

Maria was late, but the chapel services were running later. The deceased's friends and relatives, an official said, were gathered in the appropriate waiting-room. Maria pushed open the heavy Gothic door: it groaned. Blank and hostile faces looked back at her. Angela was bright in her shiny blue. Maurice came out to be with his mother. Maria and Maurice leaned against the chapel wall. Maurice smoked a cigarette. Maria hoped Bernard would not come out and catch him.

'Angela's pregnant,' Maurice said. 'That's the only reason he's marrying her.'

Maria didn't say, 'Well, I was pregnant, too. That's why he married me.' Or perhaps he made me pregnant in order to be obliged to marry me and then blame me.

'Angela shouldn't be here,' said Maurice. 'It isn't fair. She never even met my grandfather.'

'I expect she just likes to be with your father,' said Maria, 'wherever he goes, and so she should. Try to like her, Maurice; it will be better if you do. We have to be civilised.'

A clutch of hearses approached, passed: following after them, on their black coat-tails, came a cream Rolls-Royce, which parked in a space clearly marked 'Official Parking: hearses only', and Maria's mother stepped out. She wore a pink turban and a yellow suit, and all around were the colours of brick chapel, concrete paving, a dull sky, and bare branches on which buds still struggled to provide a hint of the new season. It was such a late spring: no one could understand the weather these days.

'Mother? All this way!'

'I didn't want Maria to be defeated by a funeral,' said Maria's mother to her grandson. 'I was defeated by a wedding once. It doesn't do to be defeated by rituals.'

'He brought her here,' said Maria, suddenly tearful. 'He had no right to do that. He was my father-in-law, not hers. How dare they?'

'Pull yourself together; you're not a child,' said Maria's mother, out of some kind of dim maternal memory, 'or I'll wish I'd never come.' Maria was sobbing and gulping. Bernard and Angela emerged from the chapel. Bernard seemed disconcerted. Angela was pink and angry.

'I have every right to be here,' Angela said, stopping to face Bernard, taking in the presence of the first wife, his ex-mother-in-law, her soon-to-be stepchild. 'I love you and you love me and I want every single part of you, and that means your past as well. If you loved your father, I loved him too, he's my baby's grandfather, and I'm entitled to come to his funeral, so I don't know what you mean, Bernard, by my "cashing in". I don't want to hear that kind of mean, miserable thing from you ever again. I've heard far too much of it from you lately. I don't know what gets into you sometimes.' Then she turned on Maria. 'What are you doing here, anyway? An ex is an ex, as you'll find from now on. You depress the hell out of me, to tell you the truth. That godawful grey suit is a case in point and no one's worn a scarf for years. Self-pitying bitch.'

The nasal voice stopped. It had come bursting in like some destructive gust of wind, thought Maria; everything settled, everything you clung to, was up in the air, whirling. They were all looking at her, waiting for a response. Maurice hovered halfway between Bernard and herself. Oh Eleanor, Eleanor, help me now. I married Bernard in the spring, but then the day was bright and clear. Eleanor smiled and drove my maternal mother out. Let me re-phrase that: together, Eleanor smiling, myself scowling, we held the whip that drove my mother out. Perhaps Eleanor was a false ally, after all. If she smiled it was because now she'd have my father to herself. Of course my stepmother lent me a dress. And afterwards she could afford to be generous. She'd won. Angela wants Bernard to herself, of course she does. She uses different methods, that's all – sulks not smiles. And Bernard just spreads his hands and thrives in the warmth of our squabbling.

Even as I hesitate, I see Maurice drifting over to Bernard's side. Mother love? What's that? What's required? I want Maurice to grow up to be the best of his father, not the worst. We aren't meant to be on sides: we are meant to try to be civilised. All my life spent understanding and forgiving – but these are matters of life and death; desperate things. Red on black, black on red: understood but not forgiven. Has my mother come here today to explain that to me? She can't forgive me, she won't forgive me, she must not forgive me because what I did was unforgivable; nor can she understand it. But she can still instruct me. She won't look me in the eye, she never will, but she came today to set an example, to help me.

'*My* father-in-law,' said Maria to Angela, 'mine. And it's you who have no business here. You can have Bernard's future, you're welcome to it, but you can't have Bernard's past. That's mine. You will not unravel my life from this moment back. Why don't you just go back to the house? Go on back, let me mourn in the peace I deserve. I came first and you came second, all you are entitled to is the dregs –'

'Bernard!' wailed Angela, but Bernard just spread his fingers helplessly, and licked his lips.

'It's her or me,' cried Angela. 'I'm warning you, Bernard.'

'I do as I like,' said Bernard. 'What you do is up to you.'

'This is our business, not yours,' said Maria's mother to Angela, as once she should have said it to Eleanor. 'You go, we stay.' And she looked Angela's suit up and down as if to say this is a funeral, not a wedding; can't you tell the difference? I'm old enough to do as I like but you're not. Whoever can have brought you up?

Angela looked at Maria's mother's attire and curled her lip.

'Mutton dressed up as lamb,' she actually said.

'Excuse me,' said a group of black-suited, sleek-haired men passing through, bearing a coffin on accustomed shoulders. The little cluster of mourners had to part and re-form. Maria wondered if the body inside the coffin were male or female, young or old; how they'd lived, how they'd died. Whether they were persecutor, self-interested and invalidating; or victim, understanding and forgiving, this was the outcome. Since there was no justice in death, you'd better find it in life, however disagreeable it made you in the eyes of others, in your own eyes too.

'Just go away,' Maria said to Angela, with a snap of anger so sharp and severe it all but cracked and slivered the sheltering bell-jar; or at any rate a breath of cold, fresh, lively air suddenly whipped around their legs: a memento of winter in the presence of spring. Everyone looked startled.

'Go away,' repeated Maria, 'and take Bernard with you.'

Bernard said, 'I can't do that. I'm the chief mourner. He's my father. I have to stay. But you don't have to, Angela. Really it's best that you don't. Wait in the car.'

And Angela walked meekly off to wait. Maurice moved over to stand by his mother's side.

'That's better,' said Maria's mother. 'At last!'

'What's more, I'm not living beneath a baby,' said Maria to Bernard, 'let alone you, Angela and a baby. What do you think I am?'

'That's okay,' said Bernard. 'Now my father's dead I can afford to move out. You can have the whole house.'

They stood together in the chapel, and afterwards went their separate ways. Bernard and Angela and a new baby, Maria and Maurice back home, Maria's mother back to her cards. Red on black, black on red; red on black, life on death.

Helen Dunmore

SPRING WEDDING

'OH, GOD, I don't know what's the matter,' groans Jorma. His pale fluffy cheek vibrates against hers. He's crying.

No, he's not. The second she peeks up, timid with concern, he throws himself back on to her and they roll over in his narrow pine bed until Ulli's head and shoulders are tipping dangerously over the edge and Jorma has to haul her back on to the mattress. The quilt slides off on to the floor.

The room's warm, but even so Ulli feels exposed. If he wants to, Jorma can see all of her. She had kept her baggy T-shirt on as she ducked under the quilt, then somehow that had got rolled up over her head and now it's lying in a ball in the corner of the room. Jorma's bedroom. Jorma's lucky. His father is an architect and he's made a huge low room up here for his two sons, with wide, sweet-smelling pine-planked floor and pine-panelled walls. A blonde room, cupping light even when it's grey outside. A steep window set in the roof, and a long desk underneath it, for Jorma and Jussi to study.

Jorma has the room to himself this weekend. His parents and his brother are away at a family wedding, but Jorma's got out of it because he has a test coming up on Monday, an important test in English and maths for which he'll be able to revise in the peace and quiet of the empty house. Can his parents really believe one word of it? Ulli asks herself.

She doesn't know what to make of Jorma's parents. They are effusive on the telephone, ostentatiously welcoming when she comes to their house to listen to records and drink coffee upstairs with Jorma and Jussi. They have managed to let her know that Jorma has lots of little girlfriends who are always ringing up or calling round, and that while of course they're perfectly happy about that, it's rather hard for his parents to tell one little girl from the next. One time they'd had friends round for drinks when she'd been there. Jorma's mother had insisted on introducing Ulli to everybody, even though Jorma had clearly been trying to edge her past the open sitting-room door and up the stairs without attracting anybody's attention. Ulli had come on her bike and she was out of breath and conscious of sweaty hands. She had her jeans on, and a sweatshirt which she'd tie-dyed unsuccessfully. Jorma's parents and their friends were dressed in expensive buff and white and cream playclothes that cuffed the women's care-fully waxed legs. Jorma's mother had a plain gold chain round her neck. She wore a yellow linen dress and shoes of soft peach-coloured leather, and her pale hair was coiled into a knot at the back of her neck. Not one wisp slipped loose.

'Did you do this yourself?' she asked, fingering Ulli's sweat-shirt. 'That's marvellous, isn't it, darling? You young people are so creative.'

Beside Ulli, Jorma scowled and darkened. 'It's not a work of art, Mummy. You don't have to make such a thing about it.'

His mother slid her eyes sideways towards her guests in mock-despair. Her fingers touched Jorma's cheek coolly, lightly.

'What about that revision, darling? I'm sure Ulli's got work to do as well. I don't want to get in your parents' bad books for letting Jorma distract you from your studies, Ulli.'

'You don't need to worry about Ulli, Mummy. She's about a million times brighter than me, ask anyone. And she's got two more years ahead of her.'

'Gracious, Ulli, are you only sixteen? I'd never have thought it. Your face is quite . . . *old* . . . somehow.'

There was a silence, then 'Oh well, off you go. But don't forget darling, the Manners will be here at six. And I *particularly* want you to look after Maija-Liisa. She's such a lovely girl, but *so* shy.'

'I must admit,' cut in Jorma's father bluffly, 'I rather like to see that in a young girl.'

Ulli shuts her mind. It's all in the past and anyway Jorma's parents are a hundred kilometres away, drinking champagne or whatever people drink at weddings these days. Triple schnapps, if the colour of Jorma's father's face is anything to go by. He doesn't like Ulli. His dislike makes her skin stiffen and prickle when she has to pass him on the stairs.

Jorma is rubbing his thumb up and down the inside curve of her hip-bone. Her stomach lies slack and shallow. She feels she's scarcely breathing. Jorma lays his head on her stomach, and shuts his eyes.

'I can hear your stomach rumbling,' he says. 'Just think, I know more about what's going on inside you than you do.'

His head is very heavy. Now she believes what she has learned at school about the relative weight of the head to the rest of the body. His hair is so soft and fine, and yet it curls. She can unroll one of the curls, and he doesn't even notice. He's as good as asleep, and she doesn't want to disturb him, but she's starving.

She thinks of the big white double-doored fridge in the kitchen/breakfast-room downstairs. There's always enough juice in Jorma's house, in glass pitchers without smears or streaks on them. There are fruit yoghurts in packs of a dozen, and iced buttermilk to drink. Jorma's mother doesn't go to the market. She buys fruit the expensive way, in the supermarket, and it lies in the fridge solid and clean in its plastic wrappers, unbruised, giving off no scent.

Ulli dreams of a cheese sandwich. The lurch of her stomach juices stirs Jorma, and she tips him off her and folds her body away from his. She doesn't want to walk away with her back to him. She will feel him looking at her. She dives, scoops up the white baggy T-shirt and pulls it over her head. She shakes out her hair over it. Jorma is leaning up on one elbow, resting on his side and looking at her. His face is wiped clean with sleep, its strong irregular bones softened.

'. . . *about a million times brighter than me . . .*'

No. It isn't so. His green eyes clear and look at her. He isn't smiling, but his face brims with willingness to smile. He's waiting for her to tuck up her feet under the T-shirt and sit facing him on the other end of the bed. She is studying

Baudelaire and he likes her to recite the poems to him in French. He dropped French way back, when he was fourteen. There didn't seem any point in his going on, all the teachers had agreed. Even the private tutor his mother got hold of didn't do the trick. It was just like eating something that disagreed with him. But Ulli knows that, put Jorma in a café in a little French seaside town where they don't speak a word of any other language, and he'd come back half an hour later knowing that there's a little beach nearby you can get to if you go round the rocks at low tide – it's always deserted and you can swim with nothing on . . .

'*J'aime de vos longs yeux la lumière verdâtre . . .*'

she begins. He nods and closes his eyes.

'Don't you want to know what it means?' she asks.

'Not really. It's the sound I like. The sound of your voice. You know, I used to hate French at school, but it's nice when you speak it.'

'Don't you wish we could go there? To France I mean?'

'No, why? I like this.'

'Do you? What about this?'

She puts out a foot and stirs his ribs.

'Listen. Don't go falling asleep again. Listen to this one and tell me if it doesn't make you want to go far away, as far away as you possibly can.'

'*Mon enfant, ma soeur*
Songe à la douceur
D'aller là–bas vivre ensemble . . .'

'I suppose it might if I could understand it,' says Jorma. 'Was there something about a sister? *J'ai une soeur et un frère.* My tutor was always on at me to say that for some reason. Why is it that when you're learning a foreign language, you always have to tell lies?'

He catches hold of her foot and holds it for a moment, looking at the structure of her toes and the tan-marks from her sandals. They're still there, the marks of last summer's sun, even after the long winter when her foot's been sheathed in her brown leather boots with their sheepskin lining.

At this time of year Ulli finds it hard to remember what sun feels like on bare skin. It's mid-April. Two weeks now since she stopped being a virgin. Funny how often she's thought of it that way, since it happened. She can't remember thinking of herself as a virgin beforehand. But now she thinks of it and says it over and over in her mind, in the long quiet sunlit classroom during her maths test, or when she's gulping down coffee before she catches the bus to school. The word feels like a splinter deep inside her, not a splinter of ice but something quick and hot and alive. She's getting to love the word *virgin*.

Virgin. Non-virgin. Words in a changing-room:

'Technically, I'm sure I'm not a virgin any more.'

'No, it's all right if you do that. You're still a virgin really. Otherwise nobody'd be a virgin if they used tampons, would they?'

'My mother still won't let me use tampons. She says they give you cancer.'

My child, my sister . . .

Jorma gives the foot back to her and says,

'Come back to bed.'

'I can't, I'm starving.'

'Poke around under the bed. There might be some biscuits. Jussi's always leaving stuff around.'

Jorma puts his lips against the inside of her shoulder, just above the crease of her armpit. He kisses and sips.

'Wouldn't it be nice,' he says, 'if a sort of dew came out all over you. Ulli-dew.'

'Do you know, some people rub margarine all over themselves when they're in bed together,' says Ulli. 'I just can't see why they do it, can you?'

'There's some massage oil in Mummy's bathroom. But I think that's for older people. You know. Their skin's not as nice as yours.'

'What does it taste of?'

'Mmm. I don't know really. Not anything sweet. More like moss, I think.'

'Moss!'

'Mm. More or less. But that's not quite right. It's a bit almondy as well. You know, I could tell it was you anywhere. Even if I had my eyes shut and you were in a room with twenty other people.'

'And you went round and licked them all.'

Jorma's lips move up the shallow curve of Ulli's right breast. She tenses and pulls away from him a little. He looks up. She sees him like a diver coming up out of deep water, his face pale, the pupils of his eyes shrinking as she looks at them.

'What's the matter?'

'Nothing,' says Ulli. 'It wasn't anything really, it's only . . . I wish my breasts were bigger.'

She's never said this to anyone. At school people envy her, or say that they do, because she's slim and can eat what she likes without getting fat. Girls with big breasts hate sports. Their breasts jounce under their light T-shirts and their soft thighs chafe in their shorts. Ulli thinks they look beautiful in the showers, but they'd never believe it.

'But you wouldn't look right if they were,' Jorma says, tracing the line of her breast. Her nipple stiffens. 'Look, the way you are, you balance.'

We have a little sister, she has no breasts.
What shall we do for our sister
on the day she is spoken for?

In Ulli's Bible the Song of Songs is headed over each column of verse: THE CHURCH PROFESSES HER FAITH: BEAUTY OF THE CHURCH: CHRIST AWAKENS THE CHURCH. She'd turned over the pages one day, reading the headings, then her eyes had fallen on the words below them. It was like a punch in the stomach. She had no breath. She could hear the voices speaking and answering one another, as alive as herself, wanting what she wanted. Now she soaks in what Jorma's just said.

She won't think of it now. She'll save it for later on, as she's saved the word *virgin*, to think about when she's alone.

Look, the way you are, you balance.

The light of a midsummer dawn lies across the bathroom. It breaks on the panel of sea-green glass Mother bought for Pappy on their fifteenth wedding anniversary. Thick, sea-green glass with a pattern in it which varies according to where you stand. Ulli was six that year. Mother had told her in secret a few days beforehand, and had shown her the pane of glass, unwrapping a corner of the padded wrapping in its presentation box. The next morning Pappy was shaving and Ulli was watching his face in the mirror when a longing to tell him what his present was began to swell in her until it was so sweet and powerful that her mouth was watering with the words that she knew and he did not. Nothing else mattered. Watching in the mirror she steered mirror-Ulli and mirror-Pappy until they were touching, then she whispered the secret into his elbow.

And after all that Pappy had fitted the pane of glass into the bathroom window, which wasn't at all what Mother was hoping for. She wanted it to be where people would notice it and say how unusual and beautiful it was, and ask her where she had bought it.

'Funny sort of anniversary present, glass,' Pappy had said, as if to himself. 'Risky, I'd have thought. After all, breaking glass is a bad omen.'

'There are some people you just can't please no matter what you do for them,' her mother returned. '*You* may not be able to see it, but it's beautiful, isn't it, Ulli?'

The light of a summer dawn spreads itself across the ruck of towels, the split tube of toothpaste, the brushes with hairs in them, the dirty-linen basket. Even though all the boys have left home, there seems to be just as much mess. Nobody has the heart to tidy up, and things lie about where they've been put or dropped until at last one member of the remaining family whirls round with a plastic bin-liner and throws everything in, ready or not. Ulli has taken to cleaning the shower before she gets into it.

Ulli lays a couple of sheets of soft absorbent toilet paper across the toilet bowl, and sits down to pee as quietly as she can. This is the second time she's had to get up tonight, and her mother is restless, coughing and occasionally groaning aloud in the bedroom which is just across from the bathroom door. And the walls are thin. This house is not architect-built. Ulli won't flush the toilet this time.

It's completely light now, and Ulli looks at the watch which she's taken to keeping on all night this past two or three weeks, since she started waking first once and then twice or even three times between going to bed and the official start of the morning at about a quarter to seven. It's just gone one.

She looks at herself in the big spotted mirror over the basin. She has always loved this mirror, with its secretive look of knowing another country which lies just behind the one it is forced to reflect back at her. She leans in, looks close. Yes, she looks different. There's a shadowy filling out around her jaw. Her eyes are puffy and they have light brown stains under them. Well, of course, she hasn't had any proper sleep for nights and nights. What can you expect. Quickly, she lists to herself everything which accounts for the change in the way she looks. She's tired out. Term only finished last Friday, and it was test after test for weeks beforehand. She hasn't felt like eating much, either. It's the season of mid-summer, when usually she'd be making plans with her friends every evening, for barbecues, for trips to the beach, for long evenings with their tanned legs sprawled on the grass, long evenings sitting close to the boys they've discussed endlessly while having their showers and doing their hair beforehand. Sitting closer and closer, nearly touching . . .

But this year it's all different. She has Jorma, and Jorma's away, working as a counsellor in a summer camp two hundred kilometres to the east. It's been fixed up for ages, since long before Ulli and Jorma got together. And he certainly can't cancel now, and let everybody down, his parents are quite definite about that. Besides, Ulli knows that really he doesn't want to. He's worked there before; he knows the kids and they have a great time.

'They're terrific kids, Ulli!'

And it's a kind of social responsibility too. These kids wouldn't have any summer at all, without the camp. Jorma's mother has been careful to explain all this to Ulli. There's a taste of tin in Ulli's mouth. She looks down at her watch. One-fifteen. She ought to go back and try to get some rest, even if she can't sleep. If only she could sleep properly, she's sure she would get rid of the feeling that nothing matters except curling up with her arms around her breasts and stomach, which seem to be tender and aching all over . . .

She stares deep into the mirror again, then with a decisive tug she sweeps the big yellow T-shirt she sleeps in up and over her head, and stands there naked. No, she can't deny it any longer. Her nipples are dark and soft. Her breasts are bigger.

No Jorma here to whisper to. No Jorma to tell her it's nonsense, she's imagining things. No Jorma to wrap her around with himself so that it doesn't seem to matter any more what's true and what isn't, because the rest of the world is floating off somewhere with its dates and deadlines suspended.

But the mirror just hangs there, waiting for more. What hasn't it seen? Things Ulli can't even begin to dream of.

'You'll have to try harder than this, if you want to impress *me*,' says the mirror, '*my child, my sister . . .*'

Paul Henry

THE BREATH OF SLEEPING BOYS

Something is about to happen.

Legs are crossed fingers.

A cup falls from its handle.
A wall crumbles into the road
under the weight of a flower bed.

In their dreams
something is about to happen.

Saved and damned, saved and damned –
the breath of sleeping boys.
One wave breaks. Another inhales

and something is about to happen.

Shrubbery trembles, blatantly.

November the 5th in Lilliput Road.
The introvert is out of its lid,
reads and repeats the word BANG
until the tarmac sky translates
madness back into stars, a life
into mute, mouse-like slippers.

Something is about to happen. *Sh*.

Here is the sound (let it pass)
of young blades, wading through grass.

The town's terrarium anticipates
that something is about to happen.

The wind adjusts its volume.

Peace carries a wicker basket –
the kind the stork brings babies in.
Her dress takes in the new breeze.
With each step she's moving out,
reinventing the sucked light.

Something is about to happen.

Winged eyes in a blameless dark
beat inside their own hemispheres.
Their lashes are feathers dipped in oil.

Deeper than ocean beds, their dreams
rebuild Atlantis in domed air.

Saved and damned, saved and damned –
the breath of sleeping boys.

Michael Hofmann

RIMBAUD ON THE HUDSON

Some kill somewhere upstate. Bud light,
a gutted mill, three storeys of brickwork,
mattresses and condoms, elder and sumac,
child abusers fishing for chub in heavy water.

DIRECTIONS

The new   south east cemetery
is approximately   nowhere
ten stops by underground   then bus
zigzagging   through the suburbs
as bad as Dachau   and you end up
still getting out   a stop early
at the old   south east cemetery
on which it abuts   tenements
market gardens expressways   and then
it's huge   carp in the ponds gardeners
drunks rolling on the paths   fighting
lavender and roses   round the corner
is a café   with an upstairs
long long tables   and slabs of cake

INTIMATIONS OF IMMORTALITY

Have a nice day and get one free –
this is retirement country,
where little old ladies

squinny over their dashboards
and bimble into the millennium,
with cryogenics to follow;

the shuttle astronauts
hope to fluff re-entry and steal
one last record-breaking orbit;

where they give a man
five death sentences
to run more or less concurrently.

I take turns in my three chairs,
and try to remember two switches for lights,
the third for waste.

My eyes sting from salt and sunoil,
and I drink orange juice
till it fizzes and after.

The sight of a cardinal
or the English Sundays on Thursday
make it a red letter day.

Lizards flirt in the swordgrass,
grasshoppers bow their thighs
at six sharp, and quite suddenly,

after seventy-five years,
the laurel oak crashes out.
See you later, if not before.

Christopher Hope

TITO'S DREAM
A Serbian Journal: Easter 1993

YUGOSLAVIA WAS TITO'S dream. To picture Tito's dream it helps to think of a great new house with many rooms to accommodate the united family: Serbs, Croatians, Bosnians, Slovenes, Montenegrans, Macedonians, ethnic Albanians, Serbian Muslims and ethnic Hungarians.

As if to emulate the dream of the master mason, everyone felt obliged to build a new house: the *Gastarbeiter*'s reward, the peasant's desire. First I gave you bread, said the dictator, then I gave you breezeblocks. Dozens of new, bulky houses dotting hillsides and valleys. Driving through Serbia now is like moving through a dead dream. Because when Tito died, his people woke up from his dream. The building stopped. The houses you pass are unfinished, achingly empty.

They are big houses. A dozen rooms or more. Each seems to be trying to be bigger than its neighbour. They jostle for space on deserted hillsides, they crowd the green fields beyond Belgrade. They spring up in orchards and vineyards. Between the football field and the empty factory, on the edge of a village stands another abandoned house. Concrete stairs begin climbing confidently towards the unbuilt doorway. And suddenly stop. Empty eye-pieces await wooden window-frames, which were in short supply even before the collapse of Yugoslavia. The only clue that someone is still trying to live in this abandoned hulk is a line of washing strung across a half-built bedroom.

It is Easter-time. The roads are increasingly deserted, except for horsecarts, bicycles and long-distance pedestrians. The queues for gasoline are at least a week long, trailing back from the service stations. Everything is slowly drawing to a halt. Except the implacable hens hunting worms in the cherry orchard. In a deserted railway siding, a forlorn willow hangs its head. Out in the fields this spring, farmers are trying to recall the difficult trick of turning a hand-held plough behind a single horse.

Strangely enough, there are still Muslims in Belgrade. But it is difficult. Muslim women in Yugoslavia have not been obliged to don the veil. But since the wars started, Muslim women in Belgrade have taken to wearing raincoats as a form of religious camouflage. Not to hide from fervent moralists among their own people, but to disguise themselves from their neighbours. There is a war going on and the Serbian belief that they are unwitting victims is so bitter it sometimes leads to the horrible pleasures of revenge.

At the Centre for Applied Arts in central Belgrade, an exhibition of atrocities has been in progress for some time. Colour photographs show the mutilated remains of exhumed corpses: in close-up, the burnings, eviscerations, gougings, amputations and the myriad brutalities carried out against Serbs in Bosnia by their Muslim and Croatian enemies.

This exhibition is a mirror image of the sort of thing I saw in Croatia a year earlier. The dead look no different. They are bad nationalists. They do not stand up for their country. The horrible wounds add nothing new to the catalogue of cruelty. Skeletons are not good propaganda. They all look alike. What makes such relentless exposition even more barbarous is its shrill didacticism. The dead become weapons of war. They are clubs used to beat the viewer into submission. They are ammunition. They are resurrected from their shallow graves in order to be aimed once again at the 'enemy' on 'the other side'.

When asked how much longer the exhibition of war crimes against the Serbian people would continue, the organisers advised menacingly, 'For as long as it is necessary.'

Latest news suggests that the President will stop traffic across the borders from Serbia into Bosnia, he will impose arms sanctions against the scattered republic of Serbska which has been carved out of the ruined Bosnia. This seems rather like a man intending to apply a tourniquet to his arm or leg because that limb has failed to obey him. The ventriloquist has decided to strangle his dummy.

It is not a particularly credible gesture unless you take the view, sometimes put about in Belgrade, that the President comes from a suicidal family and has succumbed to the same urge. The trouble with this speculation is that it tells one nothing new. The President shows no sign of preparing to fall on his sword; instead he is asking his country to do it for him. The President invokes the glories of the past – the Serbian genius for suffering and defeat. Kosovo! Serbs hold sacred their legendary attempts to stop the Turkish invasion at the Battle of Kosovo, a suicidal endeavour that has passed into literature. Another field of abandoned dreams.

They made from it a great poem, a Serbian *Iliad*, that celebrates their defeat. There is no escape from the long view of history, the relentless explanations. It makes no difference whether the speakers tend to one side of the government or the other, whether they support it or disown it. A Serb will tell you, as I have been told, that he will not allow a bunch of crypto-Fascist nationalists in Belgrade to speak for him. But in the next breath he will be telling you of the long agony of the Serbian nation. The Battle of Kosovo was yesterday. The Nazi atrocities in the Second World War took place only an hour before. And now the Western world, the New World Order, the Americans, the Germans, the Catholics, an unholy cabal of foreign forces round once more on the long-suffering Serbs . . .

While it is true that there are Serbs who disown their government's paranoia, you begin to wonder why the average Serb needs government propagandists when any number of individuals, from poets to priests, will tell you exactly the same thing, quite unaided by official prompting.

In the little town of Ušče, in western Serbia, a muddy river turns abruptly to the right and flows beneath an old iron bridge in the centre of town. There are graffiti on the walls which read *Mortuus* and *Amadeus*. Death and music – and the beloved of God.

Death is not far away. The army convoys rumble past to the nearby Bosnian border. The appropriate music might be provided by the great Serbian laments from the Kosovo song-cycle that recalls in blood and tears the defeat by the Turks in 1389, accompanied by the one-stringed instrument of mourning, the *gusle*: I would choose the great curse from the Kosovo epic:

> *Whoever is a Serb and shares Serbian blood and does not come to fight at Kosovo, may he have no children, let his crops fail, his wheat, his vines . . . Let him wither into oblivion . . .* *

And God? Little sign of Him. In this part of the world they have swapped God for guns.

The bridge across the river at Ušče is a rarity: an iron bridge painted dark green and still carrying some of the last insignia of the Communist era, a hammer and sickle, and the sacred star of the old religion. We paused to view the bridge with the last remaining red star, a remnant of an exploded universe.

The station commander took our passports, cameras, details and made a flurry of phone calls to superiors in distant cities asking for further instructions. Diplomatic number plates were no help. What did he say to the news that we were spending the orthodox Easter under the protection of the Bishop of Žiča? You might as well have talked poetry to a pop singer. The bishop, well, he was OK – you could see the distance his imagination had to travel to consider a universe in which bishops featured at all, and if they did they were about the God thing, right? OK. But bridges were state security. Quite different. *Real*. Not long before, he told us,

* Poems quoted are taken from *A Green Pine: oral poetry of Serbia, Bosnia and Hercegovina*, translated by E D Goy, Belgrade, 1990.

his men had trapped three Romanians running guns to Bosnia. You could not be too careful in these times.

In and out of his office tall policemen, like gun-happy basketball players, swaggered and paused and dropped in on the conversation. God and bishops and bridges. But only guns counted. Everyone knew that – didn't they? Heads full of hair, belts full of guns, and the curious swagger they seemed to have learnt in the movies. Come to stare at the freaks who photographed bridges and talked of Easter. Surely we knew there was a war going on?

I wondered what had happened to the smugglers. The police commander crossed his wrists, a pair of bony manacles. 'We didn't pat them on the head. They thought that they were in Croatia, when we arrested them.'

The commander smiled at the thought of these idiot gunrunners who could not tell Serbia from that distant enemy country, on the far side of Bosnia, on the far side of the world, on the far side of a darkness so profound that Serbs find it difficult to name that benighted land, except to say 'the other side'.

Which is how those in Croatia refer to Serbia. And what could be more angrily reciprocal? For the great enemies once spoke the same language, Serbo-Croat.

There is a problem of nomenclature in Serbia today. Will the real Serbia please stand up? Or shall we speak of a Greater Serbia? Or the Republic of Serbska? Or simply of the 'Serb Nation'? Or is one to become more bureaucratic about it, as witnessed by a vehicle identification notice on a line of trucks heading for Bosnia: 'Republic of Serbia – Sarajevo Division'?

Whole sections of the map may not be mentioned because they have ceased to exist. Where today is Zagreb? Or Ljubljana? And where is the shared literature of a thousand years? Obliterated at a stroke. Like so much else, the ancients' songs they sang in the villages from Montenegro to Macedonia have stopped:

In Hercegovina lived Ali pasha
The lovely Mara far off in Bische.
Ah, they were so far from one another
That each of them caused sorrow for the other.

Serbs like to honour their dead by laying out cemeteries on high ground. The finest views of the surrounding country are granted to the dead. Fresh graves and flags scar the hillsides above towns and villages. Tito's dream has gone underground. Families who have lost a relative nail paper death notices to trees. The fading photographs of the departed gaze wanly at the passing traffic.

In the fourteenth-century monastery of Žiča, where Serbian kings came to be crowned, the nuns are preparing for Easter. As guests of the nunnery, we fall under the patronage of the church, a form of protection so scorned by the station commander at Ušče.

The nuns who once owned great estates here, and saw them confiscated by Tito's communists, keep very much to themselves, reclusive and elusive but now slightly more visible as the long Lenten season comes to an end and preparations are being made for Easter. On Ash Wednesday, in the monastery garden, a young novice has been set to cracking walnuts. She swings her hammer in the late afternoon and the monastery gardens echo to the sound. Shards of exploding walnut shells land amongst the flowers.

There is bread and nettle soup at midday, Lenten fare. And the Mother Superior shows us to our cells. Later, she will report our presence to the police. It is not a hostile gesture, merely a formality they practise in these parts for, despite many attempts at exorcism, the ghost of Tito still haunts this country and despite an upsurge of interest, particularly amongst the young, in the Orthodox Church, the state continues to place its faith not in God but in the police.

On Maundy Thursday there is fish to be cleaned and bread to be baked. The paschal lamb is selected from the fold to be prepared for the great feast on Easter Sunday.

On Good Friday no bells ring, instead wooden clappers are sounded in mute commemoration of Christ's death on the cross. Eggs are boiled by the dozen in cauldrons. The nuns begin to paint them. Painting Easter eggs is an ancient tradition and the pictures made by the Žiča nuns are miniatures of the monastery or yellow oak leaves on a burnt sienna ground.

On Easter Saturday I set off for a number of smaller monasteries, little churches off the beaten track where the forsythia was in bloom in the monastery gardens and two or three people showed up for services in the churches on draughty hillsides. The Orthodox Church may be reclaiming its faith and its territories but it is an uncertain procedure. Under Tito's long and Machiavellian rule, the sacred monasteries of the Serbian church were decreed to be 'cultural monuments'. And as a result some began to feature on the tourist trail. Spanking new hostels were built beside the churches, holy motels for the travelling ecclesiastical enthusiast, and many of the churches themselves became rather quaint museums to a vanished faith. Shrines out of season.

You reach Blagorešterije monastery by an old suspension bridge thrown across the Morava River. Below, in the ravine cut by the river, an empty swimming pool stands open to the sky. In the sheer face of the rocky mountain above the monastery there is a cave, once occupied, like so many of the caves in these mountains, by a holy fugitive who clambered halfway up to heaven. There is also just a hint of fashion to this religious resurgence. Just as it was once 'orthodox' to belong to the Party, now it is 'democratic' to return to the Orthodox fold.

With it goes a great upsurge in vulgarity, newer frescoes of bare-toed archangels with swords and scales, down-at-heel desert saints and anchorites with spear and book. There is a musty obscurantism in a good deal of current Serbian orthodoxy, apparent in the aggressive vulgarity of some monastic enclaves and in the sense of fear and loathing felt by numbers of monks and nuns for the outside world. Over honey and coffee, with which the monks customarily welcome visitors, it is not uncommon to see displayed packages of furious religious tracts inveighing against the 'New World Order', that Luciferian conspiracy widely believed to have at its heart the desire to crush the Serbian nation and church.

But at Blagorešterije monastery on Easter Saturday there was no sound except for the prayers of the worshippers in the church. The housekeeper nun had left her kitchen where she had been stirring the Lenten soup of haricot beans and, in a hurry perhaps, had hung out her dishcloth to dry over the wooden cross of a grave by the church door. Death and domesticity, a peculiarly Serbian mingling.

An hour on foot up a steep track takes you to one of the more remote monasteries in the mountains high above Kraljevo, the fifteenth-century walled church and nunnery of Sretenje. The nuns seldom see foreigners in this remote place and in the early icy spring there are few pilgrims. The sisters sat in the kitchen slicing onions and carrots for the Easter feast.

Sister Katarina, a beautiful twenty-year-old, was mourning the loss of her brother, Miloš, in the war in Bosnia. Miloš, she said, had been 'very free'. A great-hearted boy who liked jokes. And not many years out of school. When the war began he took to the woods with his comrades. Their only source of food was the sheep they raided from Muslim villages and Miloš enjoyed the dangerous game of hiding in the woods and sounding the sheep bell to tantalise his hungry comrades in their search for meat. Miloš played the flute, he danced, and his heart, said his sister, was so soft that he could not bear even 'to see a lamb killed'. Miloš was a musician, a singer and a prankster, one who remained on friendly terms with his Muslim enemies, boys who had once been his schoolfriends back in the village just a few years before. The two sides liked to taunt each other, using their school nicknames. 'Hey, Murat,' Miloš would call to the Muslim enemies across no man's land during a lull in the fighting, 'bring me some water!' And young Murat would call back,

'Here it comes, Chedo!' And then the rifles would open up again.

It's clear from Sister Katarina's testimony that, in the beginning at least, the Bosnian combatants on both sides were boys, playing at war. But the bullets were real enough. It was unfortunate for young Miloš, who enjoyed the flute and liked playing at being the lost lamb, that after a seven-day leave when he'd sung and danced and celebrated his saint's day, his *Slava*, with his sister, he was ordered back to the front. This time to guard a strategic bridge. When the Muslims attacked, he survived. But the Serbian militia sent up as reinforcements mistook the defenders of the bridge for the Muslim enemy and Miloš fell to a bullet from his own side.

Some miles away, hidden halfway up a mountain track, lives Monk Sava. This spry hermit is in his seventies now and has literally moved mountains beside his small church to increase the sense of space and light.

'The hillside made things gloomy, so I moved it.'

He lives alone except for the distant company of a small handful of nuns. An energetic, irrepressible man who is, by his own cheerful admission, an anti-Communist, a monarchist and a Chetnik.

'Are you a German?' he demanded cheerfully when I arrived. 'I don't like Germans.'

His church is difficult to reach, at the end of a muddy track. He refuses to pave the road. 'If I did that people would come and visit me. And what good would that do me?'

Imprisoned under Tito, his hatred of communism colours his conversation and his life. Monk Sava is, in the way of those who move mountains single-handedly, a man of strong opinions. And he asks questions to which he has already supplied his own answers.

'Is he a Catholic?' This in a loud stage whisper as I sat over honey and a glass of his slivovitz, in the tiny kitchen of his ramshackle house. 'I ask this question quietly because I don't wish to hurt his feelings.'

Monk Sava waits daily for the restoration of the monarchy.

Though which king is to be chosen from the two possible contenders for the Yugoslav throne is not certain. Either one is preferable to the present government in Belgrade who are, every man of them, crypto-Communists and Monk Sava advises all who will hear him to avoid them like the plague. There is only one thing which will rid the country of this present godless regime and Monk Sava knows what it is:

'Revolution!' His fist descends on the kitchen table and the slivovitz glasses tremble.

I asked him what he planned to do with the ground he had won by moving the mountain and he answered, as if it were the most natural thing in the world, that one of the first things he would do would be to build a graveyard by the church door. And then he kissed me three times and I had the impression that each of the kisses absolved me of my trinity of errors: he forgave me for looking German, excused me for being a Catholic and even overlooked the fact that I was a foreigner.

On Easter Sunday, the Bishop of Žiča offers lunch. The painted eggs are handed around the table. It is the custom to play with the painted eggs the sort of game English school-boys play with chestnuts. You crack your egg against your neighbour's to see whose egg will shatter first. Together with the game goes the traditional Easter greeting, 'Christ is risen!' to which the response, heard again and again on Easter Sunday, is 'Christ is risen indeed!'

Earlier that morning, a visitor to the monastery of Žiča had not played the game. Rather she had played it with a certain variation, one seldom heard perhaps, but probably very ancient and certainly much closer to the heart of the Serbian perplexity over love and war. As egg met egg and one shattered, the young visitor pronounced not the jubilant affirmation of Christ's resurrection; what she said instead was much more to the point: 'Kill the Mussulman!'

The Bishop and I crack eggs. It is Easter lunch. 'Christ is risen!'

The salad goes around the table. The Bishop apologises to the guests for serving them Russian salad. He reminisces of his time in Sarajevo, to which he cannot return – that place which the anonymous mediaeval singers of Serbian folk-songs apostrophised:

> *Sarajevo, wondrous city,*
> *Wondrous, most fair!*
> *In you are white castles*
> *Bright as the sun!*
>
> *To which no one can now return.*

Without a pause the Bishop recollects the horrors of the last war, his parents hanged by the neo-Nazi Croatian Ustaše forces. He has just discovered that before they died their eyes had been gouged out. 'We must forgive,' says the Bishop, as the Easter lamb goes around the silent table, 'but we cannot forget.'

On the evening of the Easter Sunday we reach the thirteenth-century monastery of Gradać, high above the Brvenića River on a wooded hillside. Mother Maria has large, capable hands and a preference for plain-speaking. A philologist by training, she was once a Wantage nun in the Anglican Church. Received into the Orthodox Church in 1976, she has lived in Serbia for the past ten years. She is, in her own words, 'an Englishwoman alone in Serbia', a Serbian nun who holds a British passport – but partly of French extraction, like Queen Hélène of Anjou who lies buried in Gradać. Her friends back in England and her colleagues at ecumenical councils find her position ever more difficult to understand. 'I was made to feel a traitor for living in Serbia.' She did not so much convert, she says, but attached herself more closely to the Christian faith, choosing Orthodoxy because it carried her 'higher up and further in'. She is critical of Western attitudes to Serbia. 'The West is wildly unaware of the Serbian character when they impose sanctions.' She is critical of what she refers to as 'one-sided Western reporting'.

But she is refreshingly candid in her views of the Orthodox Church hierarchy. Many churchmen in high positions are 'time-serving placemen, twisting the souls of people in Serbia. We long to hear the Church proclaiming God's forgiveness. We have made our forgiveness too small.' The church hierarchy, she says, should stand back from the present government, it's too confused. And it does not speak with a clear voice. She is withering about the intellectual bankruptcy of much church militancy, and about the phobia felt for 'the New World Order'. She scoffs at the orthodox cleric who declared that the Muslim President of Bosnia was controlled by a 'collusion of homosexuals'.

Easter Sunday: 18 April 1993. Today the United Nations accepted the surrender of Muslim Bosnian forces in Srebrniča. The UN is to disarm the defenders of the town, and destroy their weapons. If the Serb forces besieging Srebrniča break the ceasefire and attack once again, the defenceless Muslim defenders will have the dubious satisfaction of knowing that they are dying under the protection of the United Nations.

Serbia has its Muslims too. These are not the ethnic Albanians of the Kosovo but simply Serbs of another faith, who live in the west of Serbia, in the Sanžak.

'Look at this!' In the market place in Novi Pazar, Youssef showed me the Serbian government's latest shot in the paper war. 'I have to register in Cyrillic. Why? We use Roman script here. I have many friends among Serbs. But in Belgrade they are different. Some people are stupid.'

We spoke German, the *lingua franca* of Eastern Europe, just as the Deutschmark is its common coin. Two foreigners meeting in a foreign tongue.

The owner of the single hotel in Novi Pazar welcomed us

with open arms. 'God, I'm bored,' he said. 'We haven't seen anyone in months. Of course you can have a room! Pick any room you choose. No, there is no hot water.'

A room beside the café, walls covered with photographs of dancers in national costume, houses the folk-dance section of the Liberal Bosnjak Organisation of Sanžak. A young man was leading a dozen teenage girls through the steps of a traditional dance. He wants them to revive their ancient cultural traditions. The girls giggled and pulled at their T-shirts, shuffling in loose-laced modern trainers as they tried to follow the dancing master's steps.

A few doors away, Ljutvo, the potter, wiped his hands on his leather apron, packed clay on his wheel in his wooden shed in the garden and set the wheel spinning. Another batch of cooking pots and water-jars was on its way. Ljutvo is in his sixties. When he retires there will be no more clay thrown. His son runs a coffee shop next door. It's easier, he says. Ljutvo is the last potter in Novi Pazar.

It is when you move into the countryside of Sanžak that the temperature rises. This is a land fit for revolt. At a remote farm, several families are working to get in the potatoes, and to round up the black water-buffalo for ploughing. The petrol shortages are biting deeply. Sitting beneath a tree, at a circular wooden table, the men talk in short angry bursts. They are puzzled, bewildered, scared. They paint what seems a picture of an ancient idyll. In fact it endured until a year ago, when the war in Bosnia, across the mountains, started in earnest.

They talk of times when Muslim families moved across the valley to salute their Serbian friends on saint's days; when they received visits, in return, on Muslim holidays.

The farmer pulls at his woollen cap and points to the farms of his Serbian neighbours across the valley: 'During the war we dressed their women in our clothing when the Germans came looking for them. The Serbs did the same for us during the First War. Once we saved and protected each other. Now

they send their troop convoys down the roads at night, singing, shouting and shooting. What they provoked in Bosnia
they will try and provoke here. We take the blame for what
is happening over there.'

I asked the farmer what he wished for.

'We don't want to live without Serbs, or Jews. Only Hitler
wanted that. We would not want it. That would not be
interesting for us. But we will not be foreigners in our own
land. We do not ask for separate states, we ask for justice.'

As you move south into Kosovo province the police presence
multiplies. The royal blue Yugos of the local force outnumber
the occasional passing cars. And the weapons carried by the
militia grow heavier. There are checkpoints at the door of
every town. And army barracks on the outskirts. Kosovo,
the Serbs will tell you, is the sacred Serbian heartland: a long
narrow strip of contested territory, backing on to Albania,
hedged in by Montenegro and Macedonia, and now, to all
intents and purposes, an occupied territory.

The numbers of Kosovars (the ethnic Albanian Muslims
of Kosovo) are disputed. Some will say that they comprise
over ninety-five per cent of the population. Others say less.
What is clear, however, is that all the police and the troops
are Serb. Tito gave the Kosovo provincial autonomy. The
present government revoked it. In most of the shops of the
market, in the town of Peć, the owners remember Tito fondly
by displaying a framed photograph of the lost leader – a way
of framing insults to the present governors.

At the top of town, around the only hotel, the Serb administrators fight back with a furious display of photographs of
their current national leaders. In Serb restaurants you will
eat schnitzels named for the hero of the Serbian revolt against
the Turks, the *Karadjordje Schnitzel*. In the Muslim eating
houses you may enjoy the *Skanderbeg Schnitzel*, named for
the legendary Albanian champion. The meat is the same.

I sat in a coffee shop in the market of Peć and talked to a
student with blue eyes and skin the colour of milk, and to
a teacher expelled from the school system after quarrelling

with the Serbian authorities who refused to allow the teaching of Albanian music, history and literature. Nearly all the Albanian students in Kosovo boycott the state schools and get what education they can in private, peripatetic colleges held in rooms and houses around the town.

The market at Peć is crowded: the goldsmiths lounge at their counters; the money-changers flap great sheaves of dinars. The rate to the dollar has nearly doubled in a week. The cooper hammers staves in a barrel, and in the simple blacksmith forges the bellows fan the furnace to a livid pink inferno.

Yet business is bad. Young Dr Fisnik is exceptional among local Albanians since he has held his job at the local hospital; he is a specialist in diseases of the lung. His brother was not so lucky and, in the Serbian purge of suspected troublemakers, he was fired from his post in the only hotel.

'Certainly,' says Dr Fisnik, 'my people have too many children. But the answer to that is education. The authorities once suggested increasing the air pollution levels because they hoped this might lower fertility rates.'

His brother, behind the shoe counter, nods towards the narrow market alley beyond the window.

'Have you seen your shadows? Ever since you set foot in the market, your shadows have followed you.'

Two men outside the shop are making a long and thorough study of the shoes in the window. Up to thirty-five police agents circulate through the market each day. And every one is known.

It is a lesser programme than genocide that has been launched against the Albanian Muslims of Kosovo. It is a campaign of humiliations punctuated by arrests, beatings and banishments. The Serbian obsession in the Kosovo is the corrosive fear that the 'enemy' (no other word will do) will somehow manage to procure arms.

I sat in a small office, within sight of the mosque, and listened to the local politicians of the Kosovo Democratic League try to make their demands plain. What did they want? Independence? Not entirely. Autonomy? Something like that. Secession? Not necessarily.

'Talking to the Serbs is difficult,' says the chairman of the Democratic League. 'They always break their promises. That is their style of life. It is one of their Asian characteristics.'

He produces two thick dossiers of colour photographs. Because the League is determined to document the attacks on Albanians, they have photographed every victim of police beatings. They can vouch for over 800 cases this year alone.

The photographs show bruises, contusions to the neck. Marks of truncheons and belts. A man shows bruises from his chest to his knees. A woman with bloody eyes shows parallel red weals running across her breasts.

As I walk down the shabby stairs, the muezzin is calling the faithful to prayer. A man watches me from the gate of the mosque. 'I see you have brought your shadow,' says the interpreter. 'That officer arrived when you did and has waited patiently.'

On the road out of Peć we pass, in succession, a derelict Muslim cemetery where a flock of sheep are keeping down the grass between the leaning headstones; the customary police check, officers in flak jackets, carrying sub-machine-guns, rifling through the boots of occasional cars; and an army barracks where a gun-emplacement pit has been dug recently and hastily covered with camouflage netting.

The Serbian nerve that detects enemies everywhere is becoming increasingly raw. The big guns aim into the empty sky; the police rummage in empty car boots; thirty-five 'shadows' in the bazaar at Peć silently pursue enemies of the nation; beyond the mountains there is the war in Bosnia; beyond Bosnia another enemy, Croatia, plots the Serbian downfall; and then there is Germany, the Vatican, the Americans and the New World Order. But there is another enemy more powerful than these: the memories, myths, legends of past defeats. It is history that has Serbs by the throat.

About twelve miles from Peć, on the road to Prizren, is the grandest monastery in Serbia, the fourteenth-century church of Visoki Dečani with its marble entrance and guardian lions and over a thousand frescos. Visoki Dečani was one of the few churches to escape the centuries-long Turkish occupation that followed the Battle of Kosovo.

From a window of the monastery there hangs a large banner of white plastic, stamped with blue triangles.

I asked the monk what the banner represented.

He took a deep breath, and began. The banners had been issued to all places of cultural value by the United Nations, through the Serbian government in Belgrade. The instructions were to display the white and blue banners on the roofs of monasteries throughout the country so that foreign bombers would not attack these priceless monuments.

The young monk studied the blue skies with perplexity. His voice rose and his words grew furious. Serbia was being unjustly blamed for the ills of the world. Serbs were ringed by enemies. They had brought nothing but peace to the Kosovo and now they were accused of throwing Muslim Kosovars out of their jobs. Had I been to the market in Peć? The shops were bulging with everything from shoes to cigarettes. Had I been to Belgrade where people were going without? The world was wicked and mad. Who could say for sure that bombs would not rain down on Visoki Dečani? It was, perhaps, possible, after all.

Though he did not mention it in his fiery sermon, the young monk might have remarked on the fact that flying objects once saved the monastery of Visoki Dečani and showed that there were times when God was on the side of the Serbs. It is said that a plan to convert the monastery into a mosque during the Turkish occupation was thwarted when a Turk, praying to Mecca in the monastery entrance, was killed by a falling stone.

In the Kosovo town of Prizren the shoeshine man said: 'Sure, I speak German. I learnt it from a book. Listen to this: Hello, how are you? I am married with a wife and six children. And no job.'

There are Catholics in Kosovo. The tiny village of Glloxham is entirely Catholic. In the parlour of the village priest, Dom Kelmen Spaqi, the talk grows angrier as the slivovitz bottle goes around the table.

'One of our parishioners lay dying. The police came to his house and searched for weapons. When the family told the police they had no weapons, they took a sick child and beat him. People become so frightened that they even make weapons. And hand them in.'

The road to the monastery is frequently blocked by snow or landslides and the final kilometres of the steep ascent must be covered on foot. The path is strewn with shell fragments from the painted eggs of Easter. The monastery is carved into the sheer cliff face, reached by a wooden bridge across a rushing stream.

My guide, Paul, shows me the tiny church built entirely inside the cave; the small room where the mentally-ill were locked, until they miraculously recovered; and the cell where the saint once lived. From an enamel basin he produced an old, brown skull with a gash across the centre of the cranium. The skull was found in a cave and Paul believes it belonged to some holy recluse who met his death from the blow of a sword. The skull might of course be that of a Turk, or an Albanian. But Paul has decided he was a Serb saint. Reverently he kisses the skull and returns it to the enamel basin.

One thing is sure, someone cracked this man's skull like an egg. Whether the blow brought death to the 'Mussulman', or death to the Serb, cannot be known. But the realities of ex-Yugoslavia depend not on facts but on faith, and even more especially upon the names you give to things: from schnitzels to skulls.

Kosovo Field, where in 1389 the great battle between Turks and Serbs took place, is fenced, empty, guarded by a small modern house beside the entrance. The Albanian gatekeeper of the memorial warns strongly against photographs. After 600 years, it seems, Kosovo Field, where the red peonies evoke the blood of thousands of slaughtered warriors, is still a military zone. In the distance one may dimly discern the outline of what looks like a radar installation. For the rest, the great plain is deserted but for the smoke-stacks of power stations and giant electric pylons.

In the Grand Hotel in nearby Priština, capital of Kosovo, the lobby sees a continual mingling of soldiers, security men, spies, and disconsolate administrators sent from distant Belgrade to govern the rebellious southern province. With Serbian menus, and Serbian music and Serbian home comforts, they eke out their tours of duty among the unruly, ungrateful Kosovars.

The water heaters have failed. Only one of the six lifts still works, depositing guests in the kitchen, when it does not fail altogether. All night the lift shafts echo with the shouts of guests trapped in the lift. The neon letters on the roof of the hotel are dying one by one. The night-time sign now reads GRAND HOT.

The establishment is neither.

Back in Belgrade, at a reception for St George's Day held at the residence of the absent British ambassador, a Serbian journalist suggests what might be done about Kosovo.

'What they really want, those people,' says the journalist, 'is for someone to turn off the light for a while and let them kill each other.'

The British Press Attaché has another idea. The Albanian Muslims of Kosovo are forever sending faxes to the embassy, complaining of arrests, beatings and sundry brutalities for which they have little or no evidence. He knows what should be done about this. It simply has to stop.

Stephen Gray

FORMERLY

I ARRIVED, NEVERTHELESS, at the village the name of which had been remembered – if little else had, beyond peasant colour – from my great-grandfather down. This hanging place, in a nation of emigrants long dispersed to find their fortunes and a better life.

His marketable skill was butchery. At first he spoke a dialect of Italian unique to himself, which in exile withered in his mouth. At dynastic weddings when his descendants attempted to keep themselves together he would bellow recollected snatches of it, before the drink slouched him back into depression. Before his death I was granted permission to research his past: a month in my great-grandfather's village with all assistance. To reclaim as legendary what had become merely quaint and obscure. The accordions and floral wreaths were now too folkloric to be believable. I needed to return to him that something of his was still intact, and that I did value it.

Hooting and waving his flag out of the window, the taxi-driver got me through the no-fire zone. There would be no shelling over the weekend: not clemency, but shortages. That was the library building where I would formerly have been accommodated. Now the side wing had been broken off, fallen down the mountainside. Shelves of school atlases ready to follow. The village which once in its fastness had been impregnable lay all the more open to enemy targeting. Its history spilled forth, as it were.

Immediately I was befriended by the librarian who had been expecting me ever since she was sent down from the capital, some years before. She had almost given up hope on me. We developed hand signals to use between our few common words, as if we were swatting flies on our shoulders: ah, *before* the war . . . previously, used to be, were once: but today . . . difficult, sticky.

The few people left in the village clustered in their own cellars among dusty gilt-framed portraits of Tito. A gargoyle from former days, like his party flag kept in tissue-paper with their family albums: blue-chinned farmers in breeches and turbans. The remaining men, as they had since the Turkish occupation, still abased themselves in the direction of Mecca at the call. To me it was inaudible, but some signal acted on them in unison many times a day. Even the wounded and dying would bundle off their pallets and pray on the stone floor. One died that way: an exceptionally direct route to heaven. I remember being deeply shocked that something natural like sudden heart failure could occur in that posture and during such grisly, exceptional circumstances.

The librarian was not Muslim, but neither was my late great-grandfather. That was the whole point: their ability in the past to live together. Even in a mechanised Western abattoir he could slaughter an ox *their* way if need be, bleeding the throat into a gutter for cleanliness: *halaal, kosher*, skilfully done with a prayer. No electric prods and stun-guns for him. The last of the chickens in the village were still killed by the hands that had fed them. The librarian and I shared one for Christmas, stuffed with herbs we had gathered on the hillside between the craters. Before a blizzard came down and really closed us off from the worst hostilities.

That librarian was a blessing in my life. The children she had been sent to serve had been evacuated, so she was pleased to pass the time in devotion to me. Although she was not from there, her knowledge of customs in that part seemed to have come to her without effort; they were 'hers' too, without any posturing or exertions at sympathy. She taught me a lot about how not to be a tourist within my own heritage, about the kind of continuity I had been taught had every reason to have been broken. That is what I had wished to discover, against myself. To be convinced.

Between us was that silent partner, the village ancestor who had held out in my life – useless, a nuisance – for as long as he could, but not long enough. Any evidence of him on paper we had exhausted within the first few days – for more than a fragment of genealogy or baptismal record a visit to a greater archive was called for: thwacks of the hands in the air – probably all gone now. Destroyed by the war. Archaeology followed: the cornerstone down the alley. They had needed the slope for drainage. This was probably *his* father's trough. He had remembered blood on the snow, blood on the snow. They would have needed that water led off the village square. Of course she was right: her logical way of bringing working lives out of the rubble, making their routines credible.

After the documents, the stones covered in moss and creeper, there was his language – the cry that had become extinct in his own lifetime. I had never transcribed what he said. Usually it was just obnoxious rumble, mixed in with a travesty of English that embarrassed us because it was puerile. Nor had I thought to tape-record him. The songs he liked – 'Sorrento', 'Funicoli funicola' – were later hits that wiped out those of his youth. She tried a few children's nonsense songs and lullabies, but they drew a blank on me.

But to her all of it seemed accessible, part of an undisturbed whole. Underground at her lodgings she taught me to play the kind of cards my great-grandfather certainly must have relished. We'd listen to the rather dim UN station playing a demented-sounding Tina Turner, over and over again, and I'd try in turn to translate for her. We would grimace awkwardly at the blatant sentiments. The wine helped. When a shell came close, we dived for cover, finding ourselves in one another's arms. Only once, and then it seemed perfectly right that we should protect each other. I now know what it was. She took my intrusion into her world of rightness, too, and rendered me more complete.

But I was not of them, in the end. I was eligible for escape by military helicopter, they were not. I promised to write to her, send the snaps, the book that would be the outcome of the visit. As I ascended over the hillside I could see them in that village square, shielding their eyes, before going in to huddle at a fireplace, together in the thick of their terrible war. In what to us was ruins, ranges, then the cover of cloud.

Hanif Kureishi

MY SON THE FANATIC

SURREPTITIOUSLY, THE FATHER began going into his son's bedroom. He would sit there for hours, rousing himself only to seek clues. What bewildered him was that Ali was getting tidier. The room, which was usually a tangle of clothes, books, cricket bats and video games, was becoming neat and ordered; spaces began appearing where before there had been only mess.

Initially, Parvez had been pleased: his son was outgrowing his teenage attitudes. But one day, beside the dustbin, Parvez found a torn shopping bag that contained not only old toys but computer disks, videotapes, new books, and fashionable clothes the boy had bought a few months before. Also without explanation, Ali had parted from the English girlfriend who used to come around to the house. His old friends stopped ringing.

For reasons he didn't himself understand, Parvez was unable to bring up the subject of Ali's unusual behaviour. He was aware that he had become slightly afraid of his son, who, between his silences, was developing a sharp tongue. One remark Parvez did make – 'You don't play your guitar anymore' – elicited the mysterious but conclusive reply, 'There are more important things to be done.'

Yet Parvez felt his son's eccentricity as an injustice. He had always been aware of the pitfalls that other men's sons had stumbled into in England. It was for Ali that Parvez worked long hours; he spent a lot of money paying for Ali's education as an accountant. He had bought Ali good suits, all the books he required, and a computer. And now the boy was throwing his possessions out! The TV, video-player and stereo system followed the guitar. Soon the room was practically bare. Even the unhappy walls bore pale marks where Ali's pictures had been removed.

Parvez couldn't sleep; he went more often to the whisky bottle, even when he was at work. He realised it was imperative to discuss the matter with someone sympathetic.

Parvez had been a taxi-driver for twenty years. Half that time he'd worked for the same firm. Like him, most of the other drivers were Punjabis. They preferred to work at night, when the roads were clearer and the money better. They slept during the day, avoiding their wives. They led almost a boy's life together in the cabbies' office, playing cards and setting up practical jokes, exchanging lewd stories, eating takeaways from local *balti* houses, and discussing politics and their own problems.

But Parvez had been unable to discuss the subject of Ali with his friends. He was too ashamed. And he was afraid, too, that they would blame him for the wrong turning his boy had taken, just as he had blamed other fathers whose sons began running around with bad girls, skipping school and joining gangs.

For years, Parvez had boasted to the other men about how Ali excelled in cricket, swimming and football, and what an attentive scholar he was, getting As in most subjects. Was it asking too much for Ali to get a good job, marry the right girl, and start a family? Once this happened, Parvez would be happy. His dreams of doing well in England would have come true. Where had he gone wrong?

One night, sitting in the taxi office on busted chairs with his two closest friends, watching a Sylvester Stallone film, Parvez broke his silence.

'I can't understand it!' he burst out. 'Everything is going from his room. And I can't talk to him any more. We were not father and son – we were brothers! Where has he gone? Why is he torturing me?' And Parvez put his head in his hands.

Even as he poured out his account, the men shook their heads and gave one another knowing glances.

'Tell me what is happening!' he demanded.

The reply was almost triumphant. They had guessed something was going wrong. Now it was clear: Ali was taking drugs and selling his possessions to pay for them. That was why his bedroom was being emptied.

'What must I do, then?'

Parvez's friends instructed him to watch Ali scrupulously and to be severe with him, before the boy went mad, overdosed, or murdered someone.

Parvez staggered out into the early-morning air, terrified that they were right. His boy – the drug-addict killer!

To his relief, he found Bettina sitting in his car.

Usually the last customers of the night were local 'brasses', or prostitutes. The taxi-drivers knew them well and often drove them to liaisons. At the end of the girls' night, the men would ferry them home, though sometimes they would join the cabbies for a drinking session in the office. Occasionally, the drivers would go with the girls. 'A ride in exchange for a ride,' it was called.

Bettina had known Parvez for three years. She lived outside the town and, on the long drives home, during which she sat not in the passenger seat but beside him, Parvez had talked to her about his life and hopes, just as she talked about hers. They saw each other most nights.

He could talk to her about things he'd never be able to discuss with his own wife. Bettina, in turn, always reported on her night's activities. He liked to know where she had been and with whom. Once, he had rescued her from a violent client, and since then they had come to care for each other.

Though Bettina had never met Ali, she heard about the boy continually. That night, when Parvez told Bettina that he suspected Ali was on drugs, to Parvez's relief, she judged neither him nor the boy, but said, 'It's all in the eyes.' They might be bloodshot; the pupils might be dilated; Ali might look tired. He could be liable to sweats, or sudden mood changes. 'OK?'

Parvez began his vigil gratefully. Now that he knew what the problem might be, he felt better. And surely, he figured, things couldn't have gone too far?

He watched each mouthful the boy took. He sat beside him at every opportunity and looked into his eyes. When he could, he took the boy's hand, checked his temperature. If the boy wasn't at home, Parvez was active, looking under the carpet, in Ali's drawers, and behind the empty wardrobe – sniffing, inspecting, probing. He knew what to look for: Bettina had drawn pictures of capsules, syringes, pills, powders, rocks.

Every night, she waited to hear news of what he'd witnessed. After a few days of constant observation, Parvez was able to report that although the boy had given up sports, he seemed healthy. His eyes were clear. He didn't – as Parvez expected he might – flinch guiltily from his father's gaze. In fact, the boy seemed more alert and steady than usual: as well as being sullen, he was very watchful. He returned his father's long looks with more than a hint of criticism, of reproach, even – so much so that Parvez began to feel that it was he who was in the wrong, and not the boy.

'And there's nothing else physically different?' Bettina asked.

'No!' Parvez thought for a moment. 'But he is growing a beard.'

One night, after sitting with Bettina in an all-night coffee shop, Parvez came home particularly late. Reluctantly, he and Bettina had abandoned the drug theory, for Parvez had found nothing resembling any drug in Ali's room. Besides, Ali wasn't selling his belongings. He threw them out, gave them away, or donated them to charity shops.

Standing in the hall, Parvez heard the boy's alarm clock go off. Parvez hurried into his bedroom, where his wife, still awake, was sewing in bed. He ordered her to sit down and keep quiet, though she had neither stood up nor said a word. As she watched him curiously, he observed his son through the crack of the door.

The boy went into the bathroom to wash. When he returned to his room, Parvez sprang across the hall and set his ear to Ali's door. A muttering sound came from within. Parvez was puzzled but relieved.

Once this clue had been established, Parvez watched him at other times. The boy was praying. Without fail, when he was at home, he prayed five times a day.

Parvez had grown up in Lahore, where all young boys had been taught the Koran. To stop Parvez from falling asleep while he studied, the *maulvi* had attached a piece of string to the ceiling and tied it to Parvez's hair, so if his head fell forward, he would instantly jerk awake. After this indignity, Parvez had avoided all religions. Not that the other taxi-drivers had any more respect than he. In fact, they made jokes about the local mullahs walking around with their caps and beards, thinking they could tell people how to live while their eyes roved over the boys and girls in their care.

Parvez described to Bettina what he had discovered. He informed the men in the taxi office. His friends, who had been so inquisitive before, now became oddly silent. They could hardly condemn the boy for his devotions.

Parvez decided to take a night off and go out with the boy. They could talk things over. He wanted to hear how things were going at college; he wanted to tell him stories about their family in Pakistan. More than anything, he yearned to understand how Ali had discovered the 'spiritual dimension', as Bettina called it.

To Parvez's surprise, the boy refused to accompany him. He claimed he had an appointment. Parvez had to insist that no appointment could be more important than that of a son with his father.

The next day, Parvez went immediately to the street corner where Bettina stood in the rain wearing high heels, a short skirt, and a long mac, which she would open hopefully at passing cars.

'Get in, get in!' he said.

They drove out across the moors and parked at the spot where, on better days, their view unimpeded for miles except by wild deer and horses, they'd lie back, with their eyes half-closed, saying, 'This is the life.' This time Parvez was trembling. Bettina put her arms around him.

'What's happened?'

'I've just had the worst experience of my life.'

As Bettina rubbed his head Parvez told her that the previous evening, as he and his son had studied the menu, the waiter, whom Parvez knew, brought him his usual whisky-and-water. Parvez was so nervous he had even prepared a question. He was going to ask Ali if he was worried about his imminent exams. But first he loosened his tie, crunched a poppadum, and took a long drink.

Before Parvez could speak, Ali made a face.

'Don't you know it's wrong to drink alcohol?' he had said.

'He spoke to me very harshly,' Parvez said to Bettina. 'I was about to castigate the boy for being insolent, but I managed to control myself.'

Parvez had explained patiently that for years he had worked more than ten hours a day, had few enjoyments or hobbies, and never gone on holiday. Surely it wasn't a crime to have a drink when he wanted one?

'But it is forbidden,' the boy said.

Parvez shrugged. 'I know.'

'And so is gambling, isn't it?'

'Yes. But surely we are only human?'

Each time Parvez took a drink, the boy winced, or made some kind of fastidious face. This made Parvez drink more quickly. The waiter, wanting to please his friend, brought another glass of whisky. Parvez knew he was getting drunk, but he couldn't stop himself. Ali had a horrible look, full of disgust and censure. It was as if he hated his father.

Halfway through the meal, Parvez suddenly lost his temper and threw a plate on the floor. He felt like ripping the cloth from the table, but the waiters and other customers were staring at him. Yet he wouldn't stand for his own son's telling him the difference between right and wrong. He knew he wasn't a bad man. He had a conscience. There were a few things of which he was ashamed, but on the whole he had lived a decent life.

'When have I had time to be wicked?' he asked Ali.

In a low, monotonous voice, the boy explained that Parvez had not, in fact, lived a good life. He had broken countless rules of the Koran.

'For instance?' Parvez demanded.

Ali didn't need to think. As if he had been waiting for this moment, he asked his father if he didn't relish pork pies?

'Well.' Parvez couldn't deny that he loved crispy bacon smothered with mushrooms and mustard and sandwiched between slices of fried bread. In fact, he ate this for breakfast every morning.

Ali then reminded Parvez that he had ordered his wife to cook pork sausages, saying to her, 'You're not in the village now. This is England. We have to fit in.'

Parvez was so annoyed and perplexed by this attack that he called for more drink.

'The problem is this,' the boy said. He leaned across the table. For the first time that night, his eyes were alive. 'You are too implicated in Western civilisation.'

Parvez burped; he thought he was going to choke. 'Implicated!' he said. 'But we live here!'

'The Western materialists hate us,' Ali said. 'Papa, how can you love something which hates you?'

'What is the answer, then,' Parvez said miserably, 'according to you?'

Ali didn't need to think. He addressed his father fluently, as if Parvez were a rowdy crowd which had to be quelled or convinced. The law of Islam would rule the world; the skin of the infidel would burn off again and again; the Jews and Christers would be routed. The West was a sink of hypocrites, adulterers, homosexuals, drug users and prostitutes.

While Ali talked, Parvez looked out the window as if to check that they were still in London.

'My people have taken enough. If the persecution doesn't stop, there will be *jihad*. I, and millions of others, will gladly give our lives for the cause.'

'But why, why?' Parvez said.

'For us, the reward will be in Paradise.'

'Paradise!'

Finally, as Parvez's eyes filled with tears, the boy urged him to mend his ways.

'But how would that be possible?' Parvez asked.

'Pray,' urged Ali. 'Pray beside me.'

Parvez paid the bill and ushered his boy out of there as soon as he was able. He couldn't take any more.

Ali sounded as if he'd swallowed someone else's voice.

On the way home, the boy sat in the back of the taxi, as if he were a customer. 'What has made you like this?' Parvez asked him, afraid that somehow he was to blame for all this. 'Is there a particular event which has influenced you?'

'Living in this country.'

'But I love England,' Parvez said, watching his boy in the rear view mirror. 'They let you do almost anything here.'

'That is the problem,' Ali replied.

For the first time in years, Parvez couldn't see straight. He knocked the side of the car against a lorry, ripping off the wing mirror. They were lucky not to have been stopped by the police: Parvez would have lost his licence and his job.

Back at the house, as he got out of the car, Parvez stumbled and fell in the road, scraping his hands and ripping his trousers. He managed to haul himself up. The boy didn't even offer him his hand.

Parvez told Bettina he was willing to pray, if that was what the boy wanted – if it would dislodge the pitiless look from his eyes. 'But what I object to,' he said, 'is being told by my own son that I am going to Hell!'

What had finished Parvez off was the boy's saying he was giving up his studies in accounting. When Parvez had asked why, Ali said sarcastically that it was obvious. 'Western education cultivates an anti-religious attitude.'

And in the world of accountants it was usual to meet women, drink alcohol, and practise usury.

'But it's well-paid work,' Parvez argued. 'For years you've been preparing!'

Ali said he was going to begin to work in prisons, with poor Muslims who were struggling to maintain their purity in the face of corruption. Finally, at the end of the evening, as Ali went up to bed, he had asked his father why he didn't have a beard, or at least a moustache.

'I feel as if I've lost my son,' Parvez told Bettina. 'I can't bear to be looked at as if I'm a criminal. I've decided what to do.'

'What is it?'

'I'm going to tell him to pick up his prayer mat and get out of my house. It will be the hardest thing I've ever done, but tonight I'm going to do it.'

'But you mustn't give up on him,' said Bettina. 'Many young people fall into cults and superstitious groups. It doesn't mean they'll always feel the same way.' She said Parvez had to stick by his boy.

Parvez was persuaded that she was right, even though he didn't feel like giving his son more love when he had hardly been thanked for all he had already given.

For the next two weeks, Parvez tried to endure his son's looks and reproaches. He attempted to make conversation about Ali's beliefs. But if Parvez ventured any criticism, Ali always had a brusque reply. On one occasion, Ali accused Parvez of 'grovelling' to the whites; in contrast, he explained, he himself was not 'inferior'; there was more to the world than the West, though the West always thought it was best.

'How is it you know that?' Parvez said. 'Seeing as you've never left England?'

Ali replied with a look of contempt.

One night, having ensured there was no alcohol on his breath, Parvez sat down at the kitchen table with Ali. He hoped Ali would compliment him on the beard he was growing, but Ali didn't appear to notice it.

The previous day, Parvez had been telling Bettina that he thought people in the West sometimes felt inwardly empty and that people needed a philosophy to live by.

'Yes,' Bettina had said. 'That's the answer. You must tell him what your philosophy of life is. Then he will understand that there are other beliefs.'

After some fatiguing consideration, Parvez was ready to

begin. The boy watched him as if he expected nothing. Haltingly, Parvez said that people had to treat one another with respect, particularly children their parents. This did seem, for a moment, to affect the boy. Heartened, Parvez continued. In his view, this life was all there was, and when you died, you rotted in the earth. 'Grass and flowers will grow out of my grave, but something of me will live on.'

'How then?'

'In other people. For instance, I will continue – in you.'

At this the boy appeared a little distressed.

'And in your grandchildren,' Parvez added for good measure. 'But while I am here on earth I want to make the best of it. And I want you to, as well!'

'What d'you mean by "make the best of it"?' asked the boy.

'Well,' said Parvez. 'For a start . . . you should enjoy yourself. Yes. Enjoy yourself without hurting others.'

Ali said enjoyment was 'a bottomless pit'.

'But I don't mean enjoyment like that,' said Parvez. 'I mean the beauty of living.'

'All over the world our people are oppressed,' was the boy's reply.

'I know,' Parvez answered, not entirely sure who 'our people' were. 'But still – life is for living!'

Ali said, 'Real morality has existed for hundreds of years. Around the world millions and millions of people share my beliefs. Are you saying you are right and they are all wrong?' And Ali looked at his father with such aggressive confidence that Parvez would say no more.

A few evenings later, Bettina was riding in Parvez's car after visiting a client when they passed a boy on the street.

'That's my son,' Parvez said, his face set hard. They were on the other side of town, in a poor district, where there were two mosques.

Bettina turned to see. 'Slow down, then, slow down!'

She said, 'He's good-looking. Reminds me of you. But with a more determined face. Please, can't we stop?'

'What for?'

'I'd like to talk to him.'

Parvez turned the cab round and pulled up beside the boy. 'Coming home?' Parvez asked. 'It's quite a way.'

The boy shrugged and got into the back seat. Bettina sat in the front. Parvez became aware of Bettina's short skirt, her gaudy rings and ice-blue eyeshadow. He became conscious that the smell of her perfume, which he loved, filled the cab. He opened the window.

While Parvez drove as fast as he could, Bettina said gently to Ali, 'Where have you been?'

'The mosque,' he said.

'And how are you getting on at college? Are you working hard?'

'Who are you to ask me these questions?' Ali said, looking out of the window. Then they hit bad traffic, and the car came to a standstill.

By now, Bettina had inadvertently laid her hand on Parvez's shoulder. She said, 'Your father, who is a good man, is very worried about you. You know he loves you more than his own life.'

'You say he loves me,' the boy said.

'Yes!' said Bettina.

'Then why is he letting a woman like you touch him like that?'

If Bettina looked at the boy in anger, he looked back at her with cold fury.

She said, 'What kind of woman am I that I should deserve to be spoken to like that?'

'You know what kind,' he said. Then he turned to his father. 'Now let me out.'

'Never,' Parvez replied.

'Don't worry, I'm getting out,' Bettina said.

'No, don't!' said Parvez. But even as the car moved forward, she opened the door and threw herself out – she had done this before – and ran away across the road. Parvez stopped and shouted after her several times, but she had gone.

Parvez took Ali back to the house, saying nothing more to him. Ali went straight to his room. Parvez was unable to read the paper, watch television, or even sit down. He kept pouring himself drinks.

At last, he went upstairs and paced up and down outside Ali's room. When, finally, he opened the door, Ali was praying. The boy didn't even glance his way.

Parvez kicked him over. Then he dragged the boy up by the front of his shirt and hit him. The boy fell back. Parvez hit him again. The boy's face was bloody. Parvez was panting; he knew the boy was unreachable, but he struck him none the less. The boy neither covered himself nor retaliated; there was no fear in his eyes. He only said, through his split lip, 'So who's the fanatic now?'

Cliff Forshaw

THROUGH THE FOREST

Minus twenty-seven. The town gives out,
trolley-buses terminate in dirty snow.
Out there it's clean. You click skis
and head towards the aching sky.
Fangs fasten upon the woods.

Rats' teeth threaded on the wind
pierce your lobes and gnaw.
Birch trees run out like barcodes
– those Western goods eyed on Arbat stalls.
Your mind is clear as that last vodka batch,
out on the sill, gripped in a handshake of ice.

Already the moon is twisting silver
like a lure where the sky fatigues.
Then it's gone, loping over your shoulder
as you slither a bend at speed
to catch the sun's last lick around tenement teeth.
The air's smudged by a single cloud:
a speech bubble erased over the lit-up factory.

At the edge of the forest, your blood is hot.
No more than a hundred heart-beats ahead of night,
you pause, pant out stars and wipe
the pelt of frost from your face.
Eyebrows crackle with static.
Ice has woven through your hair.
It breaks under your clumsy glove like birdbones,
hanging, hinged on feathered splinters from a paw.

MZUNGU

Mzungu: Chichewa for 'white man.'

He turns around, again his shadow flees him.
Mzungu's darkness giggles with children
who have marched in his big steps,
now scattered into doorways, hiding in bushes.
The look he casts over his shoulder is salt;
the taste of their world and his forever changed.
This place is always behind him: his eyes stopped by
    distance,
smiles that refer back to the red dust of a road
settling on his shoulders.
He is confused by profuse thanks for the things he has not
    done.
So many things he must accomplish before the sun sinks,
fires light up the hillsides,
and his night buzzes with worries and mosquitoes.

Mzungu never buys boiled mice kebabbed on sticks.
Women and boys wave them anyway.
Mzungu is greedy for vision,
can seal whole villages into his black trap at one sitting;
can catch us, the way we catch mice in wicker.
Mzungu with his eye and his hawk-like nose,
his steel claws, his table draped with cloud.
Sometimes Mzungu stops by the roadside bar
and buys each girl a cold one.
But lately he will only laugh with them;
no longer taking the prettiest to the back room.
Mzungu says there is something in our veins.
And now I know, we can never be brothers in blood.

113

Visitor is dew, our proverb says.
But our land remains: forever hard,
like baked clay, like an empty bowl.

Matthew Kneale

PARADISE

'SLEEP GOOD?' THAKALI'S voice was concerned. He handed Neville Ewan a tall glass of tea.

'Fine, thanks.' Neville sat up from the mattress bed – he had slept fully clothed – and took a sip. The sharp, sickly sweetness was reviving. He was a large man who, when walking, had a slight stoop, as if unusually afflicted by gravity. His face was bearded, his expression sombre, so that even in his bright yellow waterproof he looked like someone from a Victorian group photograph.

A glimmer of light beneath the door was the only evidence that the day had begun. The room was without windows as they let out heat at night and up here at twelve thousand feet all available warmth was needed.

Neville took in the scene, memorising details, putting them into sentences. The group of people were gathered about the fire, their faces lit by the warm orange glow of the flames. Like a painting. A painting, yes, he would use that. He would have to wait until he had walked out of view from the village, before he could stop and write down some notes. A pity he could not do so here, in the warm, but . . . A twinge of guilt. Perhaps he should have been more honest. Too late now.

'Breakfast.' Thakali beckoned to the fire. He was a tall, confident man – owner of this house, largest in the village – and though his clothes were tattered and mud-stained his eyes gleamed with intelligence. He knew little English and spoke in single words rather than sentences, but his meaning was always clear.

Neville took his place beside the family, drawing the heat

from the flames into his chilled limbs. Thakali's wife had been busy while Neville was still asleep, and porridge was boiling stodgily in a large metal pot suspended above the fire. She scooped out a generous helping for him, then adding around the edge of the bowl a ring of shrivelled gobbets of something.

'What are these?'

'Meat,' explained Thakali.

Yak meat. Of course. A delicacy in a poor region like this. And they were giving it to him with his breakfast. Another twinge of guilt. 'But you mustn't. It's too special. I mean how often do you eat this?'

Thakali looked indignant. 'Often.'

Worse to refuse than accept. Neville chewed one of the pieces which was like hardened rubber. 'Delicious.'

Neville felt a kind of awe of these people. They were like saints. The warmth they had shown him – a complete stranger – had been remarkable even by the high standards of hospitality he had encountered in this remote area of Nepal. The elegant courtesy that they had somehow conjured up from this poor land. How different from his own world, spoilt and depraved. Where people wallowed in their greed. Where teenagers goaded and attacked old people for pleasure. Where children were not safe from molesters. Where wives left their husbands without warning or conscience. As had Neville's own wife. No, here was something wiser, better.

He had been lucky to find the village. He had discovered it only by pure chance. Walking in the valley below, he had come across the old man sitting on a rock by the path, catching the warmth of the sun. The tattered army jacket he wore gave him a military air. He glanced up at Neville as he drew near. 'Where are you from?'

'England.'

The man nodded dreamily. 'My uncle was in your army as a Gurkha, fighting in Burma and Malaysia. He helped me learn my English.' He stroked the thick white stubble on his chin. 'What brings you here?'

Neville felt uneasy. He hated lying. 'I'm just a tourist. Here to enjoy the landscape.'

The other nodded, unsuspicious. 'Of course. And where do you go today?'

'Khorang.'

A puzzled look. 'Why not Drughat? For beautiful landscape it is the best village. And the people are famous for their friendliness.'

Neville had never heard of the place. 'Is it far?'

'Four or five hours. The path begins quite near here. If you like I can show you.'

Neville took out his map.

The climb had been a steep one, and several times he had regretted taking such a long detour. But his doubts vanished as he rounded a spur and the village came into sight. The location was spectacular. The settlement clung to a steep slope; walls of houses interlocked as if clutching one another for reassurance. Below, the land fell away dizzyingly into the main valley. Above, it steepened into a sharply pointed snowpeak, like a yak's horn. From the roofs fluttered coloured Buddhist prayer flags.

The streets were empty as he arrived, but not for long. A child peered out from a doorway, curious at the heavy clump of his boots, and uttered a cry. As if by magic Neville found himself surrounded by a mob of children and adults excitedly shouting greetings. Quite a reception. He suspected he was the first European to reach this spot in a very long time.

Thakali had soon pushed his way through the crowd, quietening them. 'Stay. My house.' When offered payment he had grown almost angry.

Neville had intended to remain only one night. In the end he stayed five. Thakali had had his two sons take him on day walks all around the area. Up towards a horn-shaped peak. To a waterfall elaborately encrusted with icicles. And a small lake, half frozen, its colour a deep cold blue. Each evening when he returned, a dinner of local food – rice and lentil sauce – was waiting.

Five days can be a long time. It was enough for Neville to feel he was almost a part of the village. He knew its routine.

The early morning began with crowing cockerels and sweet tea. As the sun warmed the frozen air, a few young men might assemble to take village-grown vegetables to the valley below, carrying huge loads on their backs, held in place with leather straps that fitted round their foreheads. Others went to tend their fields: terraces carefully cut into the steep dusty land. There was something reassuring about the sight of them working, stooping quietly over the earth, from which they could summon up food, life.

And it was so peaceful. No droning engines here. In fact no machinery of any kind. A simplicity. A perfection. But for how long? Neville thought gloomily of villages that had been open to tourism for some years, where children shrieked and threatened for sweets, and hardened house owners had learned the art of cheating foreigners. This area had been spared such things because of its nearness to Tibet. Militarily sensitive. No tourists allowed. Until the recent government decision to declare it open.

No, it would not last long. And the worst was that he, Neville . . .

He glanced at the faces beside him round the fire, sipping tea or finishing their bowls of porridge. One of Thakali's sons was listening to his Walkman, another peering carefully through the viewfinder of his camera: grown men, but with an innocence like children. No, not children. He checked himself, annoyed at so patronising a notion.

And now, finally, the moment had come. Reluctantly he got to his feet. 'I think I'd better be going.'

'Stay more.' Thakali laughed brightly. 'One day?'

He would have liked to stay. Very much. The village had moved him somehow. Made him feel at home in a way he had not felt for a long time. He smiled. 'No, I must go.'

Thakali nodded. 'Pity.' He retrieved Neville's Walkman and camera and they walked out into the sunlight. Neville's departure seemed to be general knowledge in the village, and as he and Thakali walked through the narrow whitewashed streets a small crowd materialised around them, following. It was a sharply clear morning, and as he stepped out from the houses Neville could see white peaks far away in the distance, shimmering, mysterious.

A paradise. A doomed paradise.

'Sad?' asked Thakali.

'No, no. Not at all.' How could he begin to explain? Especially after all their kindness.

'Food bad?'

'Certainly not. It was marvellous.'

Thakali nodded brightly.

They stopped on the same spur from where Neville had first seen Drughat village, only a few days before. It seemed an age ago. He shook Thakali and his family each by the hand, and tried to convey his thanks. So hard to show what he felt.

Matters would have finished there, with warm goodbyes, if it had not been for the gift. Thakali produced it just as Neville was about to turn away down the path. A medallion depicting a face: wild eyes and teeth.

'Present.' He pressed it into Neville's hand, heavy. It had to be pure silver.

Neville tried to smile. In an unreasonable way he felt almost angry. The kindness was too much, weighed on him, making him feel vile and guilty. 'Really, you mustn't.'

Thakali was not to be swayed. 'Nepal God. For luck.'

There was no way out of it. To refuse would cause deep offence. No, there was nothing he could do about any of this.

Unless . . . And then, in the space of only a moment, something in Neville's way of thinking shifted. An axiom that had seemed solid snapped. He could do as he wanted. Do what was right. If just in this case.

He glanced at the people before him, feeling excited. Cleansed. Words bubbled up inside. 'There's something I want to tell you. All of you.'

They watched, attentive. Even those who understood none of his meaning – the majority – could see that something unusual was happening.

'I haven't been quite honest with you. For that I'm sorry. You see I'm not just a tourist. I'm a writer, and now I'm working on a guide to this area, so other foreigners will know where to visit. A book.'

Thakali nodded, looking puzzled.

'Your village is something special. So calm and beautiful. If tourists come everything will change. I've seen it. People greedy. Children shouting, "One pen, one rupee".'

'One rupee,' echoed someone in the crowd. There was faint laughter.

'Everything will just be for tourists, like in Pokhara. It won't be a real village at all any more.'

'Tourist,' shouted a voice. 'Pokhara,' added another. The laughter was louder this time.

A touch discouraged, Neville ploughed on nevertheless. 'And that's why I'm not going to put Drughat in my book.'

Silence. Thakali was looking at him strangely. 'Not?'

'That's right. To keep your village perfect. To save it. The only way is to have no tourists.' Neville's words were a touch less triumphal now. He had a feeling that something was going wrong.

'No tourist?' A hubbub of voices was rising from the rest of the crowd.

Neville spoke quickly, explaining. 'Tourists are poison, believe me. They may mean well, but they corrupt. Everywhere they go, everything they touch, turns bad. I should put Drughat in my book. It's my duty as a guidebook writer. But sometimes there are more important things than work and money. And . . .'

It was Thakali who stopped him. Without any warning he stepped forward, reached out for Neville's wrist and began tugging, twisting the skin so it hurt. The medallion fell to the ground. Neville, shocked, found himself being pulled back towards the village. 'What's going on?' But Thakali offered no reply except more angry tugs. The crowd seemed to understand well enough, speeding Neville's progress with sudden shoves, so it was all he could do to keep balance. Scared now, Neville tried to look unworried, even to smile, in the hope that this would somehow help.

They did not return to Thakali's house, instead going to a smaller building at the lower end of the village that Neville had hardly noticed before. He found himself pressed roughly through the door, together with as many of the crowd as would fit. And there, sitting calmly by the fire with a glass of tea, was the old man in the battered military jacket he had met in the valley below.

Neville stared. 'What are you doing here?'

He showed no surprise. 'This village is my home.'

'But then what were you doing down in . . .?'

'Waiting for you, of course.' The man looked at him wearily. 'To send you up here. I am the only real speaker of English in the village.'

Neville was reeling. 'But . . . You knew who I was?'

'Of course. Do you think we are stupid?' He stroked the white stubble on his chin. 'We heard you were coming days ago. English guidebook man. Big beard, yellow jacket, sad face. Everyone knows you.' He turned to listen to Thakali, who was speaking volubly, in quick angry bursts of words. 'He wants to know if it was the food,' the old man explained. 'You didn't like the food?'

'The food was fine,' Neville insisted unhappily, finally understanding. So he had been set up from the very start. All that kindness had been nothing more than a ploy to get him to put Drughat in his book. An act.

The old man frowned. 'If it wasn't the food, then what?'

The village hardly seemed the innocent paradise that it had minutes before. But Neville was nothing if not dogged. He clung to the vision he had had. 'I just didn't want Drughat to be spoiled by an invasion of tourists.'

Now it was the turn of the other man to be surprised. 'Spoiled?' He considered the word for a moment. 'But I don't think this village can be spoiled. It is the most poor village in this area. The ground is too steep and it is hard to grow even potatoes. Also we are too far from the valley. And there are many accidents. People get sick or burned by their fires. They hurt their backs working in the fields. The men stumble when they carry the heavy loads and hurt their ankles so they cannot walk.' He glanced at Neville's feet. 'They don't have good shoes like you.'

'You don't understand,' Neville objected. 'Everything will

change. I've seen it happen. You'll all become shopkeepers or hotel owners. Or beggars. It'll stop being a village.'

'Quite so.' The older man nodded approvingly. 'With tourist money we can pay a doctor to visit sometimes. Also a teacher. If the children learn their lessons they may even be able to get good jobs. Leave this place and go to Katmandu.' He looked wistful for a moment. Then his eyes narrowed. 'And then you say you will not put us in your book, even though we treat you so well and give you yak meat.'

'I was only trying to help,' Neville insisted. Into his thoughts came a picture of his wife's face, spitting with anger because he objected to her taking a wooden cupboard his grandfather had given him. 'You don't know what you're throwing away. People aren't happy in the West, even though they're rich.'

The other man glanced at him sharply. 'And I suppose you will change places with a Drughat man and spend your life digging potatoes?'

Neville floundered. 'That's not the point.'

'Or is it that you are selfish and want to keep this village only for yourself? Like a pet.'

Thakali was speaking again. The other man listened, nodded, then took a piece of grimy paper and a pen from a pocket in his military jacket and rested them on his knee. He began writing, forming the letters carefully, in the manner of one creating an important document. When finally finished, he slapped the thing down in front of Neville.

I, Neville Ewan, promise to write many words about Drughat village in my guidebook on Nepal. I will tell of its beauty and famously friendly people. Also its nearness to the village path, and many interesting places that can be visited in one day. Also the delicious food. I will encourage many foreign tourists to come to Drughat village and stay.

Neville knew the document to be absurd. It could bind him to nothing. But still he resented its coercion. In his clean, glum life he had not suffered coercion since he was at school.

And he felt angry with Thakali and the other villagers for having somehow let him down. 'No,' he announced abruptly. 'I won't do this. It's not right.'

Thakali's eyes hardened. 'Sign.'

'It is better that you do,' agreed the older man.

Neville was adamant. 'You can't make me.' But when he tried to stand up – difficult with the heavy pack still on his back – the crowded airless room broke into uproar. Hands began pushing, slapping. He felt blips of pain rain against him. His knee was pressed against something metal and hot. Winded, he found himself pushed back to his place on the floor.

'Sign,' advised the old man. 'If you refuse we will not understand.'

Fear proved stronger than shame. Neville signed.

Thakali inspected the signature, then called out to the crowd. A hand reached out with the silver medallion. Thakali took it, then shoved it into Neville's shirt pocket, dismissive. There was no mistaking the object's changed status, from gift to payment. Or had it always been a payment?

The deal was done. At Thakali's instruction the crowd pressed back, allowing Neville to leave. He walked slowly at first, then, stepping into the sunlight, his step speeded almost to a run.

Only when he was clear of the houses did he glance back. He could see no figures at all, only the walls of the buildings, linked together, closed. Up ahead were the white peaks he had noticed before. But now they were different. The shimmering mystery had gone. Now they looked only cold and sharp.

D. J. Enright

SENTIMENTAL TRAVELLER

What Tel Aviv brings to mind is Alexandria
The same air, the same light, the same water.
Alexandria once waited to be bombed by Tel Aviv
Once Tel Aviv expected to be bombed by Alexandria.
So much in common in so many places you perceive.

In an alley just around the corner
From the Singapore Methodist Book Shop
Lighted by coconut candles
Stands a hawker's glittering barrow.
The wares laid out so lovingly
When at last you recognise them
Are not for humdrum or unseemly uses
As foiling conception or fending off diseases
But designed to *ENHANSE THE MARRITAL PLESSURES*.
Some akin to vacuum-cleaner fittings
Sprouting circlets of frisky goat's hair
Or the painted feathers of little birds
While others are stoutly buttressed
Or bulge with beads in garish colours –
Knick-knacks and gewgaws set out neatly.
A Sikh presides, ancient and sleepy
With sacred appurtenances and saintly smile.
Were you a woman, you reflect
You'd gather up your skirts and run a mile.
The guru flicks a pack of faded papers
Affirming the contentment of *MARRITAL CUPPELS*

Whose names are past deciphering.
Many are the matrimonies he has saved
Just around the corner from the Methodists
But peoples of now, he warbles sadly
Are too much working to joy their blessings.
Only bats play curiously about the barrow.

The main thing is, not the famous yellow cotton
The main thing is, that many people
A great many people were killed here once
(So much is beyond dispute)
They were good people
Consisting of men, women, and children
100,000 of them (a conservative estimate is 60,000)
While 40,000 women were raped (alternatively 20,000)
Though this is not why they call it the Rape of Nanjing
All of which was the work of Japanese soldiers
(Reportedly they were bored and tired, but not sufficiently)
In those days the Japanese were not good people
Of course it was a long time ago
(Though some do not consider fifty years is all that long)
But it is the main thing
One's attention is drawn to it repeatedly
Right up to the next scheduled meal
In a famous Buddhist restaurant as it happens
Where smiling monks serve elegant dishes
Totally vegetarian, which does not inhibit beer
Yet it would not do to enjoy oneself too much
Despite the manifest attractions of this beautiful city
Which it is only right to admire openly
On the banks of the Yangtze River
With its abundant greenery and temperate climate
And (the guidebook hints) its 'unharried pace'
Which brings us back to the main thing . . .

Andrew Motion

Europa: A Fragment

I must have been a woman once – it doesn't matter.
Now I'm speaking from a plastic cup: in fact I am the cup,
thrown down behind a boulder – dust and olive leaves.
Tomorrow I might switch to one of them, or be a crow
above the site, if not the site itself – perhaps the temple
where the priestess stoked the fire and told her lies,
perhaps the relics of the labyrinth where once that freak
roared round and round. Don't ask me where, exactly,
I don't know. What's more, I couldn't care. They thought
he might have been my child! But then, we all hate children:
how they drain us of our only life to fill up theirs
and then say *Oh! – too much!* or *Oh! – too little!* Nothing fits.
Not this age with another. Not the sense of who you are
with what you might have been. Not then with now, or now.

The one thing to rely on is yourself. Just think of me
out drinking in the café of a careless life, the sort of life
you might lead in the Boul Saint Mich (alone and young
and pretty but a franc or ten too short to meet the bill)
the very day – the moment – that the German soldiers came.
What would you do? Hail one I suppose and make him pay?
Of course you would. Now think of me five thousand years
or six before all that – when I had argued with my father
– nothing big, just one age chaffing at the next – and left
to give myself a talking-to, calm down, and have a swim,
when *crash!* the second that I stepped up to the waves
the whole sea went berserk: enormous hairy breakers,
fish flung panting on the shore, a fiery oven-door of water

wrenching wide, then wider – so I thought I'd see the earth
torn open to its centre, where the creatures live in dread –
and then a stretched-out second's endless hush, and then
a bull four-square before me. Yes, that's right, a bull.
Who says the universe is humourless or gods are dead?

Ah, I know what you're thinking now. You're thinking:
Bull? I'll say a bull invented and passed down to us
by some philosopher of caves and bone-head tribes
who thinks a beefy fuck is all we need to know.
Of course that's mad. You don't believe me? Well, I say it is.
I came here almost witless, inside out with grief.
I hated living where the music drills a hole into your head
and dances with your brain; I hated how my father reached
his hand from miles away to squeeze my dusty heart
then called it love. And yet I learnt to live. I did that
and still do. I kept my place until the place was me.
My wide horizon narrowed as big cities I can't name
sprang up and closed their ranks. New nonsense languages
poured in through doorways and the shelter I call mine.
It didn't matter; I had suffered and survived before.
You still don't get it, do you? Watch me. This is how:
I hid my heartbeat in the murmur of a stone becoming dust;
the simple fact of sunlight shines like my immortal soul.

Jonathan Treitel

GRAFFITI

HALF PAST NOON. Rome is snoozing. A black cat, spray-painted with a pink curseword on its rump, scurries across the Via dei Fori Imperiali, and disappears down an alley. A decent peace resumes. Not absolutely though: dilapidated wooden shop-fronts creak, and a purr emanates from the electricity cables. Moreover there is a sense of perpetual restless motion as if the city were stirring in its sleep: dust rises and falls in the hazy air; there is an illusion of motion in the graffiti daubed across the façades of buildings.

Eventually, into this cityscape, Umberto comes marching, a clipboard tucked under his right arm. He is a person whose respectability is manifest from his premature baldness, his pale severe suit, and the sunglasses clamped over his eyes. He is advancing at a fair pace. He is trailed at some distance by three shoplifters, four pickpockets, two football hooligans and a public nuisance. 'Come along, boys!' he barks. 'We haven't got all day.'

Umberto is an assistant supervisor in the department of juvenile correction. His charges, boys in their early teens, are each carrying a large plastic pail in whatever way seems most convenient: whether balanced on a shoulder or clutched against the belly. They are having to circumnavigate rusty cars abandoned along the way. They are sweating and struggling to keep up. Occasionally, when crossing a paving slab rendered slippery by graffito paint, one or another of them stumbles, but nobody actually topples.

A stocky football hooligan calls out, 'Can't we take the bus?'

Umberto retorts. 'You are not supposed to be enjoying yourself. You are paying your debt to society.'

A skinnier hooligan says, 'I shouldn't be here, signore. I'm innocent.'

Umberto echoes, '*Innocent*' – raising the pitch of the word a little, not quite making it into a question.

Meanwhile a group of pickpockets, while nudging one another, happen to be bumping up against the locked shutters of an *osteria*. Somehow their hands slip inside and emerge with fistfuls of a *fritto misto* of brains and zucchini.

Several shoplifters are trying to avoid stepping on the cracks.

And the one who is not quite all there (the public nuisance) is laughing to himself.

At last Umberto and his charges have departed in the direction of the Foro Romano. Once more the boulevard is silent. Briefly, an upper storey shutter is opened; a woman in black peers down: she makes the sign against the evil eye, then draws her head in; the shutter is closed.

Umberto moves his hands as if stretching an imaginary cord, indicating that the delinquents slow their pace awhile. They are on the Via Sacra, between the temples to Saturn and to Castor and Pollux. Ahead stand the great broken arches of the Basilica di Massenzio. All the ruins are overpainted with graffito upon graffito, great gaudy swirls of luminous paint, winding around the old stones like (the classical allusion springs into Umberto's thoughts) the sea serpent seizing the sons of Laocoön. He asks the boys if they think the Foro has always looked like this.

They do not comprehend his ironic tone. They reply, 'Once it was all in one piece, signore.' 'Once it was newer, signore.' 'I'm innocent, signore.'

'Once it was all *clean*,' he stresses. 'I remember, when I was young back in the 1990s, there were hardly any graffiti here, or anywhere in the city, or in any city in the whole wide world!'

The delinquents stare at him blankly. He realises they can't even conceive of the picture he is presenting. For them, graffiti are a natural feature of the city, as common as litter or stray cats. The act of creating it is neither good nor bad. It's only normal that citizens carry cans of spray-paint in their pocket, and leave their mark, on which are superimposed other people's marks, and hence every wall and every door, every roof and shutter and public statue and fountain, every permanent surface indeed, is bedaubed with letters and ideographs.

The delinquents approach the Arco di Tito. The more literate among them read out extracts from the messages visible on the surface: love declarations and soccer slogans in a medley of languages. 'AC Milano is magic and Roma is tragic.' '*Billy te amo*.' 'We won Mondiale.' A pickpocket points out the cartoonish phallic figures painted atop the arch, tracing the shapes with his fingertips in air. The public nuisance presses his palms over his eyes.

Umberto says, 'Can't you see what lies underneath the graffiti? The carvings! Look. They were made by an emperor, to show him conquering Jerusalem. You can see the booty he seized from the Temple, for instance that candelabra over there . . .'

A shoplifter shrugs. 'Just another kind of graffiti.'

Umberto sighs. At the university he had studied philosophy. He had been fascinated by the teaching of Vico: that the universe is subject to recurrence. Recurrence, not repetition: history is a kind of spiral . . . This doctrine comforts him in his work. True, few of the delinquents he supervises are discouraged from committing further crimes, and in any case there are always more boys growing up, but in the fullness of time all the villains will grow old and die, and the world will be much as it was in time past.

How can he explain this to the boys in terms they will understand? He searches for the right words. 'Every creature has a natural enemy: birds eat worms, dogs kill cats, and dogs can die from worms – and that is a good thing, because otherwise we would be overrun with a plague of one animal or another. So it is with weapons. Every instrument of offence is countered by a defence. The sword can be stopped with the shield. Poison gas with a gas mask. A bullet with a bulletproof vest. And just so with graffiti too. Of course people have been scribbling on walls ever since antiquity – you can see the marks on the oldest remains in Ostia or Herculaneum; indeed there is reason to believe we Italians invented the practice of graffiti, which explains why our word for it is borrowed by so many other languages. But, traditionally, there was always some way of wiping the marks off, or covering them over, so they never became too much of a nuisance. A new kind of paint appeared in the 1970s, the cellulose-based sprayable kind, which was hard to erase, so graffiti multiplied in the cities. But the plague was cured with enzymatic solvents. Graffiti went on the retreat. But then, towards the end of the century, SuperPaint was invented, removable by no known solvent. Now anybody could make a mark which could never be obliterated, other than by tearing down the wall it was painted on, or splashing another graffito on top. Within decades graffiti had spread round the world. And I don't know if you understand how pernicious the plague is: every city is a mess, nobody can think clearly, the place falls apart. To people of your generation the state of things seems universal and permanent – but is it?'

The delinquents gaze down at the ground or up at the sky.

'Look over there, at the Colosseo! A writhing mass of Technicolor maggots! That's what it looks like. You can hardly make out its shape even . . . But I remember it was not always like that . . .'

It was not always like that. Umberto then was about the age of these boys now. He had a full head of hair, but he already wore sunglasses for his eyes were always sensitive. SuperPaint existed, of course, and graffiti were common but not absolutely universal. It was possible to discover a public building which had entire walls, entire halls even, untouched by a single graffito. For instance the Colosseo, an obvious target, had been daubed along the accessible parts, but higher up you could still see the original naked stones. One summer evening he and half a dozen of his closest friends had set out on an expedition. The gang had entered the Colosseo, rolling in under the tall iron gates. The arena was dim inside; just a snip of moon overhead, plus the perpetual urban glimmer; and the shining eyes of innumerable stray cats. It had all been planned carefully. The ropes and the crampons and the spray-cans of SuperPaint were strapped to their belts. It was not difficult to clamber up the levels of the building, and then ascend the irregular outer wall, right to the top. The friends sprayed their names in huge letters on the summit of the building. How proud they had felt then, established up there above the audience of thousands of howling felines, yet even at the moment of triumph they had been aware how pointless it all was – like a team of gladiators bowing to the crowd: *Morituri te salutamus* – We who are about to die salute you. The gang had descended the difficult way, down the outside of the building. They had danced the night away in a disco in Trastevere. In the morning the sign of the exploit was clearly visible. Of course, in the years since, many other graffiti have been set on top of theirs . . . Umberto thinks he can still make out the pattern of his own name. He consults his clipboard. He marches the delinquents off down the Via della Conciliazione, heading for the river.

Less than an hour later Umberto is striding into the Piazza San Pietro. The boys are panting behind; their faces are sticky with dust. Ahead lies the great cathedral itself. Naturally it is wrapped in several layers of black polythene. Indeed the cathedral looks much like every other church or museum or historic site of note in the world – now and during the era in which graffitoing is universal. No serious work of art has been put on public display ever since that incident some decades ago in which the Mona Lisa was irrevocably moustached. It is still possible to enter San Pietro, but the interior floor, walls and ceiling are boarded over, so the effect is like standing inside an irregular packing case; only a handful of dedicated tourists or pilgrims are present in the Piazza.

'This way, boys!' Umberto jangles his host of keys. He leads the group through a side-entrance into the Museo. The place smells musty; spiders spin in the corners of the boarded-over rooms. It is dim: he pushes the sunglasses up on his shiny pate. He was taken here as an infant, before the place was covered up: he has the vaguest dreamy memory of gorgeous grandeur . . .

The delinquents dawdle.

'You are not doing this for pleasure. Along this corridor, quick!'

His air of command belies his uncertainty as to where exactly he is. Instructions and a sketch map are on the clipboard, but there are so many rooms here, and the corridors all look identical. True, hand-painted signs are nailed up by the intersections: arrows pointing to STANZE OF RAPHAEL / MCDONALD'S / WC . . . but it seems unwise to put too much faith in them. 'Down here, boys. Come along!'

He clears his throat and sneaks another look at his sketch map. He waves the group on through a doorway.

At last everybody is gathered in a tall, quite long, not very wide room. The walls are boarded over. Scaffolding has been erected as high as the ceiling, and evidently an effort had been made to drape plastic sheeting there; however it has fallen down and the black polythene lies on the floor in crumpled waves.

Umberto holds his arms out like a policeman stopping traffic. He clears his throat and announces. 'This must surely be the . . . ah, cafeteria.'

The boys put down their loads.

'What happens,' he asks, 'when an irresistible force meets an immovable object?'

The delinquents avoid his gaze.

He gestures at the plastic pails. 'What do you suppose is in there? Can you guess?'

No response.

'Did you suppose the era of graffiti would continue for ever? Of course not. Nothing is immutable. Everything rises and falls, and comes back in a different manifestation. Industrial chemists have been at work. They have solved the problem, as they were bound to. It was only a matter of time. You are each carrying a full load of the SuperSolvent, capable of removing any kind of paint!

'Our task today is to expunge the graffiti in this room.

Even as we speak, other teams of delinquents doing community service, and volunteers, and hired clean-up crews, are busy eradicating graffiti elsewhere in the city. Soon we shall have eliminated it all. And not just here: the whole world will be free of this menace. At last we will be able to see our cities for the rational, orderly places they were meant to be.'

He points upward. He flicks his fingers under his chin in a gesture of distaste. 'That mess has got to go.' He secures his sunglasses over his eyes, to mute the sight.

The delinquents stare upward. They have never seen graffiti quite like this. Luminous, throbbing colours; words and twining shapes; representations of creatures of fantasy and of virtually naked humans . . . To them, the vision appears beautiful. They look at it in silence; even the skinny hooligan forgets to protest his innocence; even the public nuisance makes no noise. They are very still, while the images soak into their heads. It seems as if the boys are trapped in stasis, like figures in a painting, doomed to gaze up for ever.

But Umberto makes the clip on the clipboard spring shut with a noise like a cracking whip. 'You are not going to leave until the place is completely spotless!'

And duly, the delinquents climb the scaffolding, with their pails of SuperSolvent and bunches of rags.

Umberto stands beneath. He observes. A contingent cat is slinking between his heels. He has a sense of his own glorious isolation as he watches the underlings do his bidding. He feels a kind of power, and a supreme joy which might be compared to that of an artist in the throes of creation. The football hooligans and shoplifters are dunking rags in the pails, and passing them forward to the pickpockets who, deft-fingered, are performing the act of erasure. The public nuisance is urging his comrades on by means of a hearty cackle. Certainly the SuperSolvent is living up to its promise. A simple wipe with it dissolves all the paint. The boys have already swabbed a good tenth of the ceiling clean, as far as the spark where God's finger touches Adam's.

Peter Porter

BELLA PROSPETTIVA

Would you address yourself
to the ending of the world
with unpaid bills on the mat
and a moulting budgerigar?

So many of your friends
think poetry consists of
clever lines stopping short
of the edge of the page.

And libraries stand up
like the Step Pyramid or
cemeteries in São Paulo,
room for one more inside.

But existence has always seemed
stupid to idealists,
a mess appealing only
to short-circuiting tycoons.

Getting-on-with-things counts:
your 127 quintets,
68 quartets and
101 trios will outlive you.

Like Archimedes you need
a point to be looking from,
a perspective to continue
the known unknown forever.

A LONG PURSUIT

The artist has recourse
to the Dictionary of Popes
to remind himself that they
whether virtuous or vile
rarely mounted Peter's throne
till so old their reigns were short.

Unlike some Kings and Caesars
who being inheritors born
ruled, regented or not,
while yet to come of age,
on horseback facing mobs
or playing the fipple flute.

'Grow old along with me'
is not an artist's creed,
and daisy-chaining sonnets
or carrying size in buckets
our youthful makars toast
their fellow-bohemian, Death.

Once back in Papal courts
we read about Formosus,
Conan, Stephen the Sixth,
'The Cadaver Synod', even
Pius the Twelfth, and see
age obsessed by hate.

Both long-sought power
and early frenzy will,
in perturbation of saints
or wiles of Popes and pimps,
help us recognise
how irrelevant happiness is.

A SERMON FOR SEMELE

This is the justice of the afternoon,
All those hours in an atelier
Trying to make some sense of skin,
A reticent god whose only cross
Is boredom, breakfasting angels ready
To discuss their chief's engagements,
And a girl enticing fire with love.

And so they'll call her feather-headed,
An archaic and affectionate
Rebuke this side of real estate,
She suspecting that her lovely pelt
Is condom to a spirit but
Watching nude and chatty on a stage
Outside the stitch-ups of the season.

If it's Thursday it must be Zeus.
Thunderer (but Clamourer
To his Press Team), he's out to prove
Creation can be classless and forgets
That she's a beauty and like him
Can condescend: all play and no
Work makes Jack a celebrity.

Only duty can be truly serious.
It's the transformation scene
Which fires the fiction-makers, stirs
The Stendhals to compose biographies
Of their penises, buys old pictures
To delude its heirs and states the Commune's
Just another way of having sex.

Better though than falling back on words
Which, Semele, is your mistake –
The clear calligraphy of touch
Is always readable, unlike
Some black embroidery of tones
Exclaiming 'Love and I are one'
Or looking through his wallet while he sleeps.

We know her tale, this season comes
Too late, but just like Congreve, Handel
And Euripides we want
A happy ending, so we play
The 'rough-beast-slouches' card and from
The bedroom fire there struts downstairs
A God of Grunge, young for eternity.

VERDI'S VILLA, SANTA AGATA

Within a radius of fifty miles
round Reggio and Modena
the landscape smells of shit.
Miracles are never kind
and Emilia-Romagna's cooking
is renowned throughout the world.

The sun turns steadily
over the standing fields,
imported Kiwi fruit
replace the orchard crops
and dry-course rivers sleep
below heraldic bridges.

They farmed their art one time
with the same intensity,
and still you see the turbid
fruits of death and nature
in Dosso's boskiness
or buttocks by Correggio.

Where though to find that grand
ordinariness which marks
the few world-eating geniuses?
Great families shrink at last
to names on famous forts
and visits after lunch.

Verdi's villa has every touch
of provincial stylelessness –
cramped rooms, dull views,
the decorations of
a Paymaster-General's widow,
glassed memorabilia.

In the garden a sluggish pond,
a tumulus for ice,
rambling paths leading
to a prairie gate
and a melancholy cat
prescribable as noon.

Glenn Patterson

HOMELANDS

Paper presented at the 3rd Dublin International Writers'
Festival, 22 September 1993

IT SEEMS APPROPRIATE at a festival whose theme is homelands to begin by remembering a writer who is spending today, as he has spent the past more than fifteen hundred days, in the most grotesque form of exile imaginable, the there-and-not-there existence imposed on him by an Iranian death sentence. I am speaking of course of Salman Rushdie, a writer who has always had much to say on the subject of homelands. Here, for instance in his third novel, *Shame*, he interjects himself into his narrative to speculate on the meaning of belonging:

> To explain why we become attached to our birthplaces [he says], we pretend we are trees and speak of roots. Look under your feet. You will not find gnarled growths sprouting through the soles. Roots, I sometimes think are a conservative myth designed to keep us in our places.

I personally owe a great debt to Salman Rushdie. It was after reading his novel about the birth of India, *Midnight's Children*, hard on the heels of John Dos Passos's *USA*, that I decided that the novel was the form most appropriate to the subject of Northern Ireland. It was only later when I had published my own first novel, while living in England, and had returned to Belfast to live and write, that I discovered that a number of my contemporaries had likewise been inspired by his work. His stories of lives lived in one place, dominated by thoughts of somewhere else – his characters' attempts to negotiate the space in between – struck a chord with us growing up in Northern Ireland's split-personality state. He was in fact, we used to say, and not entirely joking, the most important *Irish* writer of his generation.

Shame in particular, his 'novel of leavetaking' from the East as he calls it, published the year after I first went to live in England, spoke to those of us who had shared at one time or another his emigrant condition: the irresistible impetus to leave, the unresolved concern for the country, the homeland, left behind.

Leaving Northern Ireland as I did in the year after the Maze Hunger Strike, leaving it in part because of the Hunger Strike – still to my mind among the most collectively shameful (as well as personally terrifying) episodes in the last twenty-five years of Irish and for that matter British history – leaving, as I say, when I did, why I did, I had moved to East Anglia, to Norwich, as far away from Belfast as it was possible to get in Britain without falling into the sea. I had already had an unappetising taste of emigrant communities while visiting relatives in Canada, visits which included the bizarre experience of marching alongside an Orange parade in lily-wilting heat through crowds of bemused Toronto shoppers.

I had rarely seen the Sash worn with such belligerent pride.

A happy coincidence of the move to Norwich therefore was that there appeared to be only one other person there from Belfast; I knew that's where he was from because he had very helpfully been rechristened Belfast Dave. When eventually we met he informed me that from the instant I arrived I had been known – to everyone else if not to my face – as Irish Glenn. So it is we often find ourselves, willy-nilly, defined by the very thing we are trying to leave behind.

The reasons for emigration, of course, are many and complex. Some emigrants have no desire to leave the homeland at all and hang on for dear life to its memories and rituals. The Orange marchers I mentioned are only an extreme example. I think of the men in Ciaran Carson's poem 'The Exiles' Club' meeting in the Wollongong Bar, somewhere in Australia, engaged in the Joycean task of reconstructing the Falls Road of their youth, right down to the contents of Paddy Lavery's pawnshop. Even Salman Rushdie the enthusiastic exile cannot always trust in the effectiveness of his escape. The East remains a part of the world to which, he says, he is still attached, if only by elastic bands. And of course if you force an elastic band beyond a certain point there is either an irrevocable break, or an inevitable return.

It is interesting that in *Shame* Rushdie's most strongly expressed attachment to his homeland comes when he recalls his anger on hearing of the sale of his childhood home in Bombay. This seems to me to point to something, perhaps glaringly obvious, about the emigrant's sense of homeland: it is inherently nostalgic, arrested as it is at the moment of his or her departure. Actually, the word *Joycean* just now reminded me of a talk I once heard given by Dr Eamonn Hughes of Queen's University, Belfast, on the nostalgic nature of all of Joyce's fiction. So instead of the old, familiar saying that through all his wanderings Joyce never really left Dublin, there is a sense in which Dublin by the end had in fact left him far behind. (Before, that is, they turned the city into the *Ulysses* theme park.)

Of course I have been talking up to now of homeland as an essentially individual longing. (I am tempted here to substitute the word *heart*land for homeland, both in recognition of the strongly emotional nature of the longing and for its often expressed desire to be lost once more in the bosom of one's own people.) I would suggest however that there is something fundamentally nostalgic about even the collective expression of the word. This in turn is not to ignore the sustaining potential of thoughts of homeland for people who have been displaced or who are otherwise suffering discrimination because of their race, their religion or their nationality, nor to deny the need for spatial as well as legal refuges from persecution.

This has been made even more pertinent in recent weeks by the signing of the peace accord between Israel and the PLO. For its joint commitment to a demilitarisation and for its restoration of certain fundamental rights to people who have been denied them for almost half a century, the accord is clearly to be welcomed.

It is equally clear however that the accord still faces serious opposition, both from those Israelis who see any concession as a threat to the security of their state – the Jewish homeland which the Holocaust had made such an urgent necessity – and from those Palestinians who see it as a dilution of the homeland they were deprived of when the Israelis claimed theirs. This is much more than a territorial dispute. What we are faced with are two competing versions of homeland written on to the same geographical space. Worse still, in each version the homeland can also be read as *holy* land (centred on Jerusalem) with all that term's attendant baggage of God-given rights and destiny fulfilled in soil.

Quite apart from a desire to see an end to the fighting in the Middle East I find myself drawn to the example of the Israelis and the Palestinians both as a writer – the idea of competing narratives – and as a native of Northern Ireland. In fact the parallels between the two conflicts are so well developed in the minds of most Northern Irish people as to have passed over into their own country's sectarian iconography. In various parts of Catholic West Belfast, therefore, you will come across murals depicting the PLO and the IRA as comrades in arms (and indeed throughout the 1970s the local press regularly carried reports of Republicans receiving training in camps in Lebanon); Protestants meanwhile have traditionally admired the Israelis for their uncompromising response to what they both regarded as terrorism. In my teens many Protestants wore (and perhaps many still wear) the Star of David, each of its six points being said to represent one of the counties of Northern Ireland. For a time my local Member of Parliament in South Belfast was a man, a minister of the church, who claimed, apparently in all seriousness, that the Ulster Protestants were descendants of the lost tribe of Israel and as such had an unshakeable claim to their six-county state.

One Saturday morning in 1981 five men with a very different idea of the arithmetic of homeland walked into a community centre not far from my parents' house and shot the MP, the Revd Robert Bradford, dead, along with the caretaker Ken Campbell who alternated with my brother in opening the centre on Saturdays.

Again we have two fundamentalist readings of the same territory. It is at one and the same time the country that once promised a Protestant parliament for a Protestant people and the Fourth Green Field, the piece needed to complete the picture of a unified Gaelic nation. The dispute hinges, as these disputed readings often do, on a single hard-to-interpret line: the border. Perhaps to say *a single line* is an oversimplification, for borders, as everyone knows, are a recurrent motif in Northern Ireland. (Or perhaps again the larger line is like one of those titles that only come to the writer after the book is complete, a culmination of the themes running through the text rather than their precursor. For long before there was a border, Northern Ireland was border country.)

The state of Northern Ireland itself is of course in historical terms relatively young. Even in human terms it is not that old. My grandmother at eighty-two is ten years older. But then, my grandmother at eighty-two has seen the Soviet Union come and go, has seen, to pick a place at random, the territory of Alsace-Lorraine translated back and forth between the German and French on no fewer than three occasions in her lifetime. She has, in fact, seen the formation of more new countries than I can practically enumerate here and the collapse of as many old ones.

Nor do I mean to be flippant in saying this. If the fact of our own mortality is the hardest lesson that we as human beings have to learn, then the acceptance of the impermanency of institutions we have been brought up to think of as defining who we are cannot lag far behind.

Wanting to suggest something of this belief in countries as shaping forces – as *characters* – in our lives, I called my own second novel *Fat Lad*, an acronym I was taught at primary school to remember the six counties of Northern Ireland by: Fermanagh Antrim Tyrone Londonderry (for it was a Protestant primary school) Armagh and Down. What we weren't taught until much later was that the Fat Lad could so easily have been *A* Lad, pure and simple, slimmed down to two thirds his actual size by the exclusion of the potentially imbalancing (because predominantly Catholic) counties of Fermanagh and Tyrone. There is an arbitrariness here (or rather a degree of calculation) that undermines faith in the current arrangement.

Maybe it is this more than any other factor that explains the appeal of Salman Rushdie to me and my Northern Irish contemporaries, his recognition of countries as willed (or imposed) fictions, like all fictions susceptible to editing and revision.

Fat Lad was in part an exploration of how people live with such contingency, of the psychological impacts of political decisions which redefine, however subtly, their country's *meaning*, if I can call it that. Let me give you an example from my own life. When I was eleven the British government announced a referendum, quickly dubbed the Border Poll, in which the people of Northern Ireland were asked to vote for or against staying in the United Kingdom. I was petrified. Never mind that Nationalist leaders were advising their supporters not to take part in what they saw as a mere rubber-stamping of the Unionist veto: for days beforehand I could barely sleep. I cried with relief when the result came through. This was undoubtedly, in part, a political reaction: even at eleven, even in a mildly Unionist household like the one I was brought up in (my lullaby was 'Kevin Barry'), I knew by heart all the arguments in favour of the link with Britain. There was at the same time, though, a much more irrational element to the reaction. Pull away the border and it would have seemed to me then as though the bottom had dropped out, not just of the country but of all my notions of order.

Or let me, if I may, give you another, more oblique example. My father is a sheet metal worker by trade and for many years made railings in his spare time. He had a car, a Vauxhall station wagon, in which to ferry the finished railings about. It was by far the biggest car on our street, possibly in our neighbourhood. It was a bus, practically, and could fit our entire under-10s football team inside. (The word *dismay* to me is the look on the faces of opposing teams seeing us roll up to their pavilion in my father's Vauxhall. That car was a two-goal start.) One night in September 1971 we were stopped by paratroops in the centre of Belfast on our way from Aldergrove airport where we had been picking up a Canadian uncle. We were ordered out and made to stand against the window of Marks & Spencer: my mother, my father, the Canadian uncle and me. My father chatted, as my father always did (and does – this is a man who walks sideways so as not to miss anyone he knows going in the same direction only slower). The paratroops weren't having it. They pulled the film from my uncle's camera. There went London, there went Paris. Next, they emptied the glove compartment and the boot of the big station wagon. Next, they took off the door panels and unbolted the seats and set them on the pavement.

These were *our* soldiers. This was our *car* – our family on wheels – and there it was for all the world to see on the pavement outside Marks & Spencer. It had not even occurred to me till then that you could do that to a car. My first engineering lesson and it was a lesson in deconstruction. Even after the Paras had put it back together I never quite trusted that car in the same way, but sat by the door from then on with my hand near the button, ready to bale out the instant it threatened to fall apart again.

While it is rare that the terms of the contract between the people and the state are presented in the stark terms of the Border Poll, they are nevertheless re-stated daily in a myriad small, and not-so-small ways. And if the state acts outside the limits of its power, or outside the people's expectations of it, then one of two things will happen: either the state loses its legitimacy in the eyes of the citizen, or equally likely it provokes a crisis in the citizen's sense of self. Though apparently contradictory, both responses can have the same result. It seems to me that what are called, appropriately enough, *disturbances* when they reach the street cannot be divorced from these psychological upheavals.

As a writer, especially as a writer who lives much of the time in England, I find myself confronted by two major problems when trying to deal with this situation as it relates to Northern Ireland. The first is personal, or perhaps ethical, in that the lives of the people I am writing about closely resemble those of people whom I grew up among; the second is theoretical or political: in focusing on Northern Ireland as an imperfect fiction, how do I avoid giving the impression that I am trying to write it out of existence? So far as the personal question is concerned, perhaps this is something writers never resolve. We draw heavily on the communities – families even – which nurtured us and even when we write out of a desire to inform, in the broadest sense, it is hard sometimes not to feel, in the narrowest sense, like an informer.

As to the political question, it has always seemed to me that what writing about Northern Ireland could do – and by writing I suppose I am talking about the novel – was find ways of portraying the events there, not as existing in a vacuum, but in their historical, political, geographical, even geological context; as a part of the broader currents of European and world history.

At the same time I repeat over and over to myself a formula that I think is necessary for anyone who would seek to effect change there, namely that two things can be simultaneously wrong; or put another way, by drawing attention to the frailties of one system of belief, you do not automatically espouse its opposite. Indeed even to think in terms of opposites in a place like Northern Ireland is to perpetuate the problem. Militant Republicanism is not the opposite of diehard Loyalism; the union of Northern Ireland with Great Britain is not the opposite of a United Ireland. Nor for that matter, to take an example from elsewhere in the world, are an Orthodox Serbia, a Catholic Croatia and an ethnically segregated Bosnia the opposite of Yugoslavia.

It is, however, one of the most depressing aspects of the current turmoil in Europe that so often change can only be envisaged as a return to a previous – or even to a supposedly original – state.

This picks up on something I said earlier, about the idea of homeland, even in its collective expression, being inherently nostalgic. The nostalgia I had in mind was what I would call the nostalgia of nationalism. *Homeland*, as it is increasingly used in our present political climate, presupposes a nation, or rather a people; it connotes, more and more, exclusive possession and at its most extreme adopts the deadly rhetoric of racial purity. There is at the moment, I am told, one Serbian politician who claims the Serbs have descended, not from the lost tribe of Israel, but from *another planet*. A joke – I think – but one which merely takes to its logical conclusion the extreme nationalist's dream of the uncontaminated people. This yearning for pristine states is, I would suggest, ultimately infantile in nature. (It is worth remembering perhaps homeland's synonyms: fatherland, mother country.) It is a desire for the familiar, for the uncomplicated state. As such it is anti-organic. People move, have always moved, over the earth's surface. The *land* moves over the earth's surface. The present configuration is as fleeting as a snapshot: a billion years from now the earth will hardly recognise itself. Preposterous of course to think in terms of such a time-scale, but not half as preposterous, or as vain, as the argument of absolute proprietorship.

No man, as the saying ought to go, can set a limit on the progress of a continental drift.

Nor is the west of Europe free from this charge of exclusivity, as the recent resurgence of overtly racist groups in Germany, France, Britain and Italy makes abundantly clear. Yet even leaving this worrying trend aside it seems that we are unable to expand our concept of homeland without explicitly excluding other groups of people. So the lifting of internal borders within the European community has been accompanied by a strengthening of its eastern and southern frontiers. Buffer zones are established, holding countries for refugees; immigrants are classed with terrorists and drug traffickers as suitable targets for surveillance.

During the time that I was thinking about this paper I began to get confused, the way you sometimes do looking at the same words for extended periods, about the precise meaning of some of the terms I was using. I thought I had better go right back to basics and start again with succinct definitions. People. Nation. Race. All the big concepts that are used to describe and divide us. The more I looked, though, the more elusive agreed definitions seemed to become. The one defining characteristic of a people that did recur was a shared belief in a common history (shared language apparently being an optional extra). So on that basis I set out to try and establish who my people were. My family, obviously. But who else after that? The people in the part of Belfast where I grew up? Well, accepting the very particular family history we could not possibly share, yes, them too; in fact by the same reasoning *all* the people of Belfast. What then of the people in the rest of Northern Ireland – the rest of Ireland south and north? Didn't the common history extend to them? Well, a little more tenuously perhaps, but yes, to them too. And to Britain? Yes. And beyond that . . . And beyond that . . . And beyond that . . . ?

I started to grow very excited; each time I considered drawing a line under this idea of a common history there seemed to be an equally strong reason why I should extend it a little further. I was reminded of one of those moments of insight you sometimes have, waking suddenly in the middle of the night with a thought that seems to have come to you perfectly formed, irrefutable in its simplicity. Of course these thoughts rarely survive exposure to the corrosive light of day and more often than not turn to nonsense in our mouths when we try to communicate them.

But anyway.

One night a couple of years ago I woke with what I thought was some kind of wonderful Zeno's paradox in my head, only instead of motion it was difference between people that it proved was impossible. And it went like this: difference between peoples cannot exist because the closer you approach any notional dividing line the more, not less, alike people actually become. (In the same way borders are least necessary in border country, well away from the respective –

that word again – heartlands.) And this would hold no matter how far you journeyed throughout the world. You would never perceive change occurring, all you experience would be a continuum.

As I say, my sense of well-being at this night-thought did not last much past breakfast, but it has come back to me more than once lately, watching the news and thinking with dismay that, in our ever more minute distinctions of ourselves as a People, we are losing sight of everyone else as human beings.

(Again Bosnia, but Belfast too, and Brick Lane in London.)

We all have need at some time in our lives of the security that a sense of belonging to a community can give; few of us are entirely free of emotional attachment to the places where we were born or grew up. The retreat into homelands as a political model, however – into national or racial self-interest – obscures the connections between us, prohibiting the development of a critique that might indeed radically alter the distribution of power and resources to the benefit of all people, and deferring the moment when we can truly enter into an accommodation one with the other.

Ruth Padel

DOG

Plastic visors half-cock
over the nose. Rifles
over each camouflaged pelvis
like an invisible hose.

My countrymen. Each set of hands
in one line, the same line,
straightening the spine

of a viper between them
on Platform Four. Aliens,
trying to get a retriever,
all plumy shivers to her tail,

to clock the bouquet
of every white coffin
backing every bench: a banquet

of Braille, the poodle
who peed in French,
the peatfill of bush-rose,

ivy, primula for the Belfast
Central flowerbeds, downline.
She gets called back
if she skips one. On the uptrain

we watch from our windows.
What was the tip-off?
Does it all depend on one dog?

Carol Rumens

ANY CITY DEATH
Extract from a novel in progress

WHO WAS IT in the coffin? A hard line down each side of
the mouth and a furrow in the brow, the cheekbones blush-
ered and the hair perfectly centre-parted? Cathal hardly knew
what a comb was. The scalp was white as Tippex. No, whiter:
blue-white.

At least his face was rosy like flesh. But the throat in the
open-neck shirt and the single hand were blue-white. The
whole of his body like that, bloodless? Just the make-up
pretending he had blood? That wasn't Cathal's body.

He looked like Rasputin, I thought, or some icon-saint,
fierce, angular, fanatic. A man who could die for a cause, or
kill for it. Cathal couldn't have done either.

Where was the wound that had killed him? That he'd lost
a hand proved nothing. You can live without arms, without
legs. I wanted to see the ugly purple death-thing, however
terrible: a wound I could believe and feel and scream at.

If only his lovely eyes had been opened I might have known
it was Cathal.

The priest had an arrogant, Englished Dublin accent and
sounded as if he was sucking gobstoppers. It was plain he
had never met the 'Cathal' he referred to so familiarly, and
all he knew of his life was the authorised west-Belfast-to-
Queen's-University-to-fabulous-job-as-tea-boy-at-the-*Irish-
News* version. Nothing real.

Nothing about how this year he was studying Japanese
and how it had been Russian the year before, when he'd

learned to make *blinis* and sing all the verses of *Stenka Razin*. And how the year before that it was Irish and he spent three months in the Donegal *Gaeltacht* when he should have been working for his philosophy degree, trying to have conversations with the bemused locals, catch fish and translate Ronan's Lament.

I didn't recognise Father Gobstopper's Cathal, bland and careerist and stripped of his hunger for languages and places. I didn't recognise the 'Fee-awn-say', either. I sat on my hands (why are my hands so cold all the time?) and couldn't feel the ring at all, and floated on the meaningless pompous gush about tragic young lives and manhood heedlessly slaughtered in its prime, and the mercy and justice that waited, nevertheless, just the other side of pain. I realised I was waiting for him to say: if anyone should know of any impediment as to why this young man should be buried, speak now or forever hold your peace. I was ready to spring to my feet and say clearly and loudly: because Cathal is not dead, Father, and it's a crime to bury a live man, even in Belfast, shite-hole of the universe.

Imagine saying 'shite-hole' here.

I was going to giggle. I was quaking. I made a noise like a choked sob. Dad frowned at me. Fortunately there was a diversion. His Purpleness swept himself aside, the Youth Group lined up in front of the altar and raggedly strummed their guitars and lifted their sweet, husky, childish voices to make further encouraging assertions about immortal life. Hankies came out in profusion, then. I had no urge to cry. But I hated the young faces for being so alive.

Rustly silence. We got to our knees: a soft thunder-clap in the filled church. The organ whined to itself, *why, why,* and the long box floated by, between three lowered faces I'd never seen before and one I'd only seen in a photograph.

And it was all over. I hadn't made my speech. People were moving, whispering, even smiling. I might have shrieked or fainted if the crowd hadn't surged up around me and muffled me like a human ambulance and swept me out into the bright blue light with the flashing silver blots that meant the Press.

Faces bumped into mine. Hands perched on my arms, steered me this way and that. I felt I was going to suffocate.

Better the see-all-see-nothing eyes of the cameras than this clinging, scented, breathing, peering-into-the-soul pity. I made my face a mask and twitched and shrugged my shoulders to get rid of the big flies.

An inky-eyed woman in a Dracula-cape kept apologising in a stage-whisper: 'She's heavily sedated, she's had pills *and* an injection!' This was Beth, supposedly my mother.

The women surrounding me were MacNamaras. I knew them by their expensively shaped and coloured hair, their tailored jackets, their heavy mounds of flesh, decently constrained and parcelled but sometimes leaking out in cheeks and chins and ankle-flab that overflowed their shoes.

The women on Cathal's side were less uniform. Some, like his Auntie Byddi, were much smarter and sharper than any of ours; others, much dowdier. They kept their distance from me, though I could have borne them closer. They watched me too, but more delicately, more curiously. Secretly, they would have liked to take me in their arms, and I would have clutched them so I felt their bones: bones that were like Cathal's, twigs from the same branch.

I am standing by the edge of the open grave, looking in. A coffin, I think, is the evillest shape in the world.

I've been left alone at last. Why can't I cry? I'll make you cry, so. How like you this, and this, and this? I jab the red-rose thorns into the pads of my thumbs. I want to get blood on the rose, so my blood can go into the grave with Cathal. That way we shall be together in our dark little starter-home.

I want the rose to fall on the wood exactly above his heart.

Finally, my thumbs smear and dampen and a few mean, thin tears of pain sting the backs of my eyes.

Pressure on my shoulder, deepening gently. *Oh no, not again.* I turn my head as if my neck was clogged with rust.

A long hand, with smoker's kippered fingertips. Plum scarf blowing in the wind. The gaunt face that had not looked like its photograph, as it moved beside the coffin.

'Cleo, isn't it? I'm sorry I didn't get a chance to meet you earlier. I'm Owen.' He stops, hoping that's all he needs to say. The shock of the familiar, dove-grey eyes is almost like love.

'Yes, I'd have recognised you.'

'I'm surprised!' Smiling, he grips my hand. He doesn't notice the blood. I study his eyes: they are smaller than Cathal's. The hair is lank brown. Cathal's shone, even uncombed. It was starling-black.

He goes on gripping my hand and I wish he'd let go. 'I'm so very sorry, Cleo.'

I can't stop looking for Cathal in him. The bone-structure, the personality, the manners, are quite different. It's as if someone had done a pencil sketch of Cathal first and rubbed it out and drawn Owen on top, leaving faint lines of the earlier sketch still visible. He is kind and sincere, probably, but he lacks intensity. The edges of his eyes crinkle. He's over thirty, he's smiled too much and refused to see too much.

'You just got over from London.' My voice is sullen, uncoloured by a question, but, kindly, he treats it as a question.

'Yes, my flight left two hours late. I didn't think I was going to make it. Heathrow's an almighty bottleneck these days.'

The rose drops from my fingers. Owen notices at once, stoops and hands it to me.

'It's for the coffin. I hate the look of that bare wood.'

He nods and pats my arm very lightly and kindly.

I am beginning to trust him. 'I think the devil must be shaped like a coffin.'

'Do you believe in the devil?' he asks. The wrong question, that. My heart closes. I've been typecast: Protestant, heathen. No, that's not fair, it's an English question, probably: theoretical. Or embarrassed. 'I do, now.'

He bows his head. 'It's a hideous thing. A terrible, terrible tragedy.' His voice fades and returns more softly. 'Some words are so big they don't mean anything, do they? Yet what other words are there?'

I am silent, thinking. 'Words of hate and revenge, I suppose.'

'Ah yes. But what's the use?' He touches the rose. 'The flower's beautiful, anyway.'

'It won't be for much longer.'

Bold now, I toss it into the grave. What does it matter where it lands: it will rot soon enough.

The red of it vanishes as it rolls into a little ravine of black earth.

I squeeze my eyes shut. I'm not crying, not praying. Just not seeing.

When I open them, Owen has moved away, though he's watching me. Others are coming, to surround him, to surround me.

'I'll see you at the gathering,' he says pronouncing gathering with a hint of irony. And he disappears amid those shy, stiff-shouldered men who helped Cathal to his last bed. The brother who got out: the lucky leaver, waving goodbye again.

The gathering is at Byddi's, on the Lower Falls.

It is, of course, an historic occasion for some of the older MacNamaras. They cast appraising, uncertain glances at the O'Neills, and at each other. The meeting of the clans was to have taken place in our house, a big neutral house near the Malone Road, smelling of orchids and bright with new suits and dresses, a marquee on the lawn, with white linen and silver and the band playing Beatles medleys because all ages like the Beatles. The strangers would have raised their glasses to the bride and groom, and got sentimental and relaxed and eventually danced with one another. Well, perhaps. This little house is very nice, so it is. But you can't forget the name of the road outside.

The O'Neills are subdued, still. Is something smouldering between those who stayed and are on home ground and those who moved away and are just back for tonight? I can't quite pick up the scent. Anyway, I prefer to study my own clan's behaviour: it's more amusing. Uncle Jimmie and Auntie Heather, for example, late arrivals, who lower their bottoms on to the sofa with enormous care and indecision, as if there might be a Provie lurking under the Laura Ashley cushions. They receive their teacups with dignity and clutch them for a long time before drinking, looking them over now and again as if they suspected an incendiary device concealed somewhere. Or perhaps they're just checking the quality of the china.

There are young people here, too, of course, whose only religion is youth. Most of them are Cathal's friends but there are several students from my year: Paula-Mary, Liz, Sean, Rebekah, Sachiko. They must be my friends. They hug me and pat me: they cried in the church, those who came, and their eyes are always ready to fill kindly again. I try to be receptive, but I've never felt at ease with people my own age. Real friends would know that and keep their distance.

The O'Neill family does not conform to stereotype. It's a poor, thin fabric full of holes, the holes tearing ever wider. Probably most of the people that I think of as 'O'Neills' are not: it's politer to think 'O'Neills' than 'Catholics'. But they're just neighbours or friends or distant, distant relatives with other names.

I find I'm at the female end of the room. In spite of Byddi's liberated protests, we have gradually divided by gender. I'd rather have sat with the men, though Owen isn't among them: he hasn't bothered to show up. The men are really beginning to get on, pouring out cans of stout and lager, discussing sport and holidays, trying to laugh quietly and look solemn when they remember. But I'm squashed on the sofa with Mum, Auntie Heather and some neighbour with a spiral perm, a mini-skirt and the fidgets. Byddi and a bunch of elderlies are holding forth and we are the captive audience: goggling like we're watching *Brookside*.

'Has poor Marion been told?' Marion is Byddi's sister, Cathal's mother.

'Has she, Byddi? When did you visit her last?'

'There's no point in telling her, she's incapable of understanding.'

'Really? Is that so?'

'You'd never believe she was only just turned sixty. She's like a little old woman with the shakes,' the fidgety neighbour eagerly asserts.

'Parkinson's, is it?'

'Early onset Alzheimer's,' Byddi says coldly.

'Och, that's a horrible thing, so it is.'

'It was the drink that brought it on.' The fidgety neighbour wants to stir things. She plucks restlessly at the hem of her skirt, her rings glittering.

Byddi compresses her lips in sisterly solidarity: her small dark brow grows fierce. 'The doctors say the drink had absolutely nothing to do with it, Louise.'

'She was a drinker in her time, though, all the same, and what does that do to you?'

'She hasn't taken a drop in ten years, which is more than you can say for some people.' The neighbour flinches at Byddi's hard, jade look. Perhaps she drinks. Maybe her husband does. Who cares?

'It's Frank that's the disgrace,' a wizened elderly remarks. 'How could he not find the time to be here?' There is general agreement about Marion's former husband. He was always thoroughly selfish, of course. No wonder, poor Marion . . . And poor Patsie, no wonder . . . She was only sixty-three when she died, asking for Frank.

Only sixty-three? That's old, I want to shout, Cathal was twenty-seven.

'Cathal adored his nan,' the elderly says. 'She practically reared him, of course.'

I hold my breath: that's the first time his name has been mentioned. Now they will talk about him. Now they will talk about his death. They will speculate about the driver of the grey Audi, and if he was drunk, and if the old man, the only eye-witness, could really be trusted to tell an Audi from an army Land Rover. (Will some want to believe it *was* the Land Rover?) They will talk about blame and fault: Cathal could be reckless on that bike of his, the driver might not have been able to help it, still, it was dreadful not to have stopped. I've heard it all at home, over and over, and it will be just the same here, the same words, the same futile twisting and turning.

There's a long pause. And then Mum says in a loud voice with a wobble in it: 'Little Robby would have been fourteen next month. Fourteen. Can you believe it?' She's talking to Heather but wants us all to hear. And all eyes are drawn to her, the knowing eyes and the guessing eyes, flickering towards me, some of them, to gauge how I feel about this other loss.

I feel as if I'd been punched in the gut, softly but sickeningly. Just because I didn't want to talk about Cathal's death in that meaningless way, doesn't mean I want to talk about Robbie's. I don't give a shit about Robbie. I was eight and I didn't want a brother and I was glad he only lasted six months. Cot Death was the name of the angel with big black wings who answered my prayers and came to visit our house. My friend.

Yes, death can be a friend. The small cold crystal which I've clutched for days suddenly multiplies, glitters, branches all over my mind, and everything else is blotted out.

You can do it.

When? Now?

Yes. You can't bear it any longer, can you?

No, not for another minute.

I have my pills. I have the key: *my* key, stolen back from Mum's bag, wearing its newly-inked tag. 12, Rose Street. My house. It has to be done there.

I'm standing by the door, though I don't remember getting up and crossing the room.

'Cleo, your mammy's a bit upset.' Byddi touches my arm. Byddi is so good with people, so clever, so natural, with her jade-green eyes and her shiny brown bob. I'd have liked to be her: I told her that once. She said I could come and work for her when I graduated. She runs a small company called Cross Community Enterprises. She's both true to her past and free of it, utterly rooted, and utterly modern.

I drag myself to the sofa and pat the warm hooped back. The pink flesh and the black bra show through, equally obscene behind the coy veil of the blouse. God knows why she dressed herself up as a tart. It isn't her usual style. Maybe she thought it'd be camouflage among the O'Neills.

'It's all right, *Mammy*.' My voice, cold and unnatural, grates with sarcasm. Nobody notices. Dad, relieved of his duties, fades back among the men. There now, Cleo's here, the women coo. Mam looks up at me with grateful, welling eyes. You always upstage everyone, you bitch, I think. 'I'll make a cup of tea' is what I say.

'Good girl,' Byddi responds. 'The kitchen's a tip but pretend you haven't noticed.'

How strange that no one can see I'm blazing with rage.

I pushed a handful of buttered crusts into my mouth and opened the back door. There was still a glow of blue light on the sky. The moon was a sliver of honeydew melon. It was cold for the end of May but I was sweating and the air was as good to me as iced water on a hot day. Quietly I slid the bolt on the back gate. The grass alley beyond would take me round to the main road. It was easy to escape. But suddenly I remembered: I had no money. I hadn't needed any, till now: since Cathal's death I had become a child who slept and cried and was fed and taken out before crying and sleeping again.

There was no way I could walk from Falls Road to Rose Street. The search party would reach home before I did.

Tears of self-pity threatened. The smallest thing was so difficult now: how could I ever accomplish the big one?

I upended my bag among the crumbs and crusts on Byddi's counter-top. I had exactly twenty-one pence.

I must check my coat-pockets, maybe there'd be a lurking pound or two. I crawled back down the hall. The living-room door was open, spilling the restless, the young, the smokers. There was a party-noise now. I dived into a scrum of coats on the hall-stand. I was terrified I'd be clawed at and sucked back into the room, and have to struggle all over again to free myself.

The pockets yielded only tissues at every stage from water-logged to dessicated. I grabbed a clump so anyone could see I was legit, and hurried back to the kitchen.

I picked up my bag decisively. I could still get a taxi, jump out without paying or tell the driver it was an emergency and leave my name and address. I had identification. He couldn't get me arrested for that.

Behind my reflection in the back-door window formed a taller, more solid shape. Shit shit shit.

Owen breathed a sweet blast of drink at me.

'Going already? Is it that bad?'

I went out into the yard and cursed at the unbolted gate. Owen stood at the doorway, watching me.

'D'you want some tea?' he called.

I didn't reply. Go, run, I told myself, but I felt leaden. It was too late. I came back into the kitchen and slumped at the counter, shoving a big stale crust into my mouth.

'You hungry?'

'I'm sick of all this,' I said loudly through the bread.

He banged around with the kettle. 'I know. It's no joke.'

'You've only just got here,' I said angrily. 'It's fine for you.'

'Well, I'm already sick of it.'

'It's gross. They talk about everything but Cathal.'

'I'll talk about him. If you want.'

I didn't want. Owen's Cathal would not be mine. Owen was drunk: he would be flippant, patronising, know-all. 'I wish to hell I could go home.'

'Can't you?'

'I've no money for the cab.' A hope flicked inside me.

'Can't your dad leave you home?'

'I don't mean that home. I want to go to the house. Cathal's and mine.' I made my voice shake a little.

'I can give you the fare. No problem.' He watched me with his grey-eyed stare, not really intense but darkened by curiosity, perhaps, and Byddi's dusty, failing fluorescent light. He saw my hesitation and thought I was scared.

'What's wrong? Changed your mind?'

'I'm not really allowed to go there.' Now I sounded like a stupid little girl and I blushed. 'I couldn't tell them in there, you'd have to make an excuse for me.'

He went back to making the tea. 'It's your house, isn't it? Why would they stop you?'

'They think I'll do something stupid.' I'd said it before I could check myself.

'Would you do something stupid?' He turned off the kettle and came and sat on the stool next to mine.

'No, of course not.'

'What would you do?'

'Look about. Sit. Remember.'

'Sounds OK to me. More sensible than what they're doing here.' He got up abruptly and emptied the scalding kettle over the sinkful of dirty dishes. My heart seemed to be banging against my forehead.

He came back and said: 'Would you mind if I came too, Cleo? I'd like to see the house.' I was leaden again. Relieved? Perhaps. But at least I was going home.

You can find a way to get rid of him later.

'No, I don't mind,' I said.

We picked up a black cab with no trouble, that time of the evening. The last time I'd been in one had been with Cathal, three weeks ago.

If you can get a black cab to the two of you, there's nothing like it. And we had, the whole way to Ligoniel. It was like being in our own little room – better, really, because it was moving and because it was not quite private; there was a tiny thrill in the thought that the driver would guess, turn round. We were thrown close on the big shiny seats as we rocked and swung along half-lit streets I'd have feared to walk in. Cathal slipped his hand under my skirt and nuzzled my crotch. With his other hand he laid my hand across the packed front of his jeans. Desire brought saliva to my mouth. But we didn't go any farther. We suffered and eased apart. We were going to an eighteenth-birthday celebration: two bottles clinked together in the Winemark bag. It was our last full evening together and we wasted it.

Owen and I sat a polite, wide distance from each other. We were soon away from west Belfast, and rolling down Stockman's Lane into the leafy dusk of the south. I felt almost happy: it had been a narrow escape from Byddi's parlour. They'd all been mortified that we wanted to leave them. Owen had been very mature, taking the Ma and Da aside and murmuring about the therapeutic effects of a change of scene. According to him we were just going to get a breath of air and maybe a pizza. ('So my sandwiches aren't good enough? Byddi smiled.) They trusted Owen: it was something to do with his soft voice with its hint of posh English, his elderly crinkled eyes and the fact he's a solicitor, even if only a shop-front one, at the Hammersmith Citizens' Advice Bureau, where the poor people go. You don't argue with solicitors if you're first generation house-owners.

He rubbed the window and peered out on to the Lisburn Road. 'At least this part of Belfast hasn't changed. I hardly recognised the city centre this afternoon. It could have been Toronto. Well, almost. I suppose the suburbs never change so much.'

Oh I say, I thought, *Toronto*. Man of the world! I've been there too, but why boast?

We turned off by Sam's Stores, and stopped. I cried out softly at the sight.

It was the most beautiful front door on earth. Solid oak stained green with the number in brass but that of course wasn't why it was beautiful. Owen paid, I fumbled in my bag. First I couldn't find the key. Then when I found it I couldn't turn it. I cursed Da, convinced he'd changed the lock.

'Steady. Let me help.' But as Owen's hand came over mine the mechanism loosened and the door swung open.

I found the light-switch without fumbling. The house was in my blood, as I'd known it would be.

Our lovely room blazed into being. I caught my breath. There was still a faint smell of paint and factory-fresh carpet. Nothing had been spoiled.

'You did a class job,' Owen said. 'I know what these places were like before.'

It had been such a sad, dark, dirty little house. The woman from Moss and Kimberly Estates said it was the ideal thing for a young couple prepared to do a bit of work. I remembered how keen Dad was as she showed us round, and how disappointed I was.

Dad saw the way I was grimacing at Cathal.

'Where's your imagination, you kids? A lick of paint and it'll be grand!' Dad loves to be generous and he loves a bargain, as he was convinced this house was, at £11,500.

He'd managed to knock the agents down from £13,000. It was ours – his wedding-present, if only we'd say the word.

There was a tiny lobby, two square feet of tatty lino. Grit and ash and litter had blown in under a big gap where the door and pavement parted company. The parlour was miniature too. It had a broken venetian blind at the window and a bar of fluorescent light overhead: someone's pathetic attempt at modernisation. ('But you've got your open fire-place, look,' Dad reassured us.) The staircase went straight up from the parlour. There was a stair-carpet, filthy and floral-patterned like the parlour carpet, but in different colours, to make matters worse. The banisters had been painted over and over, thick layers of various creams and yellows. Cathal thumbed off some of the paint and remarked on the quality of the wood beneath. I knew he didn't hate the house like I did.

Dad was examining a saddle-board which looked black and rotten. 'Aye, it's all good underneath.' He patted the splintered board. 'Just needs sanding and varnishing.'

'Though it wouldn't cost much to have new boards,' the woman from the agents said.

We wandered about the tiny, creaking bedrooms. Cathal said it was amazing how many people used to squeeze into kitchen-houses like this. I'd never seen anything like it myself, although we live only a few minutes up the road. I'd always thought the houses on the 'wrong' side of the Lisburn Road were cute and cottagey. I'd never have bothered to come and look if I'd known they were so squalid inside.

Outside in the car, we sat and rowed.

Because there was already an offer on it, we had to act quickly. I didn't want to be pushed. I wanted to look at other places, too.

But Dad's mind was made up, and Cathal had begun to fantasise. We'd turn the three tiny bedrooms upstairs into one big room and bathroom, we could extend the parlour into the kitchen and have the kitchen where the out-back bathroom now was. We could plant flowers in the yard. We could work wonders.

Working wonders costs money, I said, but Dad said it was such a bargain he'd throw in a couple of thousand towards redecoration. It could cost a bit more than that, I said, guessing. Cathal said no problem: he'd so many friends in the building trade he could get loads of materials at cut-price.

In the end it was me against Cathal and Dad.

She's just squeamish, so she is, Cathal said. Get rid of the spiders' webs, she'll be fine.

I did loathe cobwebs, but it wasn't just that. I didn't really want Dad to be buying a house for us at all. That sounds ungrateful, I know. But I felt he was buying control over our lives. I had dreams of much bigger horizons than south Belfast. So had Cathal, of course. But they could begin here, for him. For him, this was the first leg of the journey. It was freedom.

I would hate to think about Mam and Dad, just up the hill in the Big House. Kind of looking down on me and Cathal in our little house the wrong side of the tracks. It was stifling: it was like they were saying: OK, you can go ahead and marry your handsome Catholic, just so long as you stay where we can keep an eye on you. The generosity was partly about power.

Cathal didn't see it like that and I couldn't spell it out to him. He was totally awed by the concept of a father buying his child a house for a wedding-present. It was like *Dallas* or something.

'Think how much we could sell it for,' Cathal said later, when we were alone. 'We'll sell it for triple the price and go round the world.'

'When?'

He laughed at my eagerness. 'Whenever. After your finals. How about that? Can you wait?'

'Just about.' I trusted him again, his instinct for escape.

'You did a grand job,' Owen repeated.

He followed me upstairs. I peeked into the hot-press. An old shirt of Cathal's was crumpled on a shelf. I clutched it to me, breathed in the odours of sweat and decorating. Too rich, too much. Not the time, yet. I shoved it back and shut the door.

'It's a good size,' he said, meaning the room, though he had glanced towards the bed.

'There were three bedrooms. This is two of them, the bathroom's the third.'

I went downstairs, leaving him fingering the shelving. Because our bedroom was going to double as my study, Cathal had lined half one wall with bookshelves. The desk fitted underneath.

I went into the kitchen. Dad – it must have been Dad – had left an empty can of Harp on the counter. I binned it with a curse, and rinsed the glass he'd left in the sink. There was nothing to eat and only water to drink, but that was all to the good: I would not have to pretend hospitality and encourage Owen to overstay his welcome.

I sat down on the sofa and imagined I'd had my wedding. Now we were home and Cathal almost beside me. I touched the arm gently, stroked it, leaned my face to kiss its cool coarse skin. But I heard Owen on the stairs and sat up straight and calm. He had to see I was in control.

He had brought a book down with him: *Home of Your Dreams*. He sat in the armchair opposite me, nursing the unopened book against him, afraid for me to see the title.

'Listen, if you want to be on your own, that's fine with me. I can sit here and read up on the DIY – smoke a cigarette, if you wouldn't mind.'

'You can smoke,' I said. 'I haven't got an ashtray but there's a can in the bin outside.'

He fetched the empty blue can, and lit up.

'OK, I'll go upstairs for a bit,' I said.

'We could talk if you wanted to,' he said shyly.

'I'm sorry, but I really don't want to.'

I took my bag and the glass from the kitchen and went and sat on the bed. It didn't feel private, with Owen downstairs, able to hear the slightest sounds I made.

Very stealthily, so as not to rattle them, I took the two boxes of pills from my bag. They were beta-blockers, Dr

Casey had said. I studied the ingredients: the long chemical names meant painlessness, freedom, peace. But they also frightened me. Would it simply be like going to sleep? Or something more difficult?

Certainly Owen would make it more difficult. How long would he give me on my own? Surely not much longer than it took him to smoke a cigarette or two. Then he'd get suspicious. He'd come up and find me, still alive: he'd force water down my throat, he'd push his fingers down and make me sick, and he'd call the ambulance. What chance of painless sleep and freedom then?

'Were you jealous of Cathal when he was born?' I'd gone downstairs again: I couldn't die, I couldn't rest.

'I don't remember being jealous,' he said in an eager voice. 'No, I don't think I was at all. Our mam was in a bad way fairly soon after, so I got to take a lot of responsibility at an early age, and that was fun, at the time. I was proud, pushing him in the pram, taking him to our gran's or showing him off to the other kids in the park. He did what I told him when he was small. Later on it was different. We'd disagree, slug each other now and then, but basically we were too different for it to matter much. I ran around with the gang, he sat in Patsie's kitchen, colouring or writing adventures.'

'Did the lads make fun of him?'

'Not really, he wasn't soft. He could fight if he had to. He was just quiet. We liked his wee adventures, we respected that. Later on there was music. I bought the records as I was the older one. Sometimes he'd say how can you listen to that crap, but sometimes he'd like the stuff and we'd have fun, listening. I had a great collection: I wonder where it went.'

'I hate the way things just disappear. And time. And people.'

'I just wiped myself off the Belfast map,' Owen said thoughtfully. Cathal always said he left because the kids in his gang were graduating to a more professional organisation and he didn't want to be pressured into joining them. But I didn't want Owen to go on about it. 'That expression,' I said, 'wiped off the map. I can't stand it.'

'I don't regret London. Not one bit. I'd never go back here to live. You should come over some time.'

A dark energy of hope and cunning surged in his face. I turned away.

'There's one place in Belfast I'll never go. Never, never. I keep on wondering if there's anything left. In the cracks or the drains or somewhere.'

'It would have been washed away by now,' Owen said, no longer looking at me. That would have been true of blood, saliva, urine. But I had meant something tinier: molecules.

'I'll tell you a secret,' I said. 'I've got this fantasy where I scrape a few cells from the tarmac and take them into some lab where they can be grown into Cathal again.'

'Ah, Cleo, don't.'

'D'you suppose it would ever be scientifically possible?'

'I hope not, or there'd be a mega overcrowding problem on poor old planet earth.'

'I wish so much I could put some flowers at the spot.' I meant this, I could meet his gaze head-on. 'I'm certain some part of him's still there.' He almost didn't flinch. He's used to people *in extremis*, I thought. They're homeless or in debt and they cry and curse and Owen doesn't flinch because he has good professional advice to give. Like now.

'You have to accept it, Cleo,' he said pedantically. 'Cathal was knocked from his bike, he was killed, he is dead and we have buried him.'

Pains shot through my whole body. 'You couldn't see the pavement outside Sean Graham's,' I said. 'It was covered with flowers, after the massacre. If Cathal had to die, why couldn't his death have meant something? I wish he could have died with people knowing and caring and honouring it – even strangers.'

Owen didn't know what to say. 'His death means fuck all,' I said angrily.

'It does not mean fuck all.' He sounded as if he was going to cry.

I got down on my knees in front of him. He moved as if to embrace me, then he saw I didn't want that. I took his hand. I could see he was in pain, and I was sorry for him, but I was sorrier for myself.

'Owen, please, do me a favour. Go there now, take some

flowers. I'll tell you exactly where. I've been there, it's just where the track turns off up the mountain. Please, Owen, please. I can't be at peace until the place is marked.'

'Tonight, Cleo? The Antrim Road? It's miles away!'

'No it's not. There are loads of buses from here. Or get a taxi. I'll owe you the money. You can get the flowers at Sam's. Red carnations, just one bunch. Please.'

I began to cry.

Owen bowed his head. 'We'll go together,' he said at last, in a choked voice.

I wasn't hearing this. 'No, I'm not going,' I said. 'Don't you think I've suffered enough for one day?'

'Yes, but so have I. I can't do it alone.'

'Why not?'

Owen shook his head silently. At last he said: 'Cleo, I think you want to be left here by yourself.'

'Why the hell should I?'

'Listen. We either go to the Antrim Road together. Or we go back to Byddi's. There's no way I'm leaving you alone while you're in my care. I shouldn't have brought you here.'

'Your care! What do you fucking care? I hate you!'

He went to the telephone and, it seemed to me, calmly dialled. 'Lower Falls,' he told the taxi people.

I sobbed, useless, on the sofa. He sat and stared at me, white-faced. I hated him and he probably hated me, but what did it matter?

I was in Cathal's arms. Hush, he whispered: later. Later.

Because I had made my decision, I was calm and sane and everybody thought I was recovering. 'She's young, she'll bounce back,' as Dr Casey had said, handing Mum a scrip for a month's supply of Surmontil.

Dr Casey said it would still be a good idea to see the counsellor. Mum was alarmed. 'A psychiatrist?' she said, as if it was a bad word. But Dr Casey rang the students' union and made an appointment.

'Will it go on her record card?' Mum wanted to know. And later she said: 'Those people don't do any good in my opinion', as if she'd like to talk me out of going.

'You don't have to come with me if you think it's such a stigma. I'm quite capable of going on my own,' I said.

Eventually I wore her out with my insistence. I was so much better. Whereas she was feeling awfully down.

I left at one: my appointment was at two. I told her I'd probably go over to the School of English afterwards and talk to Dr Rabbit about going back next term. I said I couldn't be home much before five, and not to worry if I was later. I might bump into friends, after all.

Mum was perking up by the minute.

How could she believe in this sane, sociable, forward-planning person? It wasn't me, even at the best of times. Maybe she thought I'd been chemically reconstituted? She might not have had faith in psychiatrists but she had faith in tranx.

I took off my shoes and lay down on the bare new mattress. Someone had stripped the bed but the room was warm, and I had my coat for covering. The crumpled shirt that smelt of sweat and decorating was pressed to my heart. Poor thin shadow-Cathal. Poor rag of life, let me warm you.

Under cover of my coat, a hand moved.

He entered the first door. So easily. No pain. Moved up the stairs and slid under the coat. Cleo, Cleo.

He stroked my hair and my cheek, moved quickly to my breasts, then to my belly. Young and impatient, he laughed at the word *foreplay*.

Why do girls wear such tight pants?

What do you mean – *girls*?

His fingers wander the edges, that foresty roughness.

Don't, it's too much. Talk to me first, make me believe in you first.

I listen to the darkness a long while before his words come out like faint stars.

'Only the old are able to die. If you die before you've finished living, you can't leave. You look for another body to fill. This is why the violence doesn't stop. All the young undead are searching for their lives, vengeful, getting in the way of the living. The young men here are full of ghosts. I wasn't like that. I got clean. For a while, I had Declan O'Neill. My one Republican ancestor – or the only famous one. Gun-running, blood-stained hero-ghost of my early teens. But mine wasn't a body built for ghostly heroes. I learnt to pity my relative: martyred at forty but so much younger than me.

'The ghost left me, and now I'm a ghost myself. I died in no cause, I wanted no revenge. I am the boy who told his ghost: tomorrow isn't yours, Declan, it's mine. You can keep it, he said. It's wasted on you, caring only about yourself, never for Ireland. Too right, I said. But for all my care, I lost my life and my tomorrow.'

Ah Cathal, you haven't lost them. Touch me now, sweetly, sweetly.

A wave flows over my belly and down my legs and strokes my ankles. I lift my feet and am free.

The finger drinks at the spring that seeps up between the rough grass in the deepest thicket of the forest. Far away on the Lisburn Road a high-throated siren calls. I hear only the intimate little tongues of wetness.

Lips brush my nipples, a path of warm breath glows from neck to clavicle to belly to mons Veneris.

For a face to rest here is the greatest act of worship. So you taught me. So I believe.

He slides into the clutch of tight hot ridged skin.

You were the first and you asked what does it feel like and I whispered the word, too ashamed to say it with my full voice, and you laughed and said: but isn't there pleasure in shitting? And a child long murdered came alive in my adult skin.

It's you I'm in and it's you that's in me, oh Cathal, you, you, you.

I came for a full minute, maybe longer. Great luxuriant waves, going on and on and on. Never before like this. Oh, don't go away.

Come to me, Cleo.

I want to, I want to, I'm scared, I don't know how. Will you show me how?

I pour the capsules into the palm of my hand.

It's like a big dark eye with a hundred white irises.

Don't be afraid.

I kiss my hand, I suck down as many capsules as my throat will take and flush them on with a draught of cold water. My heart is beating too fast. I do it again. And I won't listen to the argument beginning in my gullet, I am fiercer than my body, and my friend, the black-winged angel, is on my side. He is the river that sails the death-boat home.

I bury my head in the T-shirt. Such thin stuff, so tiny a remnant.

A swimming nausea. But Cathal fills my head now, big and powerful and his other name is Death. In the racing of my mind I name cocktails. Harvey Wallbanger, Black Velvet, Margherita, Screwdriver. I read paint-names from the card: mint-green, moss-green, jade-green, emerald, avocado, lime, marine, aquamarine, citrus green, primrose. I reel off poetry. Oh happy dagger. This is thy sheath, there rest and let me die. Copacabana, Pina Colada, Bloody Mary, Buck's Fizz, White Lady.

E. A. Markham

AT PAUL AND DEIRDRE'S, DUBLIN

I'm not the warm knife exxing through
your butter . . . My mantra: I'm not the warm knife . . .

And now I think of lunch with friends pleased
to talk of healing things, discovering
new plants in the garden when a guest
arrives with a story she wants to tell.
But she, like you, will yield to prior
claims of garden, and promise her story with the sweet.

New thoughts of knife and butter,
and our own escape from the worst that might happen;
and wine and dinner and children served,
and everyone says yes please, let's have the sweet –
which is magical, like something tropical in the garden.
Like your pruned storybeds, sprouting again.

Peter Reading

LEASTS

This is a shoddy compromise: Muscle
    Beach and the big boys;
grudgingly granted the only unwanted
    space, a barbed kampong
(somewhat resembling that in which Nippon
    hosted the Old Chap)
wherein a few remaining Least Terns
    hack an existence.

Joan Michelson

RECONSTRUCTIONS FROM A DUTCH CHILDHOOD

Extract from a novel in progress

Prologue

*There is no doubt that stories buried deep in the past
are easier to tell because less is known about them.*

Rolf Hochhuth

I WENT AFTER him. Because of this, I am to blame. Or his
spirit is to blame. Now he has to cling to me, and wherever
I go, I have to have him with me, so much weight and
mystery (an aura under the skin). Is this what I should tell
you first? I can no longer judge. I've made so many wrong
starts. I hear myself repeating myself and I fall through time
as if pulled by his weathered stone. I know where I am going
because I've been here before. I have been past his death and
dying and through the forty years of his wanderings. He is
born again and again, my Aart with the double 'a', Aartur
van Zoog.

Today is the 10th of June, 1989. (No it isn't, not any more.
Let us imagine then . . .) I am beginning again at the Wiener
Library, a library which was moved from Amsterdam to
London because of its dedication to documenting the 'Final
Solution of the Jewish Problem'. This move took place fifty
years ago, only weeks before the Germans occupied Holland.
The librarian who assists me remembers. 'Ya,' she says as
she hands me the grey box containing the microfilm.

I begin this time with a film of stained wrinkled yellowed paper. It is indexed under 'Central Jewish Committee Bergen-Belsen, Residential Camp near Celle (Hanover). Names of Jewish survivors in English and American Zones in Germany, 9 July 1945.'

History takes hold of me. I start wheeling the film on its two-inch reel and peering at the magnified words. Instructions for those seeking lost persons come first. Number one: 'No Jew is obliged to return to his native land.' This fills me with confusion. Where was everyone to go? Who was to help the nearly dead to begin their lives again? The names of the countries of Europe crowd into my head in an overwhelming tide. I have to hurry to avoid my own avoidance. I dial to the double column of names. I feel a wave of heat, my skin turns rubbery with sweat, my mouth dry as the Sahara. A Dutchman tops the left-hand column, an Aardweck, Dawid, born 1912, the same year as Aart's parents. Could he be a relation? 'Should you find a name in the list and wish to contact the person, send a note to your camp committee.' I speed the alphabet towards 'V' for van and 'Z' for Zoog. But it goes slowly as if the names themselves are a bulk of bodies inching along in a crowd. I try to distract myself with spellings of names I recognise as foreign forms of English and with birth dates of others who were children like Aart. There is a Josef Roubel, for instance, born in 1931. So he was fourteen when the war ended. What happened to him? Feigel W, another Czech, then a Greek, a Frenchman, an Italian, and Poles, Poles, Poles. And then – mine! The letters wheel into view after a section so worn several names are obliterated. He is the only doubled 'a' Aartur, the only Arthur, the only van Zoog. Altogether there weren't very many Dutchmen. All in all after the war only 5,000 returned from the camps, less than five per cent of those who had been arrested.

Although no one was required to return after the Liberation, most of the Dutch went home because Holland sent trucks into Germany and Poland to carry its survivors back. Later on, much much later, you'll see Aart standing high in one of those trucks heading for Amsterdam. He's eleven years old, tall and thin with a disarming smile. When I see him there, I hear him singing. How can I hear him? How can he be singing? I feel like singing, like riding in that truck and singing under the July sun.

I discovered Aart again this morning. There he was on the microfilm, his name, his birth date (9.21.34), his country (Netherlands).

Red Sea

They were going to England. 'There's nothing to be afraid of,' Aart's mother said. 'We'll be together, my duckling, you and me and Grandpa; and your father and Auntie Dola.'

'I'm not afraid,' Aart said. 'England's only across the Channel. It's not like going to America or Africa or Australia.' It wasn't far. That was true. But he was worried all the same. The Germans had dropped bombs and then they had fallen from the sky like white birds and now they were on their way over land.

The next afternoon his father and Auntie Dola arrived in Auntie Dola's brother's car. It was shiny and black with a rumble seat which pulled out of the back. Aart wanted to sit in the rumble seat but his father filled it with luggage. There was luggage tied to the roof and inside too, packed against their legs. He was too big to sit on his mother's lap but all the same he sat there, squeezed between his grandfather and his big-boned Auntie Dola. The good thing was that he could see through the front window. The cars in front were just as jam-packed. The bicycles were too. Boxes and bags were tied to the baskets and hung bumping against the wheels. Everyone was bent over with a pack on his back. People were pushing prams heaped to the sky and carrying their babies. People were carrying all sorts of things, a blanketed bird cage, a heavy radio, even a cello. A man with a horse and cart was taking his precious cello.

Everyone was in a hurry to get to England. Princess Juliana with her children and the Queen had already gone. Aart wanted to see both queens, the Dutch and the English; and also, the changing of the guard. England! England! There would be lots of Amsterdammers in England, lots of Dutch. One day they would come home again. Of course they would come home again. Everything would be all right.

Only they were moving so slowly. They were hardly moving along the road. It was so hot, his clothes were sticking to him. His skin was prickling. 'Mom, take my sweater off.' Why didn't she do it? 'Mom, are you listening?' It was happening again. She was not listening. He bumped back against her. 'Mom!' he exploded.

Her voice roared back, 'Be patient. Nearly there.'

'Mom,' he whimpered, a few minutes later, 'I feel sick.'

'How sick?'

'A bit.'

'Are you going to be sick?'

Auntie Dola rolled down the window on her side. 'Take a deep breath,' she ordered. He started to cough. 'What's the matter?'

'Smoke,' Grandpa said. 'Something's burning.'

'Grandpa, what is it?'

Grandpa shook his head. 'You never know what may come to pass.'

The smoke thickened as they crawled through Ijmuiden towards the harbour. Suddenly Aart could see the galloping flames. It was the tanks. Someone had set the oil tanks on fire. The sky was smoke and smoke wrapped around the anchored boats. Smoke rose and fell in waves on the surface of the sea.

Manus took two bags in each hand and led them to their boat. They found places on the deck. Manus spread out blankets. Rachel and Auntie Dola unpacked a picnic. 'It will be several hours before we sail,' Manus said.

Aart watched smaller craft slip away into the darkness and disappear. He wanted their boat to be on its way too. He couldn't wait to get to England. How much longer would it be? Everyone was wondering the same thing. How long?

How long? – everything. Who could have imagined it? – the way they fell out of the sky, the Germans in white parachutes. It was Holland's blackest day.

All night the oil burned. The light licked the sea around them. The sea glared with a glassy glaze of red. The smoke got in the way of the stars. The sky heaved and billowed with this new blackness. People coughed. They were sick over the railing and they were sick over their shoes. They held each other and whispered. Some wept. Some fainted. Grandpa held Aart's hand and helped him to pray. 'In times like these,' Grandpa said, 'how the face of the Lord God can change.'

Aart looked for the face of the Lord God to see for himself but there was too much smoke. Worn out, he rested his head in his mother's lap and went to sleep.

In the morning they were told that the ship wouldn't leave. Not ever. Because of the surrender. Ijmuiden was also now occupied territory. 'A day too late,' Manus said. 'A day too late. Just one day.' The veins on the back of his hand stood out, blue. Smoke-smeared blue, Aart thought. They carried everything back to the car and squeezed in again with their bundles. Some of the oil had stopped burning. Aart thought the sea itself looked burnt. A burning sea. A red sea. 'Like the Red Sea,' he told his grandfather.

At home in his grandfather's house, Aart drew a picture of the Royal Family watching the Changing of the Guard. He put lots of red in it. Lots and lots. 'More red than the sea.' He was so absorbed with his red colouring that he didn't hear the telephone when it rang. But he heard his mother's hoarse cry, 'Shot himself. Oh Lord my God, Misha.'

Yellow Star

He couldn't live at Grandpa's now except on the weekend because only Auntie Dola was permitted to take him to school. She wasn't Jewish. Not at all. She didn't have even one Jewish grandparent. That's why she didn't have any yellow stars stitched to her clothes. Aart had helped with the measuring and the cutting out and with the sewing too. He had threaded the needle for his cousin Loes because his eyes were better than hers. Loes had tied a final knot and broken the thread with her teeth. 'How does that look?' she'd asked, holding up his school jumper to show the star on the left breast.

Rachel had snorted strangely. 'So now we're official.'

Rachel was at home most of the time because Mrs de Jong, the milliner, was not permitted to keep her in the shop. This was by order of the new edicts. Mrs de Jong was sorry but what could she do?

'Being home with Grandpa is making Mom's tongue too sharp,' Aart told Manus and Auntie Dola.

Manus laughed. 'What is the meaning of too sharp?'

Aart said, 'Sharp like a needle. It means it can cut you. Words can hurt, you know. People say things and other people feel what they say. That's how it is.'

'What kinds of things?' his father pressed him.

'Really Manus, I don't feel like talking about it just now. Shall we see if Auntie Dola is waiting for us to have our supper?'

The three of them ate at a table in front of the window. Now it was winter and the dark arrived in the afternoon. Manus lit the oil lamps. After the meal, Aart did his school work at the table. He liked the work. 'But I keep making mistakes in Hebrew,' he said. 'Grandpa goes very fast. Or maybe it is my mind that is too slow. Sometimes I think my mind thinks it's like a bear and it can hibernate all winter.'

There was a box-room in the apartment which just fitted a bed. So in the morning he'd use the sitting-room. He'd get dressed, help himself to milk from the jug in the ice-box, and then he'd see what Manus had left for him. There were always special assignments: pictures to be drawn, numbers to work, problems to be solved.

'If the Census Office receives half a guilder for each registered Jew and there are 140,000 Jews in Holland, how much money does the Census Office receive in total? This looks like a simple addition but there are some factors to take into account. Some people can't afford to pay the one guilder for their registration card. Now these people divide into two groups. The first group is made up of those people who belong to the Israelitic congregations. The congregation has to pay for them. The second group is made up of those who don't belong to any congregation. These people are issued with cards free. In order to determine how much money the Census Office can expect to receive, you need one more piece of information. What additional information do you need?'

Daylight was just beginning when Auntie Dola wrapped a double-knit scarf around his neck, pulled his hat over his ears and pulled up his mittens. Then they went downstairs for her bicycle. He sat in his own wicker seat. She pedalled steadily and carefully along the icy roads. 'Hallo,' her neighbours called. 'Off to school?' Aart waved his red-mittened hand and smiled. He didn't mind the wind. He didn't even mind the cold. He was well wrapped up and sheltered by Auntie Dola seated high in front of him. There were houses and shops to look out for, the names of the roads, people at the tram stops, other children on their way to school, adults going to work, the milkman, the breadman, the postman, and the herring vendor with his horse and cart.

'Good morning, Mr Herring Vendor,' Aart called.

'Good morning yourself, schoolboy.' The herring vendor had a small red face.

It took a long time to reach his new school which was special for Jews. Aart shared a bench with Jacob who had already turned ten. Jacob made his own way to school. He walked for nearly an hour. 'I like my old school better,' he told Aart. 'My old school is a real school with six classrooms and a big hall for assembly and plants in the window. This is just a room, you know. It's any old room.' Jacob was right. They were packed into one room with old double-desks pushed together. 'Take a look at these desks.' Jacob ran his finger around the gouges in the desk top and then he took out his pen knife and started carving his initials.

'You're making it worse,' Aart said.

'Doesn't matter. It's all rubbish. Mr Simon isn't even a proper teacher, you know.'

'Yes he is too.'

'No he's not. He's a student.'

'How do you know?'

'My father said. Holland doesn't have enough Jewish teachers to teach in the special schools. It happened too quickly. Just on one day the Germans made another edict. Jews had to change to special schools right away. So the Jewish Council changed student teachers into teachers.'

'Well, I don't mind,' said Aart. 'Mr Simon is nice and he's smart and I hope I get him again next year.'

'There isn't going to be a next year.'

'That's a daft way to talk.'

'No, it isn't. My mother said so. I heard her talking with my aunt.'

Aart was quick to work out a solution. 'Well, I guess that would be all right. I do have my grandfather, you know. My grandfather is very clever. He can be my teacher.'

'You should get smart.'

'I am smart. I'm clever like my grandfather. He told me so himself.'

One day he showed Jacob the special things he kept in his pocket. Then another day Jacob wasn't there. And he didn't come back.

Where had Jacob gone? Someone said Switzerland. Someone else said Indonesia. Aart said, 'But the Germans won't let you.'

Finally someone else whispered, 'Dived. His family dived.'

That was what happened. You could go under like a seed for the winter. Go under. Dived, they called it.

The Jewish Theatre

They were ringing the doorbell, butting the door. Beasts. They came up the stairs stomping and shouting. Aart heard his mother's voice. He was already out of bed, his heart thumping. 'Just a minute,' Rachel said. 'Let me tell him.' Tell him what? He already knew. Hadn't they been waiting and waiting and waiting?

His mother was carrying a pack on her back with a green blanket tied to the top. 'Hurry up,' the SS policeman said. 'Get a move on.' But they were already moving along the cobblestones.

'Get a move on yourself,' Aart said to himself. It was strange walking like that through the dark. It was quiet save for their footsteps. It was so quiet it reminded him of going to watch the ducklings with Manus. The little fluffy ones paddled out from the reeds keeping close together. Manus and he kept very still. There were so many different kinds – pochards, mallards, grebes, moorhens, dabchicks, and the coots with their red beaks. There were geese too all the way from Canada and oh! the swans. Manus and he always went together to the park. Suddenly he was crying.

Rachel said, 'Give me your bag. Hold on to my sleeve.'

They came to a place he recognised, the Jewish Theatre. It was already crowded full of people yet more kept arriving, pushing in through the doors. A soldier told grandfather it was forbidden to have two bags. Aart went with grandfather to look for a place to leave the extra ones. They found a corner in the back of the main hall where it was dark. But as they walked away, someone else put a bag there too. And then someone else the next minute. Soon there were so many bags piled on top that Aart was worried. How would they get theirs out?

'It's not important,' Grandfather said, leading him back to Rachel.

Grandfather punched Aart's bag to make a pillow. Rachel helped him out of his coat and spread it on the floor. 'Lie down now. Try to sleep. If you can't sleep, rest. Close your eyes.' Grandfather covered him with the green blanket. Aart lay in the darkness listening. Then he suddenly sat up. 'What is it?' Rachel asked.

'Monkey. I want monkey.'

'Monkey?'

Aart untied the sack he was using as a pillow and pulled

out his rag monkey. He hugged his monkey to his neck as if he were three years old again. He hugged the rag animal to him and, snuggling under the blanket, he whispered a song into its ear. It was a song Auntie Dola had sung about a white bird flying through white sand and sand flowers blooming.

'Hurry up. Up. Get up. We have to leave now.' People were moving around him, a great dark throng with bulging bumping bundles.

'Where are we going?'

'You'll see.'

Where were they going? Someone said Palestine. Jews for Palestine. How did you get to Palestine? Flying on a white bird. Fools said Palestine. Were they fools? Who knew?

Aart was thirsty and hungry. Rachel gave him a sip from the bottle she carried in her bag. 'Just a small sip. We have to save some for later.' And she gave him the last potato, half of it.

Then he needed to do a wee. 'Over here,' said his grandfather, pulling him towards an outside wall.

'I can't do it here. Everyone will see.'

'You'll have to do it here.'

It had started to rain. They were herded towards the central station in the rain and put on a passenger train. It rained all morning. The rain slashed at the windows. It turned colder as if winter was returning. The rain darkened and thickened with sleet. When they reached a wayside station named Hooghalen, they were ordered out. Hooghalen was Dutch but where in Holland was it? East, they had travelled east; that much they knew. They were in East Holland, in the province of Drenthe. 'Egypt,' someone said. But the camp was called Westerbork and in the sandy wilderness lay the dark greens of heather, scrub pine and woody gorse. There was a long muddy road between the huts. This was called the boulevard, the *Boulevard des Misères*. Beyond it, on both sides stood watch-towers and on the outside of the grounds, a wire fence.

Aart wanted to go with his grandfather to the men's hut. 'Why can't I?'

'Because you're a child.'

'I'm not so small.'

'No, you're a big boy, my duckling. But there are rules. Twelve and under with the women.'

He was nine. Nine went with the women. Women and children were to live in the Westerbork women's barracks.

Muriel Spark

THE DARK MUSIC OF THE RUE DU CHERCHE-MIDI

If you should ask me, is there a street of Europe,
and where, and what, is that ultimate street?
I would answer: the onetime Roman road
in Paris, on the left bank of the river,
the long, long Rue du Cherche-Midi,
street of my thoughts and afterthoughts
and curiosity never to be satisfied entirely, and
premonitions, inconceivably shaped, and memories.

Suppose that I looked for the street of my life, where I
    always
could find an analogy. There in the
shop-front windows and in the courtyards,
the alleys, the great doorways, old convents, baronial
    properties:
those of the past. And new
hotels of the present, junk shops, bead shops.
Pastry cooks, subtle chocolate-makers, florists of intricate
wonder, and merchants of exceptional fabrics.
Suppose that I looked, I would choose to
find that long, long Rue, of Paris, du Cherche-Midi, its
    buildings,
they say, so tall they block out the
sun. I have always thought it worth
the chase and the search to find some sort of meridian.

187

From 1662 to the Revolution:
No. 7, owned in 1661 by
Jérémie Derval, financier, counsellor,
and master of the king's household.

All along the street:
Marquises, dukes, duchesses,
financiers, mathematicians, magistrates,
philosophers, bibliophiles, prioresses,
abbesses, princes and, after them,
their widows, generals, ambassadors,
politicians. Some
were beheaded and others took over. In essence
none has departed. No. 38:
there was the military prison where Dreyfus
first stood trial, in December 1894.
At No. 40 resided the Comte de Rochambeau until
he was sent to help George Washington;
he forced the English to surrender at Yorktown and took
twenty-two flags from them. What a street, the Rue du
   Cherche-Midi!

Here, Nos. 23–31, was a convent where a famous abbess
   reigned,
disgusted in girlhood by her father, a lecher,
she imposed a puritan rule and was admired,
especially when, great lady that she was,
she humbled herself to wash the dishes.

Beads and jewels of long ago look out
from their dark shopwindows
like blackberries in a wayside bramble bush
holding out their arms:
Take me, pick me, I am dark and sweet,
ripe and moist with life.
The haggard young girl in charge of the boutique
reaches for the beads, she fondles them, sad, sad,
to part with such a small but
undeniable treasure. Rose quartz:

she sells it with eager reluctance.
Listen to my music. Hear it.
Raindrops, each dark note.
She has not slept well. Her little
black dress was hastily donned, and the half-
circles are drooping under her eyes.

They say the Rue du Cherche-Midi,
with its tall houses set at shadowy angles,
never catches the sun.

Still, in the shop, that
raddled, dignified young girl –
frugal, stylish,
experienced – will, with bony fingers,
pick out a pile of necklaces:
the very one that you want, those
opals, those moonstones.

Dark boutiques, concerns; their shadow falls
over the bright appointments of the day.
It is a long, long past that haunts the street of Europe,
a spirit of vast endurance,
a certain music, Rue du Cherche-Midi.

Michèle Roberts

MAKING IT UP
Extracts from my notebooks on writing Flesh and Blood

Notebook dated December 1st, 1991

I'm starting to speed up now. Here we go. Towards a new novel. The beginning of one, just beginning to be marked on my windscreen.

Write the novel according to some surrealist game – use randomness, the unconscious, very deliberately, in its construction? Make this clear in the text? I don't know yet.

paper with the graininess of porridge, or polenta, or purée of chick peas

a woman's desire for passion freely expressed, for personal freedom power autonomy – at the beginning she thinks that to have this she'll need power over others? So she founds her convent? The Order of the Dark Star

a light in the darkness
illumination; radiance
the burning bush
light in the trees; in the grass
light held by darkness and enclosed by it, irradiating it
arise, shine, for thy night hath come

n.b. fifteenth-century narrative paintings of saints' lives

all the living and the dead can be in it, and all the present and the past

She'll found her new religion out of rebellion against the mother, very much, as well as against the father. Rage and resistance. She'll play a ritualised battle of the Mothers against the Daughters – tournament joust.

Her mother closed her eye against her, refused to see or acknowledge her reality, and her father opened his eye of sex upon her and pronounced her *his*. So her only identity was as her father's fantasy sex object. Nothing from her mother to fall back on. She needed her mother to stand by her during her Oedipal crisis but her mother couldn't. She feared she'd damaged and done away with her mother. So part of the myth of her new religion will re-enact this family drama and attempt to resolve it. All she knows is power relationships. She seeks to dominate others in her turn. She's frightened of power yet longs for it. She's full of sadistic fantasies. So have the mother damaged in some way – and a miraculous cure.

To write a maternal narrative – that lets a mother speak, that creates a text about pain and grotesque comedy and confusion, that can face all this, that can contain it – so the text somehow enacts motherhood. Form and content are mother-daughter. The text expresses that. The surrealism in the novel will come from details being heightened from the ordinary and the mundane just a little into the bizarre – so you'll still see the connection to the everyday.

Write the novel as a series of contrasts between family history, the 'real', and the mystical mythology? Which is the mythologising of the former? Write the novel in layers, it'll have to be layers, can't just be one narrative, layers of mother and father on top of the child like a mille-feuille.

Dream: a silver angel flying very fast across the heavens at night with her hands clasped sort of cannibalistic eucharistic ritual – the eating of the body of the mother – and then her magical re-generation, restoration

a central mystery in which people change, are metamorphosed, into the opposite sex? and one woman becomes two and then back to one again?

The narrative voice *enacts* this metamorphosis, *is* polymorphously perverse.

a religion about the meaning of birth and death, food central to express it, food growing in the ground; the garden of memory

Usually I write about the unconscious erupting into reality, using a sort of psychoanalytical model. This time write about the unconscious *as* reality, with 'reality' breaking in occasionally. Hence, I now see, my current interest in surrealism.

We took Beewee to Etretat, sea like blue milk, warm as summer, the grey pebbles, later as the sun began to sink the stones on the beach glistened blue, the cliffside went golden, we lay and looked at the smooth water, the waves draw in and out, hiss and drag over the shingle, nutcracker death has got Beewee in his curved claws

Notebook dated March 13th, 1992

Somehow connected to my idea of maternal narrative: one aspect of this novel's text is to be something written by a mother for her daughter – to delight and instruct her; a gift; a pattern book; a courtesy book; inventing a world fit for a daughter to live in. Jokes too. Also erotic and bawdy. And then – the idea of a sex-change as part of the narrative technique, part of the subject of metamorphosis, part of the plot. Put side by side different people, different pieces of story and story-telling, play with that, let the reader work out the trick, the illusion, that what looks like a simple sequence may not be. Patch it in.

Layer after layer to go through: sheets of paper, clothes, skins; so make the stories themselves do the metamorphosing, one into another, one enclosing another; all to do with change; so the reader has to experience something bisexual – both penetration (into the heart of the book, its hidden centre) and enclosing, being enclosed (cf Sidney's *Arcadia*).

One story will be someone who is one sex in England and another in France, set in Etretat on the shore, fishing life, the Impressionists coming to paint; also an eighteenth-century story about reason versus emotion, vice versus virtue, with the Marquis de Sade in it.

Each story is the mother of the next one/the deceitful narratives of the turncoats!

It's on the level of image, of symbol, that she heals herself and finds her mother again; and that's where it happens – in the dark room, at first she thinks it's empty but then –

sudden scary surrealistic change is the stuff of childhood – that's the experience

I'm scared of writing about religion, of being mocked, of sounding twee, and I'm scared of all the letting go involved, the plunge into chaos, not-knowing, wildness, loss of self, in order to write

Dacia was saying today, quoting Barthes, that writing is playing with the body of the mother – well, is that why I feel so blocked, because I feel not allowed to play that play? She was suggesting daughters too, not just Barthes the son, could play with the mother's body. I'm not so sure! but it was a very powerful, very sweet, evocation she made. I'm writing about the consequences of the absent mother: grotesque women; oppressed women are not necessarily *nice*. NB: I suddenly realised why I am reading de Sade – my desire to write about feminine masochism – though so far his female characters appear to be solely emblematic, representatives of Virtue and Morality opposed to Man. Boring.

Notebook dated July 3rd, 1992

We drove to Etretat early morning, no cars or people, utterly empty, grey-blue and sparkling, sun on rain. Then returned via Vattetot and Bénouville, tiny coves and hamlets, mad Edwardian summer houses sprouting turrets and balconies. Now in Domfront on its high hill. We nearly bought a presbytery, seventeenth-century with gun emplacements, a *potager*, holy pics, huge cellar full of cider. Sunset like a bloom on fruit. Milky golden light and the crackle of sun. People working with pitchforks on the verges, raking cut hay. We looked and looked. Also of course you see modern France, its bureaucracies and agrobusiness, etc; tho on this journey I encountered no racism; yeah I speak as a sloppy sentimental lover of my homeland I expect; but the peace and quiet, well. Something to cherish. Back in London's grime and traffic jams and noise oh I hated it, I wanted to go back to France. OK I love Soho, I even love the Holloway Road because of the people I meet in the shops, but I hate the noise booming around, the dog turds, the aggressive mad driving.

The form of the novel will make it appear it goes in in in – but in fact the worlds revealed could just as well seem to be external ones: what is 'inside' and what is 'outside'? NB: try to go right beyond Catholic imagery this time, right through it and out the other side.

RIP Beewee died October 28th at 5 a.m.

Finally the spirit left the house, that noisy angry one, she upped & went in the middle of the night, my fear evaporated when something else – a warm close maternal voice – took over and calmed me down. I felt I'd re-connected with all the childhood waking terrors I'd ever had in that house at night – and I was a small child again, and then at last consoled, a warm presence was near to me. I fell asleep at last.

Walk through a hidden valley to the sea, empty secret beach we discovered, fell down on to it, like being born Jim said. It was Le Tilleul – which I knew as a child.

Notebook dated January 1st, 1993

A corpse arriving in a sledge drawn quickly across the packed snow, the girl hears the sledge arrive at night, it whistles in over the snow

remember the huge rainbow that arched over the house at Criquetot after Beewee's funeral, remember the wild violets in the woods and the anemones and the primroses, the coarse salt we scattered under our feet to melt the black ice, those two deer we saw fleeing across the track in the Bois des Loges, and how at the end the house smelled of chocolate and yeast

the pattern of the novel: each bit told by a different character; are they all linked; collecting up all the bits, joining them up

loss: try to find that lost place again; paradise regained; this is the novel tugging ahead wanting to get written; supposing the novel's shape were a spiral?

Female narrators in the first half and then male? The female ones can't really see themselves, their shadow; and the male ones see women in a particular way.

Hard to make something out of nothing, haul it out, form it. I feel tired all the time, I want to escape, into sleep. Difficult narratives, writing in the third person because for some reason I feel I must for these parts of it. When you're using the first person and become possessed by a voice then it can really flow. Chaos and muddle and confusion and despair and difficulty. I don't know what I'm doing. I'm writing badly and superficially. Terrible thick lethargy. I'm not giving myself to writing with love and abandon, I lack love and commitment. You have to give yourself to the writing for the sheer love of it, there is no other way to do it, that's what it demands. I fear that, because it brings up the pain rage terror of childhood, writing makes me re-experience that, too painful. I couldn't just leave the pain and terror at Criquetot, by deciding not to buy the house, because it's inside me.

What am I frightened of? That I shall die. That I'll jump in, give myself totally, and there'll be nothing and no one there and so I'll die. Do all writers have this terror? I don't know. I don't know anyone to discuss it with. It's only novels that tap these deep-seated feelings of insecurity, this terror; never poems. Is it masochistic to keep plunging back into it? Can I learn somehow that writing, diving into language, is not the same as being a terrified angry child? Could I learn to give myself to language, to writing, without these fears and terrors? I thought I'd dealt with them and yet again they re-surface. In *Daughters of the House* I wrote about material things, in Léonie's inventory, I anchored myself that way. Things I could *touch*. It got me over the worst. Beewee's death ended my repression, my childhood in that house – I no longer had to be just the good niece, the good loving girl, I could begin to accept how *angry* my child-self was.

Notebook dated May 18th, 1993

Trying to use something slippery and unfixed as words, where the signifiers are arbitrary, invented, to express something I feel is *true* – to find some deep truth – the truth of the lives of our bodies in this world – to express it – the words themselves feel sacred and true to me, not arbitrary at all. I've got a religious attitude to language and I always have had. Religion's in the unconscious and erupts up from there.

Chaos and uncertainty – that's what I'm living in. Hold it,

contain it. Didn't Mr Keats have something to say about this? Stick with it dear.

How would I like to live? It's not a question I've felt able really to ask myself before when I was homeless, with little money. Free in a certain way, very unfree in others. Now I've *got* to think about it, because the choices are opening up. I've also *got* to think about what I really want to write about in order to get going again on the novel which got stuck while I was feeling a bit taken over by others, that I was writing for them now, not for myself any more.

Now I've bought La Poivière I want to go and live in it for ever and work in the garden, that's what I want to do.

Notebook dated October 1st 1993

When I'm here at La Poivière, sitting on the front step looking at the view of fields and hills or stacking wood or slashing brambles or staring into the fire or painting the walls or just pottering about, I'm in a state of happiness – ordinary – this is my spot on the planet, I belong, I am meant to be here. That bliss of childhood: being free out of doors, being out of the house, not needing to think about myself, being able to let go and just be part of the landscape, a happiness born in the body like the warmth of the earth, the earth's warm breath.

My fears and doubts about writing when I'm doing it – because of those childhood feelings of: what I feel is not valid and must not be spoken. Repression. Prohibition. Don't forget this. So it's not just fear of going mad when the self dissolves in order to create; it's also fear of what's inside me coming out, that it's bad because critics (e.g. Grandpère the old patriarch) said so in childhood. Don't forget this.

Days spent alone here writing. The house to myself all day long completely empty and completely silent. I sat in the sitting-room so that I could have sunlight to write and see the birds on the bird-table, and the novel just rushed out like a river underground spouting out, pages and pages every day. Very convent-like, that was the image I kept getting; long hours of silence and work. I invented a new sort of *gnocchi*. I cook much better out here because I'm so happy, I've got a light touch, it comes right. Now that feels true for the writing too. I've never ever felt such pleasure in writing as I do here. Partly I know because I've reached the magic half-way point from which you survey the end, unwritten yet, but you know you're on the way, yes it's like knowing an orgasm is building and you will come, but I do think it is being able to live here in this house that makes all the difference. A home of my own, a place to live I can't be thrown out of. Now I feel I belong in the human race. Planting my French root back into France, finishing my novel.

Janice Elliott

CONSTANTINE'S EGG
Extract from a novel in progress

Chapter One

THEY HAD BEEN a long time getting there. Through air and snow and sand and history.

The hotel was grand. Or it had been grand, and would be again. It was amazing now: done up for the millennium. There was even talk that the proprietor might show his face. They were not sure how they felt about this prospect. There was curiosity, of course, but apprehension too. The tone of his memos and directives had always been peremptory and arbitrary.

Ovit was up first as usual. He stood on tiptoe on a box to brush his stiff blond hair. He flattened it neatly to his scalp with a speck of white shoe-cream from a tin he had found in a wastepaper basket after the German gentleman left. Herr Brunner came at least once a year. He was getting on now. The rumour was that he lived in Damascus, as a retired doctor of private means. Ovit liked the old man. But then Ovit's willingness to think the best of everyone was fabled.

The small pockmarked mirror was hung too high. Ovit had considered lowering it but chose instead to grow taller. Four foot nine was short but not as short as your average dwarf. In Ovit's view, he had only ten inches or so to go, eight perhaps, and he would be satisfied. The rest of the staff, in particular Tancred the cook who was also the butcher, teased him. 'Still growing, Ovit?'

The chambermaid Greta clucked when she heard Ovit being teased like this but for himself he did not mind. A harelip or a hunched back he would have found a painful mark of distinction but being small was not so bad. If one person tried to persecute you, there was always someone else who would stick up for you because few people felt threatened by smallness and in many it aroused an instinct to kindness.

Women tended to be nice to him. Greta, for instance, said that little people were known for their virility. She told him this when they were alone. She did not shout it around to make others laugh. All the same, Ovit blushed.

When Greta said this, she was making up the beds and he was cleaning the windows in the Imperial Suite. He blushed again when she added: 'You'd better watch out for big Utta. She's got her eye on you.'

'Utta?' Ovit shuddered at the name of the giant washer-woman with her cart-horse haunches. His nose was about level with her waist and she had a smell that choked him: at once acid and meaty. Given his height, or lack of it, he was as sensitive as a dog to the way people smelled. He supposed it was the same for children, obliged to live their lives around the adult stomach, though at least they grew out of it. 'I thought Utta and Tancred were friends?'

'You think one's enough for her?'

Ovit would have liked to forget this conversation. He preferred instead to remember the neat flicks and smoothings with which Greta made up the ornate, clawed bed with the gilt cherubs and brocade hangings; and Greta's particular scent of crisp sheets and fragrant soap. She smelled of the air here, clean and piny.

He peered closer into the mirror and scratched his chin. Still nothing to shave. He thought regretfully of the magnificent cut-throat razor in the blue box with the silk lining in his top right-hand drawer, at the back. It had been his father's and was very nearly his entire inheritance in this world. Every week he sharpened it on the leather strap, just in case.

Ovit got down from the box, put on his green apron and rubbed at the frost that had formed overnight on the window-pane. What a view. He never tired of it. The mountains. The swathe of conifers fingering the huddled village below. High above were the icy peaks, such a cold sight it was hard to believe that not so many miles away there was desert stretching as far as the Euphrates. He could not quite imagine that, though he did have a picture in his head of the great river. There would be chattering monkeys, he felt sure, deep wet green and crocodiles.

No one had come from that direction for a long time.

Ovit sighed. Fond as he was of the view, it sometimes made him homesick for his lost family and the village he had left in country much like this, though flatter.

A rising sun of yellow oil was just appearing between the dark trees. If he were late he would be in trouble. What time was it? He shook the cheap metal alarm clock but it had stopped again at five minutes to twelve, the time the war was supposed to begin.

In the big kitchen that was both the warmest room at this time of day on account of the vast cooking-range and at the same time the pumping heart (or perhaps stomach, guts, liver and lights) of the hotel, Ovit was tempted by the idea of a sliver of blood sausage from the pantry and a hunk of fresh-baked bread. But if he were to avoid Tancred and big Utta, he knew he must not linger.

To quiet his hunger as he laid the fires in the Bestiary beneath the melancholy heads of elk and stag and moose, Ovit, now vacuuming the stuffed wolf frozen in anger, told himself the story of his life. He would have enjoyed another story but this was the only one he knew. Perhaps even that one was not true. Still, lacking an author to correct him, he told his favourite beast – the big bear rampant – how he had lived through wars he did not understand, with nine brothers and sisters in a cellar that smelled of apples.

Years passed, then an entertainment came to town. He thought the bearded women were sad and terrible, he was sorry for the ponies with their sequinned shivering flanks, the clowns frightened him and he was in terror for the trapeze artists. Knowing there was no safety net he could not bear their heroic flight and left the tent, crawling under the flap just as he had got in. It was dark outside but a warm summer's night. So he wandered into the only booth that made no charge and stumbling in the darkness felt his ear most painfully seized by the master who was to take his destiny in hand: the Magician.

'I was terrified,' Ovit said, as he dusted and polished the great black claw chair. 'You can imagine.' He knew that the bear could imagine nothing but there was something grave and listening about its posture and its beady eyes were so real they followed you around the room. Besides, to Ovit there was nothing sad or peculiar about talking to himself. If anyone came in he would pretend he had been humming all the time.

'You can imagine. I was not so tall then – only four feet – and the Magician was nearer six, though skinny and bent. He wore a black cloak with appliquéd stars and other signs I took to be cabbalistic. His feet were very narrow and long, pushed into soft leather slippers I guessed to be Arab. He had long, dirty grey hair which I discovered later he stuffed sometimes into an eastern turban, sometimes a hat of animal fur with flaps that covered his ears and hung down well below his chin. These flaps might have been rabbit ears.

'Anyway, once I had given up wriggling and struggling, he sat me down on a wooden stool. I could still have tried to run but the intensity of his gaze held me.' Ovit could have sworn the bear nodded but that was, of course, impossible. Or was it? He always felt happier in the company of the bear. When he had talked to it, he was calmer and more cheerful. Ovit dreamed of the bear. When there was no risk of anyone catching him, he would lay his face against its flank, which was as high as he could reach without a stepladder. He could not imagine life without the bear. If he ever had to leave this place he supposed he would have to take it with him, if only for the bear's sake. No one else, not even Greta, would climb a ladder every week to brush the fur and inspect for moths.

'Talking to that bear again?'

Ovit jumped and blushed but it was only Greta.

'Ungerberg says I've got to polish the brass in here. Go on with your story. I couldn't help hearing. What did the Magician do next?'

'D'you really want to hear?'

'Yes, if the bear doesn't mind. What was the Magician's name?'

'Hieronymus. Outside the booth there was a notice that said *Hieronymus, Doctor and Magician.* He was very nice to me. He gave me black bread and goat cheese to eat and some of his tincture to drink. That was the same stuff he sold in bottles wherever we went. It was supposed to make barren women fertile and cure all sorts of things: Dr Hieronymus's Famous Tincture.'

'And did it?'

'I don't know because we always moved on somewhere else. I liked it. When I had drunk it I stopped being scared and when he offered me employment as his assistant and apprentice I agreed at once. At home I was only another mouth to feed. Besides, in the village they called me a dwarf. My mother would look at me and pull her apron over her eyes. I knew she was crying. The dogs barked at me. In the circus I was treated with respect, as a little person. And with the help of the Magician's tincture, I began to grow. Or perhaps I'd have grown anyway.'

At this point, Ovit's telling and Greta's listening were interrupted by the under-manager, Ungerberg. The first guests were expected at any time. Ovit and Greta were to do the flowers for the Presidential suite. The gladioli were on ice in the cellar. Now this minute, or he, Ungerberg, would know the reason why.

As Ovit finally sat down to breakfast on burned porridge, the bell rang in the kitchen.

Frangel from front-desk reception looked at the board.

'The tower suite,' he said. 'Lady Hester. On your feet, Ovit. You're her pet.'

Ovit knew why Frangel lowered himself to enter the kitchen – he fancied Greta almost as much as he fancied himself.

Ovit knew, too, what would happen next. He ducked as

he always did but as ever, too late. Frangel clipped him on the ear: the same ear by which the Magician had captured him.

In his office Ungerberg slicked back his starling-black hair, studied his reflection from centre parting to tiny feet, poured a glass of hock, took a Turkish cigarette from the jade box and settled behind his desk.

At his hand was a screen from which he could view the goings-on of the Hotel Crac, both public and private. He checked his fingernails, brushed an invisible speck from his jacket, and sighed with satisfaction.

Only European management – possibly only his management – could have rescued such an improbable hotel, built on and among the ruins of a Crusader castle on a mountainside several hundred miles from the nearest airstrip.

Of course, there had been some luck. It was probably the very remoteness of the place that had saved it through the troubles of this last decade of the century. Through the Balkan wars, the upheavals in what had once been the Soviet Union, and the Islamic revolutions, no one had bothered to lay claim to this mountain site or the valley below with its small town of a few thousand souls.

But it had taken Ungerberg's patience, firmness and inspiration – backed by Bok Group money secured by the proprietor – to transform what had once been not much more than an archaeologist's guesthouse and second-rate historical site into a five-star hotel.

When he recalled the work and the years it had taken, Ungerberg shook his head in wonder that anyone could have seen it through, could have clung to the vision now realised around him. The conversion of what had once been underground stables into kitchens, boiler-rooms, utility rooms, laundries. The intricate central heating system of Byzantine complexity. The double-glazing of window-embrasures from which the foolish knights had once poured oil on Saladin himself. The new buildings. The trouble with the decorators

– their ideas, their chilblains, their waspish tempers. The trouble with the gangs of slave-labourers from Eastern Europe. The trouble with transport of supplies.

All these problems Ungerberg had overcome. He loved his hotel as he had never loved woman or child. It was an organism with which he was inextricably entwined. If its heart stopped, so, he felt, would his. So only on rare occasions did he permit himself to imagine that his dream fulfilled might be imperilled, that the hotel's position between the Lebanon on the one side and the Syrian desert on the other, was in any way vulnerable.

From the last trouble – that of enticing guests – Ungerberg had been saved by history or time, whichever of those two monitors you chose to mark the coming of the millennium. Ungerberg had little patience with history. He considered it an art rather than a craft, and one that had become as ephemeral as the ever-changing maps. Thus he had consulted the proprietor by fax and settled for the clock-time of what had once been western Christianity.

While the hotel in the foothills of the anti-Lebanon range made itself ready for their coming, the guests approached from all points of the compass and by various means of transport.

In the muddiest part of Turkey one couple had ditched their Russian car. The woman with the nose like a knife, dressed in a fur coat that had once been good, if ugly, stamped her foot. By virtue of her Uzi sub-machine-gun, she had obliged the miserable peasants to wheel out a farm wagon. There were no horses because they had eaten the horses. Instead a bent and ravaged man, with hair quite white and hollowed cheeks, stood meekly between the shafts. Obediently he accepted the harness.

'Gee up, Nikolae. Get a move on.'

The peasants watched, understandably sullen. The woman had taken their last round of goat cheese, the blankets from the bed of a dying grandmother, six living hens in a cage, one pig and their entire supply of bottled figs.

Nikolae took the bit between his teeth.

Ilena Ceauşescu cracked the whip.

Of the others who came not all had darkness in their hearts. Some did not even have invitations.

Wesley Hinde, for instance, aspiring author and confused traveller, had first found mention of the hotel in a book he picked up in Marrakesh. More precisely, groaning with amoebic enteritis in a squatter lavatory off the Square of the Extinct, he had rescued the paperback abandoned by some fellow-sufferer who had torn out a number of pages to wipe his bottom. Wesley was obliged to make use of the introduction for the same purpose but took the rest back to his room.

So, as darkness fell and in the square below the story-teller began his tale and the snake-charmer dozed on hashish and the fire-swallower yawned, Wesley slept like the dead and woke feeling empty but better. His sleep had been so deep that for a matter of minutes he could not remember who he was.

Then it came back to him all at once. The bliss of Oxford in an undergraduate summer. The purgatory of the Isis School for the Teaching of English as a Foreign Language where he languished for twelve months in a tutor's job that would at least keep him in Oxford.

Well, not entirely languished, he supposed, as the yowling of the muezzin in newly fundamentalist Morocco announced the sunset and the cooking smell drifted upwards of something like spice and urine. There had been the foreign girls. But there was something so glum about German sex, so suicidal about the Swedish sort, and anyhow, you could go off sex if you got too much. That is, you could go off what was popularly supposed to be male sex, the purely mechanical kind.

So Wesley had woken one morning beside a female whose name he could not remember, crept from the bedroom, dressed in the kitchenette, posted his resignation to the Isis School, gone for a walk in Christchurch Meadows before even the ducks were awake, and in that beautiful, wistful

Oxford dawn, decided he was a romantic: a difficult thing to be in this exhausted and complaining country, at this time, in this century.

Thus it was that he came to Marrakesh and read of a valley and a castle and a mountain. A place that contained a secret; though what the secret was he could not tell, since at that point the rest of the pages had been torn out.

Wesley did not exactly decide to go. He would say later, it was more as though he had recognised his destiny.

In her mirror Serafina pulled a face at her long pale hair which fell and folded beneath her chin like sad wings. She drew it together with an elastic band.

Serafina painted walls. She was an American princess.

At home in the forgotten palace on the Hudson River she would sleep all day in summer in the hammock slung between the apple trees and at night she would wander through the empty rooms looking for dreams. She was not afraid of the way the night creaked and scuttered, nor of the sadness of ancient drapes, though the dust made her cats sneeze.

Sometimes she heard the yip of a tug on the river or a great jet labouring up to heaven.

A whole winter she spent the nights looking into the eye of the television and eating popcorn, until the mysterious electronic heart flickered and died. That was when she started looking for dreams. But they were all someone else's, left over. Her grandfather's fat rich dreams, her mother's mad, sad ones. So she started to paint her own on the walls but they were too big. All the same, Serafina knew that she was on to something.

One spring morning walking with her cat through the shining tall grasses, Serafina found a tramp sleeping curled up in rags.

The bag-lady was well-spoken. Her name was Glory. Serafina took her indoors, gave her a soft-boiled egg and Russian tea.

Glory put in a set of cast-off teeth and told Serafina about the streets of New York.

'No place for a lady,' Glory said.

She was a read woman. It was amazing, she said, how many stories you found in garbage bags. Proust, Tolstoy, Hieronymus, Nabokov.

'Who's Hieronymus?'

Glory sat back in the rocker.

'You never heard of Constantine's Egg?'

Serafina shook her head.

Glory struck a bargain.

'You do me a fine dinner with silver candles and a duck-down pillow to lay my head, and I'll give you some education. Where you been brung up, anyhow?'

Serafina wondered if this was a Southern-born lady. There was something about the way she made her vowels very long.

'And I do Tarot, too.'

Glory rocked then she slept then she took a tour of Serafina's paintings.

Serafina showed her the tall blue sunflowers and the red sky and the little house with small people sheltering. Then she took her into the big room where her great-grandfather had entertained old Joe Kennedy and others who had turned Prohibition into gold. Here, she had painted a clearing in a forest. The grass looked mown and safe. Kind animals peered out from the lush foliage. A lion drank from the stream. In the centre of the clearing a couple sat on a park bench. They were naked except for a wreath of flowers in the girl's hair, and something shy and posed about their posture suggested they were just married. Perhaps someone was painting them, or taking a photograph. Serafina had imagined Henri Rousseau with his big black moustaches and his easel set up.

'I can't get the giraffe right,' Serafina said. 'I use house paint. It was in the cellar. It's supposed to be the Garden of Eden.'

'You been there?'

'No.'

Glory grunted.

'Where's the serpent?'

'I don't know. I suppose he's watching.' She hesitated. She liked Glory but was not sure how much to confide in her. 'I

208

paint these because I can't dream. D'you think that means I'm mad? My mother was mad. I wonder sometimes.'

Glory shrugged.

'Madness is relative. I was in Bellevue myself. All great artists are insane in one way or another because they don't see the world like other folk. That's what I told them. I didn't want no cure.'

Later, while Serafina cooked, Glory rocked. It was a wonderful evening. The wild greenery crowded the window. There was a coin of golden sun on the wooden table. The small cat teased it with her paw.

Glory said: 'Stand still. Let me look. You're tall. If you did something with your hair it would be just wonderful. You remind me of the daughter I never had. You should go out into the world. You're a princess.'

'I'd be scared. And besides, what would I do?'

'First polish the silver candlesticks, finish cooking that dinner and find me a duck-down pillow.'

The old house creaked with happiness now as Serafina swept away the cobwebs in the great dining-room, polished and lit the candelabra, brought up champagne from the cellar she had been afraid to enter, and put on a silver dress, like mermaid scales, that was hanging in her mad mother's wardrobe.

After dinner, they blew out all the candles but for one. Glory lit a cigar and told Serafina all about Constantine's Egg.

When she had finished, Glory said: 'So you see, it must be found by the pure in heart. You must leave soon.'

Serafina said: 'What I'd like best would be to stay here with you. We could have such good times.'

'And I with you, child. But I have no right to keep you.'

Serafina kissed Glory on the cheek. She smelled of ashes and flowers and fine Havana tobacco.

She left the bag-lady sitting by the hearth.

That night, for the first time, Serafina had a dream. There was an egg in it, encrusted with gold, and a man whose face she could not see, and a dwarf.

Charles Tomlinson

EPIDAUROS

Into the circle of the theatre
at Epidauros, faced
by its absent auditors
ten thousand strong, I launch
through acoustic space
the ship I have most in mind –
Hopkins' 'Deutschland' – and can hear
(his verses, thewed
like an Attic ode)
syllabic echoes cut into the atmosphere
climbing on ancient feet
the limestone tiers
where listening cyclamen have pushed their way
between the slabs
up out of Hades

APOLLO AT DELPHI

Darkness – as if it were the shadow of a cloud
    The wind was hurrying away – slides
Visibly off the plain, already sails
    Up the grey sides of the mountain to the peak
And leaves its high stones naked as Apollo.

SWALLOWS

Swallows outshout
the turbulent street:
swallows are messengers
where the day and night meet,
bringing news
from gods older than those
who pose in the gold interiors,
on the tiled cloister wall;
and a swallow it was
that arrowed past
threatening to graze you,
but delivered itself instead,
disappeared into
the dark slot above
a lintelled doorhead.

(Oporto)

Adam Thorpe

THE FIRST DAY

HE CALLED ME when the rains cleared. The mountains lost their grey hoods and smiled. They pushed back their hoods and exposed their heads and smiled. Mushrooms pushed up in the forests, under pines and stuff, even in the scrub they pushed up, because the sun shone. The sun warmed the wet mould of the forests and lo and behold! up they came, the poisonous and the good. I took my pharmacy chart but made mistakes. I never fried a button before checking with the old dame next door.

It was on one of these mushrooming hikes that He called me. I was on a not too steep flank facing north, in amongst the ilex, ducking and stooping because the ilex never grow tall enough, they just twist and keep modest, something to do with the temperate climate, something to do with the sap not reaching down, or up, or whatever. At any rate, they look dry and old when they're not. Whole forests of them look stooped and dry and worn out exactly where the old dame assures me there was nothing but goats thirty years ago, nibbling at clean grass, white goats spread out in herds and tinkling over the bare mountain.

I was up there, on this northern flank, stooped down to cut a big fat flap mushroom the colour of teak cabinets when I got this rush of blood to the head and I had to straighten up. I stood there straightened up, looking out through a hole in the ilex and blinking, hoping I wasn't growing old, the mould stuck to my gloves, the whole forest sweet and rotten after the rains – when I saw them.

I saw the Twins.

The Twins being the polite term. Let's keep to the Twins. They've always been there and they always will be there, forever and ever, almost. They're not identical twins. One mountain is a little more pointy, a little taller, a little more nervous, somehow. He was first out, I'll bet. The other's in his shadow. (Why a he? No idea. That's how I've always seen them. Brothers. The old dame next door thought of them as two old dames, knitting or something, keeping an eye on us all. Her fat nephew saw them as breasts, he'd giggle and stuff. And so on.) I blinked amongst the humus and the low ilex branches and God did an amazing thing.

First, a necessary item of information. You all know my first name, but you don't necessarily know my full name. My full name is Michael Mallinson Matthews. My sister's name is Miriam Mallinson Matthews. My father's name was Morgan Mallinson Matthews. My uncle's was Matthew Mallinson Matthews, which is getting as ridiculous as he was. Someone somewhere – probably my grandmama, bless her – was keen on the alliterative thing. Maybe it's a Welsh tradition. I don't know, having never ever set a toe in Wales. One day I will, if God lets me. Hit what half of me'd call the Home Patch.

Where was I?

Hey, where I've been ever since. Because where I have been ever since, symbolically speaking, is in that sweet forest, looking out over the fall of the flank to where the twin mountains rear up, rear up out of the shadowy valley and make the letter M.

I wept. That's a very unusual thing for me. It was then, anyway.

For, let's be straight about this, He had done an amazing thing.

The letter M. From that angle. Out there on that flank. Bare limestone heads, bluffs, sloping green sides, a soft cleft – it all came together. My mouth dropped open and the tears ran into it.

The letter M.

For Michael Mallinson Matthews.

Or just Michael.

I didn't mean to put it like that. What I meant to say was:

God spoke to me through the mountains. This is His way. He uses mountains and rivers and trees to speak to you. To His Chosen. He can also use ants and things, little teeny things, but that's not usual. Dirk says his own Call was put through one of those little metal plates at the back of the old-fashioned type of electrical socket, but that's Dirk. I reckon, on reflection, that Dirk might have been electrocuted to death and instantaneously brought round by Him in a miracle. It's conceivable. Lilian was spoken to through a hairbrush, if you remember. If she was spoken to at all. Because I might say now that I have never been too sure about this.

I went back home straight away. I got in and sat down for a few minutes. I still hadn't let go of my plastic bag full of damp flap mushrooms. Then I got up and looked out of the window. OK, it wasn't quite as clear. But they were still calling.

Michael, they said. Michael Mallinson Matthews. Or just Michael.

Those mountains are extremely ancient. They're so ancient that the tops have lost their grass and stuff. They kind of poke up out of the green and when the sun's out at dawn or sunset these rocky tops turn to gold. Imagine what I felt about that, looking through the window. Not content with bringing me to a place where I could look out and see my name shaped against the sky – not content with that, He'd gilded me. He'd given me the deluxe edition, tooled in gold. Every dawn and every dusk, He reminded me how expensive I was.

I say reminded, because I doubted His munificence, after. Those were difficult days. I was in alien country. I'm speaking literally but maybe figuratively too. Mind you, I'm not at all sure what isn't alien country, speaking personally for once. I don't want to indulge too much, but really I don't have a country I can walk into and feel, at the bottom of my soul – Hey, I'm home. Maybe there's an island mid-Atlantic where the surf would curl about my ankles and say, Hi there, pal, we've been waiting for you a long time. Maybe. My parents were Home. I mean, wherever they went I was towed like a little trailer with all their stupid quarrels stuffed in. When they split, after the fifteenth or something boutique had failed, I split too. In both senses. The trailer had no motor. I dragged it around with me. For fifty-five years I dragged it round with me. Then there was a tap on my elbow and the Lord said, Allow me. Now I'm in the trailer. In the Lord's chariot. And boy, do we zip.

I was working on my book, of course, at the time. My book. Hey, does that seem a dusty concept! But at the time it shone – my guiding star, my phantasm, my wrap-around all-purpose glitter-suit. I ripped it off me (off of me, as my mother would say, needling my Dad, who was British and pukka and drank too much) – I ripped it off of me that very same night. The same night of the day, I mean, when God first sculpted my name against the heavens. That night was starlit. Big, frosty, mean-looking stars. I stood out in the scrappy little garden and gazed until the bulk of the mountains stood out dark against the stars. Dark, but clear, even clearer than in the day. Like a voice sounds at night, in the middle of the night, because the busy crappy things of the world are stilled.

Michael. This is your call, Michael.

I went back in and grabbed my files and ran back out and – I just chucked them up. Chucked them up and away as hard as I could. It was unbelievable, really it was unbelievable. Months of work. Months of headaches and sweat and cramp in the wrists scattering through the night sky, falling down into the scrub below, like thrown garbage. I cried, of course. I got down on my knees and cried. Dogs yowling far off. Bats whittering. The old dame's TV too loud as usual – some dubbed Brazilian soap or something yacking and whining. A cat fight somewhere. And me, sobbing with gladness, weeping my thanks under the ripped-up glitter-suit of the far-away stars.

Oh yes, I'm receiving You, oh yes.

The next day I doubted it, I doubted the whole thing. Incredible. I opened the shutters. They squeal. I'm the type that doesn't oil things. Anyway, they're ancient. The old dame was out on her terrace, reading her paper. She looked up. There was a little olive tree between us and the olives were nearly ripe. I could have leaned out and picked one. In fact, when I opened the shutters they would scrape against the branches. Olives'd fall to the ground. (I can't say lawn. It wasn't a lawn, not yet, not until the big rains had gone deep.) I waved to her over the shimmer of olive leaves and she nodded back, like she usually did. She pointed up at the sky. I looked up. There was a black sack of storm, ready to empty itself, to empty the stuff it had sucked out of the sea, to offload it the minute it split against the mountains behind us. It blocked the light and the olive tree went dun. I went to the other side of the house and the mountains had their hoods back on. I'd thought the rains were over. The glass started to quiver with the rain hitting it, because it wasn't so much rain as hail. The hail smashed against everything, including my faith. I thought of my book, and saw the papers out there, getting smashed into the humus. I had slept badly. I felt the tarry brush of despair (as Dirk has put it, somewhere). I swore. And at that moment, that very moment, the mountains, the two brothers, the two old knitting dames, the two big paps – OK, let's say, the two twin peaks of revelation – cleared. The hail was hitting us but the mountains had cleared. They shone. They glowed. They were very, very beautiful. They were the letter M.

Michael . . . ?

Effulgence. Effulgence entered my head. The plastic bag was at my feet where I'd left it the previous night and I looked at it. I don't know why I looked at it just then but I did. Super U, it said. Super U! Imagine! My heart hammered. I picked it up and looked inside. I don't know why I did this. I don't know why I was writing a book on International Liquidities, either – except that it was all I knew about: that, and how not to run a boutique. No, I lie: I was writing a book on International Liquidities because I had wasted my life in high finance, and I liked gold. I liked gold and even more than I liked gold I liked the idea of gold reserves. I liked the idea that in all that crap and chaos, right at the bottom, there was this hard stuff that didn't tarnish.

Now it had flowed up and into my head, but it had No Intrinsic Value (that was going to be the title – imagine!). It was itself. It was clean.

So I looked into the plastic bag with God's gold in my head and I saw my flap mushrooms. They'd wept in the night. They were covered with a moist weeping, and smelt dark and rich. I can't describe to you how I felt just then: well, OK. This is a sort of poetic approximation: I felt like the olive tree in the sun, with its roots deep down in the decomposing darkness and its head glimmering and full of light. See how hopeless it is. How I really felt. Describing it, I mean.

The next bit is pretty difficult. I've been debating with myself how to put it across, or whether I had to put it across at all. I think I have to. Just bear with me.

I'm not young. I'm not old, either. I'm still not old. I still think of that old dame next door as my grandmother. When I work it out, though, I'm cutting it fine: she'd have to have been a child mother, if you get what I mean. That's weird. My temples are grey. My pate shows through. But I still have a youthful sheen and a good grip, and go jogging for the Lord every time I have to. I do, though, have an inefficient digestion. It's probably genetics rather than senescence. Anyway, the fact is that in my moment of supreme presence I wanted to go to the toilet.

So I did. I sat there on the toilet, and I have to be frank about this: a doubt crept in. I disgust myself, saying this. What does God have to do to get us strong? How many more mountains and clouds does He have to shove around before we get the idea? But there in that dark and huge area (the toilet is way over one end of what used to be the silk-worm nursery, and it looks like a barn, but my architect friends had pretty weird notions), the gold started to leak out of my head. I started to think – Hey, the mountains (by the way, I've been calling them mountains, but they were more like outcrops, the *mesa* kind of thing you find in Arizona, New Mexico, Utah – but outcrop sounds so dopey) – Hey, the mountains were always like that! They're very old and I'm reading into them! I'm projecting!

217

My faith was tarnishing.

I don't suppose I'd be here now, gladdening the angry and the lost and setting the world aright, if I hadn't had this habit, this very animal habit, of looking back into the bowl after I'd passed my motions. I reckon He was giving me my last chance. He uses every which way He can but only for so long. He of infinite patience doesn't waste His time. Oh yes, that was Last Chance Saloon, all right.

M. In the bowl. I don't know how things are with you, but over there they don't have water over it. Your soil sits on the china. It's primitive, I suppose, and less discreet. But it made it clearer. The letter M. It looked biologically impossible, given I hadn't shifted my position, but that's what my motions had made.

The letter M.

Michael . . . ?

I prayed. I got straight down on my knees and prayed. I really apologised, and I committed myself, like I'd seen on TV when I was switching channels and had always mocked. Then I stood up and flushed. It didn't quite flush properly. It left a mark.

M.

Michael.

I went straight out because I wanted to run and laugh. I bumped into the old dame. I couldn't not have bumped into her, because the easy way out passed her little house, while the other way'd got a barbed wire gate tied up by a piece of twine the goat shepherd would knot so tight it'd break your thumbs trying to loosen. Anyway, I bumped into her as usual and she said, after moaning about the hailstorm, something about her nephew. I didn't get on with her nephew. He'd buzz up like a fat fly on his little moped and start to fiddle with things in my garden, saying my friends had paid him to tend it. He was a drinker. He reeked. He'd look in at my window when I was working and do a tee-hee wave with his fingers. Big fat fly on the pane.

So she went on about her nephew having to come up with his chain-saw and do a bit of cleaning up. I didn't like the sound of that. I didn't like the sound of cleaning up. Even

the olive tree rustled at that. But I was in a fine mood. I felt
sorry for the old dame anyway. She was a widow. Her husband had blown his brains out in the middle of a meal. Don't
ask me why. It was just before I came, about a month or so
before. The nephew told me about the brains being all over
the walls, all that stuff. In the food, in the soup, and stuff.
Hey, and I'd come looking for calm and tranquillity! I mean,
I was paying my Swiss friends a whack for calm and tranquillity!

Madame, I said, do you know what has happened to me?

I had to repeat it, because up to now we had only shared
platitudes, and we were the only human beings for a long
while around.

She looked quizzical, even suspicious. I pointed at the
mountains, at the Twins, at the paps, at the two old dames
knitting – you get the idea. There were little shreds of cloud
clinging to them, against the wind, against all the odds.

God has spoken to me, I said. *Le bon Dieu.*

Oui monsieur, she said.

She said it as if I'd just told her it would probably rain
this evening or something.

When I look at the mountains, I continued, God says to
me, Michael. He doesn't say Michael, exactly, but he says
the first letter of my name. What is the first letter of my
name?

Oui, monsieur, she said.

Either she'd understood, or she was too perplexed to
answer.

M, I said.

I traced the letter, my finger following the peaks. It was
obvious. I could hear God mouthing it. The paps and the
twins and the two old dames knitting or whatever disappeared, it was so obvious. Against the sky was my name. It
was exactly how the monks used to do it, the hooded monks
a thousand years ago, bent over their illuminations. The huge
initial and then the rest of the word. I could see ICHAEL
like it had been written out by a monk. I really could. It
was like on the beach when you look up and see the little
plane writing a commercial in the sky, and slowly it blurs

and drifts away into cloud. Only this didn't blur and drift away into cloud.

You see? I said. I was really excited. You see it?

She turned round and beamed at me, though her eyes were full of what I can only call distress.

Oui, monsieur, she said, nodding. *Allez, allez*.

That's what she always said. It was a kind of sigh. We must go on, we must. *Allez, allez*. I pretty well danced down the track and up into the forest and then turned to look back at the farmhouse. She was still there, on the terrace, staring up at the mountains. A tiny blue dab staring (I'm sure of it) up at the mountains.

It may seem stupid, but I only thought of it then. I only thought of the obvious thing – the obvious Moses thing, the slap-across-the-cheek-it's-so-obvious thing – when I'd hit the densest part of the forest. I turned right about and dipped down into the valley and then jogged gently along the road until I struck the path. Not any old path, but the path that ascended. That ascended not any old place, but The Place. Well, two places, in fact.

M for Michael!

Up I went faster than a billy-goat. I could hear the billy-goats, actually – I could hear them tinkling their neck-bells down in the valley. I could hear the bell of the village ringing out the hour, too. Then I could hear nothing but the wind. The path was steep but easy. It was wide, it was generous. Hey, I thought, this isn't as difficult as I imagined.

Are you listening, all of you?

I repeat. This isn't as difficult as I imagined.

O fool.

The fact is, I'd been scared stupid at the thought of climbing up there. My Swiss friends had left a note about where to get bread and stuff and who to ring if the drains bubbled over and so forth, and at the end they'd mentioned some hikes, big hikes and medium hikes and little hikes. (If you can have little hikes.) Climbing the Twins came first, right at the top, number one. I'd not given it more than a second's consideration. I have very bad vertigo. From down at the bottom it looks like you have to be a tightrope walker or something even to stand up there. From down at the bottom it looks like there isn't enough room to put two feet down. It looks like you'd have to inch up the bluff and then just sort of cling there. Even thinking about it gave me the heebies.

But here I was, thinking this isn't as difficult as I imagined, clambering up that big path and scattering stones and breathing in the spacey scents of wild thyme and mint and stuff and saying out loud, Thank you. Thank you, God. May I prove equal.

Then I came to the fork. Well, I had to decide which one to climb first. I looked up and the thinner one towered to my left with a tiny buzzard or something circling the rock slowly just like in *McKenna's Gold* when they're digging for treasure and dying or whatever they are doing. I felt giddy for a moment, because it struck me that the buzzard wasn't really tiny, it was just that it was extremely high, and its extreme highness was equal with the peak. The fleshier twin, the second one out, the calmer one, towered to my right. It had no buzzard. It looked flatter at the top. It looked like there was a toehold at the top. I started out on the little path to my right. Almost straight away it got awkward. I had to duck down under the dwarf oaks and got facefuls of juniper and wild holly and other spiny stuff I never once learned the names of. I kept going. I slipped because not only was it ducking time but it was also slippery rock time. Soon I was using hands. I mean, I was *climbing*. Get this: I didn't feel vertigo. Through gaps in the brush I saw the valley and further mountains sweeping away from me. It was all hazy down there, hazy and blue like a Japanese print. Up here it was clear as a diamond. Loud and clear. Moses clear.

And there were these big white rocks, big white boulders toppling over it seemed, toppling over on to my weak little form as I grabbed them for a handhold. I stopped looking down, now. Hey, I wouldn't have fallen anywhere, not really far anyway – but I didn't want to risk it. I just kept on up. Up and up until there wasn't any more up to go.

Sky.

Sky and bare white rock and a bit of heather and sky again. Sky all around, higher than the buzzard way over there circling. I was higher than I'd ever been in my life. Symbolically speaking. I was so high I didn't feel dizzy, like I don't feel dizzy in jet aeroplanes.

OK. I don't want to labour this. You've heard it, you've probably read it a lot of times. You've no doubt, some of you, heard other people talk and write about it. What you don't know is what happened immediately after this moment.

The fact is, immediately after my high, after I'd spread my arms and hailed the Lord as loud as I could, feeling my voice and my spittle taken by the wind, I started to come down. Symbolically speaking. I started to look. I started to look at the plain below spread to what I reckoned must be the argent blade of sea. Like the argent blade of faith. I started to look at the other mountains behind me. I started to look at our valley, and at our incy-wincy bit of settlement in its tuck of green, like a tiny leaf had fallen. And everything was flat. I mean, it wasn't beautiful. It wasn't fundamentally beautiful. What I mean by this, is that it was the world and the world was lost. If I could've looked out on a virgin land long before the human race came along, I might have seen something beautiful.

But it wasn't virgin. It was dotted and smudged and here and there it glinted. And not with water. Even the vines, all ruby and gold, got at my throat. It was all so old and new, old and new at the same time. But it wasn't old enough and it wasn't new enough. Only I and my mountain were very old and very new. Hey, I've never mentioned this before, but I felt low up on my mountain. I'd gone right up high only to see everything lowered, everything flattened. That's the way it is, I suppose, when you go real high. You flatten everything else.

I started back down. And then this other thing: I couldn't stop thinking about fatso nephew. I circled fatso nephew like the buzzard was circling the other peak. This is ridiculous, I thought. But I couldn't get fatso nephew out of my head. He'd burrowed right in and was really sniggering away in there. He'd got to me. He'd got in the way of the Lord. I'll bet Moses never had a fatso nephew type clouding his peak moment. But I did, I have to admit it, I admit it right here and now.

I say I started back down, but this is the other thing I've never mentioned before and no one else has mentioned before because I've never told anyone before. I should have done. It was and is very instructive. The fact of the matter is, I couldn't find the way down. From up there, it was just big white rocks tumbling away on all sides with tufts of lavender and sprigs of heather and the tops of crooked little ilex and that was it. I started down one way, only to find myself staring into what has to be termed an abyss. I started down another way, only to end up on the wrong side of the mountain facing a thicket. I couldn't find the path. I couldn't remember which boulders I'd climbed up and over. They all looked the same, big and blinding white. I thought, Hey, I'm stuck up here on my mountain. I can't get myself down.

I got scared.

I got scared at that. The wind was frankly cold. I was hungry. I needed to relieve myself but the wind would have blown it all over and maybe back into my face. My vertigo was creeping back. The Lord had brought me up here to die. That was it. I'd die up here. Either I'd die and be taken up that way or he'd translate me intact, which I didn't think likely. I didn't feel that latter thing coming on, not at all. I didn't feel anything much except scared.

But I didn't die, I can assure you of that. I looked over at the other peak and felt the sweep of my name, my letter, my call, up and down and up and down back into the lost world the Lord had plucked me from. Then I looked to my left and saw it. Under the boughs of an ilex. The path: concealed by the ilex I never even remembered diving up out of. I clambered down over the boulders and slipped a little. I got scratched on the cheek. I relieved myself into a thicket. My ankles hurt. My hair was caught several times. I plucked a juniper berry and chewed it. Something big scuttled off in front of me. I guess I looked scary, by now. I met no one, which was probably just as well, in several ways.

Eventually I made it down. I looked up. My initial towered, toppling against the high, racing clouds. And then my name.

That was my supreme moment of transfiguration, looking back. Even the buzzard had vanished. I panted. I spread my arms, panting. I am equal to it. I was shouting. The mountains stayed themselves. My voice came back.

I didn't even need to climb the other one.

When I reached the house, still dancing, still laughing and saying yippee and so forth because I was so full of what I must do, how I must serve Him, that meany little whine I'd heard from up in the forest turned out to be the nephew. Who else?

He shouted at me. He had to shout at me. He didn't switch the thing off.

Your friends requested it! he yelled. The olive tree shuddered and fell, nearly striking me down. True, it was scraping the shutters and maybe growing too close to the house or something, but it was doing no harm, no real harm. (My friends were Swiss, which might have had something to do with it.) Anyway, I called him an ass. He called me a madman. He started waving his chain-saw about.

Then it stuttered and fell silent.

He looked at it. He looked at it for about ten seconds and then he unscrewed the fuel-cap. I shook my head, and wanted to laugh a glorious happy laugh. But I didn't, and neither did I tell him why it had stopped. He muttered madman again, under his breath.

Why do you say that? I asked. Because I could tell what he had said from the way his lips had puckered.

He looked at me keenly.

I know all about madmen, he said. Oncle Martin was mad.

He jerked his head at the Twins, then put a fat finger to his temple and imitated the report of a shotgun, grinning all the while. I nodded. I was in a fine mood. I fancy I know what he'd have gone on to tell me, given the chance. But I walked away, fast, over the wreckage of the olive tree into my house. I know how the Opposition works.

At least, I know now how the Opposition works. They've got the numbers, we've got the Will. They've got will too, but not The Will. Between will and The Will there's more than a little definite article and a shed pair of horns. At any rate, I didn't know much about anything in those days except I was being Put On Alert. I sat in the big oak chair by the fire and felt discomfited. When I feel discomfited I have a twitch. Some of you have seen it. It's not a big ugly spasm like my mother'd have when a boutique was running dry and the spasm making it worse because she'd put off the customers, but it's a delicate thing to do with the corner of the mouth having to touch the ear-lobe. Of course, no corner of any human mouth can actually touch an ear-lobe, unless there's something pretty anatomically remarkable about someone – but you get the idea. I would imagine that it was touching. At least, the corner of the mouth would imagine it was touching, because I'm not sure I'm fully responsible for this action, rather like I'm not fully responsible for everything Dirk and some of the others get up to, the ones who think Dirk has the edge on Michael, and are trying to tell Dirk he has the edge on Michael when Dirk knows inside he doesn't and never will have any kind of edge on Michael. Hey.

Hey, I didn't want to go on and on about this, this thing of mine. Stop it there.

The picture is just so, then: I'm sitting in the chair staring into the fire and twitching a little. I'm trying not to think about this Oncle Martin guy. I'm trying not to think about the fact that his brains ended up in the soup next door. I'm trying not to think about big fat nephew's fat finger pointing at the mountains and then at his temple. I'm particularly trying to forget the fact that his uncle's name begins – sorry, began – with M. What I am doing is enjoying the silence, while all these gibbering idiots are taking their axes to the door of it. Then the chain-saw starts up.

The corner of my mouth damn well nearly does it. I practically rick myself.

I leap up and go to the front window. He's out there, slicing the olive tree into neat parts. I find myself counting rings. He's that close. I count fifty-five. Fifty-five! The olive tree was exactly my age, give or take a missed ring or two. Some years it swelled real good, others it got nowhere. After all that effort, it went and got zilched in about five minutes. Hey, I thought, that's cruel. That's crazy.

Crazy!

Then it came to me.

It came to me watching the fat nephew bent over that trunk, slicing it up. Wood chips flying out like sparks from a welder. His whole fat body quivering. No wonder I've got a thing about fat people. No wonder I have this very strong notion (Dirk and Lilian and even Maurice agree with me) that fat people are the Horned One's sidekicks. Not every fat person, of course, but the odds are truly on that fat people, especially the ones that can actually help it, are working against us. My mother was fat. It's incredible, but I've not considered that truth until right now. Hey. She was, too. She'd sit there in the boutique (they all looked the same, my parents' boutiques, with tacky art nouveau china stuff and some moth-eaten dresses at the back and Peruvian jewellery clunking your forehead at every turn) – she'd sit there at the back with her mean twitch and she'd spread all over the chair like she was melting. When things were really bad she'd switch off the lights to save money which made things even worse, turnover-wise. There'd be this kind of dim mountain in the corner, snuffling. I was already packing my little suitcase with my little treasures, upstairs. Why? Because when it was time to up and go she'd try to save on space, and pick on my stuff first. I didn't get there fast enough once. I was out at school or something, I lost my woolly chipmunk.

Old Joey, he was called. One ear sucked real small. That's how I'd get to sleep. Sucking Old Joey's ear. Old Joey the chipmunk, who heard all my secrets. I must have bored Old Joey with my secrets. He'd get damp. His neck'd taste of salt. You just guess why Old Joey's neck'd taste of salt. Old Joey my woolly chipmunk.

Oh yes, she was a fatso, all right.

OK. Back to me at the window. As I said, that's when it came to me. That's when it came to me how, in actual reality, the world out there was crazy. Fundamentally crazy. Fat nephew slicing up the olive tree with his ridiculous machine was fundamentally crazy. The old dame, even, was crazy –

even crazier than Oncle Martin who, thinking about it, was probably sane. And then it spread out beyond the forests and the hills and the vines and all that stuff between our little place and civilisation, it spread out to include all the towns and suburbs and cities and parks and the ships on the oceans and the crazy jet aeroplanes floating about in the sky and everywhere you'd find people, basically. We had created a completely crazy thing. Count the rings. Two million, three? It had taken that long. It had taken that long to end up crazy. Look out of your window, Michael. What do you see? You see a fat man slicing up My Creation with a thing that gets your ear-lobes quivering and your fillings singing. No wonder you're ricking yourself with that mouth of yours. Hey, you've got yourself – no, we've got Ourselves one heck of a cleaning-up operation, Michael. Michael?

I was nodding. Of course I was. I was Receiving loud and clear. The question came to me, though, because I was still weak. Fundamentally weak.

OK, but where do I start?

The room was filling with smoke. I'd only just gotten to use the chimney and the wood was too green, or perhaps I'd laid it badly. My Swiss friends hadn't left me a stick. I hated the idea of buying it in, but I did. It was expensive. The fat nephew had brought it over in his brother's truck. Two tons of it. Of course, it was green. It hissed. It bubbled sap out the ends. I see that, now. So I was coughing. The wind was picking up and blowing down the chimney and the smoke couldn't compete. I opened the window. I had to. The chain-saw scream invaded. Fat nephew looked up. He must have heard the window opening. If I'd been the kind of picky person that oils, or the wood hadn't been green, or the wind hadn't blown as hard, none of this might have happened. But that's not quite right. He had arranged these things, He'd made pretty sure they were arranged so as I had no choice. That's the extent of His commitment to me.

Stop, I said.

Fat nephew looked quizzical. The chain-saw whined down. His back was stiff. He looked like a crouched beast of some indefinable but far epoch. I like that. Some indefinable but far epoch.

Stop that, I emphasised.

Fat nephew gave a sort of derisive chortle and spread his arms out.

Don't give me that, I said. (My French was suddenly flowering, I might say. I even had a bit of a local accent coming in.) Don't give me that crap. From now on, things are going to change, things are going to stop being crazy and slowly, very very slowly, things are going to start turning sensible. And things are going to start turning sensible right here. You should be very content. The world is starting to turn right with you. You are the first to turn right.

I couldn't help my twitch activating again at that point, because the idea of the world starting to turn right with this guy was frankly unpleasant – it was as if I sensed what I now feel I know about fatsos. But He never makes things too easy. The harder the wall, the stronger the fist, as Maurice puts it.

Hey, I yelled, are you listening to me?

The guy had backed off. He was walking backwards, as if I was the Lone Ranger and he was some schmuck of a rustler. OK, he was chortling, but the fact is that I had scared him. And let me tell you something. Some of you might find this hard to swallow, but that was the very first time in my life I had scared anybody. Least of all a big fat guy with a chainsaw. I am, let's face it, physically speaking, a shrimp. I have very thin wrists and varicose veins. My ears stick out. I'm what some people call scrawny. In a few years' time I'll get to be called sprightly. Now I'm just plain scrawny. But my fist is very hard. Our fists are very hard. Symbolically speaking, of course. The body is a shell. By itself it's zilch.

He'd gone. I'd banished him from my garden. OK, he'd wrecked my garden, but you can't have it all ways. I went outside and stood by the wreckage. The trunk was limbless. It was in three parts. Big branches sat in their own sawdust. The leaves, the nice blue-green silvery leaves, were limp. Their colour was gone. They lay in a heap of branches and were nothing. Hey, this is going to take some time to clear up, I thought. For a second I actually made to go over to the old dame and ask when fat nephew was next on the job. Can you believe it?

But I didn't, of course. He was banished. I heard the meany whine of his moped ringing over the valley and bouncing off the hills. I looked up. M for Michael was clear as a diamond against the blue sky, polished good and bright by the cold wind. I gave the mountains a thumbs-up. Then I set to, opening my arms and hugging the olive branches and the olive leaves and getting grazed again but not caring, not caring. I knew the old dame was watching from her terrace, pretending to read her newspaper. *Allez! Allez*! I knew the whole world was waiting, pretending to read its newspaper. *Allez! Allez*! By nightfall I had cleared the garden. I hadn't even stopped to eat. I turned to the old dame's house. There was some dubbed Australian soap or something, yacking and cackling away. Olive twigs crawled up my shirt. Olive leaves sat in my hair. If I leaned and stretched my arm out, I could have scraped the shutters. Instead I just stood there, feeling the fifty-five rings it had taken to grow me, knowing how nothing could chop me down, not ever, not ever because my name was up there, tooled in the gold light of the close of the first day the world turned right.

Patricia Beer

AT PÈRE LACHAISE

October evening. Leaves swoop down like owls
And stun themselves upon the paving-stones.
A skip stands ready for a year of plague.
Patches of fake fur begin to sprout
Upon the clothes of mourning visitors.

Here death smells pleasant, dry like wine not drought.
This cemetery is not a killing field.
It sanctions those who like to make love here
Rather than at home. Its dead are safe.
Their tombs can tumble down above their heads,
Lie there and do no harm. It passes time
Pampering its trees and hierarchy of beasts:
A cat composed of mice and birds and rain
Turns his head, as scornful as a lighthouse.

When is darkness deemed to fall in France,
When do its cemeteries close down for sleep?
Deep in the city, bells are suggesting nightfall
And suddenly beyond a bend in the path
A whistle blows, less loud and much more peevish
Than the Last Trump. A man with a cross face
Comes round the corner, shooing us along.
Husband takes the speckled hand of wife
And they walk back into the world together
Happier than they were, perhaps, in spring.

CHURCH OF THE HOLY FAMILY

A hot dry afternoon in Spain.
We walk through space that will become a large cool
   church,
A group of architects and their partners
One of whom mutters that it is ridiculous,
Seeing that religion is on the way out.

There is much talk of what will be where and when,
Less of what is already built:
Rooms full of plans and schemes and models,
Stairs which visitors climb
To look solemnly out of holes
Getting a bird's-eye view
Of a man's dream, rising.
There is nobody working on the site
Who could possibly live to smell the incense.

Tomorrow we go home, back to work,
Back to back in the art galleries of Britain.
And in my case back to the cathedral
That I have walked through on and off
For the best part of one of its five centuries
Sheltered from rain and traffic and nonconformists.

My forefathers, soaked to the skin,
Came into market from the sea and the fields
Crossing the transept from south to north
Not for a few seconds like passing under a thick tree –
There was no roof yet –
But because it was the nearest way
To Fish Lane and Colewort Row,

Hallooing to their friends, clanging away above them,
Gossiping about progress
And what their sons and grandsons
Might come to know at last

When air turned into incense
And there was a new king
And perhaps peace and better weather.

William Trevor

A DAY

IN THE NIGHT Mrs Lethwes wakes from time to time, turns and murmurs in her blue-quilted twin bed, is aware of fleeting thoughts and fragments of memory that dissipate swiftly. Within her stomach, food recently consumed is uneasily digested. Briefly, she suffers a moment of cramp.

Mrs Lethwes dreams: a child again, she remains in the car while her brother, Charlie, visits the Indian family who run the supermarket. Kittens creep from beneath inverted flowerpots in the Bunches' backyard, and she is there, in the yard too, looking for Charlie because he is visiting the Bunches now. 'You mustn't go bothering the Bunches,' their mother upbraids him. 'People are busy.' There are rivers to cross, and the streets aren't there any more; there is a seashore, and tents.

In her garden, while Mrs Lethwes still sleeps, the scent of night stock fades with the cool of night. Dew forms on roses and geraniums, on the petals of the cosmos and the yellow spikes of broom. Slugs creep towards lettuce plants, avoiding a line of virulent bait; a silent cat, far outside its own domain, waits for the emergence of the rockery mice.

It is July. Dawn comes early, casting a pale twilight on the brick of the house, on the Virginia creeper that covers half a wall, setting off white-painted window-frames and decorative wrought-iron. This house and garden, in a tranquil wooded neighbourhood, constitute one part of the achievement of Mrs Lethwes's husband, are a symbol of professional advancement conducted over twenty years, which happens also to be the length of this marriage.

Abruptly, Mrs Lethwes is fully awake and knows her night's sleep is over. Hunched beneath the bedclothes in the other bed, her husband does not stir when she rises and crosses the room they share to the window. Drawing aside the edge of a curtain, she glances down into the early-morning garden and almost at once drops the curtain back into place. In bed again, she lies on her side, facing her husband because, being fond of him, she likes to watch him sleeping. She feels blurred and headachy, as she always does at this time, the worst moment of her day, Mrs Lethwes considers.

Is Elspeth awake too? She wonders that. Does Elspeth, in her city precinct, share the same pale shade of dawn? Is there, as well, the orange glow of a street lamp and now, beginning in the distance somewhere, the soft swish of a milk dray, a car door banging, a church bell chiming five? Mrs Lethwes doesn't know where Elspeth lives precisely, or in any way what she looks like, but imagines short black hair and elfin features, a small, thin body, fragile fingers. An hour and three-quarters later – still conducting this morning ritual – she hears bath water running; and later still there is music. Vivaldi, Mrs Lethwes thinks.

Her husband wakes. His eyes remember, becoming troubled, and then the trouble lifts from them when he notices, without surprise, that she's not asleep. In another of her dreams during the night that has passed he carried her, and his voice spoke softly, soothing her. Or was it quite a dream, or only something like one? She tries to smile; she says she's sorry, knowing now.

At ten, when the cleaning woman comes, Mrs Lethwes goes out to shop. She parks her small white Peugeot in the Waitrose car park, and in a leisurely manner gathers vegetables and fruit, and tins and jars, pork chops for this evening, vermouth and Gordon's gin, Edam, and Normandy butter because she has noticed the butter is getting low, Comfort and the cereal her husband favours, the one called Common Sense. Afterwards, with everything in the boot, she makes her way to the Trompe l'Oeil for coffee. Her make-up is in place, her hair drawn up, the way she has taken to wearing it lately. She smiles at people she knows by sight, the waitress and other women who are having coffee, at the cashier when she pays her bill. There is some conversation, about the weather.

In her garden, later, the sound of the Hoover reaches her from the open windows of the house as the cleaning woman, Marietta, moves from room to room. The day is warm, Mrs Lethwes's legs are bare, her blue dress light on her body, her Italian sandals comfortable yet elegant. Marietta claims to be Italian also, having had an Italian mother, but her voice and manner are Cockney and Mrs Lethwes doubts that she has ever been in Italy, even though she regularly gives the impression that she knows Venice well.

Mrs Lethwes likes to be occupied when Marietta comes. When it's fine she finds something to do in the garden, and when the weather doesn't permit that she lingers for longer in the Trompe l'Oeil and there's the pretence of letter-writing or tidying drawers. She likes to keep a closed door between herself and Marietta, to avoid as best she can the latest about Marietta's daughter Ange, and Liam, whom Ange has been contemplating marriage with for almost five years, and the latest about the people in the house next door, who keep Alsatians.

In the garden Mrs Lethwes weeds a flowerbed, wishing that Marietta didn't have to come to the house three times a week, but knowing that of course she must. She hopes the little heart-leafed things she's clearing from among the delphiniums are not the germination of seeds that Mr Yatt has sown, a misfortune that occurred last year with his Welsh poppies. Unlike Marietta, Mr Yatt is dour and rarely speaks, but he has a way of slowly raising his head and staring, which Mrs Lethwes finds disconcerting. When he's in the garden – Mondays only, all day – she keeps out of it herself.

Not Vivaldi now, perhaps a Telemann minuet, run Mrs Lethwes's thoughts in her garden. Once, curious about the music a flautist plays, she read the information that accompanied half a dozen compact discs in a music shop. She didn't buy the discs but, curious again, she borrowed some from the music section of the library and played them all one morning. Thirty-six, or just a little younger, she sees Elspeth as; unmarried of course and longing to bear the child of the man she loves: Mrs Lethwes is certain of that, since she has experienced this same longing herself. In the flat she imagines, there's a smell of freshly made coffee. The fragile fingers cease their movement. The instrument is laid aside, the coffee poured.

It was in France, in the Hôtel St-Georges during their September holiday seven years ago, that Mrs Lethwes found out about her husband's other woman. There was a letter, round feminine handwriting on an air-mail envelope, an English stamp: she knew at once. The letter had been placed in someone else's key-box by mistake, and was later handed to her with a palaver of apologies when her husband was swimming in the Mediterranean. 'Ah, *merci*,' she thanked the smooth-haired girl receptionist and said the error didn't matter in the very least. She knew at once: the instinct of a barren wife, she afterwards called it to herself. So this was why he made a point of being down before her every morning, why he had always done so during their September holiday in France; she'd never wondered about it before. On the terrace she examined the postmark. It was indecipherable, but again the handwriting told a lot, and only a woman with whom a man had an association would write to him on holiday. From the letter itself, which she read and then destroyed, she learnt all there was otherwise to know.

There are too many of the heart-leafed plants, and when she looks in other areas of the border and in other beds she finds they're not in evidence there. Clearly, it's the tragedy of the Welsh poppies all over again. Mrs Lethwes begins to put back what she has taken out, knowing as she does so that this isn't going to work.

' "Silly girl," I said, straight to her face. "Silly girl, Ange, no way you're not." '

Marietta has established herself at the kitchen table, her shapeless bulk straining the seams of a pink overall, her feet temporarily removed from the carpet slippers she brings with her because they're comfortable to work in.

'No, not for me, thanks,' Mrs Lethwes says, which is what she always says when she is offered instant coffee at midday. Real coffee doesn't agree with Marietta, never has. Toxic in Marietta's view.

'All she give's a giggle. That's Ange all over, that. Always has been.'

This woman has watched Ange's puppy fat go, has seen her through childhood illnesses. And Bernardo, too. This woman could have had a dozen children, borne them and nursed them, loved them and been loved herself. 'Well, I drew a halt at two, dear. Drew the line, know what I mean? He said have another go, but I couldn't agree.'

Five goes, Mrs Lethwes has had herself: five failures, in bed for every day the third and fourth time, told she mustn't try again, but she did. The same age she was then as she imagines her husband's other woman to be: thirty-six when she finally accepted she was a childless wife.

'Decent a bloke as ever walked a street is little Liam, but Ange don't see it. One day she'll look up and he'll be gone and away. Talking to a wall you are.'

'Is Ange in love, though?'

'Call it how you like, dear. Mention it to Ange and all she give's a giggle. Well, Liam's small. A little fellow, but then where's the harm in small?'

Washing traces of soil from her hands at the sink, Mrs Lethwes says there is no harm in a person being small. Hardly five foot, she has many times heard Liam is. But strong as a horse.

'I said it to her straight, dear. Wait for some bruiser and you'll build your life on regrets. No good to no one, regrets.'

'No good at all.'

Of course was what she'd thought on the terrace of the Hôtel St-Georges: a childless marriage was a disappointment for any man. She'd failed him, although naturally it had never been said: he wasn't in the least like that. But she had failed and had compounded her failure by turning away from talk of adoption. She had no feeling for the idea; she wasn't the kind to take on other people's kids. Their own particular children were the children she wanted, an expression of their love, an expression of their marriage: more and more, she'd got that into her head. When the letter arrived at the Hôtel St-Georges she'd been reconciled for years to her barren state: they lived with it, or so she thought. The letter changed everything. The letter frightened her; she should have known.

'We need the window-cleaners one of them days,' Marietta says, dipping a biscuit into her coffee. 'Shocking, the upstairs panes is.'

'I'll ring them.'

'Didn't mind me mentioning it, dear? Only with the build-up it works out twice the price. No saving really.'

'Actually I forget. I wasn't trying to – '

'Best done regular I always say.'

'I'll ring them this afternoon.'

Mrs Lethwes said nothing in the Hôtel St-Georges and she hasn't since. He doesn't know she knows; she hopes that nothing ever shows. She sat for an hour on the terrace of the hotel, working it out. Say something, she thought, and as soon as she does it'll be in the open. The next thing is he'll be putting it gently to her that nothing is as it should be. Gently because he always has been gentle, especially about her barren state; sorry for her, dutiful in their plight, tied to her. He'd have had an Eastern child, any little slit-eyed thing, but when she hadn't been able to see it he'd been good about that too.

'Sets the place off when the windows is done, I always say.'

'Yes, of course.'

He came back from his swim, and the letter from a woman who played an instrument in an orchestra was already torn into little pieces and in a waste-bin in the car park, the most distant one she could find. 'Awfully good, this,' she said when he came and sat beside her. *The Way We Live Now* was the book she laid aside. He said he had read it at school.

'I'll do the window-sills when they've been. Shocking with flies, July is. Filthy really.'

'I'll see if I can get them next week.'

There hadn't been an address, just a date: September 4th. No need for an address because of course he knew it, and from the letter's tone he had for ages. She wondered what that meant and couldn't think of a time when a change had begun in his manner towards her. There hadn't been one; and in other ways, too, he was as he always had been: unhurried in his movements and his speech, his square healthy features the same terracotta shade, the grey in his hair in no way diminishing his physical attractiveness. It was hardly surprising that someone else found him attractive too. Driving up through France, and back again in England, she became used to pretending in his company that the person called Elspeth did not exist, while endlessly conjecturing when she was alone.

'I'll do the stairs down,' Marietta says, 'and then I'll scoot, dear.'

'Yes, you run along whenever you're ready.'

'I'll put in the extra Friday, dear. Three-quarters of an hour I owe all told.'

'Oh, please don't worry –'

'Fair's fair, dear. Only I'd like to catch the twenty past today, with Bernardo anxious for his dinner.'

'Yes, of course you must.'

The house is silent when Marietta has left, and Mrs Lethwes feels free again. The day is hers now, until the evening. She can go from room to room in stockinged feet, and let the telephone ring unanswered. She can watch, if the mood takes her, some old black and white film on the television, an English one, for she likes those best, pretty girls' voices from the nineteen forties, Michael Wilding young again, Ann Todd.

She doesn't have much lunch. She never does during the week: a bit of cheese on the Ritz biscuits she has a weakness for, gin and dry Martini twice. In her spacious sitting-room Mrs Lethwes slips her shoes off and stretches out on one of the room's two sofas. Then the first sharp tang of the Martini causes her, for a moment, to close her eyes with pleasure.

Silver-framed, a reminder of her wedding day stands on a round inlaid surface among other photographs nearby. August 26th 1974: the date floats through her midday thoughts. 'I *know* this'll work out,' her mother – given to speaking openly – had remarked the evening before, when she met for the first time the parents of her daughter's fiancé. The remark had caused a silence, then someone laughed.

She reaches for a Ritz. The soft brown hair that's hardly visible beneath the bridal veil is blonded now and longer than it was, which is why she wears it gathered up, suitable in middle age. She was pretty then and is handsome now; still loose-limbed, she has put on only a little weight. Her teeth are still white and sound; only her light-blue eyes, once brilliantly clear, are blurred, like eyes caught out of focus. Afterwards her mother's remark on the night before the wedding became a joke, because of course the marriage had worked out. A devoted couple; a perfect marriage, people said – and still say perhaps – except for the pity of there being no children. It's most unlikely, Mrs Lethwes believes, that anyone much knows about his other woman. He wouldn't want that; he wouldn't want his wife humiliated, that never was his style.

Mrs Lethwes, who smokes one cigarette a day, smokes it now as she lies on the sofa, not yet pouring her second drink. On later September holidays there had been no letters, of that she was certain. Some alarm had been raised by the one that didn't find its intended destination: dreadful, he would have considered it, a liaison discovered by chance, and would have felt afraid. 'Please understand. I'm awfully sorry,' he would have said, and Elspeth would naturally have honoured his wishes, even though writing to him when he was away was precious.

'No more. That's all.' On her feet again to pour her second drink, Mrs Lethwes firmly makes this resolution, speaking aloud since there is no one to be surprised by that. But a little later she finds herself rooting beneath underclothes in a bedroom drawer, and finding there another bottle of Gordon's and pouring some and adding water from a bathroom tap. The bottle is returned, the fresh drink carried downstairs, the Ritz packet put away, the glass she drank her two cock-tails from washed and dried and returned to where the glasses are kept. Opaque, blue to match the bathroom paint, the container she drinks from now is a toothbrush beaker, and holds more than the sedate cocktail glass, three times as much almost. The taste is different, the plastic beaker feels different in her grasp, not stemmed and cool as the glass was, warmer on her lips. The morning that has passed seems far away as the afternoon advances, as the afternoon con-nects with the afternoon of yesterday and of the day before, a repetition that must have a beginning somewhere but now is lost.

He is with her now. They are together in the flat she shares with no one, being an independent girl. At three o'clock that is Mrs Lethwes's thought. Excuses are not difficult; in his position in the office he would not even have to make them. Lunch with the kind of business people he often refers to, lunch in the Milano or the Petit Escargot, and then a taxi to the flat that is a second home. 'Surprise!' he says on the doorstep intercom, and takes his jacket off while she makes tea. 'I'll not be back this afternoon,' is all he has said on the phone to his bespectacled and devoted secretary.

They sit by the french windows that open on to a small balcony and are open now. It is a favourite place in summer, geraniums blooming in the balcony's two ornamental con-tainers, the passers-by on the street below viewed through the metal scrolls that decorate the balustrade, the drawn-back curtains undisturbed by breezes. The tea cups are a shade of pink. The talk is about the orchestra, where it is going next, how long she'll be away, the dates precisely given because that's important. In winter the imagined scene is similar, except that they sit by the gas fire beneath the repro-duction of *Field of Poppies*, the curtains drawn because it's darkening outside even as early as this. In winter there's Mahler on the CD player, instead of the passers-by to watch.

Why couldn't it be? Mrs Lethwes wonders at ten past five when a film featuring George Formby comes to an end. Why couldn't it be that he would come back this evening and confess there has been a miscalculation? 'She is to have a child': why shouldn't it be that he might say simply that? And how could Elspeth, busy with her orchestra, travelling to Cleveland and Chicago and San Francisco, to Rome and Seville and Nice and Berlin, possibly be a mother? And yet, of course, Elspeth would want his child, women do when they're in love.

Vividly, Mrs Lethwes sees this child, a tiny girl on a rug in the garden, a sunshade propped up, Mr Yatt bent among the dwarf sweetpeas. And Marietta saying in the kitchen, 'My, my, there's looks for you!' The child is his, Mrs Lethwes reflects, pouring again; at least what has happened is halfway there to what might have been if the child was hers also. Beggars can't be choosers.

At fifteen minutes past five, fear sets in, the same fear there was on the terrace of the Hôtel St-Georges when the letter was still between her fingers. He will go from her; it is pity that keeps him with a barren woman; he will find the courage, and with it will come the hardness of heart that is not naturally his. Then he will go.

Once, not long ago – or maybe it was a year or so ago, hard to be accurate now – she said on an impulse that she had been wrong to resist the adoption of an unwanted child, wrong to say a child for them must only be his and hers. In response he shook his head: adoption would not be easy now, he said, in their middle age, and that was that. Some other day, on the television, there was a woman who took an infant from a pram, and she felt sympathy for that woman then, though no one else did. Whenever she saw a baby in a pram she thought of the woman taking it, and at other times she thought of that girl who walked away with the baby she was meant to be looking after, and the woman who took one from a hospital ward. When she told him she felt sympathy he put his arms around her and wiped away her tears. This afternoon, the fear lasts for half an hour; then, at a quarter to six, it is so much nonsense. Never in a thousand years would he develop that hardness of heart.

'I have to go now,' he says in his friend's flat. They cease their observation of the passers-by below. Again they embrace and then he goes. The touch of her lips goes with him, her regretful smile, her fragile fingers where for so long that afternoon they rested in his hand. He drives through traffic, perfectly knowing the way, not having to think. And in the flat she plays her music, and finds in it a consolation. It is his due to have his other woman: on the hotel terrace she decided that. In the hour she sat there with the letter not yet destroyed everything fell into place. She knew she must never say she had discovered what she had. She knew she didn't want him ever not to be there.

Lovers quarrel. Love affairs end. What life is it for Elspeth, scraps from a marriage he won't let go of? Why shouldn't she tire of waiting? 'No,' he says when Elspeth cheats, allowing her pregnancy to occur in order to force his hand. Still he says he can't, and all there is is a mess where once there was romance. He turns to his discarded wife and there between them is his confession. 'She travels, you see. She has to travel, she won't give up her music.' How quickly should there be forgiveness? Should there be some pretence of anger? Should there be tears? His friend set a trap for him, his voice goes on, a tender trap, as in the song: that is where his weakness has landed him. His voice apologises and asks for understanding and for mercy. His other woman has played her part although she never knew it; without his other woman there could not be a happy ending.

She sets the table for their dinner, the tweed mats, the cutlery, the pepper mill, the German mustard, glasses for wine because he deserves a little wine after his day, Châteauneuf-du-Pape. The bottle's on the table, opened earlier because she knows to do that from experience: it's difficult later on to open wine with all the rush of cooking. And the wine should breathe: years ago he taught her that.

In the kitchen she begins to cut the fat off the pork chops she bought that morning, a long time ago it seems now. Marietta's recipe she's intending to do: pork chops in tomato sauce, onions and peppers. On the mottled Formica working surface the blue tooth-beaker is almost full again, reached out for often. The meat slides about although, in actual fact, it doesn't move. It is necessary to be careful with the knife: her little finger is wrapped in a Band-aid from a week ago. On the radio Humphrey Lyttelton asks his teams to announce the Late Arrivals at the Undertakers' Ball.

'Of course,' Mrs Lethwes says aloud. 'Of course, we'll offer it a home.'

At five to seven, acting instinctively as she does every evening at about this time, Mrs Lethwes washes the blue plastic beaker and replaces it in the bathroom. Twice, before she hears the car wheels on the tarmac, she raises the gin bottle directly to her lips, then pours herself, conventionally, a cocktail of Gordon's and Martini. She knows it will happen tonight. She knows he will enter with a worry in his features and stand by the door, not coming forward for a moment, that then he'll pour himself a drink, too, and sit down slowly and begin to tell her. 'I'm sorry,' is probably how he'll put it, and she'll stop him, telling him she can guess. And after he has spoken for twenty minutes, covering all the ground that has been lost, she'll say, of course: 'The child must come here.'

The noisy up-and-over garage door falls into place. In a hurry Mrs Lethwes raises the green bottle to her lips because suddenly she feels the need of it. She does so again before there is the darkness that sometimes comes, arriving suddenly today just as she is whispering to herself that tomorrow, all day long, she'll not take anything at all and thinking also that, for tonight, the open wine will be enough and if it isn't there's always more that can be broached. For, after all, tonight is a time for celebration. A schoolgirl on a summer's day, just like the one that has passed, occupies the upper room where only visitors sleep. She comes downstairs and chatters on, about her friends, her teachers, a worry she has, not understanding a poem, and together at the kitchen table they read it through. Oh, I do love you, Mrs Lethwes thinks while there is imagery and words rhyme.

On the Formica worktop in the kitchen the meat is where

Mrs Lethwes left it, the fat partly cut away, the knife still separating it from one of the chops. The potatoes she scraped earlier in the day are in a saucepan of cold water, the peas she shelled in another. Often, in the evenings, it is like that in the kitchen when her husband returns to their house. He is gentle when he carries her, as he always is.

Philip Hensher

A GEOGRAPHER

BRUNO WAS A nice boy of thirty-seven. He had kept his
looks, and his size in trousers. He had learnt English to a
certain firm expertise, of which he was proud. He had lost
his hair, which he considered unimportant. He had gained a
moustache, about which sometimes he thought one thing,
and sometimes another. These were the different opinions he
held about the principal changes in his state since the time
when he was young.

For five years he had lived in a flat in Golders Green on
his own, and worked for five days a week in the London
office of a large Italian bank. His mother still lived in
Mantua, and was fond of her respectable unmarried banker
son as of her respectable dead banker husband. Bruno sent
her one thousand pounds every month, of which he knew
she saved one half, and did not mind; and every day, in the
early evening, he telephoned her.

He had decorated his flat in a style which was briefly
fashionable, and which he considered looked attractive in
photographs. His cupboards were of polished steel, and his
bookshelves were of polished steel, and his lights were spot-
lights from a stage, and his curtains were not curtains, but
metal blinds, and black. His occasional visitors found it
impressive, but not comfortable. He smiled if they expressed
this view, since he knew with perfect security that not comfort, but ease, was his aim. He knew this. After five years of
living in the flat he owned, he only sometimes thought he
had allowed himself, five years before, to be persuaded of
the merits of this style by people he would never meet. He

only sometimes wondered if he altogether cared for it, and very occasionally he knew he did not. Bruno was fondest of his stiff-jointed dog, from whom he had only once been separated, when he had first come to England and the dog had stayed in grim, institutional quarantine, with only occasional visits. In black moments he wondered if he could bring himself to buy another dog when Pippo died.

Once a week, generally on Friday nights, Bruno allowed himself to put on a black leather jacket and go to Hampstead heath. There he permitted strangers to perform sexual acts upon him, and, more rarely, he performed sexual acts upon them. His looks, enhanced by his small, distinguished blond moustache, seemed to make him a good deal in demand among the other men who frequented Hampstead heath on Friday night. He spent a good deal of time during these encounters calculating the quickest way to escape from the police or from hooligans seeking victims to injure. He knew that men were sometimes arrested, or assaulted by other men.

These occurrences he knew about by repute, but nothing remotely dangerous had ever happened to him, nor did it ever. He did not calculate risk; he merely saw that it was real. Because of this, he did not seem entirely at ease to his temporary sexual partners, nor was he. He was on the heath for pleasure, and not for ease. They occasionally told him, his temporary sexual partners, that he should relax, or asked him to remove more of his clothing than he judged wise. Bruno smiled, and did not act as they suggested.

Bruno did not feel guilty or worried about his participation in open-air orgies each Friday; nor, if a colleague or acquaintance asked him to dinner on Friday night, did he feel he would prefer to be on the heath. It was something he often and regularly did, but it could not be considered a habit. It gave him pleasure of simple and several kinds; he enjoyed the lack of emotional complication in the sexual gratification, but also the beauty of the heath and, occasionally, an encounter which would begin wordlessly and would develop into an intimate, romantic conversation between strangers, looking at London.

When Bruno came back to his flat, his dog Pippo did not seem to look at him in a reproaching, but in a fond way. Bruno rarely thought what was the case, that he had never slept with a man. Nor, if this thought had come to him, would he have thought anything of it.

One Sunday morning, towards the end of May, Bruno was emptying the pockets of a pair of trousers in preparation for sending them to the laundry, when he found a note, in handwriting not his own. The note said Simon, and a telephone number. It was an odd scrap of paper, and next to his name, the boy who had written it had, out of habit, written a cross to signify a kiss. He put it on one side while he unravelled his shirts and pulled out his socks from their pulled-off balls and did not think about it.

In itself this was not unusual, this note. From time to time boys on Hampstead heath with whom he had engaged in conversation pressed their telephone numbers on him. He always accepted their telephone numbers, and out of civility gave them a false telephone number, as he had already given them a false name, in return. Once a man at a colleague's dinner party had suggested, when the colleague and his wife were out of the room, that they exchange telephone numbers. Bruno had done so, as if it were a normal thing to do. To Bruno's relief the man had never telephoned him. Perhaps the man, he thought later, had noticed his nervousness. He had been relieved, not because he had not found the man attractive, but because he had.

What was unusual – what caused a tiny rippling eruption in his thoughts, like a bubble bursting in viscid black water – was that he had no memory of this card, or of a boy named Simon, or of the note being given to him.

Bruno went to work the next day. His desk was as tidy as his flat, because he never left work hanging over from day to day. He arrived at eight thirty, and worked until his lunchtime sandwich which he ate, reading a newspaper, in a bar near his office. He returned and worked until he had finished what he had to do. His secretary went at five, and he left at half past six. All the time he generated work for those around him and beneath him, and he did not think about what he was doing. Once, after lunch, he took out the piece of paper from his pocket and began to dial the telephone number. He stopped one digit from the end, and replaced the receiver. He worked hard; he knew people who worked harder.

The next day he did call the number. It was not easy for him to see why he should. If it was a man from the heath, there were certainly other men who would be prepared to have sex with him on the heath. The fact that he had no recollection of the man suggested that the man was not worth recalling. He had almost decided definitely not to call the number when he found that he was pressing the digits of the telephone number in sequence.

'Are you a friend of his?' the voice at the end of the telephone said, bluntly.

'Yes,' Bruno said. He was not easily daunted on the telephone.

'He's in hospital.'

'Oh, I'm sorry.'

'Nothing serious. He's had a bit of a bashing. I'm sure he'd welcome a visit, though. He isn't getting many visitors. His mother's going to come in a day or two, but he's a bit low, to tell you the truth. What did you say your name was?'

'Bruno,' Bruno said.

He permitted the man to tell him the name of the hospital and the ward number where Simon, whose name he knew from a note from a pocket, was recovering, and even asked the man to slow his speech, as if he were writing the information down. He felt a little twinge of pity at the boy with so few friends, lying in hospital waiting for a man neither he nor his flatmate knew. When he put the telephone down, he held the information in his head for a moment, and then, surprising himself, he did write it down.

The man against the white sheets was bruised around his mouth and chin. On his forehead was a large flushed patch, like the ambivalent cursing kiss of a giantess in a fairy-tale. It was impossible for Bruno to say if he recognised the man or not. His face was considerably damaged and misshapen. The man looked up. Only in his eyes was there an unbruised softness. Simon – if it was Simon – did not recognise Bruno, since he lowered his head and went on reading his book. When Bruno drew up the chair, he laid the book down on the bed, face down, and looked up with a sigh.

'I'm not religious,' Simon said flatly.

'Nor am I,' Bruno said, surprised.

'You're wasting your time.'

'What do you mean?'

Simon sighed heavily.

'I mean, I don't believe in God, and I'm not likely to, and I don't care how long it takes you to get round to it, I'm not going to listen. So you might as well go away now and talk to someone who doesn't mind it.'

'But I came to see you,' Bruno said. He didn't know what else to say, and it now struck him that he was in an embarrassing situation. 'I found your name in my pocket. I thought you must have put it there.'

Simon looked at him properly. He reached to the small light cupboard to his side, and took a grape from a plundered bunch. He sucked the grape, spat out the pips on the floor.

'I don't care,' he said, referring to the grape pips. 'I'm that sort of person. I thought you were a vicar or something. We get that a lot, here. There was a rabbi yesterday, and he went away when I said I wasn't Jewish, but you can't say anything to the vicars to make them go away. Some of them wear their clothes, but most of them dress like you, in a suit and that. That's what they say in the ward.'

'How long have you been here?' Bruno said.

'Since Saturday,' Simon said, apparently surprised. He seemed to think Bruno must have known that he was in hospital. 'I'm glad you came, though. No one else has come. They all say they hate hospitals. I remember you now. Your moustache I remember. What did you say your name was?'

Bruno thought of answering the question, but then he decided to tell Simon what his name was. 'Bruno,' he said.

'Bruno,' Simon said. 'My mum's coming to see me, on Friday.'

'I'm glad,' Bruno said. 'I came because your flatmate said I should.'

'He's not my flatmate,' Simon said. 'I haven't got a flatmate, actually. I used to, but he went. He was going to be here for a week, the boy you spoke to, but that was two weeks ago and he's still there. He says he's going to go, but I don't think he will.'

'Do you want him to go?'

'Yes,' Simon said. 'Well, maybe. He's being quite useful, sorting things out, and that. You know why I thought you were a vicar? I've just realised, it's because you didn't come with anything.'

'What should I have come with?'

'Well, nothing, really. What I mean is, when people come and visit you in hospital, they usually bring something for you. Like a bunch of grapes or something. Or a magazine. That's what I'd really like. There's a trolley here that sells magazines and newspapers, but by the time it gets up here there's only *Titbits* left. It's only vicars that turn up in a suit and not bringing you anything. And you, which is nice.' He grinned, suddenly, inconsequentially. They looked at each other for a long pleasant time.

'Would you like me to bring you something?' Bruno said.

'Well, only if you were going to come back anyway. The thing is, my mum was going to come tomorrow, but now she isn't coming until Friday. It would be nice if you could fetch me a magazine to read.'

'What do you like to read?'

'*Vogue*,' Simon said, surprised, as if there were only one magazine to read. 'I don't know how long I'm going to be here, or I'd ask you to bring a book. They think when they did me over, they fractured my skull, what they call a hairline fracture, and they're just keeping me to see if I die or anything.'

'They think you might die?'

'No, of course they don't,' Simon said. 'They just think they'd better keep me here. It's really boring, though. It's nice of you to come. What did you say your name was?'

'Bruno,' Bruno said.

'Oh yes.'

Bruno looked at the bruised boy in bed, and suddenly he felt a wave of sex come over him. He liked the boy's white hospital gown, against which his flesh was furred and dark, when the men in the white beds around him wore pyjamas which they owned. He liked even that he did not understand what had happened to him, since he did not know what the boy meant when he said *they did me over*, and he did not understand what his flatmate had meant by *a bit of a bashing*, and, shy, did not feel he could ask for an explanation. The boy looked back with his special gaze, tender.

'Can I have your phone number?' he said.

'Yes,' Bruno said, and took a piece of paper, and on it he wrote his name, and he wrote his telephone number. It occurred to him to lie, and he did not.

'In case I think of anything else you could bring,' Simon said. 'Come back tomorrow.'

'With *Vogue*.'

When Bruno smiled, it was as if he could see himself smiling with all the charm and pleasure he had never been able to see in himself in photographs. He went directly home in the underground train. He got on the first train he saw, without noting its direction. He sat and looked at the progress of black thick wires in tunnels as the train progressed, and the embarkations and departures of the people. His mind was blank, or it was not blank at all, and he noted the pleasure he felt, with pleasure. It was only after some time which he could not account for that he saw the station the train was drawing into. He had to get off the train and reverse his direction, to take it again.

When he reached his home it was too late to telephone his mother in Mantua, and, rebellious, he did not. He invariably telephoned her at half past seven. She never complained if he did not, but he always regretted it subsequently. He knew this; still he did not telephone. Instead he sat with his stiff dog on his lap and played foolish good games with Pippo, and when Pippo wished to, he put a lead round his neck, and together they went for an eager tottering walk. How good Pippo was and how easy. Like Simon.

'Hello,' Bruno said, on the telephone.

'This is Mauro,' the voice said.

Bruno knew no one called Mauro in Mantua who would

announce themselves in English, and he waited for confirmation from the voice.

'I spoke to you the other day,' Mauro went on.

'Oh yes,' Bruno said. It still meant nothing.

'I'm Simon's flatmate.'

Bruno recognised the voice, although Simon had said he had no flatmate. 'How did you know my telephone number?'

'Simon gave it to me. He just wanted to know if you were going to see him tomorrow.'

'Don't telephone me at home, please,' Bruno said. 'I don't know you.'

'Are you Italian?' Mauro said. '*Sei italiano?*'

'Don't telephone me, please,' Bruno said, and put the telephone down. Terror came upon him. The pleasure he had felt was quite gone.

The next day, he did not go to work. It was unusual for Bruno, although not for the other people whom he worked with. He called his secretary and told her he was unwell. She seemed to accept his word, and asked him if there was anything she should do or any appointments she should cancel. He told her that she should examine his appointments diary, and that if she wished to reach him, she should leave a message on his answering machine, which, since he would be in bed recuperating, he would not answer.

Only afterwards did it occur to him that he had not told his secretary what was wrong with him. Nor had she asked. He did not go to bed, but he switched on his telephone answering machine and went out. When he came back, he dialled Simon's telephone number, firmly. But the pip of a ring made him put the telephone receiver down, and he did not know if Mauro was there to be spoken to. That day for him was blank and after it he had betrayed his mother and his firm both.

The next morning he did go to work. There was a pile of mail on his desk. While he prepared to deal with it, he sent his secretary out to buy a copy of *Vogue*. He telephoned his bank and checked the balance in his current account. Having done this, he requested them to transfer two thousand pounds to his mother's bank account in Italy. He knew she preferred money to presents; he felt that about himself, too, that he had no interest in a present which he might not need or want. Money was better.

'Lovely,' Simon said when Bruno gave him the copy of the magazine. 'It takes me all day to read *Vogue*, sometimes.'

'All day?' Bruno said. 'I read it this morning. It only took twenty minutes.'

'I don't think you can have been really concentrating,' Simon said. 'It's easy to read things quickly if you don't really look at them. Anyway, I bet you had other things to do. In your office, I bet.'

'How do you know I work in an office?'

'Your suit, it just screams office. I used to have to wear a suit, but that was in a shop, and it wasn't a proper suit. I never thought you would wear a suit when I met you.'

Bruno felt a violent blush like a slap, unfelt. It was the word *met* that did it. Simon looked at him in a way which is always described as innocent, and is knowing.

'You don't remember me, do you?' he said finally.

'No I don't,' Bruno said. 'It was very dark, of course.'

'I remember you. Your moustache, mainly. Of course, I've got a bit of a beard now.'

'Don't they let you shave here?'

'They do, but it's nice not shaving sometimes. Of course, it's not much of a beard, but I thought I'd let it go for a while, just to shock my mum, when she comes. She's always saying something like this is going to happen to me, and she'll be pleased to be proved right now. Maybe she won't recognise me either, with the beard, or think I've turned into a real man or something. You know. What does your mum think of your moustache?'

'What happened to you?' Bruno said, finally.

'They did me over,' he said. 'They beat me up. They kicked my head in. They hurt me.'

'They hurt you,' Bruno said.

'It doesn't matter,' he said.

'What's your name?' Bruno said. 'Your real name.'

'Simon,' Simon said. 'It always was.'

They were there and stayed there for a while.

'Come and lie down,' Simon said. 'In your suit.'

The ward was full of people. It was full of white, and the boy was asking him to lie on his bed with him. Bruno stayed in his chair and smiled, and he knew before he blushed that it was the smile he once brought out and let stay on his face when people said things to him that he did not understand. But, drained of embarrassment, Simon did not mind.

'Who is Mauro?' Bruno said.

'My flatmate. You spoke to him, then.'

'He spoke to me. I didn't know how he knew my telephone number. He just phoned me up.'

'He wants to come and stay with you.'

'He wants to come and stay with me?'

Bruno looked at Simon, but he seemed to be quite serious.

'You see, my mum's coming to stay. She was coming to stay the day before yesterday, but now she's coming tomorrow. He can't stay if she's coming, of course.'

'I've never met him,' Bruno said.

'You'd like him,' Simon said. 'He just needs to get out of my flat and he's nowhere to stay. He doesn't know anyone in London. It wouldn't be for long.'

'I've never met him,' Bruno said. 'I've only met you twice.'

'Three times,' Simon said. 'Here's my telephone number. It would be ever so nice of you if you did.'

He produced a card with his telephone number and his name written on it. This time there was no kiss after his name. Bruno realised he must have had it prepared, as he had prepared the conversation.

'You've given it to me already,' he said, handing it back. 'I don't need it.'

When he got home, he had decided to telephone his uncomplaining mother. He knew she worried sometimes, and knew that, if he did not telephone her, she would not presume to telephone him. He wondered sometimes what fits of sulk and pique she diagnosed in him, and did not speak about; he thought about the reasons she would have for seeing a mood in him not to telephone.

It was his habit not to dial the number of his mother, but simply to press the last number recall button. It was rarely necessary to do otherwise. He did it without thinking and without thinking he heard the English dialling tone. Only when the ring stopped and he heard, not his mother, but Simon's recorded voice, did he realise that the last number he had dialled had not been his mother.

'Hi there,' Simon's voice said. 'This is Brett. I can't get to the phone right now. I'm at the gym, pumping up my body just for you. So if you wait till the tone, and leave your number, I'll get back to you, and we'll plan some fun, okay?'

There was a short silence, and then an electronic noise. Bruno said nothing; he put the telephone down.

In the fridge there was some meat and some mushrooms. With some onions and a bottle of red wine and a little fennel, Bruno cooked himself some dinner, a heavy delicious dark stew. This was something he sometimes did; tonight he did it because it gave him a chance, which he felt he needed, to telephone his mother and ask her how a beef stew could be cooked best. She gave him the information he asked for and then, fond, they had a conversation in which nothing was said and nothing was left out. She did not reprimand him for not having telephoned, and in the end, he apologised, and she admitted she had been a little worried. He did not tell her about the money he had sent her; he looked forward to her surprise and her unsolicited thanks, which for him were, he thought, enough.

When the stew was ready, he realised he had cooked far too much; enough for two, really. He wondered, while he ate, whether it could be recooked and eaten the day after-wards. Then it occurred to him to give the rest to Pippo, who was, elderly, nuzzling his ankle as if he could not quite identify what the thing he could smell and wanted to eat was. He put some out on Pippo's dish which, since he was a puppy, he had always eaten from, and by the time he had finished, it was cold enough to be given to the dog. He set it down in front of Pippo, who truffled around it for a while, and then hobbled away. Bruno wondered what was wrong with it; he wondered whether Pippo disliked the fennel, or the red wine, and, speaking in dog-Italian, as to his dog he always did, he asked what was wrong. The dog looked, but did not answer.

He left it, and the next morning, when he got up, the meat had been eaten and the plate licked quite clean.

Bruno went to the hospital, for the last time.

'What do you do?' Bruno said.

Simon seemed to be determined not to blush and not to display embarrassment from the directness of his gaze.

'I'm an escort,' he said. 'A masseur. I once took a course.' Then he saw that Bruno's way of looking didn't register understanding, and, his eyes not dropping, he didn't say what he meant.

'I didn't have to do it,' he said. 'I enjoy it. I wanted to go to university. I liked geography, I wanted to do that. I like what I do now. I won't do it much longer. It's a bit dangerous.'

'Is Mauro a masseur as well?'

'Sort of. He's stupid about it. He gets people off the street, and afterwards they won't pay him. They're trouble, sometimes. That's what happened to me. I tried to get involved and he hit me with a chair. Not Mauro. The man off the street. It wasn't Mauro's fault, not really, except for being stupid. I'm cross about the chair. That's why I'm here.'

Simon reached for the bowl where the grapes had been, but it was empty.

'I should have brought you some fruit,' Bruno said.

'Anyway he's gone now,' Simon said. 'This came this morning.'

He handed over a postcard. In capitals it said Simon baby Don't worry about your mother because I'm going Don't worry you won't have to see me again See you again one day I don't know where I'm going I'm sorry about what happened Get well Mauro. Kiss my fat speedy ass honey remember!!!!

On the side of the postcard where there was the space for an address, it said only Simon, and the number of the ward where he lay.

'He just handed it in at the desk,' Simon said. 'Downstairs. Half the fucking staff read it before it got to me. They gave it to some old cunt called Simon halfway down the ward. I suppose he couldn't remember what my surname was, the stupid cow.'

'I've got to go,' Bruno said. 'I'm sorry. I hope you get better soon. I can't come back again, I'm afraid.'

'I knew you were going to say that. Every time you meet someone you like and it doesn't work,' Simon said. 'It seems like your last chance. Your last chance for a nice house and someone who loves you. But it's not like that really, there are always other chances.'

Bruno looked at him. He couldn't think of anything to say. He did not know if Simon was talking about him, or if he was talking about Mauro, and he could not ask.

'There are plenty more fish in the sea,' Simon said, and giggled. 'The thing is, Mauro needn't have gone after all. My mother's not going to come. She never was going to come, I suppose. I thought she was, but you can't trust anyone to do what they say they're going to. So he could have stayed in the flat till I came out of hospital. Still, I can't pretend I'm not glad in a way to see the back of that one. Never visited me.'

He stopped, inconsequentially.

'Do you know how to get in touch with him?' Bruno said, finally.

'I don't,' Simon said. 'I can't think where he could have gone. He can't afford a hotel or a flat or probably even a room. He can't afford to go back to Italy even if his family would have him. I don't care, though. He'll turn up again like a rotten apple. I'm sorry he phoned you up that time.'

'That's all right.'

'You might as well go now.'

Bruno got up, but instead of going, he sat on the white sheets of the hospital bed and put his arms round Simon. Then, as Simon had once asked him, he lay on the bed, pulling Simon down with him into an embrace, his face into the small haired hollow beneath his jaw. He was glad, in a way, to see the back of this one.

They stayed like that for a moment which went on, before it was time for Bruno to get up and go. He felt Simon, in his stiffness, not especially willing to continue with the embrace, but, as in other circumstances, and other rooms, he was paid to tolerate the embraces of others, he put up with it. Nor did Bruno especially want to continue it, and he did not quite know why, in this white ward with strangers walking by him and observing the two men in an embrace, he did so.

Like a bullet his knowledge that Simon would get better, and his love would find other chances, was in him, lodged; and it was in goodbye that he craned around the face, so strange at this angle, and his furred mouth found the professionally fond corner of a smile, and kissed its partial and plural goodbyes to a man, and to more than that, to a chance. He had never known Simon, never known his life or the rooms he lived in, and it was to something in himself that Bruno was kissing goodbye. And, before he said goodbye, slower than the break of slow thunder after bright distant lightning came the thought, like no words, of hands moving over flesh in order to know it; like the hands and minds of geographers swarming over the maps and lands of remote and unvisitable continents. They were going to live; forever; severally.

For Luiz Paulo Stöckler-Portugal

Rebecca Gowers

A SMALL ROOM

WEBSTER AND GRAHAM sat hunched over a couple of cans of beer in a cramped bedsit, unavoidably close to one another, Graham on the bed itself, and Webster in a small yellow armchair. In front of a deal desk stood a pair of upended milk crates with a thin piece of foam on top. There was nowhere else to sit, apart from the floor.

'Sure, Dr Quinn had talent, and excellent taste; but I wouldn't call him a genius,' said Webster.

He leant his head against the worn seat-back and gazed up at the ceiling.

'What, he wasn't a genius?'

'No,' said Webster.

Graham sighed. 'Oh right,' he said.

The gas heater was on High. Condensation trickled down the inside of the window-panes. Unwashed crockery and dirty clothing lay dumped across the carpet and wedged into the bookcases.

'I was fond of him, but let me tell you,' said Webster, 'universities stink! Jesus. Quinn.' He bit the lip of his beer can and sucked the liquid in through his teeth. 'You walk into an English university with ideas of your own, and they just sit there talking rubbish. Quinn was okay, but most of them made me sick. Not sick, but annoyed you know. They want you to be dim because it saves them effort. I hate students. I don't know why I stayed a year even.'

Graham wiped the sweat off his upper lip. 'Anyway,' he said, with an inconsequential laugh.

Webster smiled, stuck a cigarette in his mouth, and lit it,

keeping his head angled back as he did so. 'Okay, say I decided I wanted to write a thesis: no problem,' he said. He winced and shifted his neck from side to side. 'What's the problem? Man, I don't need them. Shit, who needs that kind of help? I can do whatever I want. It's what you yourself think that's important. No one listens to anyone else any more anyway. The main secret is knowing how to think.'

'Oh right,' said Graham.

'It not only doesn't matter; it not only doesn't matter,' said Webster, his voice rising, 'it's honourable to get out of there. People don't mind about the right things any more. Some people scarcely mind about anything at all. Dogma! Who has courage nowadays? Who gives a shit?'

He finished the last dregs of his can of beer, opened another two and leant forwards to put one at Graham's feet. Daylight was fading fast.

'But this way, you see, I'm free,' he added bitterly, after some thought. 'I'm free. I'm free. I can do whatever I like. I haven't been indoctrinated. Poor sods. I can read what I like; think what I like. Here, listen to this.' He heaved a book up from the floor and skimmed through the pages. 'Yes: "How many birds start so diseased, or become so weary, during the great migrations, that they tumble down, from the sky, to the ocean, to death? Do they die because they fall, or fall because they die? Do they die on water, or in the air?" '

Graham picked up his new can of beer and took a slow mouthful. 'Are you asking me a question?' he mumbled.

'You know,' said Webster, 'it's largely the case in life that we choose what we try to answer. Okay; right, listen to this.' He lifted up another of the books that lay around him on the floor. ' "An old woman is vastly improved by having a large nose." '

Graham stared at the water trailing down the window-pane.

'You see, when do we ever visibly see stillness? That's what I wonder,' said Webster. 'If you're indoors you're going to be conscious of your own nose moving around in front of you, right? Maybe out in a city somewhere without trees; but there's always writing up in some form or another; writing on the walls. Find me a city that doesn't have writing all over it. Nobody asks us if we mind. Words are not static visual material. Blank sheet? Really? Did you know, when a Buddha's feet are parallel he's dead?'

He leapt up and turned on the overhead light.

Graham blinked awkwardly. 'What about going out?' he asked.

'Isn't it raining?' said Webster, slipping back into the chair.

'So?'

'Look,' said Webster, but he didn't finish the remark.

Graham leant forwards.

'No, don't even ask me. Don't nag. Jean will be back soon,' said Webster. 'You stay. You should meet her properly.' He raised his hands towards the ceiling. 'What's so wrong with being self-conscious?' he cried.

Graham gripped his beer can. 'Jean's a student, isn't she? What about her?' he asked. 'You don't like students. What about her?'

'Oh well, we aren't ants,' replied Webster vaguely. 'You know, you put a couple of ranging animals in a small space and they'll circle for a long time.' He started to cough. 'You use a battery; it runs out; you get a new one. You don't use your brain; it runs out; you don't get a new one.'

'Webster,' said Graham.

'Right, Jean's at university, she is, okay, because it's good for her to be taught certain things. She's not exactly a spark-ler, fine, but then some people don't even know what they don't know. She tries hard: I like that. You know, you start by being interested in something, then you want to be the best at it; then you want to be the best at anything at all; then finally you just want to be better than the people you know, or even just the person who's with you.'

Webster drank some more and then added, with comic pomposity, 'We will be successful in only the most paltry and ridiculous ways. You and me, sir: a part-time phone-sales rep, and a reader of books.'

Graham stared at the window. 'Jean must be more intelli-gent than me,' he said distantly.

Webster tried to clear his throat. 'Well yes, in a way she

is. Okay, yes,' he said, 'but it depends what you mean by intelligent.'

They fell quiet. Jean was coming slowly up the stairs. She entered the room exhausted. Her fringe was stuck in wet streaks to her forehead. Her skirt was soused below the line of her coat. Her brown leather shoes were stained black where she'd stepped in puddles.

She bent down to kiss Webster on the top of his head, but he stiffened away from her, so she stood up again fast leaving rain in his hair.

'Graham,' she said.

'Oh hello, Jean,' said Graham.

Webster jerked himself out of the armchair.

'No, no,' said Jean.

'No, you,' he said. He sat down on the floor beside a line of bottles with his back to the wall, and pulled a dirty mug towards him for an ashtray. He coughed again.

Jean stood in front of the two boys, momentarily poised, then took off her coat and flung it across a plastic screen in the corner. There was a tiny kitchen area beyond, with a mini-fridge, a sink, an old Baby Belling, and an electric meter by the skirting board. Something crashed.

'Well, Graham, my my,' she said, lowering herself into the chair and letting her arms dangle over the sides.

'Hello,' he said again. He blushed and Jean smiled.

Webster blew out a lungful of smoke. 'So, Female Archetypes in the Nineteenth-Century Novel,' he said.

'After all that I didn't make it.' Jean shrugged. 'I'll get notes off someone else later. I should have gone of course, of course. I went to the library instead and wound up reading in the downstairs café. I met some people.'

She lifted up her eyebrows and opened her eyes wide as if suddenly realising they were drinking. 'Beer. Beer?' she said. 'You know, I could do with a beer.'

Webster silently offered her the remains of his can. She looked down at him with scorn. 'Great. Thank you very much. They were mine,' she said.

She slumped backwards, hissing dejectedly, and examined the ceiling. The gas fire rattled.

'Well,' said Jean after a while, 'I suppose I'll just have to hit the old bottle then.'

'Ah, here we go; your whisky-drinking women,' said Webster. He passed over what was left of a half litre of Black Label, twisting off the cap for her.

'You remember I told you about the really thin girl?' Jean raised the bottle to her lips. 'I heard the most disgusting thing today. It's really weird. When she feels hungry she goes to the nearest petrol station and breathes in all the fumes to kill her appetite. Isn't that disgusting?'

'I should think it kills more than just her appetite,' said Webster.

'I know this bloke who sniffs drains,' said Graham, and he blushed a second time.

Jean held the whisky bottle square in her hand, like a trooper, or a drinker; like someone for whom this felt good. 'So what have you both been up to?' she asked. 'Something amusing? There's an incredible fug in here. Do we really need the heat on?'

'We were discussing intelligence, and what to do with it,' replied Webster.

'Oh really?' said Jean. She simpered at him.

'Okay, what's the difference between a dimwit and a nitwit?' said Webster. Graham was staring bleakly at the window. 'Any takers?' asked Webster. 'Jean? No? I only just found this out. This is a medical theory: lice. A dimwit is someone who's dim, but a nitwit is a child so plagued with nits that it can't concentrate on its lessons.' He looked Jean straight in the eye. 'I think you're a kisswit,' he said.

An expression of tired dismay passed across her face. She looked hastily at Graham, and then turned back to Webster. 'Have you done any work today?' she asked.

He shouted with laughter. 'Yes, actually. I've had an amazing idea for a cartoon. Would you like to hear?'

'Have you drawn it?' she asked.

Webster dismissed the question with a wave. 'Okay, there's this girl in full leather gear; whips, chains, handcuffs, fishnets, high heels, right: the full works. And she's screaming, "I hate you. I hate you." And you can't tell from her face if this is part of her act, or if she actually means it: you're not sure. And she's in this poky little room, a bedsit-type room, and it's in a real mess. There's old cups everywhere, knives, plates with crumbs on them, bottles, cans et cetera; clothes all over the floor. And in the armchair there's this young man. All he has on is a pair of Y-fronts. He's just sitting there slouched over looking at the floor, and he's either looking really listless or really unhappy; or maybe a mixture of both. And underneath it says, "Where did it all go wrong?" '

Jean smiled and then pursed her lips, spreading her fingers carefully over the frayed arm-rests of the chair. 'You,' she said, 'are a moral pervert.'

'Wait a minute, I like that,' replied Webster. 'That sounded really natural. "You are a moral pervert. You, are a moral pervert." ' He laughed and tapped his beer can on the floor.

'Anyway, I don't hate you,' said Jean, half smiling too. 'I don't hate you. I mean, shall we go to a concert or something? I don't know what's on. We should go out. Would you like that? I mean I'll pay.'

'Oh yes?' Webster snorted. 'All three of us? Where and what? Moldo's Penny Aquarium Ballet? My God; from now on I reject all concerts. Jesus! I've realised recently that I hate concerts. Why? Because I hate audiences. I hate them. I don't want to be part of that sort of thing. I can't stand all those pale, middle-class, whitey, ugly-looking people all doing the same thing at once. From now on I'm not going to any more audience events. It's too much.' He frowned. 'Music, music,' he added, 'we have music here. I'd rather talk to you. I hate seeing those people enjoying themselves. It offends me.'

'Oh,' said Jean.

'Good,' said Webster. 'Hot days in Dogtown.'

The phone started ringing on the floor next to him. The three of them exchanged glances. Webster didn't move. 'You're a pro: you answer it,' he said to Graham.

Jean got up and leaned against the wall so that Webster had to breathe in the sodden smell from the cloth of her skirt. She drooped down and picked up the receiver. 'Hello?'

she said. She listened for a moment. 'No. No, I'm so sorry. I'm afraid you must have a wrong number.'

Webster ran a finger up her leg.

'Touch means take!' she cried wildly, but he recoiled at once, and so she forced a bright laugh. She gathered up the spiral phone cord, which slithered loosely out of her hand at once, and moved the telephone over to the desk. There was an abandoned game of patience laid out between her sheets of notes. She sat down on the milk crates, got up to fetch her bottle, sat down again and drank some more.

'Look, we have a guest. Let's drink the vodka, why not? There isn't much left,' said Webster, picking it up to show her. 'May we? Let's celebrate life, longing, and friendship. What's the time? Jesus. Let's have a proper drink.'

Jean gave Graham an inquiring look, but he declined, agitatedly flapping his hands.

'Be a man,' said Webster.

'No,' said Graham.

'Just one,' said Webster. 'What are you, a man or a fly?' He lit a new cigarette and took a long shot of vodka, swishing it round like mouthwash. 'So,' he said, turning back to Jean. 'So. Graham and I were wondering: who do you think's more intelligent, you or me?'

'What?' she replied nastily. 'At least I work. At least I work, you know. What is all this problem with concerts anyway? Some kind of pathetic style problem? Are you ashamed to be an ugly, middle-class whitey yourself? What audience do you think is out there judging you? Who cares about you at all?'

'I'm not middle-class,' replied Webster, 'I hate audiences,' he paused, 'and the only audience I fear for myself is me.'

'Oh well, we're honoured,' said Jean flatly.

She toasted Graham. He blinked and looked away from her. He picked up his first can of beer, finished it in a long and awkward series of swallows, and then started methodically to drink from the second.

Webster regarded them both through narrowed eyes. 'I'm lonely,' he said; 'and you're both lonely. Who's the loneliest? Who cares about me at all? I don't know. There are various things I don't know. At the same time, somehow, sometimes I'm actually frightened by what goes on in my head. This is the thing. You know? Nothing else has the same impact. It's wrong, I'm sure. Not even the loveliest woman could move me the way my thoughts sometimes do. What work do you expect from me? The way my mind is at the moment, I'm moving into broad sweeps, into the fat levels. I feel incredibly excited sometimes, some mornings, as if there were no really insurmountable difficulties.'

Graham flinched.

Jean glared sideways down at Webster. 'Tell me something,' she said, 'these thoughts, which you can't put into words; are these thoughts thoughts which you can articulate to yourself, or do you just know they're there, without knowing what they are?' She took a large mouthful of whisky.

Webster yawned and continued to smoke. At last he said, 'Here I am. Look at me, swilling back your money, or more accurately your father's money. Unlike you, Graham and I are not supported by our parents.'

'Especially since I don't have any,' whispered Graham, putting his head in his hands.

'No,' said Webster. 'Leaving that aside, right, leaving money aside, where we get it from, by what, dole-scrounging, handouts, work, the question is: what will become of us, and what do we want for ourselves? I proposed to Graham earlier that we all want to be the best. At what? Who cares? We want to be launched, released, recognised, remembered. It's all a stupendous form of laziness. Nobody thinks properly any more.'

'Tell me more about your thoughts,' said Jean, wide-eyed.

'You really don't get it, do you?' Webster hit his fist on the floor.

'Get it, schmet it,' she shouted. 'Birmingham Bertie from Bow; the more you sing, the higher you seem, the sicker, the sicker they get below.' She lost impetus and laughed weakly.

Graham gave a faint, peculiar laugh too. 'Below,' he whispered, between his fingers.

Jean turned to him. 'Can I say something?' she asked. He sat up straight, sweating. 'I mean, I know this must sound incredibly rude,' she said, 'but do you think you could possibly allow me to spend a bit of time with Webster; you know, alone. It's been a really hard day. It's been a hard week. I'm sorry. You know, really.'

Graham stood up at once. He rapidly clenched and unclenched his hands. 'Anyway,' he said, and walked to the door.

Webster seized him by the trouser leg, twisting the cloth round so his grip was tight. 'Wait, wait a minute, I want you to stay,' he said. 'You go if you want,' he said to Jean, 'but Graham's invited here. He's my oldest friend. I invited him.'

Jean got up, and then sat down again. 'Oh shit,' she said, laughing hysterically. 'Why don't I just pop out and get some more beers; or some vodka.' She stood back up. 'Is that a good plan? Beers all round; or we could go to the pub.'

Webster shrank from looking at her. She waited uncertainly.

'Let me go,' said Graham. His voice trembled. 'You let me go now. It's time for me to go.'

He yanked his leg free, ran down the stairs, and out into the night, ran through the rain, along the slippery pavements, ran and ran, until he was many streets away.

Tibor Fischer

THEN THEY SAY YOU'RE DRUNK

THE MORNING'S NUTTER was there.

Brixton, Guy decided, must have more headcases per square inch than any other place in the world. He had sojourned in the great cities of the continents, had seen some sorry, deformed, trashy sights, but for multitudinous loonies Brixton was unassailable. It was a pity he couldn't find a way of profiting from it: then it occurred to Guy that since so many of them ended up in custody as clients of Jones & Keita, he did make a few quid off them.

Today's guest nutter was black and massive. Could easily bounce into any bouncer's position. That was the other thing about Brixton, not only plentiful in barkers, it had the biggest barkers he had ever seen.

Walking up to the bus stop Guy reflected that someone with his trousers around his ankles, trying to eat his shirt wouldn't normally have troubled him much. It was the size of the shirt-eater rather than his activity that was perturbing. Six three and big, big, big; they obviously didn't spare the carbohydrates at the bin. What concerned Guy was that if the shirt-eater wanted something to wash down his victuals, and mistook Guy for a can of Tennent's and tugged firmly on his ring-pull, Guy couldn't do much about it, apart from croaking pathetically. The shirt-eater was huge enough to do anything he wanted to.

They were very keen on taking off their clothes. A week ago Guy had peered out of his window and spotted another whopper obsessing outside. Guy found using the window very stimulating; it was an eventful view: riots, accidents, robberies. The strapping loony had been fastidiously garnering items from dustbins and then arranging them in the interior of one of his neighbours' cars; having installed the objects, he climbed in and joined the rubbish, sitting there peacefully in his *pinacothek*.

Phoning the police was the usual concomitant to looking out of the window. Working for a solicitor and asking the police for help was a mite odd; it seemed unnatural. Guy had been especially reluctant to phone for the law on that occasion because he hated his neighbours, and the owner of that car in particular.

Whether it was his job or merely living in Brixton, Guy found himself painfully short of warm, goodwill-like emotions. He'd watch his neighbours and get extremely annoyed by the way they walked. He hated Brixton, he hated his neighbours, he hated the clients and, the truth be told, he wasn't too keen on himself.

Although he had been longing for the refuse-arranger to cause some expensive damage to the car he was in, because the nurse's car was next to it, Guy had phoned the police. The nurse was ensconced in duodom, but you had to plan ahead. If the refuse-arranger wanted to extend his display to the adjacent car, there was nothing Guy could do about it on his own, and bearing in mind it took the police half an hour to turn up (the police station was ten minutes' walk away) it was best to book in advance.

Two police officers appeared: a policeman (five seven tops) and a policewoman (five six) with nothing in the girth department. Guy estimated that between them they could just about restrain one limb. They tried reasoning, not having much choice. Guy had time to make a cup of tea and another phone call while they implemented mateyness and coaxing. The refuse-arranger refused to budge and responded by pulling off his clothes. Guy observed the policeman speaking into his shoulder to summon reinforcements. Four larger policemen dragged off the refuse-arranger while the original pair retrieved the strewn clothing.

On the bus, one stop closer to Peckham police station, Guy watched a drunk attempting to buy a ticket; Guy wasn't late yet, but the drunk had been fiddling in his pockets for four minutes in a search for coin, holding everyone up, until the passenger behind him volunteered to pay his fare.

Guy had been convinced that the drunk had been sent to multiply the unpleasantness of his trip to Peckham, but he latched on to an African woman sitting towards the front, and leaning forward in the confidential manner drunks have (despite their shouting), battered her with his breath. The woman tried for the wrapping-all-her-senses-in-one-spot technique; however, the drunk was so on that Guy was sure that even sober he was unbearable. 'But I don't want to BOTHER you with MY PROBLEMS,' the drunk promulgated with projection that would have got him a contract at the National.

In his coat pocket, Guy checked for his knife. Despite being over-familiar with the law on offensive weapons, he had started carrying a flick-knife. Not in case of being mugged. If anyone wanted his money, they could have it. He wasn't going to risk injury over a few quid. No, what worried him was being selected for ring-pulling by one of the barkers.

The longest he could go now without encountering a barker, once he was out the door, was twelve minutes (the time it took to get to the tube where there was a minimum of one on duty).

The shortest time had been thirty seconds, one morning when he had stumbled out to get a newspaper. As he was carrying out the phenomenally onerous task of paying for his paper, he was shoved in the back, shoved in that very definite and violent manner that tells you someone is shoving you deliberately. Guy had turned round to see a lithe black teenager wearing a T-shirt with cut-off sleeves and an Arab headdress. 'You should be more careful,' he said to Guy. Virtually asleep, Guy realised it was going to happen; he could see other people in the newsagent's staring at them with the keen interest that presages a splash of blood. He was going to be beaten up multiculturally. Wonderful.

They shoved each other for a while, Guy struggling to

work himself into a rage. Then, without a word Arab-head walked out of the newsagent's, crossed the road smartly and went into a greengrocer's, presumably to find someone to shove there. Four minutes later, when Guy was fully awake, fully furious and fully armed, he had gone into the green-grocer's looking for him, but he had vanished.

After that, he resolved never to go outside untooled up. If he had to use it, he would say he had just found the knife on the street and was on his way to hand it in when . . . Guy didn't see why the role of the only honest person in the United Kingdom should fall to him.

As he got off the bus, an elderly black man spat at Guy. The comet of phlegm trajectoried a couple of inches past Guy's chest. Then the man grinned at Guy. If it had made contact, Guy would have been forced to do something about it, but this wasn't worth it. If you stopped for everyone abusing you or gobbing at you, you'd never get to where you were going.

Guy entered the reception area of the police station. And waited while the constabulary deigned to acknowledge him. In the streets, in the courts, in the newspapers they might have to take it, but here, here was their domain. 'Solicitor's rep,' Guy announced when they felt they had let him ripen enough, 'in the matter of Scott.'

With most clients you discerned a batting average in favour of criminality: that there would be a few months of good living before they got nicked. He always had the intention of asking the Scotts why they did it, because they were always caught. They were dependable clients, and had even started asking for Guy by name.

Part of the reason why Guy hadn't asked the Scotts why they did it, was because, despite their always being caught, they always claimed they hadn't done it.

In an age where family bonds were often sundered in ugly fashions, or simply didn't exist, it was rare to see a father and son so close. Scott senior and Scott junior were unusual in other ways. Street robbery was suited to the nifty. It was an offence much favoured by failed athletes, those who hadn't got it right at county level, but who were happy to have a chance to put their training to use.

Scott junior wasn't right for this line of work. So fat he wobbled like a water bed (born too late for success in freak shows), you couldn't imagine him crossing even a bathroom with speed. This was where Dad came in, providing a chauffeur service.

Peckham police station, after one of their early (if not initial) forays, was where Guy had first encountered them. No charges were preferred because Scott junior had attempted to snatch a bag from a lady who turned out to be his former PE teacher (he obviously hadn't recognised her from behind, otherwise he might have recalled her judo classes). His PE teacher did recognise him, and apart from loudly naming him tautophonically and clinging on to her bag, she had thrown him to the pavement and having pronounced 'This isn't school, sonny,' knowingly started to kick him senseless. Dad piled in and simultaneously joined his offspring on the pavement.

The Scotts were rescued by the police. Scott senior's version was they had been assaulted by a demented woman and he was outraged that a number of witnesses maintained that Scott junior had made a grab for the bag. Taking their contusions into consideration and the feeble nature of the snatch, they were cautioned.

In one respect, the Scotts fitted the profile of street robbers – they were exceedingly dim. Bag-snatching was not a crime which attracted the calculating or imaginative. There was some craft in finding the right sort of victim in a favourable environment: small, skinny females with no fondness for the martial arts or a predilection for carrying concealed weapons – in a badly-lit car park or sequestered side-street or secluded subway. The technique didn't require much study: the handbag was grabbed and the victim pushed or thumped to the ground (though there were those who esteemed the method of shoving the victim to the ground first and then grabbing the bag). If nothing else, you could envisage Scott junior excelling at the shoving part.

Then came the Balham High Street job. Scott junior

plucked the bag cleanly, leaving bagless lady gaping, and jellied his way to the car. The Scotts sped off chuckling and, turning the corner, drove into a police checkpoint (a biannual event). No tax. No insurance. No MOT. No licence. No brake lights. No tread on the tyres. Arguably, they might have fronted it out if it hadn't been for Scott junior sitting in the passenger seat with the contents of the crocodile-skin handbag spread out, scrutinising a powder compact.

Patiently, Guy had listened while the Scotts had protested that the bag had been thrown into the car by a mysterious stranger who had hotfooted it out of their lives. They had just been making their way to a police station to hand it in. They were stumped as to how the woman's description fitted Scott junior perfectly, down to the 'Whip me and cum on my tits' logo on his T-shirt.

Out on bail, they had another whirl. The snatch went okay, the getaway was okay, but the car broke down on the way home. By the time they returned by bus, the police were waiting for them, after surmising from the description furnished by the victim ('out of work Sumo wrestler') who the culprits were. The Scotts: fit-up, victimisation. The jury: guilty. The judge: suspended sentence. Moral: get good wheels.

Though you could go over the top, Guy concluded, remembering Palmer's smash and grab on an antique shop (which had been staked out by armed police, presumably on a tip-off, which was bizarre since Palmer had never been known to think more than fifteen minutes ahead). Palmer had been transported to the scene of the crime in a bright red Ferrari, just nicked by his friend who was driving.

According to Palmer, he had visited his friend who had offered to give him a lift to another friend. When, during the journey, it had emerged the car was stolen, Palmer had instantly demanded to be let out. The car came to a stop coincidentally in front of the antique shop, where, incensed by his friend involving him in a criminal act, Palmer altercated with him and directing a brick at him (which had suddenly come to hand), the brick had missed the friend but had hit the antique shop's window. Palmer had been solicitously examining the goods in the window for damage, when the guns had materialised.

There were a few clients with whom you developed a matey rapport, with whom you could have a chortle. Guy had thought about voiding the thought: 'You don't mind if I laugh, do you?' But Palmer wasn't the sort of client who encouraged levity, he was the sort of client who would bite off your ear if he detected the slightest diminution of respect towards himself, no matter how much legal training you had had. Palmer was a non-laugher; he had been absolutely earnest about this line of defence.

Guy had excused himself, left the interview room, laughed till he cried, composed himself and had returned to resume taking instructions.

Sadly Palmer was another devoted client, although no one wanted to handle him. Most clients had their territories, their proclivities, their patterns. Not Palmer. Palmer did everything: moody money, arson, plastic, burglary, molesting young girls. He was an all-round entertainer. Handling cases like Palmer's, Guy couldn't avoid coming to the view that if he had any moral fibre he'd be doing something to sabotage Palmer's defence, not that it was needed in the antique shop matter. Palmer was looking at some bird, all the more if he demanded a trial, though there were judges stupid enough to give him probation.

Reading Palmer's palm as it were, the future was easy to tell: he'd revolve in and out of jail, blighting lives like botulism until he unloaded a major viciousness, a rape or murder, when even a judge would be forced to put Palmer away long enough to study for an Open University degree.

Someone out there was waiting for Palmer to excise the happiness from their life.

Finally admitted, Guy had a word with the arresting officer, who had that very jolly bearing that policemen have when they have a perpetrator on the charge sheet within hours, and have the perpetrator so bang to rights that the entire legal profession working in unison (having resurrected and roped in every lawyer that ever lived) couldn't do anything about it.

The Scotts were improving; they got the bag, got rid of it and got home without incident. They went unrewarded for their improved efficiency since the crime had been recorded by a new high-quality colour security video camera, and the Scotts had been instantly recognised by the investigating officer.

The Scotts were very popular. There was nothing the police liked more than criminals who caught themselves. The officer was very chatty, revealing that the Scotts had disposed of the handbag but luncheon vouchers had been found on the sofa and (here the policeman gave a contented snigger) the victim's credit card had been discovered in a coffee jar.

Guy instructed the Scotts to go no comment, because that was usually the best policy, doubly so with the dopier clients, who would invariably create more work for counsel if they detoured from those two words. And it was a stance you couldn't be faulted for; it might not always be the best, but it was never wrong. You could always talk later if necessary. The Scotts would be better off putting up their hands in light of the videotape, the handbag's contents making themselves at home in the Scotts' home and the victim's vivid recollection of Scott junior's 'Kill them all and let God sort them out' T-shirt.

Yet the Scotts clung on to their innocence like a pit bull to a favourite leg; somewhere, by someone, a long time ago, the Scotts had been advised never to cough and this motto had stuck in their minds like a hunk of hair blocking a drain, blocking out any prudent assessments of their predicament.

There were, Guy reckoned, three main categories of stupidity. There were the nervy types who still reverberated from the shock of school and who liked to keep out of people's way in case anyone asked them to add up something or tested them on the capitals of South America. They only got involved in crime by accident since they knew they would fail. Then there was the more practical group who realised what their limitations were and worked round them. Lastly, there was the category that the Scotts were domiciled in, the too stupid to realise they were stupid, those who spent all their time wondering why everyone else was so stupid.

The conference with the Scotts was affable, apart from their inability to comprehend why Guy thought bail was unlikely.

The Scotts had fitted in with unprecedented convenience. Guy strolled down the hill leisurely with time to kill before his appointment at Brixton Prison. He popped into a shop and bought some cigarettes for Bodo. The Scotts had been disappointed that Guy hadn't been able to offer them a smoke. Guy usually carried ten Benson & Hedges, but it had given him a surge of pleasure to have been without them.

Further down the hill, there was a fresh drunk (unlabouring Irish labourer variety) with the question-mark posture of the profoundly inebriated. He held a can of blue-label and guttural in the gutter was declaiming 'and then . . . and *then* people say to you, you're drunk . . .'

They were relaxed at the prison. They normally were unless someone had gone over the wall in the previous week. Guy sat down in the interview room and waited for Bodo (currently the favourite client) to appear. Bodo's problem: close association with seventy ks of marijuana.

From Augsburg he had come to London to play guitar. Short of readies, he had met a man in the pub one evening (no, he really had). The man got chatting with Bodo and offered him three hundred quid to make a delivery. This was one of the reasons Guy liked him, it was such an easy mistake. Bodo knew perfectly well what was involved, but had thought, one run, three hundred quid. Guy sympathised with him; he had been in a similar situation when he had met Gareth who had persuaded him to try outdoor clerking for his firm. It could easily have been the man in Lewisham who had hired Bodo.

Duly arrived at the rendezvous, Bodo had found an edgy van-driver who wanted to rid himself of the bales as swiftly as possible. Bodo had been flabbergasted to find the transfer being conducted in the open, to wit, the car park of a

McDonald's, and that the bales weren't even disguised, just wrapped with a few shreds of newspaper. Bodo was greatly worried about the sloppy packaging since only a few of the bales fitted into the boot of his car and the rest had to be stacked up on his passenger seats.

Shaken, Bodo started off for the address he had been given (verbally), having been also told a car would be following him. Bodo watched as the red Lotus which had been cruising twenty feet behind him, sped past after he had been pulled over by the police who wanted to talk to Bodo about the red light he had burned ('I didn't even notice the lights, I was checking the map').

The prospect of Bodo, sweating in conditions close to freezing, and a car replete with gargantuan bales of marijuana roused the suspicions of the police officers.

'Can you tell me what these packages are, sir?'

'A very long jail sentence, I think,' replied Bodo in the way to win policemen's hearts.

It didn't look good for Bodo. He had put his hands up, though in a situation like that it didn't do you much good. One kilo, you could pretend it had been planted and that someone else had left it there, but with seventy, you just had to start shopping for a good five-year calendar. Bodo had barely had room to drive.

It didn't look good at all. He had all sorts of disadvantages. University education. Undivorced parents. No history of sexual abuse. No history of substance abuse. No history of alcoholism. No illegitimate children. No criminal record. Flawless English. Skills. Nothing to mitigate whatsoever. The judge would throw the book at him.

In he came, wearing his 'Legalise It' T-shirt. 'Wie geht's?' asked Guy always eager to exercise his one German phrase, because it made him feel European and because that night with a German girl in a youth hostel in Rennes hadn't been in vain.

Bodo was trying to be tough about his forthcoming sentence, and being partially successful. He was settling into it; though he had some problems: he wanted to try for bail, but the only people who had that sort of surety were his parents and he hadn't shattered their serenity yet. Essentially, Bodo wanted bail for a last fling with his girlfriend. He wasn't fooling himself that she would be waiting for him when he emerged a much older and wiser man.

They discussed bail and other business. There wasn't much to discuss. Guy had attended mostly for Bodo's sake, to try and cheer him up; he knew there couldn't be much to occupy him in HMP Brixton. It wasn't as if he could learn anything: a virtuoso guitar player, a PhD in astrophysics, and he spoke and wrote better English than anyone else in the nick (the governor included).

Bodo was focusing on the future. 'I will go back to Augsburg. Teach guitar. No more big cities. No more adventures. Everyone will know me as that boring Mr Becker, and no one will believe I did crazy things in London.' He pulled on his cigarette with lag-like intensity. 'You know, by the time I get out it probably will be legal. Perhaps I should do something to speed up the campaign.'

They got up and waited for the warder to collect Bodo. 'I was looking at the moon last night,' Bodo said. 'You can see it very well from my cell. I was looking and I thought one day there will be people there and they will have jails there, because they will have arseholes on the moon. Wherever there are people, there are arseholes. Be careful, Guy, you never know when you may turn into one. Look in the mirror often.'

He got home and ran the bath. Guy locked both the locks on the door and placed his longest kitchen knife (with a nice serrated edge) on the toilet seat cover. It was unlikely, almost impossible for anyone to get in, but Guy found it hard to trust the universe these days.

He missed the police.

They had turned up the night Guy had complained about the noise next door. It had been four in the morning and Guy had learned there was something outstandingly annoying about a mighty salsa beat passing through a wall. Most styles of music he could handle, and he had nothing against people having fun, but this jarred. The police had the same effect as him: none. Either the neighbour couldn't be bothered to answer the door, or the music was too loud for him to hear the furious bangings on the door.

The police officer had commiserated with Guy, who had resolved to reciprocate the gift of insomnia by going out and slashing his neighbour's tyres after the police had gone. The police officer had looked out of Guy's window. 'You've got a good view here, haven't you?'

So Guy found himself with a surveillance unit in his front room. His citizenship wouldn't have gone that far normally, but there had been early mention of a few quid being bunged his way for inconvenience.

It was the hairdresser's they were interested in. It had impinged a little into Guy's thoughts too. The hairdresser's seemed to be closed more than was generally considered beneficial for a business, with its shutters firmly pulled down. Even when open, it didn't seem to be doing any better than when it was closed. Nevertheless, parked around the premises were a number of cars that shouted affluence.

'Is it drugs?' Guy had asked.

'We don't give a toss about drugs any more,' the DC had replied. 'They're flogging guns.' The police left after a week, looking dissatisfied. Dissatisfied, Guy gathered, because nothing of a bang to rights nature had been attained, and because while they had been doing some close-up work in The White Horse, Guy's flat had been burgled and their cameras stolen. Guy lost nothing: they didn't take his television or video which was rather insulting. They were old but serviceable.

The most grating thing was that his door had been kicked down. Guy had spent time and money fitting extra locks on the door. The locks had resisted admirably, but the door itself had disintegrated into toothpicks.

The company had been good though. Guy had enjoyed swapping tales of iniquity and vileness.

He was pleased to see his reflection in the mirror. He was going to Hampstead, that should give him a break from all this.

Strolling to the tube, Guy watched a Tennent's drinker (discharged squaddie variety) lob his empty can on to the top of the entrance way of Lambeth's Housing Section, and then proceed to urinate lavishly against the building while his girlfriend gazed on in my-hero fashion. You got tired of people distributing rubbish everywhere and dispensing substances that were not intended for public inspection, but it had to be acknowledged that it could never be wrong to hose down a Lambeth Council office.

At the tube, Guy broke through the cordon of evangelists (chiefly Christian, but with Islam closing the gap, some equipped with luggable speakers) and the selection of purveyors of politics (chiefly communist). Brixton underground station had a mysterious quality, the trait of congregating people who wanted to change your life, mostly noisily, by taking your money. And people who wanted you to change their lives, by taking your money.

In a corner of the concourse a stonehenge of drunks and section thirty-sevens were laughing at the funniest joke in the world. The king of the dossers was holding court.

The king, to Guy's knowledge, had been at the tube every day for the last five years, on a nine to five basis (a much better attendance record than any of the employees of London Underground assigned to Brixton). People still gave him money – perhaps it was his unkempt demeanour.

Because in fact the king wasn't a street person, he lived in a council flat around the corner from the tube, the new estate that had been built by the railway line after the rioting in '81. He had a variety of natty outfits and seemed to enjoy working the tube. And why not? The concourse was warm, dry, furnished with hot and cold beverages, snacks, a newsagent, a photo-booth for shooting up in and catchy rhythms pumped out by the record shop.

The king fancied himself as profound: when giving the litany of 'spare change, spare change' a rest, he would sire full-volume observances such a 'Persons! Persons! Where are you going?' with a suggestion that he was trying to elevate them to a higher plane of being.

Through the ticket barrier Guy was confronted by a black,

sunglassed Walkmanner, walking up on the first segments of the down escalator (in effect, on the spot), drink in hand. Guy paused for a second to see whether the pacer wanted to walk off or whether he would work out that he was supposed to go down. But he carried on striding happily as if the underground station were his private gym, a perception provided by wonky mental machinations, or perhaps a simple craving to infuriate those who wanted to descend to the platforms.

Guy didn't care what cortical flamboyancy had licensed this. Living in Brixton gave you a superb ability to distinguish between irksome eccentricity and hazardous lunacy. The drink was a complete giveaway – orangeade. Everyone knew real nutters and lovers of GBH drank Tennent's. Besides he was quite small. Guy shoved him out the way without bothering to add 'Sorry.'

On the up escalator an Australian, surfing expertly on the handrail, glided past Guy.

With the train rattling away, Guy opened up packets of annoyance and determination. He was annoyed because he had been thinking for months now how attractive Vicky was, and how despite her being agenda'd, he wasn't warming up her skin.

He hadn't been able to understand how she had been able to go out with that twentieth-century nonentity, Luke. Despite taking a pride in his amorous resources, Guy recognised there were males who were stronger, richer, tanneder, excitingly employeder; he wouldn't have liked it if Vicky had been dalliancing with one of them, but he could have understood it. He had wanted to say, 'If you're not interested in me, fine, but at least let me fix you up with someone proper.'

Patience was Guy's speciality; he was prepared to wait. A rebuff or two wouldn't put him off, he was prepared to stay in touch without any physical remuneration, he wasn't disheartened by polite conversation.

However, Luke had gone back to his home town of Ipswich for what had been billed as a long weekend, but hadn't come back. What had appeared in his stead was a piece of wedding-cake in a flowery box, with a wedding invitation to his wedding to an old childhood sweetheart (whom Vicky had long assumed relegated to the sporadic Christmas card league), accompanied by a short note: 'I think it best if we don't see each other for a while.'

What had amazed Guy was Luke's cruelty. Or humour. Both had seemed beyond him. Luke, a sound engineer, seemed to have such enormous respect for sound that he hardly ever uttered a word, and it wasn't even as if the words he did utter carried extra pith to compensate for his long silences. Over and over again, Guy had been through his memories to verify his impression of Luke as tedious and nondescript. He took up about eleven stones' worth of space, that had been his chief characteristic. Though of course the most vivid memories of Luke were the ones he didn't remember but could see, those of Luke grimacing and groaning as he compressed Vicky's buttocks.

Vicky had discovered that she had been matrimonially outflanked on Monday; Guy had discovered that she had discovered on the Wednesday. Congratulating himself on his diligence and the efficacy of his intelligence network, he had phoned instantly, to supply commiserations.

To his shock, he had found Vicky far from disconsolate, but about to move to Hampstead where she had acquired a position as house-sitter in a four-bedroomed wonderland (sauna, jacuzzi, gymnasium, satellite TV) as well as some chef from a Korean restaurant who was taking her for long walks and who was talked about in tones which conformed to a buttock-compressing situation.

She had sounded very chirpy; indeed, the only rain cloud that appeared in her vocal firmament was when Guy proposed a meeting. She reeled off excuse after excuse, so it was only now, a week later, that Guy was getting his slot, since Vicky was having a drink with two Dutch female friends. Guy was buoyed up by the idea of the company, although he was worried he was falling in love with Vicky.

Guy found them in the pub, and noted that Vicky greeted him with that total lack of interest that too often signified a total lack of interest; similarly the two Dutch girls were perceptibly unexcited by his presence. Far from feasting on his words, as women who are intent on a holiday liaison would, they scarcely paid any more attention to him than to any of the other people in the pub.

Studying Vicky, Guy surmised that he was part of a batch-job, that she had had to take the Dutch out for a drink, and he had been tacked on to kill two birds and one unacting actor with one evening in the pub.

Guy bought a round just in case the ladies were aroused by generosity and then they sat down at a large round table which had already acquired a hardened pubber (old single ex-door-to-door salesman variety), who sat there serenely with the tools of his trade: the never-diminishing half-pint in a pint glass, the roll-up with almost a cigarette's length column of ash, alcoholic hair, and a smile that was confident it knew what was what.

The conversation rolled on without any aid from Guy, who was sitting next to the pubber. After a couple of minutes, the pubber with the ornate diction of someone trying to disguise their drunkenness, asked Guy if he had a handker-chief. Guy replied that he hadn't, because he didn't. The pubber then tripped up the girls' conversation by canvassing them for a handkerchief. They were unable or unwilling to provide one.

A few moments later, the man asked Guy again for a handkerchief, with a trifle more urgency and an intonation that insinuated that Guy was holding out on him. Guy repeated with bonus firmness, a firmness he hoped would penetrate the boozy padding, that he didn't have one. What was beginning to irritate Guy was that it was a three-second walk to the bar or the toilet where, if his need were that great, a tissue could be obtained. The man seemed determined on annoying someone into fetching a handkerchief.

The Dutch girls were now listing with Vicky (rather insen-sitively, it seemed to Guy) which actors would be most wel-come in their undergrowth; the actors they named didn't have more talent than he did, Guy felt, but they did have advantages such as immense fame and wealth. He'd like to see how they would fare opposite the girls shorn of their

celebrity and riches: probably the same as him. This enumer-
ation of carnal preferences boded badly for him, since the
girls clearly felt they were amongst girls – it was the sound-
track of a failed evening, when their mouths ran out of words
and Guy was aware they were staring past him with the
blanched visages of road-accident viewers.

He glanced over his shoulder. The reason the man had
been pleading a handkerchief was now abundantly clear. A
strand of snot, a foot long, dangled like a dipstick from his
right nostril. The pubber's hooter was huge, which doubtless
empowered the well-racinated extension.

For any Brixtonian this was rather elementary stuff, and
Guy wasn't hugely bothered. Unexpected in Hampstead
(what was the point of paying millions for your home if you
had someone growing mucous tendrils in the local?) but in
Brixton they would have tried to lasso you with it. The
pubber was progressively more and more amused as the
pendulum parabola'd over a larger and larger area.

'Am I upsetting you?' he chuckled. It wasn't upsetting,
Guy analysed, but it was incredibly irritating. He hadn't
travelled all the way across London for this, and he wasn't
giving the pubber the satisfaction of knowing he had added
another layer of unpleasantness to the evening. Guy shut him
out of his mind, having checked that the pub (which wasn't
that busy) had no other rump havens.

Shortly after, alerted by the extra work of the revulsion
muscles on the women's faces, Guy revolved to witness the
pubber escorting with two fingers the strand on to the carpet.
This eased things a bit since he no longer had to worry about
the swinging adventures of the snot.

However when Guy was tactically agreeing effusively with
Vicky about the importance of a united Europe, he espied
horror having another outing on her face. Guy lefted his gaze
to perceive a three-incher worming its way out of its hangar.
There was another request for a handkerchief.

'Why don't we go outside?' suggested Vicky.

They went outside and sat at a plastic table. It was the end
of May but cold. Not cold enough to prevent them from
sitting outside, but cold enough to prevent them from enjoy-

ing it. Guy didn't see why they should be outside catching a chill. This was all too English for him: someone inconveniences you, so you help them make things even more inconvenient for you.

Things weren't right. There had always been revolting drunks, the insane had always been partial to public transport, but Guy recalled in his teenage years the sight had been out of the ordinary. You saw one in the street and you went home to say 'There was a really revolting drunk in the street' or 'What a nutter we had on the bus today.' Now it would be striking if half the passengers on a bus aspired to civilised behaviour. Though perhaps he should try moving out of Brixton.

Guy's reverie was terminated by the figure of the pubber lurching out of the doorway, the man with the metronomic catarrh. We're in for a reprise, guessed Guy.

'Hope you're . . . enjoying yourselves,' he said as he zig-zagged past with an inflection that broadcast this was the last thing on earth he would want. Perhaps he had been on course for home because he took a few more steps, but the group's provocative lack of response caused him to tarry. He established himself a short distance away from their table (but more than a flob or a fist away) and started emitting abuse. They tried not paying any attention, but this didn't impede the invective, in stock, blunt and unimaginative terms, but with a remarkable hatred.

And here we are, mused Guy. In a dying city. Where else would you spend your day being polite to morons whose only talent is burning up others' money in benefits, legal and penal costs? Wading through beggars, spending an hour crossing the place, only to be ignored by women and to end up sitting in the cold sworn at by a man whose secretions are no longer secret?

On one Dutch face Guy saw a look that said the man needed help and understanding. On his face Guy imagined there was an expression which maintained that the man needed to be kicked in the head vigorously, ideally until he was dead. He was close to snapping. The trouble was that the inveigher was old, puny and drunk; Guy would simply be beating him up. In a way this was the most galling aspect – that the pubber was sheltering behind their notions of decency. Furthermore, Guy's familiarity with the law conjured up charges of assault or manslaughter.

Besides which the ladies wouldn't approve of any laying on of hands. Women were funny about things like that. And there was no point in reciprocating the insults; that would only fuel the harangue.

'Some people aren't very nice,' continued the pubber, 'some people are . . .' he went on using the verb that has proved most popular on city walls since city walls had come into being.

They opted for drinking up. Guy wondered if there was a country anywhere where individuals like the pubber would be executed and if he could emigrate there. However, just as they were getting to the bottom of their glasses, the pubber shuffled off.

The Dutch contingent was staying with Vicky, and Guy accompanied them back home so that if anyone else wanted to swear at them he could assist them in ignoring it. In addition to which, Guy prided himself on not giving up. The possibility of the three girls unrobing and having a yearning for aromatic balms to be kneaded into their flesh existed. But as so often happened, it didn't happen.

A minicab was called for Guy. Having missed the last tube, he was now rounding off with an expensive trip down South. The driver was a Jamaican. Guy had barely been in the car ten seconds when the driver asked him if he could seek his advice. The driver recounted how, back in Jamaica he had met a girl, got married: he had brought her back to live in London but she had absconded after a week. 'So me had 'er deported.' All well and good, but then he had been back in Jamaica again where he had patched things up and now he wanted to bring her back again. He was thinking he should ring the Home Office.

Guy could see the Home Office relishing the call. He could see the driver walking into the office at Jones & Keita and asking for advice; like most of their customers he seemed to be in contention for some international award in imbecility.

The driver must have had an age with a four in the front and Guy could see the wife with an age that still had a one at the start; a young lady no doubt older and wiser after her deportation who would either fit in her supplementary intubations while her husband was out on the road, or who would do a more thorough disappearing act next time.

Yet, perhaps because he was feeling tired, it glinted less like stupidity, it was simply part of the on-going. What people do. And apart from the airfare, what was the difference between going to Kingston or Hampstead?

'Give it a try,' said Guy.

'Dat's what I say, give it a try.'

The minicab broke down halfway along Acre Lane. Guy waited patiently for a while in case the driver had the ability to revive it; then he paid, ready to walk the last ten minutes. 'Good luck with your wife,' he said, surprised that he meant it.

He looked up for the moon, but couldn't see it anywhere.

Patricia Tyrrell

THE MARROWBONE-AND-CLEAVER CONCERT

BEYOND THE ATTIC windows ran a narrow ledge; she climbed out to it and the 'For Sale' sign creaked above her head. She decided dreamily that the boys were right, this rusted sign must have been up a while.

Her head laughed and gurgled but her feet were steady, otherwise she wouldn't have dared walk the ledge. The effect of the purple capsules had faded quickly this time; the boys' chatter had thinned her fog. It was fortunate that these two empty houses stood together; the frames of all the attic windows were rotted, so she would easily tug one free in the adjoining house and climb in . . . *so*. She stood in the small empty room and the purple waves peacefully washed through her again.

When they receded she leaned at the window and stared down into the narrow street, all peeling tall housefronts with bow windows and doors festooned with scrollwork or carving. The ground floors were mostly shops – antiques, a printer's, art supplies – now closed and secretive in the dusk. At the far end, down near the quay, a church all squared grey stone – St Mary of the Angels, one of the boys had said. He'd grinned and made some joke about it; he wasn't high like her and the joke flew away past her like a gaudy balloon. She'd reached out her hand to catch it and everyone laughed, all the half-dozen boys and the other girl; so she'd withdrawn her hand – carefully, watching it to make sure it was still a part of herself – and tucked her body together, had hunched in a corner and let them forget her. Later they'd started thumping around, tuning their Godawful instruments – how could you tune a thighbone? – and the satiny purple flowers which were trying to open inside her got offended; enough of this, they said. You with all this beauty inside you, and them – yuck! An uncouth mob.

She leaned at the window and mourned the going of the capsules; she'd need to get more next day. The wisping tide of them laid itself along the street's end and merged into the wisping waters of the bay. Slices of waves rolled in and flattened, then the land rose on the bay's far shore. She leaned, drowsy and happy.

After a while the sunless air struck chill and she shivered. She wasn't going back next door till their damn concert was done with, no matter what. She lifted into place the window she'd entered through, and crossed the room. Along the passage all the doors stood open; the air smelled of dust and faded leather – a burnt smell – and papers which might have stood here for hundreds of years before removal.

Down one flight of creaky stairs; here the front rooms were big and the window frames solid. She couldn't hear a speck of sound from the boys, so they hadn't started the concert yet; had they all been knocked dead by whatever they'd taken earlier in the day? She chewed the cuff of her shirt and was passionately lonely, rather afraid. What would you call this room – a bedroom? Large, but whoever had this house built must have been rich. No furniture anywhere, unlike the house next door. Two weeks the boy said they'd been sleeping there already. They'd jimmied the back lock and left the huge front door untouched; a dull blue, it soared higher than any door she'd ever seen, and a filthy brown stone pillar soared each side of it. Front door fit for a king. The backyard was sly, quiet, dirt-smeared, not overlooked because of its jungly shrubs. Come sleep where we live, they'd said to her on the street corner where she sat quietly staring, legs stretched out among the walking feet of the passers-by. We got, they said, a house, lots of room. Won't bother you none, the tallest boy said, and she hauled herself far enough out of the haze to realise that they, like everyone else, found her scruffy, undesirable. We got our own bints, another of them said, and he sniggered. She couldn't speak – the drug held her too tight – but the tall boy must have understood that if she could speak she'd say Why then? He bent down and held out his cool hands to pull her up to the level of the people she wasn't – didn't want to be – like. Because, he said (while his uninterested arm around her supported her away from there), the fuzz'll pick you up if you stay sitting here, and we got plenty room, this house we been sleeping in . . . He paused to glance at jeans on a rail, dancing in the breeze, and he said as if to the lifting tough assortment, You could do the same for us some day. This pure altruism shocked her, she'd never come across it before.

This was her first evening in the house, but the boys had apparently slept there each night and tidied their belongings, and themselves, away by day in case through some miracle a buyer came to look. Their tastes were coming-and-going moods like hers, no problem. Only this whiny music of theirs set her nerves quivering, and the girl they'd brought in – Diane – stared at her as if she was dust on a carpet. No, she couldn't abide Diane.

The purple waves slipped from her and thinned on the horizon; the light in the house waned to dark grey. The windows were grimed and smeary too. The silence sent loneliness through her like a cutting-open, like when you feel in your pocket and the last capsule's not there. If she didn't hear people moving around and talking very soon she would scream, and the boys wouldn't like that. Even if she could hear them playing those damn instruments, that would help.

She ran from the bedroom and took the next downward flight three at a time; they were wide and shallow, their carved rail flaked with gilt. At the bottom she gasped, hugged herself, listened. She could faintly now – couldn't she? – past her grabbed-in breaths hear the boys. Yes, one of them laughed. She wondered what they took and when; must be well organised, to keep them hitching in and out of this house at the right times.

Suddenly dim shafts of amber pierced the dark corridor; fear hissed through her till she realised the street lights had been switched on. The electricity in these two houses was off, of course, and the water. The boys had brought in juices, Cokes and such. Candles too; the eerie clumps of those spooked her but she couldn't stand total dark either. She leapt through an open door at random into a room on the front, where the lamp-light from outside fell. Enormous room; she christened it a ballroom.

Beyond the plaster carving of the wall, and the great gaping fireplace, she heard the boys. Not to pick out words, but they were alive people; she was safe and as near being human as she wanted to get. Which wasn't all the way.

They stopped talking and after a moment their damn concert began. She'd never been to proper concerts but she knew you sat in a big hall and listened; how could you call this a concert when there was no audience? Except herself, but one person didn't seem like enough. She curled on the floor beside the hollow fireplace but the shrill squeak of those hollowed long-and-short bones, the thump of the axe (they hadn't been able to find a regular butcher's cleaver, so they'd substituted), were too loud, they wailed and banged on her bones and made her desolate; so she uncurled herself and drifted across to the tall uncurtained window. She could imagine how easy it might be to pass right through the glass and keep on travelling down the empty street to the quayside, the harbour, the waters of the bay. She'd half a mind to try it; this bunch would never miss her, and the glass needn't get in the way. She scratched at it with a fingernail – and suddenly the street wasn't empty.

The single file of humped elderly figures climbed from the quay and passed from lamp-pool to dark and lamp-pool again with the ease of a person running an absent-minded hand across stubby projections. She leaned at the glass with her ears hanging forward like shells, but the advancing figures were soundless. The receding drug had left all noises very clear and sharp in her head; she would easily have distinguished these footsteps from the bang and whistle of the boys' noise – but there were no footsteps. Heavy-set old men though, and they all wore fishermen's boots.

Up past the church of St Mary of the Angels, its stone

blocks as hard-featured as the faces of these old men. Up the other side of the street, keeping to the other side until, without glancing at the house, they crossed the road fifty yards below it; panic fluttered like a bird in her mouth. A bird with dry panicking wings, with claws which scraped; fear had never been this real. Her heart thudded out of rhythm with the boys' thudding axe; she clutched the glass and willed the old men to pass by quickly. When instead they mounted the next house's steps and stood in front of that enormous door, her mind went liquid with terror, yet she had to see what would happen. Some sort of watch patrol, to complain of the noise? What business was it of theirs?

The foremost man fumbled in the pocket of his long overcoat, then moved so close to the door that he was out of her sight; was this glass thick enough to hide the sound of their feet and of a key turning in that clumsy old lock? One by one the old men stepped forward out of her line of vision; they must be going into the house, because each side of those steps a basement area gaped. Yet the shrill waver and thump of the concert continued; the drug unexpectedly blurred back into her and suggested that the old men had melted out of existence at the moment they unlocked the door, but she couldn't believe that. Convenient if so, and the kindly drug's suggestion was well-meant, but she didn't accept it.

The piece the boys were playing arrived, after many repetitions, at its end. The boys laughed and chattered; among them she distinguished the voice of the tall one who'd brought her here. Simon, his name was. But the old men . . . the house all at once flared with dazzle; she gasped and through the chimney flue the youths' single gasp came too. Surely every light in the place was on; had there been that many bulbs in the sockets? She was – almost – sure not.

An instant's silence, then the boys scuffled around and talked low-voiced among themselves. The great blue front door opened – it threw a rectangular slab of light on the pavement, like the largest most dazzling coffin ever – and their talk stopped. Out through the door a body suddenly hurtled, travelling as she'd dreamed of, without touching the ground.

Then the body lost momentum; it jammed up against a shop-front on the far side of the street and began to whimper, to feel itself all over as if it doubted its existence. It was the youth who'd thumped the smaller axe. It tottered to its feet, all spectral and quavery, then stumbled away. Down the hill; the unflinching stones of St Mary of the Angels watched it go. Then a single shout through the flue, so instantly cut off that she couldn't tell if it was youth or old man. Two more bodies curved through the door, departing on air. They took longer to pick themselves up, and still weren't on their feet by the time they'd crawled out of sight. Silence, silence. The remains of the drug lay in her like a slammed baby and said Oh my God oh dear God oh but— And cut off like the shout had, leaving her with nothing.

Light cascaded in slanting oblongs from every window. Water ran too, it cut on and off with a terrible meaningfulness. How many youths had there been altogether? The lost drug tried to slant them like the twisted window-light, but she managed to count: one two three four five. They'd seemed like more because she'd been so drifty when they brought her here, she was flickering in and out of the world and they flickered around her, but by the time her head settled down enough for her to walk the ledge, they'd resolved themselves into five. One long marrowbone and one shorter, one big axe and the small backup, and Simon – the tall one who'd shown her an astonishing unselfishness – for sparse vocals and to fill in if anyone needed a rest. They'd planned for everything except this.

If only their being thrown, their crashing, would make some noise; if only they'd cry out. She watched the fourth soar higher, further, than the others; for a moment he hung so exactly poised above the opposite railings that surely he would drop on to them and get stuck, speared there like a piece of meat. But in falling he twisted sideways at the last moment and avoided them; he seemed to hit his head against them though. And lay, his limbs moving skittery but small at the foot of the railings.

Number five, a young-bird flutter. Yet the weak rickety flight made him safer, it landed him in the middle of the street and from there he ran swiftly, apparently not hurt, to the twitching prone one, hoisted him on his back and, bent double, stumbled away, keeping to the pavement as if this were an ordinary street and traffic a real possibility. The girl at the window sagged in relief; all five of them out and still alive. Then she remembered Diane.

Diane who'd stared as if any other girl was dirt on the carpet, Diane who hated her and whom therefore she hated. She gazed from the window and saw this last flight, so poised and apparently serene that Diane must have launched herself and truly be enjoying this . . . a flight onward, onward. To a shop window to hang across its glass front with arms and legs splayed in so undignified a pose that the watcher from above had to laugh softly. Hanging till a limping figure raced back up the street to pick her off the glass and drag her away. This time the high-up watcher was almost sure of hearing a moan, and the dark trail behind the dragged figure looked real too. All gone out, anyway; all probably still alive. Then the girl remembered herself.

Her sneaky laugh cut off short, though the voices booming in the flue wouldn't have heard it, they were talking so loud. Yet she couldn't understand a word they said. She shook her head but the drug had gone away again; the world was clear, sharp. Surely the drug had gone.

A bang and the huge door was shut, its tall rectangle of light locked within the house. Locked, yes; this time she heard the key turn. Her fingers couldn't open the window-catch, but anyway these front windows overhung the deep pit of the basement entry. The voices boomed indistinguishably and she tried to plan past them. The front door of this house she stood in was undoubtedly locked, the back door too; the windows shut and noisy in their old frames. If she pushed up a back window to climb out, surely the old men would hear her and rush to catch her there or in the garden; she wouldn't put it past them to penetrate the walls. If they caught her, what would they do? She was the last to be thrown out, and their violence had increased with each one. If, said her head, their hands touch me, I'll die, one way or another I certainly will. Not hysteria this, but the truth.

Their voices boomed and light streamed from the windows; water ran again through the pipes and was cut. Yet surely Simon had shown her how you couldn't turn the water on here; what trick had they found? Her brain – cold and hard and terrified – reminded her that although the back door of this house would be locked, in the adjoining house the back-door lock was broken; the boys had ripped it off to get access. She would have to go up the stairs of this house, along the outside ledge and in through the other attic window, down silently through the lit house (all the men seemed to be in the room beyond the flue, the room the concert had been held in), to the kitchen, the unlocked door, freedom.

One thing stopped her, it kept her scrabbling at the window and after a while sent her down through the empty house to scratch uselessly at the front door; one thing kept her scratching there while the voices boomed and the door stayed locked and there was no more point in scratching. The awful thing, the thing which barred and held her, was that she couldn't be sure of the old men's nature. If they were real, a bunch of fanatic near-murderers, that would be terrible; she didn't want to get killed yet. But if they weren't real – if they were phantoms of the drug and her own disordered brain – then she absolutely couldn't cope with that; to stay beside the door for ever and starve was her only possibility. On the distant bay the tide wisped in and out and she scrabbled endlessly at the door's thick wood, knowing she would never dare move from that spot. Because she couldn't be – would never be able to be – wholly sure.

Glyn Hughes

BRONTË

Extract from a novel in progress to be published by Bantam in autumn 1995

CHARLOTTE BRONTË STOOD on the playing field at Roe Head School, the centre of a ring of eight girls. Miss Susan Ledgard remarked that 'Miss Brontë has a face like a lion', and it was not a compliment.

Her broad face, with its wide-set, yellow-brown, soft eyes and its feline mouth, surrounded by her crimped, yellow-brown hair, was incongruous upon her tiny body. If she raised her eyes, which was not often, she had the round-eyed stare of a cat at night when surprised by a light. The look was caused by her short-sightedness, but the girls had not realised that, yet. Although she was leonine, she was not at all bold. All she managed was puzzled defiance. Hers was the look of a lioness cowed by the zoo or the circus, with only a dim memory of not being defeated.

She had started off, not in the centre, but as one of the circle. Apart from one or two of them who were related, the nine were all strangers to one another because the Misses Woolers' school near Huddersfield was a new one, but they all understood this game of throwing a ball – except for Miss Brontë, who never even tried to catch it. Therefore they had fallen into a new sport, of setting her in the centre and throwing the ball past her, but she was supposed to stop it. 'Piggy-in-the-middle' she heard them call it. Once she had managed to catch the ball, the one who had thrown it would change places with her. Charlotte Brontë, instead of feeling special, as she might have done – instead of feeling that she had been given a chance for initiative and leadership – felt humiliated and at bay.

She had never heard of the game before and she behaved like a fool. She could not see the ball when it was thrown. She saw only one among several vague movements, which might or might not have been someone throwing. She only knew for certain when the ball was a few feet from her face, and if she had been cowardly she would have ducked. Instead, she let it pass a foot above her head as if she hadn't noticed or as if she wasn't afraid of being hit. She was terrified.

She was next supposed to have her eye on the person who would be throwing it back from the other direction but she did not even turn round. She still kept her eyes mostly upon the ground. She wished she had a book in her hand. It was a frost-hard day in the second half of January and she was very cold, but she would not have minded nipped fingers if they had held a book. She wanted to think about Brannii, Emii, Glass Town, Papa and her beloved creation 'the Marquis of Douro', but the maddening game stole her thoughts.

A moment later, the ball passed by her ear from behind, and Miss Someone-or-other laughed. Miss Brontë raised her head for a second. The ball was thrown towards her yet again – from Miss Taylor, she just about recognised. Charlotte still did not move her arms or position.

This time the throw was gentle, lower, and less dangerous. Falling upon the thick folds of her woollen skirt, the ball was lost for a second, then it rolled down and settled at her feet where she ignored it.

'*Throw it back*!' shouted an exasperated but still friendly voice a dozen yards in front of her. Charlotte thought that it came from Miss Taylor, but it could have been Miss Alison or one of the two Misses Brooke. Miss Brontë saw a vague, upright shape, somewhat like a huge clothes-peg but with woolly edges.

Genii Tallii bent down to the ball then paused half way, inspecting it as if still not sure what it was. But of course it would be silly of them to think that she could not see it from *that* distance, it was just that she was hesitating over what to do.

'*Throw it!*' another of the girls repeated. This voice was

threatening and came from somewhere to the side of her. Certainly it was not Miss Taylor this time. She thought it was Miss Ledgard.

'It will not bite you, Miss Brontë!'

Yes, it was Miss Ledgard. It was followed by a chuckle from the others.

Charlotte could feel what she could not see clearly: the girls mocking her. She feared that the eight were getting to be friends by picking on her. Their homes were close together in this part of the West Riding and all were daughters of the new class of wealthy mill owners for whom, as the proprietors, the five Misses Wooler, had cleverly spotted, it was worth opening a school. Charlotte was the only pupil from far away – that is, from twenty-five miles distance – and who was a specimen of that type of freak known as a poor parson's daughter.

She felt that she could have been Zenobia, Lady Ellrington – she of her recent story, *Albion and Marina* – surrounded by the Ashantees. Where were the other genii; where were Tabby and Papa? She felt excruciatingly alone.

She snatched the ball, stood erect with her arm raised as if to touch the sky, and balanced the ball over her shoulder.

'Here you ore!' she shouted, straining after gaiety.

'Miss Brontë's Oirish!' mocked the extremely *nicely* spoken Miss Amelia Walker.

'We have a scullery maid who is "*Oirish*",' Miss Walker added, and there was much laughter.

' "Bog-Irish", as they say. They keep their pigs in the kitchen. They keep hens in the bedroom. Don't they, Miss Bron*teh*?'

In a temper, Charlotte hurled. She would have liked to be aiming a cannon ball at Miss Walker.

'Bravo!' sneered Miss Haigh.

'Oh, *sod!*' exclaimed Miss Allinson, another manufacturer's daughter.

For Charlotte had missed everybody by yards. How could she miss everybody! It landed among frozen grasses at the edge of the playing area and the group broke up to chase after it.

Charlotte Brontë burst into tears.

'Why are you crying?' asked the strong young voice of Miss Taylor, who had left the others and had come close by.

Charlotte was fourteen years of age. She had been wrested from the bed she had always shared with Emily, and from Glass Town, because her family once again hung over a precipice. Papa had been seriously ill with congested lungs. It had continued through summer, autumn and winter. As he fought for breath, just as Anne often used to – filling rooms with terrible gasps, unable to climb stairs or pulpit steps without many pauses – it was feared that he would collapse.

The issue of his daughters' abilities to earn their own livings had again *Raised its ugly head*. They were never allowed to forget the cliff close to which walked all unlovely daughters of clergymen. It was a fall into domestic servitude at best, as ladies' maids or governesses; into early graves from poorly doctored sicknesses at worst. Now they dangled over the fall again. Charlotte, because she was the eldest, had been sent for another attempt at salvation through training in the skills of a governess.

Mary Taylor was ten months younger than Charlotte, but was ten years older in her grasp of the real world. Unknown as yet to Miss Brontë, Miss Taylor had enjoyed a striking upbringing. It included a sense of sisterhood with her own sex. Mary Taylor's father was a 'heavy wool manufacturer' of blankets and army cloth, and a banker. Also he was a freethinker and a republican, thus scandalising his colleagues in these Chartist days. His home, the Red House in Gomersal, was electric with intellectual dispute, and he believed that women should be brought up to think for themselves and speak their own minds. He had done a good job with Mary.

She had been protective of Miss Brontë ever since having had the advantage, with the other girls, of seeing Charlotte arrive. On the first day, Charlotte had not put in an appearance until late afternoon by which time the others were well settled in. Mary, for example, had only come five miles. And she had arrived in a smart gig that had been polished up for the occasion and was driven by a family servant.

The strange little Miss Brontë on the other hand had turned up in a market cart. She had spent all day being passed from lift to lift, prearranged by her strategically minded Papa, from Haworth, to Bradford, to Halifax, thence to Huddersfield and up the hill to Roe Head. She sat next to the driver behind the rumps of a couple of hefty cart-horses. Although the clumsy cart was covered over, a piglet could be seen poking its nose through the open weave of a basket.

It had been a special misfortune for Miss Brontë that arrivals were visible at Roe Head through its three tiers of bow-windows. These were not where the front door was but were on the side looking over the valley; nevertheless they offered a view of the driveway. In one bay, the other eight girls were assembled. They were strangers to one another, short of amusement and of subjects for conversation. Miss Brontë provided both as she stepped down from the cart, stiff, cold, miserable, and huddled in her cloak after twenty-five miles of slow progress through the market towns and the mill villages. The other girls had put on some style for their appearance at a new school. Charlotte looked like a little old woman as she followed, not a personal servant, but the grubby, indifferent carter who carried her trunk.

'Whoever is that little fright?' Miss Haigh had giggled.

'Oh dear!' The snobbish Miss Walker rolled her eyes and waved her arms like an exasperated mamma in a Rossini opera. 'That'll be Miss Brontë.'

'*Who?*'

The strange name had been enough in itself to produce a laugh in the schoolroom. They did not know about Lord Nelson and his alternative title, any more than they knew about Glass Town.

'She is my aunt's godchild, though I have never set eyes on her before. She lives in the mountains.'

After a quarter of an hour, which was time enough for Miss Brontë's nervousness to intensify, she had been brought by Miss Margaret Wooler to the schoolroom door. The oak-panelled passages, the great doors, the wide staircase starting up from a spacious hall, had overpowered Miss Brontë and crushed her confidence as if she was a victim in Glass Town's *Hall of Judgement*. The schoolroom door swung open and she had stood there, looking down, blinking, in near-tears. Divested of cloak and bonnet, showing herself in her 'practical', old-fashioned dress, she had still looked like a little old woman to her fellows, in their pretty frocks, their lace, bright ribbons and neat shoes. They had interpreted her tense expression as hostility.

'I don't know how to play games,' Charlotte blubbered in response to Miss Taylor's question on the playing field, and she hid her face in a home-stitched handkerchief.

'Then don't play them!' was Mary Taylor's simple, smiling answer. She shone like a dandelion on a sunny day.

It was a revelation to Charlotte that she didn't *have* to cultivate the affection of her peers. Charlotte smiled back and tucked away her hankie. If Mary Taylor had noticed that it had been stitched at home, it would not have upset Charlotte now.

Miss Taylor might well have remarked upon it. She remarked upon anything she wanted to, candidly.

They stood out in the frost, the sun shining upon it. Beyond, Charlotte could hazily take in the valley of the Calder with its factories' smoke thawing the frost somewhat. On the far side of Huddersfield, whitened slopes reflected a warm colour that she would have known to describe as 'chrome yellow'.

When she had been part of the game of piggy-in-the-middle she had felt trapped and the wide, vague view had reminded her of it. Now she was aware of a spacious glow of beautiful colour.

She was no longer alone.

Penelope Fitzgerald

THE MEANS OF ESCAPE

ST GEORGE'S CHURCH, Hobart, stands high above Battery Point and the harbour. Inside, it looks strange and must always have done so, although (at the time I'm speaking of) it didn't have the blue, pink and yellow-patterned stained glass that you see there now. That was ordered from a German firm in 1875. But St George's has always had the sarcophagus-shaped windows which the architect had thought Egyptian and therefore appropriate (St George is said to have been an Egyptian saint). They give you the curious impression, as you cross the threshold, of entering a tomb.

In 1852, before the organ was installed, the church used to face east, and music was provided by a seraphine. The seraphine was built, and indeed invented, by a Mr Ellard, formerly of Dublin, now a resident of Hobart. He intended it to suggest the angelic choir, although the singing voices at his disposal – the surveyor general, the naval chaplain, the harbourmaster and their staffs – were for the most part male. Who was able to play the seraphine? Only, at first, Mr Ellard's daughter, Mrs Logan, who seems to have got £20 a year for doing so, the same fee as the clerk and the sexton. When Mrs Logan began to feel the task was too much for her – the seraphine needs continuous pumping – she instructed Alice Godley, the rector's daughter.

Hobart stands 'south of no north', between snowy Mount Wellington and the River Derwent, running down over steps and promontories to the harbour's bitterly cold water. You get all the winds that blow. The next stop to the south is the

303

limit of the Antarctic drift ice. When Alice came up to practise the hymns she had to unlock the outer storm door, made
of Huon pine, and the inner door, also a storm door, and
drag them shut again.

The seraphine stood on its own square of Axminster carpet
in the transept. Outside (at the time I'm speaking of) it was
a bright afternoon, but inside St George's there was that
mixture of light and inky darkness which suggests that from
the darkness something may be about to move. It was difficult, for instance, to distinguish whether among the black-
painted pews, at some distance away, there was or wasn't
some person or object rising above the level of the seats.
Alice liked to read mystery stories, when she could get hold
of them, and the thought struck her now, 'The form of a
man is advancing from the shadows.'

If it had been ten years ago, when she was still a schoolgirl,
she might have shrieked out, because at that time there were
said to be bolters and escaped convicts from Port Arthur on
the loose everywhere. The constabulary hadn't been put on to
them. Now there were only a few names of runaways, perhaps twenty, posted up on the notice boards outside Government House.

'I did not know that anyone was in the church,' she said.
'It is kept locked. I am the organist. Perhaps I can assist
you?'

A rancid stench, not likely from someone who wanted to
be shown round the church, came towards her up the aisle.
The shape, too, seemed wrong. But that, she saw, was because
the head was hidden in some kind of sack like a butchered
animal, or, since it had eyeholes, more like a man about to
be hung.

'Yes,' he said, 'you can be of assistance to me.'

'I think now that I can't be,' she said, picking up her music
case. 'No nearer,' she added distinctly.

He stood still, but said, 'We shall have to get to know one
another better.' And then, 'I am an educated man. You may
try me out if you like, in Latin and some Greek. I have come
from Port Arthur. I was a poisoner.'

'I should not have thought you were old enough to be married.'

'I never said I poisoned my wife!' he cried.

'Were you innocent, then?'

'You women think that everyone in gaol is innocent. No, I'm not innocent, but I was wrongly incriminated. I never lifted a hand. They criminated me on false witness.'

'I don't know about lifting a hand,' she said. 'You mentioned that you were a poisoner.'

'My aim in saying that was to frighten you,' he said. 'But that is no longer my aim at the moment.'

It had been her intention to walk straight out of the church, managing the doors as quickly as she could, and on no account looking back at him, since she believed that with a man of bad character, as with a horse, the best thing was to show no emotion whatever. He, however, moved round through the pews in such a manner as to block her way.

He told her that the name he went by, which was not his given name, was Savage. He had escaped from the Model Penitentiary. He had a knife with him, and had thought at first to cut her throat, but had seen almost at once that the young lady was not on the cross. He had got into the church tower (which was half finished, but no assigned labour could be found to work on it at the moment) through the gaps left in the brickwork. Before he could ask for food she told him firmly that she herself could get him none. Her father was the incumbent, and the most generous of men, but at the Rectory they had to keep very careful count of everything, because charity was given out at the door every Tuesday and Thursday evening. She might be able to bring him the spent tea-leaves, which were always kept, and he could mash them again if he could find warm water.

'That's a sweet touch!' he said. 'Spent tea-leaves!'

'It is all I can do now, but I have a friend – I may perhaps be able to do more later. However, you can't stay here beyond tomorrow.'

'I don't know what day it is now.'

'It is Wednesday, the twelfth of November.'

'Then *Constancy* is still in harbour.'

'How do you know that?'

It was all they did know, for certain, in the penitentiary. There was a rule of absolute silence, but the sailing lists were passed secretly between those who could read, and memorised from them by those who could not.

'*Constancy* is a converted collier, carrying cargo and a hundred and fifty passengers, laying at Franklin Wharf. I am entrusting you with my secret intention, which is to stow on her to Portsmouth, or as far at least as Cape Town.'

He was wearing grey felon's slops. At this point he took off his hood, and stood wringing it round and round in his hands, as though he was trying to wash it.

Alice looked at him directly for the first time.

'I shall need a change of clothing, ma'am.'

'You may call me "Miss Alice",' she said.

At the prompting of some sound, or imaginary sound, he retreated and vanished up the dark gap, partly boarded up, of the staircase to the tower. That which had been on his head was left in a heap on the pew. Alice took it up and put it into her music case, pulling the strap tight.

She was lucky in having a friend very much to her own mind, Aggie, the daughter of the people who ran Shuckburgh's Hotel; Aggie Shuckburgh, in fact.

'He might have cut your throat, did you think of that?'

'He thought better of it,' said Alice.

'What I should like to know is this: why didn't you go straight to your father, or to Colonel Johnson at the Constabulary? I don't wish you to answer me at once, because it mightn't be the truth. But tell me this: would you have acted in the same manner, if it had been a woman hiding in the church?' Alice was silent, and Aggie asked, 'Did a sudden strong warmth spring up between the two of you?'

'I think that it did.'

No help for it, then, Aggie thought. 'He'll be hard put to it, I'm afraid. There's no water in the tower, unless the last lot of builders left a pailful, and there's certainly no dunny.' But Alice thought he might slip out by night. 'That is what

I should do myself, in his place.' She explained that Savage was an intelligent man, and that he intended to stow away on *Constancy*.

'My dear, you're not thinking of following him?'

'I'm not thinking at all,' said Alice.

They were in the hotel, checking the clean linen. So many tablecloths, so many aprons, kitchen, so many aprons, dining room, so many pillow shams. They hardly ever talked without working. They knew their duties to both their families.

Shuckburgh's had its own warehouse and bond store on the harbour front. Aggie would find an opportunity to draw out, not any of the imported goods, but at least a ration of tea and bacon. Then they could see about getting it up to the church.

'As long as you didn't imagine it, Alice!'

Alice took her arm. 'Forty-five!'

They had settled on the age of forty-five to go irredeemably cranky. They might start imagining anything they liked then. The whole parish, indeed the whole neighbourhood, thought that they were cranky already, in any case, not to get settled, Aggie in particular, with all the opportunities that came her way in the hotel trade.

'He left this behind,' said Alice, opening her music case, which let fly a feral odour. She pulled out the sacking mask, with its slits, like a mourning pierrot's, for eyes.

'Do they make them wear those?'

'I've heard Father speak about them often. They wear them every time they go out of their cells. They're part of the new system, they have to prove their worth. With the masks on, none of the other prisoners can tell who a man is, and he can't tell who they are. He mustn't speak either, and that drives a man into himself, so that he's alone with the Lord, and can't help but think over his wrongdoing and repent. I never saw one of them before today, though.'

'It's got a number on it,' said Aggie, not going so far as to touch it. 'I dare say they put them to do their own laundry.'

At the Rectory there were five people sitting down already

to the four o'clock dinner. Next to her father was a guest, the visiting preacher; next to him was Mrs Watson, the house-keeper. She had come to Van Diemen's Land with a seven-year sentence, and now had her ticket of leave. Assigned servants usually ate in the backhouse, but in the rector's household all were part of the same family. Then, the Lukes. They were penniless immigrants (his papers had Mr Luke down as a scene-painter, but there was no theatre in Hobart). He had been staying, with his wife, for a considerable time.

Alice asked them all to excuse her for a moment while she went up to her room. Once there, she lit a piece of candle and burned the lice off the seams of the mask. She put it over her head. It did not disarrange her hair, the neat smooth hair of a minister's daughter, always presentable on any occasion. But the eyeholes came too low down, so that she could see nothing and stood there in stifling darkness. She asked herself, 'Wherein have I sinned?'

Her father, who never raised his voice, called from down-stairs, 'My dear, we are waiting.' She took off the mask, folded it, and put it in the hamper where she kept her woollen stockings.

After grace they ate red snapper, boiled mutton and bread pudding, no vegetables. In England the Reverend Alfred Godley had kept a good kitchen garden, but so far he had not been able to get either leeks or cabbages going in the thin earth round Battery Point.

Mr Luke hoped that Miss Alice had found her time at the instrument well spent.

'I could not get much done,' she answered. 'I was inter-rupted.'

'Ah, it's a sad thing for a performer to be interrupted. The concentration of the mind is gone. "When the lamp is shattered . . ." '

'That is not what I felt at all,' said Alice.

'You are too modest to admit it.'

'I have been thinking, Father,' said Alice, 'that since Mr Luke cares so much for music, it would be a good thing for him to try the seraphine himself. Then if by any chance I had to go away, you would be sure of a replacement.'

'You speak as if my wife and I should be here always,' cried Mr Luke.

Nobody made any comment on this – certainly not Mrs Luke, who passed her days in a kind of incredulous stupor. How could it be that she was sitting here eating bread pudding some twelve thousand miles from Clerkenwell, where she had spent all the rest of her life? The Rector's attention had been drawn away by the visiting preacher, who had taken out a copy of the *Hobart Town Daily Courier*, and was reading aloud a paragraph which announced his arrival from Melbourne. 'Bringing your welcome with you,' the Rector exclaimed. 'I am glad the *Courier* noted it.' – 'Oh, they would not have done,' said the preacher, 'but I make it my practice to call in at the principal newspaper offices wherever I go, and make myself known with a few friendly words. In that way, if the editor has nothing of great moment to fill up his sheet, which is frequently the case, it is more than likely that he will include something about my witness.' He had come on a not very successful mission to pray that gold would never be discovered in Van Diemen's Land, as it had been on the mainland, bringing with it the occasion of new temptations.

After the dishes were cleared Alice said she was going back for a while to Aggie's, but would, of course, be home before dark. Mr Luke, while his wife sat on with half-closed eyes, came out to the back kitchen and asked Mrs Watson, who was at the sink, whether he could make himself useful by pumping up some more water.

'No,' said Mrs Watson.

Mr Luke persevered. 'I believe you to have had considerable experience of life. Now, I find Miss Alice charming, but somewhat difficult to understand. Will you tell me something about her?'

'No.'

Mrs Watson was, at the best of times, a very silent woman, whose life had been an unfortunate one. She had lost three children before being transported, and could not now remem-

ber what they had been called. Alice, however, did not altogether believe this, as she had met other women who thought
it unlucky to name their dead children. Mrs Watson had
certainly been out of luck with her third, a baby, who
had been left in the charge of a little girl of ten, a neighbour's
daughter, who acted as nursemaid for fourpence a week.
How the house came to catch fire was not known. It was a
flash fire. Mrs Watson was out at work. The man she lived
with was in the house, but he was very drunk, and doing –
she supposed – the best he could under the circumstances,
he pitched both the neighbour's girl and the baby out of the
window. The coroner had said that it might just as well have
been a Punch and Judy show. 'Try to think no more about
it,' Alice advised her. As chance would have it, Mrs Watson
had been taken up only a week later for thieving. She had
tried to throw herself in the river, but the traps had pulled
her out again.

On arrival in Hobart she had been sent to the Female
Factory, and later, after a year's steady conduct, to the Hiring
Depot where employers could select a pass-holder. That was
how, several years ago, she had fetched up at the Rectory.
Alice had taught her to write and read, and had given her
(as employers were required to do in any case) a copy of the
Bible. She handed over the book with a kiss. On the flyleaf
she had copied out a verse from Hosea – 'Say to your sister,
Ruhaman, you have obtained mercy.'

Mrs Watson had no documents which indicated her age,
and her pale face was not so much seamed or lined as
knocked, apparently, out of the true by a random blow which
might have been time or chance. Perhaps she had always
looked like that. Although she said nothing by way of thanks
at the time, it was evident, as the months went by, that she
had transferred the weight of unexpended affection which is
one of a woman's greatest inconveniences on to Miss Alice.
This was clear partly from the way she occasionally caught
hold of Alice's hand and held it for a while, and from her
imitation, sometimes unconsciously grotesque, of Alice's
rapid walk and her way of doing things about the house.

Aggie had the tea, the bacon, the plum jam, and, on her own initiative, had added a roll of tobacco. This was the only item from the bond store and perhaps should have been left alone, but neither of the girls had ever met or heard of a man who didn't smoke or chew tobacco if he had the opportunity. They knew that on Norfolk Island and at Port Arthur the convicts sometimes killed for tobacco.

They had a note of the exact cash value of what was taken. Alice would repay the amount to Shuckburgh's Hotel from the money she earned from giving music lessons. (She had always refused to take a fee for playing the seraphine at St George's.) But what of truth's claim, what of honesty's? Well, Alice would leave, say, a hundred and twenty days for *Constancy* to reach Portsmouth. Then she would go to her father.

'What will you say to him?' Aggie asked.

'I shall tell him that I have stolen and lied, and caused my friend to steal and lie.'

'Yes, but that was all in the name of the corporeal mercies. You felt pity for this man, who had been a prisoner, and was alone in the wide world.'

'I am not sure that what I feel is pity.'

Certainly the two of them must have been seen through the shining front windows of the new terraced houses on their way up to the church. Certainly they were seen with their handcart, but this was associated with parish magazines and requests for a subscription to something or other, so that at the sight of it the watchers left their windows. At the top of the rise Aggie, who was longing to have a look at Alice's lag, said, 'I'll not come in with you.'

'But, Aggie, you've done so much, and you'll want to see his face.'

'I do want to see his face, but I'm keeping myself in check. That's what forms the character, keeping yourself in check at times.'

'Your character is formed already, Aggie.'

'Sakes, Alice, do you want me to come in with you?'

'No.'

'Mr Savage,' she called out decisively.

'I am just behind you.'

Without turning round, she counted out the packages in their stout wrappings of whitish paper. He did not take them, not even the tobacco, but said, 'I have been watching you and the other young lady from the tower.'

'This situation can't continue,' said Alice. 'There is the regular Moonah Men's prayer meeting on Friday.'

'I shall make a run for it tomorrow night,' said Savage, 'but I need women's clothing. I am not of heavy build. The flesh came off me at Port Arthur, one way and another. Can you furnish me?'

'I must not bring women's clothes to the church,' said Alice. 'St Paul forbids it.' But she had often felt that she was losing patience with St Paul.

'If he won't let you come to me, I must come to you,' said Savage.

'You mean to my father's house?'

'Tell me the way exactly, Miss Alice, and which your room is. As soon as the time's right, I will knock twice on your window.'

'You will not knock on it once!' said Alice. 'I don't sleep on the ground floor.'

'Does your room face the sea?'

'No, I don't care to look at the sea. My window looks on to the Derwent, up the river valley to the north-west.'

Now that she was looking at him he put his two thumbs and forefingers together in a sign which she had understood and indeed used herself ever since she was a child. It meant *I give you my whole heart.*

'I should have thought you might have wanted to know what I was going to do when I reached England,' he said.

'I do know. You'll be found out, taken up and committed to Pentonville as an escaped felon.'

'Only give me time, Miss Alice, and I will send for you.'

In defiance of any misfortune that might come to him, he would send her the needful money for her fare and his address, once he had a home for her, in England.

'Wait and trust, give me time, and I will send for you.'

In low-built, shipshape Battery Point the Rectory was unusual in being three storeys high, but it had been smartly designed with ironwork Trafalgar balconies, and the garden had been planted with English roses as well as daisy bushes and silver wattle. It was the Rector's kindheartedness which had made it take on the appearance of a human warren. Alice's small room, as she had told Savage, looked out on to the river. Next to her, on that side of the house, was the visiting preacher's room, always called, as in the story of Elijah, the prophet's chamber. The Lukes faced the sea, and the Rector had retreated to what had once been his study. Mrs Watson slept at the back, over the wash-house, which projected from the kitchen. Above were the box-rooms, all inhabited by a changing population of no-hopers, thrown out of work by the depression of the 1840s. These people did not eat at the Rectory – they went to the Colonial Families' Charitable on Knopwood Street – but their washing and their poultry had given the grass plot the air of a seedy encampment, ready to surrender at the first emergency.

Alice did not undress the following night, but lay down in her white blouse and waist. One of her four shawls and one of her three skirts lay folded over the back of the sewing chair. At first she lay there and smiled, then almost laughed out loud at the notion of Savage, like a mummer in a Christmas pantomime, struggling down the Battery steps and on to the wharves under the starlight in her nankeen petticoat. Then she ceased smiling, partly because she felt the unkindness of it, partly because of her perplexity as to why he needed to make this very last part of his run in skirts. Did he have in mind to set sail as a woman?

She let her thoughts run free. She knew perfectly well that Savage, after years of enforced solitude, during which he had been afforded no prospect of a woman's love, was unlikely to be coming to her room just for a bundle of clothes. If he wanted to get into bed with her, what then, ought she to raise the house? She imagined calling out (though not until he was gone), and her door opening, and the bare shanks of the rescuers jostling in in their nightshirts – the visiting preacher, Mr Luke, her father, the upstairs lodgers – and she prayed for grace. She thought of the forgiven – Rahab, the harlot of Jericho, the wife of Hosea who had been a prostitute, Mary Magdalene, Mrs Watson who had cohabited with a drunken man.

You may call me Miss Alice.

I will send for you.

You could not hear St George's clock from the Rectory. She marked the hours from the clock at Government House on the waterfront. It had been built by convict labour and intended first of all as the Customs House. It was now three o'clock. The *Constancy* sailed at first light.

Give me time and I will send for you.

If he had been seen leaving the church, and arrested, they would surely have come to tell the Rector. If he had missed the way to the Rectory and been caught wandering in the streets, then no one else was to blame but herself. I should have brought him straight home with me. He should have obtained mercy. I should have called out aloud to every one of them – look at him, this is the man who will send for me.

The first time she heard a tap at the window she lay still, thinking, 'He may look for me if he chooses.' It was nothing, there was no one there. The second and third times, at which she got up and crossed the cold floor, were also nothing.

Alice, however, did receive a letter from Savage (he still gave himself that name). It arrived about eight months later, and had been despatched from Portsmouth. By that time she was exceedingly busy, since Mrs Watson had left the Rectory, and had not been replaced.

Honoured Miss Alice,

I think it only proper to do Justice to Myself, by telling you the Circumstances which took place on the 12 of November Last Year. In the First Place, I shall not forget your Kindness. Even when I go down to the Dust, as we all shall do so, a Spark will proclaim, that Miss Alice Godley Relieved me in my Distress.

Having got to the Presbittery in accordance with your Directions, I made sure first of your Room, facing North

West, and got up the House the handiest way, by scaling the Wash-house Roof, intending to make the Circuit of the House by means of the Ballcony and its varse Quantity of creepers. But I was made to Pause at once by a Window opening and an Ivory Form leaning out, and a Woman's Voice suggesting a natural Proceeding between us, which there is no need to particularise. When we had done our business, she said further, You may call me Mrs Watson, tho it is not my Name. – I said to her, I am come here in search of Woman's Clothing. I am a convict on the bolt, and it is my intention to conceal myself on Constancy, laying at Franklyn Wharf. She replied immediately, 'I can Furnish you, and indeed I can see No Reason, why I should not Accompany you.'

This letter of Savage's in its complete form, is now, like so many memorials of convict days, in the National Library of Tasmania, in Hobart. There is no word in it to Alice Godley from Mrs Watson herself. It would seem that like many people who became literate later in life she read a great deal – the Bible in particular – but never took much to writing, and tended to mistrust it. In consequence her motives for doing what she did – which, taking into account her intense affection for Alice, must have been complex enough – were never set down, and can only be guessed at.

Julia O'Faolain

THE RELIGIOUS WARS OF 1944

AT DUSK, MR LACY, the keeper, eager for his tea, rang a bell to chase dawdlers home. They were hard to flush out, because the park was dotted with gazebos – 'follies' built in the famine days to provide work – and if you hid in one you could always get out later by climbing the tall iron gates. There were places, too, where foot holes had been gouged in the perimeter wall.

'I'll have yez summonsed!' Mr Lacy's peaked cap sliced through the dimness. Authority shone from his brass buttons. 'I'll tell yeer mammies.' There was a by-law – but what was a by-law? – forbidding anyone to linger in the locked, possibly perilous park.

Mysterious goings on had been reported. A girl from Teresa Dunne's school had fainted when a man did some momentous thing, appearing to her out of a bush. The *gardai* had come, but then the matter was hushed up and the girl cowed into discretion.

'I'll tell you what she saw,' Mrs Malahide offered Teresa. 'If you like.' They were in the Malahides' drawing-room, and Teresa, whose mother had sent her over with a cake, was waiting to be given back the plate. You couldn't trust Mrs Malahide to return it later. She was a bit scatty, a Protestant, and, according to some, 'a gentlewoman, though no lady'. She would say anything and was, intermittently and dangerously, Teresa's mother's friend.

'Well?'

Teresa was torn. She was reluctant to learn secrets from Mrs Malahide, who would rob them of their versatile glee.

Not knowing kept open a shiver of possibilities – but Mrs Malahide was a belittler. She could shrink the wars of Troy. 'Men fighting over a bitch' was how she once described those.

'Don't mind her,' people advised. 'She's that way because of her lip.'

She had a harelip, without which she would have been a beauty – would have stayed in England and married her own sort rather than poor, decent Jack Malahide. Instead, here she was in an Irish village, cut off by the war and living, said gossips, on 'the smell of an oil rag'. Teresa herself had seen the grey, scummy broth of sheep's lung which Mrs Malahide left on the stove for her children's meal when she and her husband took off for the pub. He, a parson's son, had served in the colonial service and now made simple toys that people bought because the Emergency had cut off supplies of better ones. Bright and two-dimensional, his hobbyhorses bounded up the village street between the legs of four- and five-year-olds whose sisters held skipping ropes by the snug beechwood handles he had painstakingly turned on his lathe. He had a marvelling smile and worshipped Mrs Malahide.

'Poor Jack,' sighed his cronies. Yet they liked her for her spirit and because, when not blasting the sour grapes of life, she was, said Teresa's mother, 'great value'. Mrs Dunne, while deploring her friend's morals, hailed in her that fine contempt for convention which titillates the Irish.

'She's great company,' Mrs Dunne would acknowledge, 'and hasn't a pick of human respect.'

That was what worried Teresa. For how could she reconcile the ideals of her school nuns with tolerance of Mrs Malahide, who must be the most brazen thing alive? Lipstick ran up the crack of her harelip, and contamination oozed from her. She had a moustache yellow from chain-smoking, and today – Sunday – her feet lazed in cinders that had spilled past the confines of her fenderless hearth. Drifts of turf ash had possibly settled in her hair, which was like the plumage of an old hen. Both hair and ash had orange streaks, like fossil memories of fire.

Scattered on the floor were the *Sunday Pictorial* and *News of the World*, banned English papers that had been smuggled past the customs inside copies of the *Catholic Herald*. Teresa read the headlines with an affronted eye. 'SCOUTMASTER FOUND TROUSERLESS . . .' a fold concealed where. 'DECEIVED MISTRESS CHOPS OFF LOVER'S . . .'

To quell the riot in her mind, Teresa told herself that perhaps no more had been chopped off than the lover's tie. But no: not in that paper, or Bunty Malahide wouldn't trouble to smuggle it in. Dirt was what she liked. Scandal. Her mind was beyond description.

'Impure,' the nuns would have said, but the word fell short. Failing to anticipate Mrs Malahide, they had sent Teresa forth into the world, unfit to cope – and were perhaps no fitter themselves. Tender rituals absorbed them, and most of last term had been spent planning the Feast of the Immaculate Conception, for which every girl had been required to buy a ten-shilling lily. Those whose families found this a strain might, the nuns conceded, substitute a chrysanthemum. But the concession was reluctant. Each donor was to say, 'O Mary I give thee the lily of my heart! Be thou its guardian forever,' and then present a bloom securely tipped with waterproof paper, lest sap stain her white uniform skirt. 'You could hardly,' said the nuns with a rueful smile, 'say "I give thee the chrysanthemum of my heart." '

'It was Mike Lacy,' Mrs Malahide had grown impatient. 'He exposed himself to her. I don't know why your mothers don't tell you the facts of life. Poor bugger's been sacked. I suppose his family will starve. Do you' – she drew greedily on a cigarette – 'take my meaning? We're not talking about the exposition of the Sacrament!' On her lips the words sizzled into blasphemy.

Teresa gaspd. Outrage released a babyish prickle of tears. Turning to hide this, she was once again assaulted by the headline 'CHOPS OFF . . .' What? *That*! What else did they keep harping on Sunday after Sunday in the *News of the World*?

'Why will Mr Lacy's family starve?' She made fast for the periphery of the story.

'You tell me!'

In exasperation, Mrs Malahide drew on her cigarette, then

emptied her lungs: *pfff!* Smoke coiled, and her harelip was very visible. 'It was his penis,' she told Teresa. 'He showed it to her. Can you tell me why that would make a girl of her age – nearly your age – faint? How old are you now? Twelve? Thirteen? Haven't you ever seen your father without his clothes? Or your brother? Well then? It's a necessary part of nature, as you'll soon discover. I blame those nuns for poisoning your minds. Sick sisters. Why hide things? Unless they're being hypocritical, which I have no doubt they are!' And Bunty Malahide began to tell how Father Creedon – a man crippled with arthritis – was enjoying the sexual favours of all the nuns in the local convent. Like a cock in a barnyard or a victorious stag. Exciting herself, and possibly forgetting to whom she was talking, Mrs Malahide worked up conviction. She always downed a glass or two of Tullamore Dew while reading the Sunday papers.

Teresa was fired by battle frenzy. The abuse of adult privilege infuriated her, and the maligning of the nuns called for punishment. 'Bear witness to your religion', she had been taught two years ago, in confirmation class, but the occasion had not arisen until now. Avenge, O Lord, those slaughtered saints whose bones . . . The spirit of old wars curdled her blood. She could feel it happen: clots blocking the flow as they did in anatomy charts. Evil was incarnate before her. Her eyes felt squinty, and the air glowed red.

The funny side would strike her later: for Mrs Malahide's flights of fancy would have been brought down to earth by a single look at Mother Dolours' dowager's hump, or at pale little Mother Crescentia, who flew into such passions about 'men keeping women from the altar'. Quite suddenly, while putting a theorem on the blackboard, this meek nun would swing around, stab the air with chalk, and launch a polemic so ahead of its time that, years later, when the issue became a live one, few of the girls she had harangued would recall her yearning to be a priest. At first, the idea was too odd to shock, and by the time it did Mother Crescentia's bones would be mouldering in the very graveyard whose soil, if you believed Bunty Malahide, was white with those of strangled babies sired by Father Creedon.

'Why else,' Bunty wanted to know, 'would nuns wear those bulky clothes? It's to hide their pregnancies! Holy Mothers forsooth! You don't think he goes there to hear confessions?'

'She needs a gag!' Teresa told her mother later. She would have cheerfully watched Mrs Malahide burn at the stake. At the very least, the Englishwoman should be forced to eat her own unwholesome words. Instead, magnified by laughter, they mocked Teresa when she rushed off, feeling, she suspected, every bit as assaulted as the girl in the park must have done when confronted by Mr Lacy. But she had not tried to argue. What would have been the point? Bunty Malahide loved a fight, and the one way to hush her would have been to agree with her. Teresa couldn't. That would have been a betrayal of sweet-cheeked Mother Fidelia, who had made her pupils promise to profess their faith without false diffidence and arm themselves against ridicule. Mother F., an ardent and pretty nun, inflamed her pupils, and for a whole term Teresa had daydreamed about her, imagining shared heroics and intimacies so private that when the dentist pulled one of her teeth she went without gas lest she babble them out under its influence. For a while, even thinking of Mother F. made her skin tingle.

What could have possessed Mr Lacy? Had he perhaps been taken short while having a pee?

The story of his fall must be true, though, for he was now doing odd jobs in the Dunnes' garden, where he looked old and bald without his peaked uniform cap. And maybe it was also true that his family was hungry, for one night, when Teresa looked out her window, she saw him by moonlight stealing cauliflowers and putting them into a sack. Poor Lacy! She remembered his old threat, 'I'll have yez summonsed', and it struck her that she could do just that to him. Not that she would! The precariousness of self – he had lost some of his – was too upsetting. Earlier, she had seen him shelter from the rain under the empty sack, and his head had looked no bigger than a fist. Falling asleep, she dreamed that someone had exposed Mother Fidelia's poor, cropped head. Nuns gave up their crowning glory when they took the veil.

Her mother had a row with Bunty Malahide over what she'd said to Teresa, and then made it up.

'How could you?' reproached Teresa.

But Mrs Dunne said you had to make allowances. Bunty's life had not gone well. That was why she lived here. The Irish were good-hearted, unlike her own sort, who despised her for marrying down. 'She's good-hearted herself,' argued Mrs Dunne. 'Look how kind she is to Greta.'

Greta was German and in need of kindness, now that Germany was losing the war. The map pins with which Teresa's father marked Allied and Axis movements had reversed direction, and the march round and round the sofa, with which he and her brother Pat hailed the theme music before the BBC news, had acquired new swagger. '*Léro léro lillubuléro*,' crowed Pat, lifting high his small fat knees. Sometimes he banged two spoons together. He was six. '*Lillubuléro bullenalà!*' The tune was Irish, and a lot of our men were fighting with the Allies, so, although we were neutral, and miffed by Mr Churchill's threatening to seize our ports, we wanted his side to win. Pat planned to kill Hitler when he grew up.

You tried to hide such thoughts from Greta, though, and even Bunty, who hung out the Union Jack when Englishness welled up in her, refrained from trampling too brutally on Greta's sore feelings. With victory in sight, she managed – most of the time – to be forbearing.

'Well, she trampled on *mine*!' Teresa blushed. The word 'feelings' reminded her of Mother F., and her anger at Bunty Malahide mingled with shame over a treason of her own. Queerly, at the height of her crush on the nun, she had felt impelled to write a mocking verse about her and to circulate it among her friends. The risk had excited her, as if she half hoped to be caught. The jingle began childishly, with the words 'The dark witch of Loreto', and, as it went from desk to desk, someone changed 'witch' to 'bitch'. That brought Teresa to her senses, and she snatched back her rhyme. She could be expelled. Girls *had* been for less – for trespassing in the nuns' part of the convent or spying on the pool where they took sea baths in long cotton dresses. Disrespect for the 'brides of Christ' was a sacrilege, and she spent nervous days wondering if a copy of her jingle had escaped her.

The reality of her fear freed her. She now felt only pity for Mother Fidelia, stuck in her make-believe – which, it occurred to Teresa, was not unlike the games she and her classmates had played when they were small. Using penny-leaves for currency, they had sold field daisies for eggs and brown dockleaf blossoms for tea. Grass became string and rhubarb leaves wrapping paper. What difference was there between that and offering the Virgin the lily of your heart? The 'brides of Christ' didn't even eat in public. If you gave one of them a sweet, she kept it for later. Everything was for later. They did nothing now, which was why it was so unfair of Mrs Malahide to pretend they did.

'If I were you,' said Teresa's mother, 'I'd talk less about feelings! Remember how you hurt Greta's at Christmas?'

How forget? It had been the talk of the village, after a dirndl-skirted Greta, her queenly braids done up in a crown, had given a children's party. As if Christmas were something on which Germans had a special claim, she had invited all the local small children to celebrate it, and, in the end, most parents had decided to let them go. After all, the woman was not thought to be a Nazi, and she and her non-German husband were desperate to have babies but couldn't. Let her have ours for an afternoon, said the villagers magnanimously. Jack Malahide supplied a bran tub to be groped in for prizes, and Mrs Dunne sent Teresa to help and to keep an eye on Pat, who was a bit of a handful.

He was also the child whom Greta knew best, so she asked him to start things off by inviting a little girl to dance: a mistake. Pat, when shy, sat on the ground. Plonk. Backside down. There was no budging him.

Greta didn't understand this. Hunkering down to coax him, she brought the fun to a standstill, and shushed the other children, who became bored. There was – people said afterwards – a German stubbornness to this, and a barren woman's pedantry. She kept on and on at Pat, while the others fidgeted and pinched each other and a boy grabbed the Baby Jesus from the tasteful German crib. It was when someone pulled the plug on the fairy lights and several children began to cry that Teresa lost her head. 'Pat,' she cajoled, 'ask Annie to dance. You'll never grow up and kill Hitler if you're afraid of a small girl.'

At first, she didn't notice her gaffe, much less connect it with what happened next, which was that Greta gave a small scream, rushed to the telephone, and told the village operator that she wanted everyone to leave. Yes. Now. At once! Parents were to fetch their children. The party was over. 'Take them away! I know now what you tell them behind my back! Oh you Irish are false! Tell the parents. Their children steal Baby Jesus and wish to kill Hitler. You hate me secretly.'

Helplessly, Teresa tried to restore order while Greta sobbed, Pat still sat on the floor, and the more enterprising small boys pocketed the marzipan crib animals, which had been cooked with sugar rations contributed by their mothers. Then someone put *Heilige Nacht* on the gramophone. It was Jack Malahide, who had borrowed the rector's car – those who had petrol during the big Emergency were expected to help with minor ones – and was now piling children into it to deliver them home. Meanwhile, his wife calmed Greta down and comforted her with whiskey.

It was only when Teresa heard Bunty say to Greta that Teresa hadn't *meant* to upset her that she knew she had. Greta, her flaxen plaits askew, was weeping over the ruins of her crib. Where, she wanted to know, was Baby Jesus? And the marzipan donkey? She looked like a wronged maiden in a tale by the Brothers Grimm.

Peace was made. But Greta was not the same. Like poor Lacy, she had lost her plumpness and her trust.

It wasn't all Teresa's fault. The Church of Ireland – Protestant, despite the name – let Greta down, depriving her of spiritual comfort, since she, who was also a Protestant, had nowhere else to go. But how attend its services? Its small, embattled, but adamant congregation prayed hard against Germany, called God to its colours, and sang in unwavering chorus, 'Thou who made us mighty, make us mightier yet'. Since 'us' meant Britain, this annoyed the native Irish as much as it did Greta. Patriots marvelled at the old oppressor calling itself 'Mother of the Free', and from time to time on a Friday night broke into the church to pee ritually on its floor.

Friday was payday, when even poor Lacy, defying the confines of his life, was to be heard smashing his own possessions, driving his wife to despair, and chanting in the spirited abandon of drink, ''Twas there that you whispered tenderly that you loved me, would always be Lily of the lamplight, my ow-w-w-wn Lily Marlene.'

This cut Greta to the quick. 'Even our songs they steal!' she wailed to her false friends, Mrs Malahide and Mrs Dunne, who consoled her with soft words and hard liquor.

January was snowy, and Colonel Williams' pond froze, which gave people a rare chance to bring out their skates. The Colonel offered to supply a barbecue. No invitations were sent, since all were understood to be welcome – all, that is to say, except Greta. Williams, an ex-British officer, would not fraternise with the enemy.

'Will she have the nous to stay away?' worried Mrs Dunne. 'I've dropped hints, but Greta's not one to take them.' Mrs Dunne sighed. Neutrality was tricky.

Teresa had her own troubles. She had, after some hesitation, suspended her feud with Mrs Malahide so as to borrow her toboggan. It was the only one in the village. Everyone else used old sheets of corrugated iron.

The Malahide attic was a trove of odd tackle: snowshoes, pith helmets, motoring veils, and other aids for facing intemperate conditions. These, like the scaly tail that is kept hidden in the story of the mermaid who marries a fisherman, testified to their owners' alien nature. The Malahides had lived in places whose foreignness clung to them. Jack Malahide, for instance, had a parasite in his blood which, according to local gossip, could only be caught on the rare occasions when it emerged to walk across his eyeball.

While rummaging up there for skates for her mother, Teresa had a shock.

'I found a poem of yours,' said Bunty Malahide, coming up behind her so suddenly that Teresa nearly let a trunk lid fall on her own neck. 'It slipped from your pocket. About a nun. It's quite funny,' she congratulated. 'I must say, you're a dark horse!' And she proceeded, teasingly, to recite it. 'I added a verse.'

This was, of course, crude. All about nuns with buns in the oven. Father Creedon's name figured in it, *and* Mother F.'s! Teresa felt sick – the more so because of something that had recently happened in school. 'I'm disappointed in you!' the nun had told her hurtfully. 'You've let me down. You're as silly and light-minded as the rest.'

What had sparked the thing off was a discussion of the seniors' Christmas play. This was about a pagan who got converted on his wedding day, then found himself in a moral dilemma when fellow-Christians wanted him to be a martyr while his bride claimed that he owed himself to her. It was resolved – predictably, if you knew convent plays – by the bride's own conversion. The thing was in hexameters. Deadly in more ways than one. A kind of trap, Teresa sensed, for girls like herself, who the nuns hoped might have a vocation. To elude this, she asked Mother Fidelia whether the converted bridegroom wasn't a bit prone to spiritual pride? What about his telling his Christian mentor, who deplored his reluctance to get himself killed, that the mentor didn't know what it was like to have a wife? This, as Teresa remarked reasonably, was only a day after his wedding. How much could he know about having a wife himself? After one night?

Mother F. blushed. Unprecedentedly. And the class dissolved in glee. Teresa, though usually quicker than the rest, was the last to see why. Sex, to be sure! The topic had, she saw with shock, invaded not only the sanctuary of school but the mind of Mother Fidelia. Indignantly, Teresa, too, blushed, and when accused by the nun of letting her down, felt that the shoe was on the other foot. Like it or not, the lily of her heart was festering and likely, as Shakespeare warned, to smell far worse than weeds!

And now here was Bunty M., source of slime and vulgarity, gleefully reciting Teresa's embarrassing jingle. Why had she ever written it? To check her own feelings for Mother F.? But there was no time to ponder this. Imagine if Bunty – you couldn't put anything past her! – were to show it to other people?

'Give it back to me,' begged Teresa. But Bunty said the poem was now half hers, and she wanted to copy it out.

'I'll give it to you at the pond, this afternoon,' she promised.

Teresa didn't dare argue.

Colonel Williams did things in style. Two small boys with brooms were keeping the ice clear of slush, and Mike Lacy had been set to mind the barbecue. Carefully pricked wartime sausages, made mostly of breadcrumbs and lard, squirted sizzles of grease into the charcoal. Anglo-Irish ladies sailed by on skates bought on foreign holidays before the war. This, noted Mrs Dunne, had been one of the villages of the Pale. Even the Lacys were of English stock, having come over, generations back, to serve in a mansion that had now disappeared. Colonel Williams lived in its dower house, which would no doubt be torn down one day, too. His sort and their habitats were doomed.

'The big-house people had their good side.' Mrs Dunne surveyed the pretty scene. 'Liked to make a show. "Showing the flag", they called it. But at home' – she lowered her voice – 'they'd live on the smell of a sausage. We had a maid who'd worked for them, and she was as thin as a lath. They starved her and themselves. Half an egg they'd give her for Sunday breakfast! Imagine.'

She spoke briskly while fastening her borrowed skates. Greta, Mrs Dunne was relieved to see, hadn't come. Neither had Bunty Malahide, for whom Teresa was anxiously looking out, refusing to be distracted until Colonel Williams begged her to help with the sausages. There was hot wine as well, which was to be kept from the younger fry. Teresa surreptitiously drank the better part of a glass before deciding she didn't like it.

Her mother skated towards her, showing signs of agitation. 'Greta's just come and gone,' she whispered. 'The Colonel cut her dead. I tried to talk to her, but she rushed off in a state. There was something bad, too – for Germany – on the one o'clock news. Somebody should be with her. Help me off with my skates. No. Better go ask Father Creedon to look after her. I saw him coming up the field. Quick! Take the toboggan and head him off. Ask him to hold the fort until I come.'

So off whizzed Teresa to intercept the priest and, having sent him on his errand of mercy, trudged back up the slope to the barbecue, where the Colonel was discussing the incident with Bunty Malahide. What could one do, he shrugged, but set an example? War was war, and it was a damn shame the Irish hadn't joined this one. They were natural fighters. A crying shame! Still, better not to spoil today's merriment. He lowered his voice, and Teresa heard no more. He was a straight-backed man who, when walking around his property, carried a long, swooping, metal-tipped tool for rooting up weeds. You had, he told Bunty, to take a stand. Stick to your guns, what? Bunty kept nodding her head.

'Yes,' she sighed. 'Yes.'

Teresa, who was keeping an eye on her, saw with surprise that Bunty's sardonic look was gone. She and the Colonel stood in a small bubble of intimacy. Of course, they were two of a kind, and maybe lonely. Maybe they found us as alien as we did them? The thought was unwelcome. She had to admit, though, that Bunty looked pinker and younger than usual. Her eyes sparkled, and Teresa remembered people saying that Bunty would have been a beauty, but for her lip. For a moment she even had a look of Mother Fidelia.

Behind Bunty, Mrs Dunne now moved into Teresa's field of vision as she cut across the field, slipping in the soft snow. She was trying to catch up with Father Creedon and Greta, who had taken the path.

'Can't run with the hare and hunt with the hounds!' said Colonel Williams, who was obviously upset.

'Just look at that!' Bunty waved towards the dip in the field where Father Creedon was trying to hold up the stumbling Greta. His black suit glowed against the snow and, as they watched, she lurched, and he caught her in his arms.

Bunty shaded her eyes with her hand. 'He's getting a feel in! Well, good for Greta. Better her than the nuns! She'd *like* a bun in her oven! A gift from Holy Ireland to take home to Germany when the war ends! That reminds me, I've got your poem here,' she called to Teresa. 'I've added another bit. Do you want to hear?'

'No!'

'It's quite racy! Listen . . .'

But she got no further, for Teresa – or was it Mike Lacy, who had been at the wine? – now shook the barbecue, so that the sausages fell onto the coals and the sudden fatty blaze had to be dealt with by the Colonel. When things were restored, Teresa dusted off the salvageable sausages and threaded them on a spit while Mike laid out a ring of fresh ones.

The way he was standing, they looked like penises sprouting at belly level from his old black suit. Or the spokes of a monstrance. Exposition, thought Teresa, and was shocked at the effect Bunty Malahide had on her thoughts. Might this be irreversible? A lasting contamination? And could it have leaked from her mind to Mother Fidelia's? Removing a split sausage from her spit, she saw that a piece of smouldering coal had got stuck inside it. Giddily, she became aware of Bunty's voice rabbiting on and, mingling with it in her head, like wireless interference, a line from a prayer: 'Cleanse my lips, O Lord, with a live coal.'

'Here. Have a sausage.' She pinched the fatty meat tight over the coal, handed it to Bunty, and watched with a thrill of horror as the harelip closed jauntily on the burning mouthful.

Paul Magrs

PATIENT IRIS

SHE HAS A friend called Patient Iris who lives at the top of the town by the Roman remains.

Irises take a good while to open. She thinks if you sit them by the window they stand a better chance.

Iris is patient. She watches men reconstructing the Roman remains.

At the top of the town you can see all of South Shields, the grey flank of North Shields, the blue sash of sea.

The Romans must have built here for the view.

Their fort is vast. When they rebuild it do they use the old stones or do they have brand new, cut into shapes they have guessed at? She and Patient Iris watch them working and the stone certainly looks fresh. Newer and more yellow even, than those private estates they've been putting up.

She feels bad about Patient Iris, who has turned bright yellow and sits all day and night by the phone. She is ready to ring out in case she has an emergency. Iris's bedsores are a sight to see. She has looked, under Iris's nightgown, at Iris's bidding. She instructed Patient Iris to sit by her window, to get some air, watch the world outside. Lying down all day can do no good for you, really.

Fat purple welts, all down the back of her. Succulent, like bursting fruit.

Patient Iris can't quite remember, but didn't the coast here once freeze entirely?

It is so high up. The Roman soldiers, with the north wind

shushing up their leather skirts, at parade on those ramparts, they must have been so cold.

And didn't it once freeze up?

Patient Iris lived at the end of a street. When it froze up, surely it was before the time that they bombed the row's other end. The houses went down like dominoes, a trail of gunpowder, sizzling, stopped before it got to Patient Iris's door.

Patient Iris is a survivor. She survived the frozen winter when, she realises now, she must still have been a child.

Patient Iris talks on the phone with her friend. Her friend phones now, more often than visiting. They both agree that visiting is not much use. There's nothing new to see. Although the Roman remains, across the way from the flat above the pub where Iris lives, grow a little higher every day.

And these two women don't need to see each other. They are so accustomed to the sight of themselves that the phone is all they need. And it saves a trip out. The trip up the hill is arduous, after all. Yet they used to walk it happily, surely, to get to the Spiritualist Church, when calling up your husband was the thing, before Bingo.

Her friend phones to check on Patient Iris's health. Both know that it cannot last the winter.

And the winter is stealing in. When Patient Iris wakes in her chair each morning, the first thing she sees are the Roman remains; blanched with scabs of frost, their outlines etched in by an impossibly blue sky.

Winters like this, everything turns to jewels. Patient Iris runs her fingers over and round her tender sores as she speaks into the receiver to her oldest living friend. Will they turn to crusted rubies, drop away, make her well and rich again? Vaguely she imagines profiting from her ailments. There must be a pay-off somewhere.

'Do you remember,' she says, breaking into her friend's flow of chatter, 'do you remember when the coast froze up?'

Her friend is thrown by this *non sequitur*, but for an instant she sees the orange cranes, stilled in the docks, useless and wading on ice. The monstrous keels of half-completed ships, abandoned, like wedding dresses on dummies with the arms not on yet and pins sticking out.

'I think so,' she mumbles. She had been telling Patient Iris about the local women, bonded in a syndicate, who won a million pounds between them on the football pools. They were all supermarket cashiers and had their photos taken for the press sitting in shopping trolleys.

'But do you remember, as well, the seals on the ice? They appeared from nowhere. Came thousands of miles south because it was so cold that winter.'

Her friend doesn't remember the seals.

Patient Iris remembers seeing grey sides of beef, stranded on the ice. She worked in a butchers. The red-faced lads joked about serving up seal chops.

The seals grew bigger. From the top of the town Patient Iris could hear them barking in the night. Not barking like dogs; grunts and coughs like old men in the park. They were getting bigger because they were pregnant. The whiskered seals with large, inscrutable eyes, beached on the useless docks.

'They were mermaids. The stupid sailors mistook them for mermaids. Typical sailors.'

'Imagine,' says Patient Iris suddenly, 'imagine giving birth on sheer ice. Imagine being born on to sheer ice. You come out of that blubbery safeness, straight on to the snow. The seals try to cover each other, but . . .'

Her friend decides that Patient Iris's mind is wandering. Tomorrow she will visit in person. She begins to end the phone call. She feels an urgent need for Iris to put down the phone, in case she wants to call out an ambulance for herself. Her friend knows Patient Iris all too well; she likes to do things for herself.

Patient Iris has been kneading the bedsores as she talks. Down the side of her leg, through stiff white cotton, fresh stains of primrose and carmine bloom.

Patient Iris puts down the phone and thinks.

One night when the seals were barking out their birth pangs, she left the house in her nightie and slippers and walked down to the docks. The dark, slumped shapes, dividing and reproducing, unabashed on the exposed span of gleaming ice. The high pig-squeals of baby seals. The mothers rolling over, moist with their own cooling gels, careful not to slip and crush the bairns.

Patient Iris met a woman, a hag, really, with great hooped skirts and a basket of herring on her back. She said her name was Dolly. She was a lunatic, screaming the odds at the clock-face when it struck the hours. In her basket the fish slipped and goggled their frozen eyes as Dolly jogged about to keep warm.

'I keep sailors inside my skirts, that's why I wear them so big. So they can hide inside and dodge the draft. They needn't have to go to sea. They oughtn't to have to do what they don't want.'

Dolly's face is like a coconut. The hairs grow thick inside the grooves so she'd never be able to shave them if she tried.

Tonight Patient Iris's oldest living friend dreams of Patient Iris turning yellow and sitting by the phone. The moonlight smacks off the stark Roman walls and drops into her room. Iris is motionless, asleep sitting up, and looking dead already. Except for the fine hiss of breath, issuing as smoke from her open mouth.

She sits awkwardly in her chair, Patient Iris, almost doubled up with her precious jumble of inner organs preserved inside a clatter of limbs.

Patient Iris sits as awkwardly as the supermarket cashiers, legs and arms akimbo in shopping trolleys, waving about their champagne and glasses and oversized cheques.

Patient Iris's friend of many years dreams that this winter will be cold. Much colder than ever before. Colder even than that winter before the town was bombed and Tynedock sheeted over with ice.

Colder still and the archaeologists decide they must down tools and abandon the Roman remains till spring. It is so cold that they become frightened. This is the kind of cold that crystallises fragments of lost souls in the air. They rekindle themselves and brighten when it comes in dark. Centurions gather on the ramparts in their leather skirts, with the wind whistling about them, their eyes dead and quartz.

In the cold imagined by Iris's friend, the Roman remains can complete themselves at the top of the town.

Old outlines glisten silver in the air, tugging at each other, stirring the air to recall what once stood there. Moisture freezes, clicks into place, recreates a fabulous ice palace on the reconstructed site, at the top of the town, above the frozen docks, above the window of Patient Iris.

Her window is open and the time is right for irises to open – unseasonably, perhaps even dangerously, mid-winter. But what does Patient Iris care for danger now?

She is open to the elements. Her sores have opened her up to the harshest the North can offer.

The cold of the North heals up Patient Iris for ever. Her gasping, fish-like, collapsing internal organs stop in their tracks and freeze. Her bedsores harden. Patient Iris reaches with one arthritic hand to splash a little scent behind each ear before she allows the cold to come over her entirely. The scent catches at each ear-lobe and dangles there in perfect cut crystals. And now Patient Iris is laminated for ever into a clear envelope of ice; the fate of those who live at the extremes, like here, at the top of the town. She decides to pop out for a walk. It is the first time she has fancied walking in ages. Perhaps Dolly will still be about, saving sailors or Roman centurions, pushing them under her voluminous skirts.

Patient Iris stops by the docks to see the seal mothers return and, sure enough, she is rewarded by the sight of their stolid, hard-working bodies.

Patient Iris is much braver now that she has left the phone off the hook and can wear her bedsores as jewels. She will skate over the ice to see how the burgeoning families are doing.

She will talk the snorting, whiskered mothers through their

difficult night, as their children are slapped out like old shoes
on to the bloodied glass.

Elizabeth Berridge
POOR MARY AND THE BOOK OF LIFE

THE FARM WAS a mixture of mellow brick, with grey stone flinty walls, built in an L-shape, adjoining the church. The village was small, with one shop, the post office counter at the back behind a kind of wire mesh. You made your way to buy a stamp or a comic around open sacks of dried fruit, oatmeal, boxes of apples or onions, coils of rope. There was a neighbourly feeling about the shelves, where boxes of matches and wicks for oil stoves shouldered tall jars of sweets. You pushed open the door to a smell of wax candles and paraffin; occasionally a barrel of fish packed in salt and ice might curdle this heady mixture. Madly unhygienic by today's standards, but nobody in the village seemed any the worse. People lived long and healthily in Bardingham, for the almshouses were always full.

I was never lonely at Priory Farm, a child among three adults – four, if you counted Hannah, too redoubtable and kind to be discounted. There was always something to be done with any one of them. I might shell peas outside the kitchen door, sitting in the sun, listening to the rattle of the pods into an enamel basin, or watch Jacopy at work in the vegetable garden, go with him to pick raspberries. I might ride on the horse-drawn wagons when the corn was cut, or walk into the cool stables and talk to the horses, watch the milking of the cows. There was an air of unhurried occupation, of tasks that were fulfilling in themselves, for each day was rounded without effort. We belonged to the country rhythm in which each of us had a place.

Aunt Mary had her special responsibilities, and I liked to

go with her when she fed the cats at supper time, filling shallow dishes by the barn with fresh milk and stale bread and household scraps. Twelve or thirteen would come running, all colours, all sizes. Their job was to keep down the rats and mice and they were never allowed into the house as pets, however hard I begged for a kitten. She also did the household mending, for she sewed neatly, and would settle down with a pile of socks or stockings to darn, or turn sheets sides-to-middle, repair pillow slips or tablecloths. Once I asked her why Aunt Lizzy's stockings always wore out at the knees. I tore my own stockings, but couldn't imagine that an adult would tear hers.

She slid me a glance, looked across at Aunt Lizzy, down again at the stocking stretched over the darning mushroom and said, with a tiny smile, 'Guess.'

I couldn't, and there was silence in the room. Soon after, Aunt Lizzy left us and Aunt Mary leant forward and whispered, 'Down on her knees to the Lord – that's what does it.' Then, seeing my amazement, she added, tapping her own knees, 'In the church. It's that old stone floor.'

Aunt Lizzy was good, I knew that, but to pray when it wasn't a Sunday gave me a lot to think about. And why didn't she use a hassock?

Deft, contained, birds and flowers growing from the tips of her fingers as if from a conjuror's wand, Aunt Mary sat embroidering a tray-cloth in the churchyard. Sent to summon her to one of the meals that punctuated the long summer days, I liked to watch her before I made my final approach. There always seemed to be a small, sneaky wind tunnelling around the tombstones, and this breeze loosened her beautiful fading golden hair from the careless bun low on her neck and disturbed the fine curls about her ears. Unsuitable to her age, said Aunt Lizzy.

Had she once – on account of this mass of golden hair, then so long she could sit on it – really been taken by the gypsies? Had she been frightened or excited by the experience? Had she really seen inside one of their painted vans and had they told her fortune?

Her answers depended on her mood. Sometimes she would say, teasingly, 'Papa saved me. He rode up on his great black horse and used his horsewhip on them as they sat round the camp fire. He threw open the doors of the van and wound my hair round his hand and dragged me out. That was the only time I cried.'

'They were kind then, the gypsies?'

'Oh yes. There was an old woman who gave me a delicious stew. That was why I cried. What with the pain of Papa pulling my hair so hard and having to leave the stew. I've never tasted one like it since.'

I never quite believed her because, on another occasion, she might tell me that a gypsy girl of her own age opened the van door in the middle of the night and told her to run. 'My father is going to cut off all your hair tomorrow and sell it. He'll get a pound at least. Run!' Another time the tale went that she broke away from the gypsy man's hard fist when she imitated an owl – strange sound to hear in full daylight – and he loosened his grip to stare round at the trees.

Aunt Mary was the only grown-up with whom I allowed myself the luxury of, no, not quite total disbelief, more the take-it-with-a-pinch-of-salt kind. She seemed to me at times a child, young as I was young, her brand of fantasy my own. Grown-ups, in those days, were like timetables, unalterably correct, telling no lies, and one's life was run along their tramlines. Like timetables they were there to be consulted, then left until needed again, for a child could live between tramlines comfortably enough if she was wise.

I always knew where to find her, for she liked to use the flat top of a table-shaped tomb as a workplace: the moss made it soft to sit on, and she could spread out her silks or wools in neat strands, her pin-cushion and needle-case and scissors.

'They're an old local family, after all,' she told me once, giving the stone a proprietory pat. 'Bancroft's father used to shoot over their land.'

I hoped she would come at once and not pause at Jock's

grave, for that would hold us up and Aunt Lizzy had said, 'Tell her to come directly, for I'm dishing up in ten minutes and I'll not have the food spoiling.' To my relief, when she saw me, she thrust her needle into her work, folded it and swept it into a linen bag. We walked together through the grasses growing high and feathery around sunken tomb-stones, avoiding the long-neglected humps of old graves. Pollen brushed off on to our shoes and seeds clung to my bare ankles and prickled my aunt's lisle stockings as we rounded the church and took the path to our narrow secret door in the wall that led straight into the kitchen garden of Priory Farm. This door looked massive, made of iron, with scrollwork and bars; yet it was all show, for we could quite easily unlatch it, and although there was a massive key it was seldom locked.

Over the door, about a foot out from the wall, was a curved wooden archway with a plaque set in at the top of the curve. It read:

> *This entry into God's piece was erected*
> *by the seven children of Hector Burford,*
> *rector of this parish 1845–63,*
> *and of his wife Sarah,*
> *lovingly remembered.*

The names of the seven children, not all decipherable, were carved into the arch itself with a flower between each name. Apparently it had been the youngest daughter's idea, for when she married the owner of Priory Farm she persuaded her husband to open up the wall and set the door there so that they could walk comfortably to church in all weathers. The arch was an afterthought, erected when the rector and his wife died. I liked the words 'God's piece', and had to have it explained, for I was not sure whether it referred to my uncle's farm or the church grounds; or even, allowing for a possible misspelling, to God's peace, which I was assured every Sunday morning, 'passeth all understanding'.

We washed our hands under the pump and flapped them about to dry before joining Aunt Lizzy and Uncle Bancroft at table. The dining-room was dim and cool, for it was panelled in old oak and the walls were thick. My uncle said grace and set to carving the cold joint of beef. He was a tall quiet man, all brownness. His face and hands were burnt to the colour of the hay in his fields, his thick hair crisp and dark, with streaks of grey over each ear, and he always seemed clad in shades of brown and dark green, like some creature of the earth needing protective colouring. I loved to watch him carve; those big countryman's hands held the knife and fork so surely and each pink slice of meat fell away equally matched in size and thickness.

Salad and jacket potatoes and butter. Everything grown or made on this farm. It was a wonder to me, used to life on the outskirts of London. At my uncle's feet, for he was never far away, lay his liver-and-cream spaniel, Prince, ears feathered on the patterned carpet, eyes alert for movement above him. From behind the door to the kitchen came stifled laughter from Hannah as she ate with the two farm workers.

'What are you planning to do this afternoon?' Aunt Lizzy asked me. 'It's going to be hot, perhaps you had better rest in the cool with a book.'

But at once Aunt Mary broke in, in her excitable way, 'I thought that Beth and I could cut the grass around some of the graves. The churchyard is a disgrace! And there are so many daisies . . . would you like to make the longest daisy-chain in the world?'

She turned her blue eyes to me and I could only nod.

'Well, dear, you might like to collect the eggs with me later,' said Aunt Lizzy. 'There's that little black hen hiding somewhere . . .'

'The one with the crooked leg?'

'Yes. The other hens drove her off. I don't know where she is.'

'Plenty of time for that after tea,' said Aunt Mary. 'What a noise Hannah is making with those two men!'

Aunt Lizzy rang the little bell beside her, and the laughter stopped. As Hannah appeared, somewhat flushed, Aunt Lizzy put a warning finger to her lips, and said she could bring in the raspberries and cream, and cheese for the master.

The only remark my uncle, a silent man, made as he rose from the table was, 'Ben's coming about the horses, off their feed,' and nodded himself and his dog away out of the room. We heard his footsteps crunching across the farmyard.

'Come along, then, we'll get the secateurs and the shears.'

I looked at Aunt Lizzy, but she only pushed up her round, thin-rimmed spectacles and sighed.

'She'll be across at the church soon, you'll see,' said Aunt Mary as we made our way through the gate again with our garden tools.

It was hot and still in the churchyard. Difficult to imagine on such an August afternoon the winds and rainstorms that had made such a shipwreck of it. Stone crosses and discoloured angels leaned at all angles. Wild rose and plum, elder and thorn sprouted in unexpected places, truer guardians of the dead than the crumbling monuments, for they clawed at bare arms and inquisitive hands. Self-seeded descendants of once lovingly tended garden plants had escaped, claiming new territory; flourishing in isolated clumps of unexpected colour. Canterbury bells and tall spikes of hollyhock, marigold, pansies, even nasturtiums, attracted bees and darting flies. The drowsy bee-noise added to the stillness, overlaid it. Bumble bees, bigger than any I have seen since, went buzzing and bumping in and out of the Canterbury bells like so many fat women anxious for a bargain at the sales. Or else they sat, exhausted, on the dry crumbly mounds and fanned themselves with their absurdly small, transparent wings.

I was glad that cousin Jock was buried here, in the old part of the churchyard. On the south side of the church lay the new graves, bright with green pebbles and flashing black inscriptions on marble, and indestructible flower vases or artificial lilies under glass domes.

We cleared swathes among the graves until we were tired and the sweet smell of cut grass enclosed us. So we sat down for a breather – naturally by Jock's grave. My cousin Jock, who had died at the age of six from meningitis. Aunt Mary's son. I was born two years after he died and I was now four years older than he was. If he had lived he would have been eight years older, too old for me to play with. This strange sum fascinated me as much as his grave.

It had at its foot a fat marble book, spread open with the pages miraculously suggested, and even a wide curving bookmark curling up like a ribbon. On the left-hand page was engraved the one word 'Jock' in a flowing hand like a signature, and on the right-hand side incised in print, 'whose Book of Life was closed too soon'.

We picked buttercups and daisies from the uncleared patch under a buddleia, alive with red admirals, and made a long chain of flowers, piercing the juicy stalks (I with my thumbnail and Aunt Mary with a pin, for she shockingly bit her nails) and pulling each stem through, right up to the head. Then we draped it across and across Jock's book.

'What made you think of it, Aunt Mary? It's so lovely.'

She was touching the J of Jock and bent her head round to me.

'Yes, isn't it? I thought of it all by myself. Jock loved books – loved reading, he learnt early. And even if Lizzy didn't approve I meant to have it. She said who was I to say such a thing, only God knew whether Jock had read enough of the Book of Life. Even the rector thought I was setting myself up too high.' She moved restlessly, pushing up her hair under the old wide-brimmed straw hat. 'But I had my way. I was upset, you see.'

Together we looked at the headstone, rising out of the crowded bed of flowers that filled the plot. All colours, all scents; the purples and white of lavatera and petunia to complement each other, the sharp pink and strong reds of ivy-leaf geranium, dark blue of trailing lobelia and the eau-de-Cologne green of mint which edged the bed. I pinched a leaf and the sweet sharp smell stayed on my fingers.

JOCK OSGOOD LAMPTON

1918–1922

God giveth and God taketh away

'There she goes now,' said my aunt, handing me a peppermint. I looked up to see a green skirt disappearing into the church porch.

'Is she going to clean the brass or do the flowers? Shall we see if she wants any help?'

Aunt Mary levered herself up on to her knees, then on to her feet.

'What a funny child you are,' she said, in a flat, tired voice. 'Lizzy gets all the help she needs in there.' All at once she pulled at the daisy chain so carelessly that it broke in two, and draped it round her neck. 'Well, that's what I wanted and that's what I got.' She seemed not to be speaking to me at all. 'It was having no husband, you see. Having no husband to guide me.' And she was up and away, her high laugh exploding like birdsong, her skirts clutched up to her knees, hat falling away as she ran. 'Race you to the gate!'

I followed with the shears and the secateurs, humping along slowly. I felt heavy and old and cast off. As I passed her hat I kicked it aside into the long grass.

For tea that day we had the damp gingerbread Aunt Lizzy made, stuck with crystallised ginger and sultanas.

'Some people ice their gingerbread,' she said, 'but that's gilding the lily, I say.'

'It's gilt you put on gingerbread, Lizzy,' said Aunt Mary, 'not icing.'

Uncle Bancroft, divining that Mary was in one of her funny moods, for once made a remark.

'I've known some women fill up the hollow in a sad fruit cake with icing,' he teased.

'That's cheating!' Aunt Lizzy was easily drawn. 'In the WI baking competitions we can always spot it. But gingerbread should be flat on top, like a good madeira.'

'I love sad cake,' I said loyally, for my mother sometimes made one by mistake.

After tea Aunt Lizzy and I collected eggs and fed the hens, a ritual I enjoyed. She was a small woman, well-fleshed, with broad shoulders and a very soft, plump face, cheeks reddened from the Norfolk winds and sun. She was easier – if less exciting – to be with than Aunt Mary, for there was a stability about her reassuring to a child. As I followed her across the farmyard, carrying a basket, I was fully confident that she would lead me to all the secret places the hens liked.

She walked slowly, clucking encouragingly and scattering handfuls of the grey, dampish mixture of meal and grain that I knew was kept in a wooden box with a hinged lid in the barn. As her bantams – which always ran loose – came stepping round us, I asked her about the little black hen.

'There's no sign of her here. We'll go round by the big ditch when we've finished. I hope a fox hasn't taken her.'

The bantams laid all over the place, in patches of nettles between the threshing barn and the stables, among the straw bales, and at the base of old haystacks. But the Wyandottes, superior plump white hens companioned by a fine cock, were in large wired-off runs. Getting their eggs was easy, we had only to open the outside of the nesting boxes along the back of the henhouses. The summer before I had told Aunt Lizzy that it made me feel like a burglar, putting my hand in through someone's window. But although she laughed about it afterwards with Hannah, she explained seriously that once a hen had laid an egg she didn't want it any more. It was left as a present. You always knew when a hen went broody, for then she wanted to sit on a clutch of them and hatch out babies.

Remembering this, I said, 'Perhaps the little black hen is broody and wants to hatch out a family. That's why she's hiding.'

'I never thought of that. Aren't you clever!' she exclaimed.

As she handed each egg to me I carefully laid it in the basket. But something else was bothering me, and I asked her straight out.

'Aunt Lizzy, why did Aunt Mary have no husband to guide her when Jock died?'

'No husband to . . .' Aunt Lizzy's rosy face was hidden as she secured the flap of a nesting box. 'What nonsense has she been telling you now?'

I explained about Jock not finishing the book of life and saw her sharp brown eyes behind the round spectacles half close in displeasure. But she answered me, as I knew she would.

'Because my brother Tom – your aunt's husband – had taken himself off to Canada a week after Armistice Day, and he's never been back since. That's why.'

Aunt Lizzy always told the exact truth. She embarrassed people by this habit.

'Why didn't he send for her, then?'

One of my schoolfriends had had to leave that term to join her father in India.

'He didn't intend to. And that's all I'm going to say on that subject. Idle gossip is for idle tongues, miss.'

I was outraged. 'It's not idle gossip, Aunt Lizzy. It's family! Poor Aunt Mary, I think it's a shame! Didn't he care about his own son? Didn't he want . . .'

'Apparently not. We were not in his confidence.' She turned and made for the straw bales. 'Life isn't all honey, you'll learn that. The good Lord knows what He's about and affliction is never sent to those who can't bear it. Oh, look by your foot . . . you nearly walked into a nest. That's two cracked eggs we'll have to use up in a custard . . . do watch what you're doing, child, and leave other things alone.'

I held my tongue. Children were not important enough to be told everything. We had to nibble around the truth and be grateful. Grown-ups held the key to all knowledge; they were omnipotent, their lives were closed books. What did they expect in return, these omnipotents? Trust and truthfulness. Affection and obedience. It wasn't fair, but then life wasn't fair; it wasn't in truth all honey. That would be expecting too much, it would be 'setting oneself up'.

I could not resist trying to curry favour.

'Aunt Mary's lucky to have you and Uncle Bancroft, Mother says.'

'She may be comfortably placed in others' eyes.' Aunt Lizzy sounded even crosser. 'But perhaps in her own soul she walks on sharp stones.' She retrieved two small bantam eggs from a half-concealed cardboard box and held them a moment, looking down. 'That's why we care for her, poor daft girl that she is.'

When we had stowed all the eggs away in the kitchen, I went out by myself to the dusky churchyard, and, in spite of the mocking ghost call of an owl, made my way to where Aunt Mary's hat lay in the grass. Chastened, I carried it back to the farm.

Susan Wicks

INCONTINENCE

I remember they taught us the future –
the great globe rolling as if in moonlight
from the ovary's cupped darkness
out into unmapped distances,
the sperm spilling like mercury
on a new world where they might settle, hungry
for life, the elastic belt stretched
across stained bench-tops between us
among gas-taps and Bunsen burners,
its flesh-coloured hooks dangling
for the loops of imagined towels
still plump in their package. In the film
the pile shrank: in black-out darkness
we watched each stainless napkin
disappear impersonally. Now when I come to visit
in this metallic landscape
of tripods and zimmers, I find myself
counting the pads stacked in your cupboard
as they disappear – folded against the future,
as if bought for you by your own mother.

John Saul

CARGOES

WALLING OFF THE end of a street called Calle Calicuchima, sitting high in the water, the freighter *Alexander* docked almost in the middle of town. A great black hull studded with rivets, a floating giant to the local people, its daytime shadow dwarfed the new P&O office and cut a slant across the pillars of the customs building. Under the stars its mooring ropes creaked back and forth, while its great wall added darkness to the night.

This was 1910, when my grandfather sailed and strode the earth.

When art told tales.

When Picasso worked with Georges Braque, making brown pictures, snipping up newspapers, painting with combs and sand and glue.

The *Alexander* had just come up the west coast from Valparaíso, at that moment, with next to nothing on board. Its crew of course were on board. My grandfather, the captain. His white uniform. His broad white cap, which he brushed at the peak and put on at the mirror. Off with his cap; it was all well and good for photographs, ceremonies, strong sunlight, but otherwise it fitted best under his arm. He combed his dark hair and stepped down the walkway to the Malecón, the waterfront, to be greeted by the Honorary Consul. Captain Jones, welcome to Guayaquil. Thank you, said my grandfather, though I have been here before.

But not to Quito, high atop the Andes. Quito via the new mountain railway, a marvel of gleaming brass and carmine, a proud flame in the fire of British financial enterprise. In

Quito he was to negotiate next year's cargoes: cacao, coffee and bananas. This much is recorded in his logbook, a document which has come to rest in my possession.

1910, when these artists stuck tin and cardboard onto canvas.

When my mother was conceived.

Captain Jones first quartered nearby, at the Hotel Bolívar, and waited for the season's loading to begin. He was given a room overlooking the flat brown expanse of the River Guayas, with its slow tides and islands of green grass. Unusually for him, he rested, having looked out the once from the balcony; just long enough to clutch at the empty air, for the rail was lower than the bridge of the *Alexander*. He then hung up his white cap, trousers and captain's jacket, and slept. On waking he was offered pancakes with fried banana, *platanos*, and tea with lemon.

When Picasso suddenly threw a banana at Braque, the story goes, he deftly caught it. Although Georges immediately returned this toss Picasso was already locked back in his work and had forgotten the banana. He was even oblivious as it slumped down his chest, and it remained dumbly in his lap all afternoon.

Yet mostly he and Georges made a finely tuned pair of jugglers, moving closely hand in hand. They used the same materials, the same signs, performed the same intellectual somersaults. When Pablo experimented with an oval frame for his cubist works Georges did too. When Georges decided to print on words and letters Pablo likewise ventured forth with the names of drinks, newspapers, composers.

The banana-throwing took place in Picasso's studio on the Boulevard de Clichy.

As it was an awkward distance from there to the nearest post office, Picasso would frequently ask Braque to post letters for him on his way home.

Merci, Georges.

From central post office to central post office one such letter arrived remarkably fast. Ten days was a short time for mail to cross the Atlantic (a feat, incidentally, the *Alexander* might also soon perform in eleven); and another eight to skirt the continent was par for the times. The communication in question, written on a brown watercolour wash, was to Picasso's cousin Sarita, and urged her to think about works of art stencilled with words and glued up with newsprint and oilcloth and wallpaper.

She was six blocks east of the *Alexander* in Guayaquil, serving a brief and torrid apprenticeship as a whore.

As the urge to think about stencilled words and pasted cloth and paper travelled that minimal further distance westwards, and my grandfather came to see the pages of this letter, indeed to possess them (and later keep them in the leaves of his logbook), he did have some notion who they were from. For while his primary source of knowledge was engineering, the stars, and men fighting hardship, the elements and each other, he none the less had a keen interest in the arts. He possessed African masks, some Pre-Raphaelite drawings and a heavenly carved commode from Burma. So he naturally became curious; but no more than curious. For if it now seems bizarre of fate to present him with a blood relation of Picasso, it may not have seemed so then. This was a different world, in which Picasso was a tiny fish; at the same time, remember too, the world then was a smaller place, of fewer people, and the number of coincidences far greater than we can imagine now.

This story, *Cargoes*, tells how my mother came to be conceived.

In 1910: when a lot got rolled into a year and the time seemed to have a way of keeping on, ticking and ticking.

Yet what does an empty freighter, a revolution in art, or strange tentacles reaching back and forth across the Atlantic have to do with my mother's creation? Was she not the daughter of Edward and Mary Jones, then dutifully dusting window-sills and waiting, an ocean and a continent away?

Well, first let me return to the Malecón and the Hotel Bolívar. There has been unpleasant wrangling on the quayside. It is now the second day without loading. And though time was less costly in those days, it still meant money. My grandfather grew anxious: on the morrow he was to depart on the celebrated train. Could the Consul be relied on to iron out the disputes and supervise the loading? In the midst of which came the pancakes and tea with lemon again. This tea, said the Captain – the same man who devoted weekends to instructing his grandchildren at draughts and patience, adorer of dogs and tortoises, who gladly lent out *The Wonder Book of Ships* and made people feel marvellous when he hugged them – this foul brew requires milk. He was begged to understand there was a problem. *No hay leche, señor capitán, no hay.* The hell there wasn't; he would find some himself. And he strode down the *Avenida*, neglecting to put on his captain's cap or the jacket with the gold rings; an oversight he regretted once he came to a likely shop, a dusty, untended stall with children asleep in baskets and the lank air stinking of meat.

He had to wait his turn. Nor was he accustomed to the relaxed pace of Ecuador. He might burst with impatience. If he missed that train there would be hell to pay. But with others paying it. The thought of the whip kept in his cabin even crossed his mind. Ticking and ticking and ticking went the time. He heard mosquitoes. He wanted this milk in that tea, which would be getting cold. So he stepped forward like a captain and demanded *leche*. Downing a pocketful of cents, Chilean escudos and heavy English coin on the counter all at once, he grabbed a bottle and left. Back on the avenue he walked fast, then ran. He had not run for months. It felt good; he felt delirious. Careering crazily round the hotel corner he slid sideways on a slab of stone.

Thus with one arm high to save the bottle, Captain Edward Jones, in a tale well known to his family, crashed on his side in a puff of dust. He groaned the once, while on the ground. Shooing off well-wishers he rubbed his now grey elbows, brushed himself down and returned to his room; winded by the thud of landing, quieted into silence; yet pleased at having saved the bottle. He drank tea with ostentatious amounts of milk only he could see. Gently but surely his naturally good mood lapped back over this strange shore of anger he seemed to have landed on. The city's five o'clock breeze stirred, freshening the room. He felt slowly better. In the evening he ate with the Consul at the Flamingo, the city's most vaunted restaurant, and retired to bed in a misted glow of alcoholic vapours, content. The following morning he was unable to rise for pain.

A doctor came. The Captain had likely fractured a number of ribs and should remain put for a week, better two. He should not travel, not exert himself, and regularly blow through a straw into a glass of water in order to stop his ribs mending inwards. He cursed, summoned his second-in-command, asked the Consul to call, and changed his business schedule. He told the Consul he would have trouble reconciling himself to a picture of the brass and carmine train setting off without him, disappearing under steam and a shroud of rain forest. The Consul discreetly suggested he receive company, and within the hour had sent a short-list of names and professions. Among these was a young lady purportedly the cousin of a painter by the name of Picasso. Picasso? he said to this man: this is a ludicrous country. And tell her to prove it, he instructed him.

This lady may have brought a treasure-trove of letters if we are to believe the scholars. For they surmise that if a celebrity is known to have written one letter to a person he will have written ten. And what plans might have been contained there! How Braque was stencilling syllables evoking beer and liqueurs, cafés, Paris, dancing, abandon; while Picasso was in love and was painting on a picture to his love, Eva, the dedication *Ma Jolie*.

And more. *Bach, Mozart*, Braque had applied boldly across his paintings; while Picasso set down *Notre avenir est dans l'air* in a flourish across the French tricolour, looking to the future.

Now, back across the globe, in the breast of a fellow

European, my grandfather, it is my contention the same spirit of optimism must have domineered; certainly for a man at the height of his powers and the pinnacle of his profession. And who could say yet it was the pinnacle? For the world's markets were yawning open, and mass products required mass transportation; was not the canal in Panama surging to completion? Steel; radio; powered flight. And there were shipping lines and huge ocean liners, pages of them later in *The Wonder Book of Ships*, waiting to be managed.

It is time now to turn briefly to the life of the young lady Sara Soria, commonly known as Sarita. First, here she was, not having known the financial resources of Pablo's side of the family. But like her cousin she had felt the need to leave Barcelona, and had sailed to Ecuador to seek a living under the wing of a distant relative. This entrepreneur in tagua nuts had died on her, however, as she still negotiated the Strait of Gibraltar.

The next fact to know about Sarita is that her meeting with the Captain had been entirely contrived by the local *Las Peñas* bordel. In coming to enter the list of suggested companions no report had been made on the suitability of her personality, age or appearance, despite her advantages of being attractively petite and darkly pretty; nor was any effort made to inform her either; no, she was there to fuck the Captain and return with cash in His Majesty's coveted banknotes. To this end Sarita had been instructed only on how to satisfy an incapacitated man. For she was by nature sleepy, someone with a drawl in her voice and step, and in each of her former liaisons had not been one jot active; but had simply shaken hands, parted her legs and lain there.

Thus she arrived on the third day of the mooring, startled to find a man browner than herself, round and smiling, with a figure suggesting the body and the muscles of a wrestler. She had expected a quite different personage: a silent admiral, a tall pale man with a black top hat and stick, an icy arrogance to make her shiver. But my grandfather welcomed her warmly because that is the way he was — even if he had suspected that this petite half-girl, half-woman, with rose in her dark cheeks, was there to rifle his pockets and make off with his silver watch (in fact almost certainly already in the Consul's safe).

It was late afternoon, and again the cooling breeze had started. The Captain rose carefully from the armchair where he had been studying contracts, directed her to the balcony and showed her the view of the river with its flat brown expanse and islands of green grass. She spread her pale skirts on the divan and they took tea with a choice of milk or lemon. He read the notorious letter, or what he could of it given his floundering Spanish. *Blériot ha cruzado el canal de la Mancha*, he had her read; though he did know this already. Speaking slowly in English he told her about his ribs; wherever he felt misunderstood, throwing in a few words of creole and the occasional exaggerated gesture. He blew her loud bubbles through his straw until she laughed, her laughter itself making a kind of light bubbly sound. Attracted by this girlish behaviour, he did this again and again until the glass was empty. *Cucha, los hombres!* said Sarita wiping a real tear of laughter. Encouraged, my grandfather suddenly moaned and clutched at his sides, staging his rendering of a man in stabbing pain. Oh, oh, *aya aya*, said his companion, laughing uncontrollably and collapsing on the divan. Debilitated from laughter, she asked to be shown where the damage was, and was shocked again into a sudden hush, and a slight, involuntary, submissive bow of her body, as she felt the unexpected warmth of his skin. And how white his shirt was. She turned away red in the face, recovering only by daring to scoop the lemon out of her teacup and suck it. They traded further babyish attempts at the other's language. Sarita Sarita, he chanted in her same infantile register. *Capitán*, she called him back. Give me that letter from France, he said, and she threw it on top of his coat rack. First you must climb the Eiffel Tower, she taunted him. Who knows what other fun or nonsense they got up to: the clock on the waterfront chimed the hour. Sarita looked towards the sound, the balcony. A goodly time had passed; the sun had set beyond the now grey river Guayas. She stood and motioned for the

Captain to rest on the divan; and since there was nothing else to be done, walked to the door and turned the key in the lock. Turning back to him she unpinned her long black hair; and without any semblance of guile took off her shoes, her stockings and her skirts.

In Paris Braque and Picasso returned ecstatic from the stairways of the Eiffel Tower. After the creation of this extraordinary edifice in this, the most modern of cities, the nub of the Western universe, what now was not possible? Thinking of Eva, Picasso set up his brown café picture and sketched in the bottle-top of *Vieux Marc* he had emptied with her the night before. He imagined her laughter and drew a half nipple amongst the rims of glasses and plates. *C'est la poésie*, said Georges looking on; Poetry dates from today, he added, citing a new poem called *Le Panama ou Les Aventures de mes sept oncles*. *Oui, je connais ce poème*, said Pablo irritably; *mais il me faut me concentrer*. He placed a window on the café table and in it a short ironwork motif from the Eiffel Tower. Elsewhere he added more nipples.

A note to his dealer declared the hope that he and Braque could disgust everybody yet; for their exploits had just begun. They would forge on, scorning fears of failure; such were the turning points, he claimed, such the attitude to accompany the great moments in human endeavour. On we ride, he said to Georges, *abandonnés*.

I wonder how my grandfather felt about being ridden gently to his orgasms, enveloped by tender skin, girlish kisses and thighs half the girth of his own. I have no way of knowing if he easily abandoned himself or if a corner of him said no, what of Mary, quiet Mary in England, her warm embrace, her tablecloths and chicken soup; her Victoria sponge cake and sensible shoes. Yet I suspect he dived headfirst into the pool of pleasures offered. Later, it is true, he played the part of devoted husband, and moreover did so to his death. But in 1910 the future, his future, felt open as never before. The

letter from France talked of the realisation of centuries of
dreams: Icarus had flown, even crossing the English Channel.
Everything was possible. Could not he, Edward Jones, be
lorded in a foreign country, Picasso's cousin straddling his
damaged ribs; and once its holds were laden the *Alexander*
might indeed make England in eleven days. Surely he could
take a lover and return to Mary, tell her this was possible
and yet their marriage had also been built to last?

Could he? I am sure Mary broke down into tears at his
confession, shattering any such speech he may have had
prepared. Then she and Edward will have made it up, in a
way, because they always found a way; on this occasion by
him taking her in his arms and imploring forgiveness, she
murmuring back something neither of them could understand, herself barely catching the odd word through the great
ache he brought back with him, through the quiet sobbing.
Mary, coping with the brutal truth not by dashing his presents on the kitchen floor but by opening to the Captain in a
bewildered mood of awkward reconciliation, tears, in her
necessity to stay close to the man she hoped she loved; while
he would be carrying her to bed and gently taking her, she
clinging to him not knowing what else to do but to cling and
be taken by him.

So it happened.

Such happenings can be deduced by combing backwards
through the generations.

By working out the implications of all manner of family
documents.

By having *Wonder Books* around for inspiration.

My mother, I might add in a footnote, being created from
her father's dark adventure, emerged with the more durable
parts of its debris. Like every child she was in part a memento
of what had gone before; a kind of human souvenir. Of both
parents. And at her core was the core of her own mother:
the anxiousness above all to be a saint. This was Mary's
way, her well-blazed path. For saints need sinners to prove
themselves, and she had Edward. The Captain, performing
the infidelity needed to keep his wife a saint and his marriage
safe.

I've often imagined this ship making a wall at the end of the street, slowly growing laden, waiting to cast off and return to England.

John Fuller

STAR-GAZING

1

This glass is open to the sky
And gives the spaces overhead
(Which only never seem to die
Because they are already dead)
Their bright particularity.

They terrify us with their roar
Of silence and their sprawling lack
Of definition. They ignore
The names we give them as they pour
Their startling shapes against the black.

And in its quivering circle they
Return our gaze with unconcern
As though they only had to burn
And burn, and might not even stay
Till all their light were burned away.

It is a stiff and heavy glass,
Turning within a thread of brass.
It is an eye to frame at night
The airy meteors as they pass
And read their signatures of light.

It has no legs on which to stand
But must be shouldered and then panned,
The eyepiece steadied with one hand,
The other acting as support,
Until the looked-for star is caught.

And this is how, in any case,
We tend to use the tilted face:
The naked eye a searching cone,
The straining neck leant back, alone
Or on a shoulder not its own.

Star-gazing is a friendly thing,
When eyes aware of other eyes
And other arms on which to cling
Seek fires of a different size
And arcs that colder clay supplies.

And that discrepancy of sense
Restores us to each other, hence
To our exalted littleness
From which we dare thus to address
The neighbourhood of the immense.

Remember when the season bid
Us wander up and down the hill,
Blinking against the sky until
Its blackness bore a Perseid,
A little spark that seemed to spill?

The dizzy heavens tried to weep
With stars, the night was nearly gold,
We clenched our fingers counting, told
Tall stories till at last the cold
Conveyed us to the house of sleep.

2

The telescope's one dusty eye
Was found beneath my father's bed,
Coffined and latched. I don't know why
He kept it there. He might instead
Have let me point it at the sky.

We could have looked for every star
Named on his little planisphere,
Making the scattered singular
And with a word brought strangely near
The very farthest of the far.

For language is this human trick
Of simply daring to presume
Upon the contents of a room,
Distinguishing, quadruple quick,
A chess queen from a candlestick.

Since we have words for the unseen
And places where we've never been,
It's not surprising we know how
We can discriminate between
Cassiopeia and the Plough.

The I and Not-I is another,
Learnt by the baby from its mother
When first it predicates the Other,
But this is going too far back
Into the Freudian zodiac.

And anyway you will recall
How Freud declared that after all
Our devious minds turn everything
To something else: imagining
A breast, we dream a piece of Ming.

Are things the same, or different?
We take our pleasure in the trope
Of metaphor, where what is meant
Is not what's said: a star is hope,
And longing is a telescope.

That sort of thing. Or maybe it's
A poem made of separate bits,
Joining the lid and narrow box
By means of hinges and of locks,
Inevitable opposites.

Or it's the closing of the light,
A deathbed of its own, the pen's
Last stroke, the useless oxygen's
Retreat, the stopped watch in the night
Sharing the darkness of its lens.

Or it's a symbol, if you'd rather,
Of the essentially unknown,
The door that opens with a groan
To leave me standing there alone
In terror, and without a father.

3

Most of us eventually
Are orphans. Now that I am one
At fifty-six, it's real to me
But is a state with which no one
Could really have much sympathy.

For when our story's almost done
The plot is clear, it never thickens:
No deeds turn up, no bastard son,
No cruel change of fortune, none,
Nor tight-lipped guardians out of Dickens.

No shocking secret brings relief,
No birthmarks, sapphires or debentures,
No equatorial adventures,
No cousin with a handkerchief
Or pretty lips to blot the grief.

The twin events were feared and fated
And they were not long separated:
After the closing of his door,
Although my mother watched and waited,
Life could not go on as before.

And so she suddenly departed
And finished what her parents started.
Her final face was broken-hearted:
That mask we never rearrange,
The one expression we can't change.

Less of surprise than resignation,
The mouth almost in supplication.
I looked in vain at that inert
Abstraction, trying to convert
It to rebuke, or love, or hurt.

And his: likewise a spurious cast
Of some imposed solemnity,
A hollow mockery, the last
Gaunt face he pulled to frighten me,
One I could never bear to see.

For all the warnings and the fuss
Death is an instantaneous
Incompetent photographer,
The moment always wrong, a blur
We never could admit was us.

We'd always go back if we could
To that authentic unrehearsed
Expression that we had at first.
We may have thought it not much good
But hadn't then foreseen the worst.

And so my orphaned task is to
Redeem that album of the living
In memory without misgiving.
The lens of death is unforgiving.
The shutter falls for me and you.

4

Perhaps the entire universe
Is something like a camera
Within which matter can rehearse
Its unconvincing poses, star
By star, self-satisfied, perverse.

An endless film is moving through
Its darkness, a grey pantomime,
A shadow of some ballyhoo
That we are bound to misconstrue:
The film is us, is mind, is time.

How can we see and understand?
How can we see and be inside it?
We haven't yet identified it.
We think it is immensely grand
Yet need to hold it in our hand.

That particle that we observe
Appears to take a likely curve
And yet we doubt its path and distance:
Is it the same, or did it swerve?
Has it position *and* existence?

We slave to see electrons glide.
We like to watch the cells divide.
We'd put the sun beneath a slide,
Even our own observing eye,
To try to see our ignorance die.

Forgetting that we found the comic
Ages before the subatomic,
Forgetting the philosophic glories
Of the wise Greeks, observatories
Showing them systems that were stories.

No theories do it half so well
As what the lifted eye can trust:
The sky itself that longs to tell
The fable of its mortal dust
That falls and burns because it must.

Now Sol inflates his fiery chest
And drives his chariot to the west.
Beneath the burning wheels and hooves
The glittering sea grows large. It moves
More slowly now, and takes its rest.

Night loses all her inhibitions
Upon the sleeping of the sun.
The dome is opened, one by one
The stealthy stars take their positions
And act as they have always done.

Their dances formally presage
The entry of the real star,
Nude Artemis, the singular
Pale presence in this theatre,
Striding across her silver stage.

5

In every sky she knows her place.
In Corsica she looks just as
She does in Wales. (In Wales the face
She sadly leans towards us has
The old Oxonian grimace).

Perhaps it's something she forgot?
Her one good eye is vacant, more
Like a bruise, a cobweb or a blot.
And we stare back. But don't know what
On earth she can be looking for.

Something immeasurably lost,
Like innocence? Or something hunted?
Does she look savage, or affronted?
She chose a vagrant's path. The cost:
Millennia of dust and frost.

The tides are at her heels, and she
Reflects a special gravity
On water. Easy then to claim
She has a longing for the sea
From which initially she came.

Here on this plio-quaternian coast
The wind has hollowed each exposed
Piled boulder to a standing ghost,
A gargoyle or a weathered shell,
A sort of lunar sentinel.

So the *tafonu* haunts the rocks,
Bathed in the very light it mocks,
A gaunt subspheric demilune,
A meteorological cartoon,
A granite version of the moon.

It takes no time for the grotesque
To normalise its strange aesthetic:
It constitutes the picturesque,
Its likenesses are energetic
And are essentially poetic.

How readily they can disarm,
These sculptures of the Notre Dame
De la Serra or Calanches de Piana!
Configurations of Diana,
Wrecked symbols of her power to charm.

They are the metaphors of change;
Of matter's endless vacillation
And dogged differentiation,
Its power to seem forever strange;
Analogies of alienation.

So we stare down the littoral,
Just as we calculate the night,
For stalactite or meteorite,
Behaviour of stone or light
Departing from the usual.

6

For we have stripped away the year
With grief and work, and found its heart,
Something with which to persevere,
Something with which to make a start,
Something we knew we might find here.

The summer shows us at its core
A state of being that might save us.
What we have lost we can't restore,
But know we have, and need therefore,
The bodies that our mothers gave us.

Our eyes, grown heavier with all
They've seen, need lifting up towards
The light. We need those major chords,
That full acceptance of the sprawl
Of nature in her free-for-all.

We need the sea's oblivion,
To dive below and gaze upon
The coloured life that knows no clocks,
The *oblade* and the *sparaillon*
Playful beneath their crusted rocks.

And where the water meets the sun,
Burnished when the day is done,
The sea and sky appear as one,
Rare stuffs laid out that no bazaar
Could sell: faded, crepuscular.

The late sky's only silhouette
Are hills that few have crossed as yet
Or wish to cross, for on each side
Are valleys where men lived and died
And never were unsatisfied.

The tumbling bat comes out to eat
And crickets open their salon.
The lizard poses at your feet,
Then moves with practised flourish on
The dust it owns and signs, Anon.

Again we light the candles and
Make shadows of our contraband
Of herb and shell, and once again
We pour the pink wine of Sartène
And hold its pebbles in our hand.

At which we come to feel, of course,
With vacillating Arnold, 'Ah
Love, let us, etcetera . . .'
But feel it with unusual force
Beneath the heavens' *feux de joie*.

And wish for it beneath their beams
And watch the orange iris burn
To black against the sky and learn
Again the names of stars and turn
From the flickering terrace to our dreams.

7

Our dreams are how the past arrives
At compromise. They come in clusters,
Like jostling men concealing knives;
Or singly, the strict loss-adjusters
Of over-accidental lives.

Just as distressingly, they go.
Whether unique or in a series
They do not, like a video,
Record the things we ought to know
Or illustrate important theories.

They are not baleful like a spook
Nor tie things neatly like a suture.
They do not speak about the future
In riddles like the Pentateuch,
Issue no warning or rebuke.

Yet sometimes out of our obsessions,
Our cautiousness, our indiscretions,
Our dreaming minds intently make
Surprising symbols of repressions
They can do nothing with awake.

Here we sleep long, remember more,
And our unconscious when we snore
Stands open like a friendly door
Revealing our individual isness
Struggling to sublimate life's business.

The frequent dream we never doubt
Or think to ask what it's about
Takes on new certainty, its theme
Acknowledged in the general scheme
Of what we recognise as dream.

That hidden staircase, undetected,
Leads to a half-remembered room.
The smouldering timbers, long neglected,
May breathe each cinder to a plume,
And break into a fiery bloom.

And yet I climb excited there
To find some sort of foothold where
I might do something to reclaim it.
I know I do not need to name it:
The stair's the thrill of being a stair.

And it is almost less surprising
Than the reality around us.
When in the morning fish surround us,
This is because we swim on rising,
Yet still our equilibrium founders.

Half-asleep we glide, mistaking
The weedy rocks for grassy vales,
See distant sheep instead of snails
And crows for the black scissory tails
Of *castagnoles* we know on waking.

8

And if we wake up in the night,
We easily feel flabbergasted:
Our dream had such vast scope, despite
Our knowing that it must have lasted
No longer than a meteorite.

A whole Victorian triple-decker
Is there, the scientists have reckoned,
All the emotion of *Rebecca*,
All the excitement of *The Wrecker*,
Contained within a microsecond.

Our dreams burn up on entering
The atmosphere of real life.
They snap shut like a pocket-knife,
Are delphic, tiny, maddening
As prisoned birds that will not sing.

What was it that my father said
To my cocooned and dreaming head?
He sat there, dazed, and I was not
Surprised to see he was not dead.
I talked on like an idiot:

The multitudinous happenings
Since he had left us, publishing,
Memorials, his personal things,
How I'd looked after their removal,
Hoping I met with his approval.

And yet all this was to protect
Him from the certain ill-effect
Of his decline, the little chance
Of permanent deliverance.
His face took on a radiance.

With all my silly chatter done,
I put my arms about him, knew
His real dying had begun
And knew this miracle was true,
Occasion for a last adieu.

But what he said, or what I made
Him say, was lost. Was I afraid
To hear, or even make the attempt?
Perhaps that moment was undreamt,
A kind of deference to his shade.

And I awoke or I was woken
By a strange consciousness of tons
Of falling stardust fired like guns
Above me, and my dream was broken
By midnight and the weight of suns.

The bright stars flipped like shuttlecocks
That lurch and fall. Each left a mark
Upon the retina, a spark,
A sudden match struck in the dark
That spurts and dies against the box.

9

Alpha Centauri in the night,
Look down and tell me what to think,
Pour out unstinting, as I write,
Over my intermittent ink
Your steady undistracted light.

You are the starting point of what
Has been an idle whim of ours:
To draw a line from dot to dot
In the right order, thus to plot
A secret picture of the stars.

370

Of light you are the principal
Among the many lights that blaze.
You are the entrance to the maze,
The illuminated capital,
The hidden theme of the chorale.

And all we need is your immense
And unconcerned magnificence
Turning and turning unrevealed,
A random point of reference,
One intersection in the field.

I mean, we simply need to start
And all else follows, part by part:
The heavens turn, and through the art
Of imitation we can feel
Them turn, and so invent the wheel.

Then nature's spiral yields the spring,
Whose impetus from tightening
Controls the otherwise hotchpotch
Of random forces. Then a notch
Upon the wheel invents the watch.

Never so simple, but forgive
An argument that goes slipshod!
My real intent is figurative:
In Lilliput it wasn't odd
They thought his watch was Lemuel's god.

For when our hour of death arrives,
We all admit it's time that drives
Us on and that our only heaven
Has been the less than thirty-seven
Million minutes of our lives.

We can't contrive perpetual motion.
Alpha to Omega is more
Than we shall ever have. Three score
And ten concludes our self-devotion,
While the stars dash upon the shore.

Forgive this clockwork replica
Of what we do not understand.
And let our fretful cells disband
In peace beneath each stopped spread hand
And still heart of our Omega.

10

Strange how our jealous star conceals
From us all other stars as though
Their coded clusters, spokes and wheels
Might point us out a way to go!
Empty and blue are his ideals.

And he intends to lull us with
A spurious sense of being free,
Dazzling the senses with his myth
Of a benevolent coppersmith
Burnishing the sky and sea.

But when the sun has gone to rest
The scenic blue gives way to night.
The constellations reignite,
Harmonious, ordered, self-possessed,
The ancient *mécanique céleste*.

Which of their portents can be true?
For me, perhaps, as well as you
There's nothing much they can foretell
That isn't just our point of view:
Stars shine *away* from us as well.

For certain, even while we're gaping,
Their light is rapidly escaping,
So which events they may be shaping
Is much in question: light doesn't last.
The present soon becomes the past.

So all our history is sent
In light-waves through the firmament,
Continuous record of mishaps,
The most extemporised of maps,
The very picture of Perhaps.

And as one scene succeeds the other,
Each generation is distinguished,
Father and son, daughter and mother,
One by one, the bonds relinquished,
And the long lives in turn extinguished.

No pattern there, except in death,
The stubborn drawing of a breath
After breath after breath that perseveres
For all of our allotted years,
The sixtieth, seventieth, eightieth.

So when we look up at the sky
And claim the interest of the stars
And when we weep our au revoirs
We know it is our turn to die.
The next black-letter day is ours.

We even know there's no reprieve
For our own daughters' generation,
Beautiful in their vocation
And individualisation.
And this is what it is to grieve.

Tim Pears

BLUE

HE KNEW HE'D died at three o'clock in the afternoon of Wednesday, July the 27th, 1988, the moment he woke up in the room that he'd come to hate. He hadn't left it for two months now, and he was wearily familiar not only with every object – with the thermometer in a glass beside the lamp and the heavy chest of drawers and the dark, forbidding wardrobe – but also with the quality of light and shadow in the room according to what time of day it was; with the way the room expanded and contracted as the ceiling joists shrank at night and swelled during the day; and how sound changed at different times so that in the morning his voice was dulled and barely reached the door but in the dark the room became an echo chamber, his daughter's name, 'Joan,' rebounding off the walls and returning to him from many different directions.

He was familiar with all these things but none of them interested him, as he declined in the starched sheets, propped up against a backrest of awkward, misshapen pillows that his daughter regularly thumped and plumped up with a ritualised but desolate enthusiasm, as if doing with them what she wished she could do for her father. He'd gradually lost his huge rustic appetite until it had become a torment to swallow even the soups and junkets she prepared in the liquidiser, and he lost weight with inexorable logic until the robust farmer was a skinny wraith whose ribs were showing for the first time in fifty years.

The pain moved around his body like a poacher in the night searching for a vulnerable deer in the pinewoods. It

374

had first attacked him in his heel, reappeared in his neck, then after a six-month respite erupted from deep cover in his back, to roam up and down his spine with sporadic, intense malevolence. He knew (and so did everyone else) that it had to be lung cancer, since he'd smoked forty untipped cigarettes a day since the age of fifteen; so why the hell didn't it just eat up his lungs and have done with it?

The pain was what had wrecked him. Joseph had always thought he was impervious to pain and his grandson, Michael, had grown up in awe of his grandfather's disdain of both the occasional accident and the regular discomfort that beset the life of a farmer. When he gashed his hand or banged his head he only bothered to use his handkerchief if the blood was making too much of a mess of everything. And when they'd unclogged the field drains the previous February, while Mike was whimpering like a child from the cold his grandfather thrust his arms into icy mud as if oblivious of reality.

But this pain was different: it gripped him in its teeth like a primitive dog, and there was neither escape nor end to its torture. He felt nauseous. He fantasised heating up a kitchen knife and cutting out whole afflicted chunks of his own flesh, that that might bring relief – but he couldn't even reach the stairs. Dr Buckle prescribed ever-changing drugs of increasing dosage, until the pain was dulled and so were all his senses and he found himself withdrawing into a small space where there was no sense and no sensation, only a vague disgust with the faint remaining evidence of a world he'd once inhabited with force and command.

Joseph Howard knew he'd died at three o'clock in the afternoon when he woke from an inconclusive nap and he looked around the room with a sharpness of vision that made his mind collapse backwards through the years, because he'd refused to wear spectacles and hadn't seen the world as clearly as this since his fortieth birthday. He could read the hands of the alarm clock without holding it three inches in front of his face, he could make out each stem and petal in the blue floral wallpaper, and the edges of things were miraculous in their definition, lifting away from each other and occupying their own precise space instead of merging into a dull stew of objects.

He pricked up his ears and heard a voice outside calling, and although it was too far away for him to make out the actual words he could recognise, beyond any doubt, the tone and inflection of his grandson, Mike. And even more remarkably, when another man's voice answered, from even further away, he knew that that was old Freemantle's grandson, Tom.

It was then that he realised, too, that the pain had gone. His whole body ached with something similar to the symptoms of flu, as if his body had been punched in his sleep; but it was such a contrast to the agony of these last months that he felt on top of the world. He got out of bed and stood up, and the blood drained from his head and made him feel faint and dizzy, so he sat back down to get his balance. Yet it was actually pleasurable to come so close to fainting, woozy and lost. It made him recall the one time he had ever fainted, as a beansprouting adolescent in the farmyard, the world suddenly losing its anchorage and drifting deliriously out of control.

Joseph had finished dressing and was tying his shoelaces, with an infant's concentration and pleasure, when his daughter came into the room carrying a mug of weak tea. 'Father!' she cried. 'What on earth does you think you're doing?' She rushed around the side of the bed but he took no notice of her until he'd finished, and then he sat up and looked her in the eyes and said: 'Joan, I feels better and I'm getting up.' Then his smile disappeared and he studied her face with a scrutiny that she found unnerving, taking in the crow's-feet and the puffiness around her eyes and the small lines at each side of her mouth, and he said: 'You're a good girl, Joan.'

He knew he'd died but he didn't care. He found his stick behind the door and went for a walk into the village. He could feel his blood flow thin through his veins and his left hip no longer troubled him. He passed two or three people on his way to the shop and they returned his cheerful greeting with manifest surprise and a certain awkwardness.

The shop bell rang and Elsie came through from the kitchen. Her large owl's eyes widened behind her thick pebble-specs, and then narrowed. 'Does Joan know you's out, Joseph?' she demanded suspiciously. 'She was only in yere just now.'

'Don't worry about me, Elsie,' he replied, 'I never felt better. Only I wants some fags. I've not had a smoke in ages.'

Elsie looked away, embarrassed. 'I haven't got none of your sort in, Joseph. You's the only one what smoked that brand.' She reached over to the shelves. 'You could try some of this, they says 'tis a strong one.'

'I'm not bothered, I'll take a packet of they,' he smiled. She handed them to him hurriedly and he felt in his pockets. 'Damn it,' he said, 'I've come out without any money. You know how much I hates credit, but can I send the lad down later on?'

'Course you can, bay,' she said without looking at him. 'You git on, now.'

As he turned to leave, he said: 'I might even bring it myself.'

Dr Buckle appeared the next day and took his temperature and checked his pulse and listened to the sounds of his insides through the dangling stethoscope. Then he declared, in a voice of scientific indifference: 'It's an impressive respite, Joseph. But you're still weak. Don't overdo it.'

He wanted to get straight back out on the farm, but Joan told Mike she'd hold him responsible if Joseph picked up so much as an ear of corn, so he left his grandfather behind in the yard. Joseph wandered around the garden and poked about in the sheds. It was a hot day, the sun rose high in a blue sky and he wiped the sweat from his neck and forehead. Sparrows swooped in and out of the eaves, a throstle sang from one of the apple trees, and when he saw a magpie in the first field he knew without any doubt that he'd see another, and sure enough there it was over by the hedge.

A ladybird landed on the back of his hand. At first the tiny creature appeared strange, only for being so distinct in his cleansed vision, but then he observed that its markings were red dots on a black shell instead of the usual other way round. He didn't think he'd ever seen one like that before, but he might well have and never been struck by it. There must be a name for it, he thought: an *inverted* ladybird, perhaps; a *topsy-turvy*. He lifted his hand and blew, and the tiny insect opened its wings and flew away.

During the months of his miserable decline Joan had climbed uncomplaining up the stairs many times a day to make him comfortable, to help him on to the bedpan and carry it off to the bathroom, to rub cream into his dry skin, eventually to spoon food into his mouth. His recovery must have meant a great easing of her burden and he was frankly glad that she let him occupy himself now without interruption. Midway through the afternoon he became aware of a curious, pleasing sensation somewhere inside him and then he realised with surprise what it was: hunger. He marched into the kitchen.

'You'll not believe this, girl, but I've got myself an appetite all of a sudden.' She didn't look at him directly but fussed around in the fridge and said at the same time: 'Sit down, I'll knock 'e up a sandwich.'

Joseph planted himself at the table and laid his cigarettes and matches on its grainy surface. He could remember his own father making it, after a huge old beech tree had come down in an April gale. He could remember the sweet smell of the shavings as his father sawed and planed in the far shed, and he could remember the way his father kept nails between his moist lips.

Joan set a plate of sliced-white-bread sandwiches in front of him and murmured that she was off shopping, as she departed from the room. He watched her through the window disappear down the lane and then he closed his eyes, the better to appreciate the texture of mushy bread and coarse ham, and to savour the sharp distraction of mustard, contradicted by granules of demerara sugar.

That evening after supper Joseph suggested a game of draughts with Mike, and they played for the first time since

Mike was a child and Joseph had taught him, after the boy's father had left. They played half a dozen games, all of which Mike spent hunched over the board uneasily, never once looking up at his grandfather, who won every game.

That night Joseph slept for eight hours solid, untroubled by the morbid, drugged dreams of those last months, and he woke fully rested. He lay and listened to the chickens squawking and to house martins scurrying. He yawned and stretched, slowly, his knotty old muscles elastic again, and he relished their pleasure.

As he got dressed he saw his older grandson, John, who always came home late and left early, drive off to work in Exeter. Joseph went downstairs. The kitchen was empty. He heard the tractor ignition and stepped outside; he called but Mike didn't turn around, as the tractor coughed and rattled into the lane. He came back in and called his daughter, but there was no reply, so he made himself a mug of strong tea and wondered whether there was any secret to making toast. And he assumed there must be because he burnt it, but he ate it anyway and enjoyed the taste of charcoaled bread beneath the butter and home-made, thick-rind marmalade. Then he took his cap and went outside.

He knew he'd died because he felt so light and so at ease. It occurred to him that that evening he should challenge Mike to an arm-wrestle, and he laughed out loud at the idea. He tried to look at the sun and it made his eyes water.

He walked through the lower fields. The wheat was high and brittle. He bit some grains and let the dry nutty flavour linger on his tongue and he wondered who first discovered how to make flour, and then bread. He entered the pasture where the dairy herd was grazing and passed among his Friesian cows, patting their flanks. He rolled up his sleeves and held out his arms, and the braver among them licked his skin for its salt with their rough wet tongues, though still like all the others eyeing him with their dull expression of fear and reproach. He wondered whether they forgave him for his life's labour of exploitation and butchery, and he realised how much he loved this farm, these animals, this rich and crooked valley.

Joseph walked into the village. As he began climbing Broad Lane he realised he'd left his walking stick behind, but he also realised that he didn't need it: he was striding forward, with his bow legs and his slightly inturned toes; his tendons and sinews and leathery veins felt invincible, and he wiped the healthy sweat from his face without pausing. For the first time in he didn't know how long, he thought of his wife, whom he once used to walk to Doddiscombsleigh to, and then court during long walks in Haldon Forest, where, while the Second World War raged far away from them, they made urgent love in the shadows of the pines on a scratchy bed of cones and needles, dry twigs crackling as they moved. But he found that, in truth, he was thinking less of her than of himself – walking, so much walking in his life; he could carry on walking now and he needn't ever stop, he felt so strong, he felt he could walk the length of the Teign Valley and back again.

Joseph looked around as he walked, peering over hedges and through gates, but there wasn't a soul around. When he got up to the phone box he thought he saw a child running along the lane in the distance, but he wasn't sure. He sat down on the bench at the top of the Brown. The improvised goalposts stood quiet and forlorn. An absurd television image leapt perfectly remembered out of his memory, of the majestic black French defender Marius Trésor lunging into a breathtakingly insane tackle during the 1982 World Cup semi-final.

Joseph felt some tiny drops of rain fall on his hands: he looked up and the sky was a clear, unblemished blue. He wondered whether they were the prickles of pins and needles and he lifted his hands and shook them, and ran them down over his face. The world was silent and empty. He knew he'd died three days earlier at three o'clock in the afternoon, and he leaned forward with his head in his hands and wept.

When he heard the church bell tolling he wiped his eyes with his damp sweaty handkerchief, which made his eyes sting, and walked up past the almshouses and then the village hall where he'd once gone to school, and he walked through the lych-gate into the graveyard. Twenty yards away they were lowering the coffin into the ground and the Rector read from his Bible but Joseph couldn't hear him. Then the Rector, still reading, picked up a handful of soil and threw it into the grave and that he did hear, faintly, granules scattering across the lid of the coffin.

He knew everyone there: Granny Sims, for twenty years his fellow churchwarden; Douglas Westcott; old Freemantle and some of his fragmented family; Martin the retired hedge-layer; Elsie and Stuart from the shop.

As to his own family, in front of the various cousins and nieces and nephews, John held his mother Joan's arm, while Mike looked like he ought to sit down, because he was leaning a little too much of his weary weight against his girlfriend, whose name Joseph never could remember.

He looked across the graveyard at them and for the first time since his death Joseph felt a sudden upsurge of anger. It swelled inside him, pure and physical: a rage of bile, while his heart pumped hot blood through his veins. Volcanic anger. Anger so strong he thought he might burst.

He closed his eyes, clenched his fists and gritted his teeth. And then he shouted out: '*Why did you not show me this world before, you bastard?*' as he lifted his eyes to the wide blue sky, and felt himself light and rising.

Stephen Knight

YOUNG SIWARD

At break of day, the smallest bird
   (My second heart) beats its wings
Against my chest then settles down
     To sing.

At first, birds bearing twigs
   Alighted, now my armour fills
With song; song spills from every crack,
     Trills

Echoing for hours . . .
   I plait my beard with worms and leaves
Repeating *crest gorget cuirass*
     Cuisse greave

For comfort. Moss embraces me.
   The branches at my elbows bud.
Step by step, meadows turn
     To mud.

All day, beneath the drumming rain,
   I watch the black clouds block the light
Then march to Dunsinane;
     At night,

I dream of empty courtyards where
   Alarmed birds rise from me like smoke
And I am naked: frightened: streaked
     With albumen and yolk.

ORPHEUS

No smile no arms outstretched no kiss, only this:
The furbelows of rubbish on the escalator's edge.

Brian Aldiss

SITTING WITH THE SICK WASPS

AN EPIDEMIC IS like a failure of electricity. All is well with an individual, until suddenly one day, perhaps in the middle of a conversation, he begins to feel unwell. The current of his health has been cut off.

As a boy I often took refuge in our bathroom. It was the one room in our house which possessed a lock. There I was safe from my elder brother. 'Nasir, Nasir,' he would cry. 'Come out and be a man.' When I did not reply, he would lose interest and go away. I would stay where I was until my parents came home in the evening.

In the bathroom was a large stone bath. In that I crouched, feeling safe with the grey stone about my body. By pretending that I was inside an elephant, I made sure my brother would not get me.

The wasps suffered an epidemic that year.

Every year, wasps built a nest in the thatch of our roof. My father, who was kind to everything and everyone, taught us to love wasps. He said that wasps were on our side. They protected us from flies by eating the maggots of flies. He also pointed out the beauty of wasps, dressed in their neat little uniforms.

Perhaps it was a child's fancy, but I used to know that the wasps respected my father. Often they would come down and crawl on my father's hand and fingers. They never stung any of us, except for my brother when he tried to tear off their wings.

As I sat huddled in the stone bath, wasps fell from the thatch to the floor of the bathroom. They were already dying.

When my parents were home and I was safe from my brother's persecution, I would stand outside our house and watch what was happening on the roof. All appeared well. The industrious wasps buzzed back and forth in the sunlight. Some carried in bees or flies to feed the next wasp generation. Some rested on the reeds, fluttering their wings as if in sheer delight with existence.

That was an external view. Inside, in the dark, all was unwell. The hidden epidemic was working, spreading, switching off the life current.

One by one, the victims of the epidemic came spiralling down to our cold stone flags. Few managed to fly off the floor once they were there. The more active ones could skid along, or crawl about for a while. Some just lay where they fell, twitching their antennae. Few survived for more than an hour. The epidemic had got them.

Sometimes the wasps dropped on me in the bath. I let them lie, knowing them to be harmless. They seemed too feeble to sting. Such energy as they had was concerned with dying as circumspectly as possible.

While lying on the floor, they suffered one last hazard. A kind of large spiders lived in the drain. They spun no webs. My mother told me they were called 'wolf spiders'. The wolf spiders would rush from their dark lair, seize a dying wasp, and carry it, still struggling with the last of its strength, into its recesses.

In this horrifying process I never interfered. My religion taught me that the spiders had as much right to life as the wasps. My main judgement was, as I stared over the little stone wall of the bath at this activity, a sort of luxurious fear that existence should have to be constructed along such lines. It struck me as unfair that the wasps should suffer this last torment.

Perhaps the spiders caught the epidemic from their victims. If they rushed, dying, out of the other end of the drain into the open air, sparrows would eat them. Then the secret death would spread to the birds of the air. And who would eat their corpses? The villagers?

It seemed the electricity was more simple to turn off than turn on.

Studying those who fell before my eyes, I saw how they suffered pain. When their time came, their legs collapsed and they lay on their sides. The fur on their shoulders became tawdry, their smart yellow-and-black armour ceased shining. So close did I feel to these humble creatures that every death seemed to make me dwindle.

Now that I am adult and able to nurse my poor mad brother, I see the epidemic is in him too. The current of his mind has been switched off. Unlike the wasps, he makes a great fuss about his plight. Often I find him cramped into the stone bath, weeping.

MAKING MY FATHER READ REVERED WRITINGS

IN THE FICTIONS of Pierre de Lille-Sully is much that is exceedingly strange and marvellous. He must have been an animist, although he professed the Christian faith; for him, even words have life and spirit of their own.

Unfortunately, I have a poor grasp of the beautiful French language. But in the year 19—, I came across a second-hand book which immediately became one of my treasured possessions; it was a translation into English of de Lille-Sully's short stories, under the title, *Conversations with Upper Crust Bandits*.

I was spellbound. One only knows such love for fiction when one is young. I dwelt in the stories. Many of them I read over and over. But not the last one in the book. For reasons I cannot explain fully, I was reluctant to read 'The Prince of Such Things'. I knew little about literature, and devoured in the main what I regarded even then as trash; being unversed in finer things, I regarded the title of this last story as a bad one. It seemed to me dangerous, even a little deranged.

'The Prince of Such Things' . . . It is the responsibility of authors to give their stories a title which invites one in, or at least promises to make matters clear. Here, de Lille-Sully seemed to be neglecting his duty.

At this period, I was a retarded adolescent of fourteen, and very much under my parents' thumb. My two sisters were high-spirited and joyous by nature. I felt myself to be the very opposite. My father's first name was William. He had had me christened William too. As soon as I was old enough to feel the smart of it, I smarted that I had been given the same name as my father. I was diminished by it; did they think I had no separate existence?

Once alert to this injustice (as I saw it), I felt that everything in my father's behaviour was calculated to deny me an individual existence. In the matter of clothes, for instance, he always selected what I should wear. The possibility never existed that he might consult me. And when I grew large and gawky, I was made to wear his cast-off jackets and trousers.

Evenings in our house were particularly oppressive. My sisters would not remain in the sitting-room. They went upstairs to their bedroom, giggling and whispering to themselves. I was constrained to remain below, to sit with my parents.

We lived then in a northern country. Now that I am settled in the South of France, I look back on those long evenings and nights with something like terror. So mentally imprisoned was I that it never occurred to me to go out, in case I should suffer a word of reprimand from my father.

The custom was that my parents sat on either side of a tall wood-burning stove. They had comfortable chairs of a forbiddingly antique design, inherited from my father's family. I sat at a table nearby, on a hard-backed chair. At that table I read books or magazines, or drew in a callow way.

I should explain that my father would not allow television in our house. And for some reason – it may have been a superstitious reason for all I know – the radio had to be switched off at six-thirty.

Prompted by my sisters, I once dared to ask my father why

we could not have television. He replied, 'Because I say so.' And that was sufficient explanation in his eyes.

Always, it seemed I was in disgrace – 'in his bad books', as the saying goes. All through my childhood years, I yearned to be loved by him. It made me stupid. It made me mute. The whole evening could pass in silence until, at a gesture from my father, we would rise and go to our beds.

It was my mother's way to sit almost immobile while the hours passed. Women are able to sit more still than men. She wore headphones, listening to music on her Walkman. The thin tintinnabulation, like a man whistling surreptitiously through his teeth, penetrated the deepest concentration I could muster.

My father sat on the other side of the stove to her. I do not recall their ever conversing. At seven-thirty each evening, my mother would rise and pour him a glass of *akavit*, for which he thanked her. Father made a habit of reading his newspaper to an inordinate degree. The frosty crackle of broadsheet pages as he turned them punctuated the hours. I never understood his method of reading. It was clear that, having stumped up a few *öre* for his copy, he was determined to get his money's worth. But the way in which my father searched back and forth among the pages suggested a man who possessed some cunning secret method of interpreting life's events.

Such was the scene on the evening I decided at last to read Pierre de Lille-Sully's story, 'The Prince of Such Things'. I set my elbows on the polished table-top, one each side of the volume. I blocked my ears with my hands, in order to defend myself from the crackle of paper and the whistle of music. I began to read.

Perhaps in everyone's young life comes a decisive moment, from which there is no turning back. A decision, I mean, not based on rational thought processes. I hope it is not so; for if it is, then we have no defence against it, and must endure what follows as best we can. The matter is a mystery to me, as are many features of existence. All I can say is that on that particular dreary evening I came upon one of those decisive moments.

The brilliance of 'The Prince of Such Things' flooded into my mind. The words, the turns of phrase, the sentences, the paragraphs and their cumulation, unfolded an eloquently imaginative story. It was a study of ordinary life and yet also a fairy story. More than a fairy story, a legend of striking symbolism, exciting, agitating, and ravishing in its effect.

In a way, its basic proposition was ludicrous, for who could believe that ordinary people in a Parisian suburb had such powers. Yet the persuasiveness of the piece overcame any hint of implausibility. De Lille-Sully gave expression to an idea new to me at the age of fourteen, that the manner in which one thing can stand for another quite different – a sunrise for hope, let's say – forms the basis of all symbolic thought, and hence of language.

I was swept along by his narrative, as branches are swept along by a river in flood. Never had I guessed that such prose existed. Even the preceding stories in the book had left me unprepared for this magnificent outburst of de Lille-Sully's imagination.

I reached the final sentence exhausted as if by some powerful mental orgasm. My mind was full of wonder and inspiration. The sheer bravura of the story gave me courage.

The longing to share this experience was so great that, without further thought, I turned to my father.

Across the expanse of carpet separating us, I said, 'Father, I have just read the most marvellous story anyone has ever written.'

'Oh, yes.' He spoke without raising his eyes from the newspaper.

'Read it yourself, and you'll see.'

I picked up my book and took it across to him. How did I feel at that moment? I suppose I felt that if we could share this enlightening experience the relationship between us might become more human, more humane . . . That we might be more like father and son.

Transformed by the story. I felt only love for him as he condescended to put down his paper and accept the volume. He held it open just as he received it, asking what I wanted him to do.

'Read this story, father. "The Prince of Such Things".' I was conscious that I had not approached him to do anything for many years.

He sat upright in his chair, set his face grimly, and began to read. I stood beside him before retreating awkwardly to the table. There I made a pretence of picking up a pencil and drawing in an exercise book. All I did was scribble, while observing my parents.

My mother had momentarily shown some interest in my action; or perhaps it was surprise. After a moment's alertness, she retreated into her music, eyes focusing vaguely on a point above the stove. My father, meanwhile, concentratedly read the miraculous story. His eyes twitched from left to right and back, as if chasing the lines of print down the page. It was impossible to gather anything from his expression. No sign of enlightenment showed.

It took him, I would say, almost two hours to read de Lille-Sully's story. I had not lingered over it for more than three-quarters of an hour. I could not tell if this meant he was a slow reader, or whether he was deliberately keeping me in suspense.

Finally, he had done. He closed the book. Without looking at me, he set the volume down on the right-hand side of his chair. He then picked up his newspaper, which he had dropped on the left-hand side of his chair, and resumed his scanning of its columns. He gave me no glance. He said not a word.

The mortification I experienced cannot be expressed. At the time I did nothing. Did not leave the room, did not retrieve the book, did not leave. I sat where I was.

Either he had regarded de Lille-Sully's miraculous tale as beneath his contempt or – ah, but it took me many a year before the alternative came to me – he was unable to comprehend it.

As I have said, this evening wrought a decisive change in my life. Without volition, as I sat there looking away from my father, I found I had decided that I would become a writer.

Cate Parish

BETWEEN THE FACTORIES AND THE SEA

The late November sun cast a light like dried blood
over the strip of land between the factories and the sea –
the bird sanctuary, enclosed in barbed wire;

But already the light was failing, the sea more loudly chewed
its dead, and a chemical fog was blotting out distances,
when a clot of starlings got stuck overhead:

They'd all rush headlong into some imagined centre,
only to burst apart as if from impact, the whole swelling
then subsiding, like a painful emotion,
the dark, amorphous heart of that place;

Or some would plummet around the periphery, as if to herd
the others in, but the others would flow out,
all of them frantically flapping, agitated with gibberish –

In London, people formed for and against
this chaos of starlings: in the squares, men beat bin lids
and played tapes of tortured birds; encircling them,

Women with petitions tried to gather together strangers
to oppose the men: there the circling and crying of birds
was not lost in fog but seemed
meaningful and exciting as some newly-hatched,
　revolutionary idea.

Lavinia Greenlaw

SERPENTINE

Those buried lidless eyes can see
the infra-red heat of my blood.

I feel the crack, the whisper
as vertebrae ripple and curve.

Days of absolute stillness.
I sleep early and well.

His rare violent hunger,
a passion for the impossible.

He will dislocate his jaw
to hold it.

My fingers trace the realignment
as things fall back into place.

Each season, a sloughed skin
intensifies the colours that fuse

with mineral delicacy at his throat.
Flawless.

Beautiful, simple,
he will come between us.

Last night you found his tooth
on your pillow.

NATURE

The night I got married, the ducks on the pond
– wing-clipped, ornamental, hardly wild –
brought us running from the house.
They were competing to grasp
the one white bird by the throat and force
her head underwater as she skidded in their circle,
climbed the surface, feathers splayed, hawking up
a painful comic cry I had not understood.

That last visit, out of season,
in the taut thread of our final year.
The air was so weak it could not carry
the smoke from the fire, which did not rise
but found its way by some freak downdraught
to settle in the baby's room.
She neither woke nor altered her breathing
but in the moment it took to reach her,

I stepped through darkness. And did not run
but sat on the step as the day contracted
to fill the window, confusing the maybugs
caught at the glass and the leaky sill of the door.
Insects I could neither kill nor touch
nor open the latch for, they bumped, collided,
swam towards light. And could not reach it.
Why? Does it have to be like that?

Joseph New

Two Spirits in the Country Park

Peace perfect peace

Tweet-tweet, tweet-tweet.

Oh!
Where?
What can that be?
What?
That snap?

Twitter, twitter.

What? I cannot hear, for all this birdsong.
Did you not catch it, from that bank where the odour of
rhododendrons springs from the blooms' cache of pollen so
strong it might stun you if you stand too close?
I think you are hearing things.
Such blossoming! As though the world's blood burst
through its skin!

Tweet. Twitter.

There, I hear it again. Let us leave the path and go down
the bank and see!

Trrrrrrrrrrrrrrrrrrrrr!

Mercy. Oh! Did you just see that bird went past nearly

pierced my ear through! I am not used to all these things flying freely through the air.

Goodness, it was only a finch.

They do not always look where they are going.

Or a lark.

I read about a man had his eye out once.

Or collied dove.

With one of their bills. They are all in a rush!

Hark! That snap again! Will you never hear it?

It is only your imagination playing tricks. I will not leave the path. Down that bank is maybe a roost for small birds where they squat among the bushes, scores at a time trembling in concert, then burst at once out like shards of ordnance in detonation over a city street: how the deadly fragments fly, shattering the shops' shining panes, scarring steel, clawing concrete, and all the poor humans standing by are blown into rags.

I really do not think . . .

Twit. Twit-twit.

Did you note it *that* time?

I have told you.

In that case I will go down and explore alone.

Oh be sensible! It is probably nothing but twigs cracking under the roll and twist of lovers in the brake, a youth and girl with nowhere else to lie alone. His one hand on her jugs and the other more private, the boy will not want you trampling on his moment of pleasure.

Nonsense. It sounds like the behaviour of some rare beast to me, and personally I intend to spot it.

Oh well go.

I will.

All right. Though wait. What if it is a stray which, weary of sniffing its food out of bins and dumps and bent and twisted cans, has abandoned the streets and run the bypass to this green belt where, lucky dog, he has discovered a fawn couched among roses and snapped its neck and now, for the first time, it cracks warm bone in place of licking the smear of processed horse, and joys in the living blood? Then you appear, like an owner come to take it back to the gutter. It might tear your skin.

Twitter.

Perhaps you are right and I will not go down this once. It was probably a starling's mimicry.
More than likely. I heard nothing.
Also they imitate motor noise and gunshot.
Cunning fowl. But come, let us follow the path to another part of the wood, and leave them to their practice.

Tweet-tweet
Churrr.
Tweet-tweet
Churrr.

Peace perfect peace.

Hiss.

What?
That sweet stink! Breathe it!

Hiss. Hiss.

Oh pardon. I am so distracted by these adders. Where is it safe to put your feet, nowadays?
Can you not smell it?
Sorry.
Was it resin or musk? Wild garlic, or the bitter tang of rue?
Sniff. Not a sausage.
The wind bore it to me out of that fruitful meadow, whose poppy-spotted golden bristling body stirs under the warm blanket of blue air.
I think you are smelling things.

No truly. Ahh, the disturbance in my nostrils makes me want to reel!

Hiss. Hiss. Hiss.

There again! Such intoxication – you have to breathe!
I won't.
You must!
I might catch a fever off the pollen.
Come, let us clamber the fence and wade through the meadow waist-high to find it!

Sssssssssssssssssss!

Shift! It nearly had my foot! I could panic! The earth's alive!
That waft again! Cannot you savour it?
Nothing but fancy.
Anything but, rather. Let us follow our noses.
I will not cross the fence. The serpents will be having a field-day in the long grass, hunting, chasing, teaching their vicious young to creep, mating in lusty knots, snapping the air with excess of animal vigour, and spraying their venom that winds through the body like gas blown into a village at night: first the tethered mules are numbed, then in their kennels the swift-footed dogs. Next the toxin enters sleeping houses and, deadening, stills the nerves of the lungs and tightens the bands on the hearts of the poor slumbering humans. Next day, successful men in masks arrive to bag them up.
I really do not feel . . .

Hiss hiss hiss.

You are mad. This odour has dropped from heaven and will not permit me to hesitate.
But use your brain. It is no doubt a woman from the city, tired after work, holidaying, who has travelled here to anoint her skin with creams and oil whose fragrance tempts the

sun's rays to light upon and cleave to her in a darkening embrace. She will not thank you for clouding her pitch and losing the thread of her block-buster.

Nonsense. It is some rare herb, or maybe the piquant stinkhorn.

Suit yourself.

I go.

Okay. Though wait. What if it is a bull fell dead, and out of its massive decay funguses, moulds, and blossoms flourish in garish splendour, and in the great crack that was once its belly the wild bees hive, metamorphosing its tripes into waxen architecture, its stinking bowels into runnels of pungent honey? Ready to die defending their sweet home, they fall upon you till you are skinned with bees, and I must beat them off and carry you home and wrap you in icy sheets for a month.

Hiss hiss hiss.

On second thoughts, the fence shows it to be a private field, and I do not want to transgress the code of the country. It was probably only the scent I spilt on my handkerchief.

The solution in a nutshell. And now let us head back treewards before the snakes grow too frisky and gnaw our heels.

Hiss hiss hiss hiss hiss.

Peace perfect peace.

What's that?
What's what?
That?
A driven leaf.
No! That spark?

Buzz buzz buzz.
Buzz buzz buzz.
Buzz buzz buzz buzz buzz.

Over where?

There. Damn these flies! Lord! Did you not notice it, there where a deer-track leads down the knoll into the blaze of deep gorse?

I think you are seeing things.

Oh there is nothing like gorse in bloom. It makes my head quite swim!

Buzz buzz buzz.

There, it flashed again! Let us go down and see!

Bizzzzzzzzzzzzzzzzzzz!

Uhh! Ohh! That one went on my lip! Ahh! Puh!

Come on.

No. It is all in the mind.

It is not in the mind at all! Again! Again! Did you not see it *that* time?

I will stick to the road. Why, the flies are a dozen times thicker down there. See how they cluster upon the thorns then break into the heavy air, howling, reeling, like armed men, troopers, shipped to the shore of some hostile island: they start from their craft to scatter over a smoking unmapped beach. Shying from tracer, they dodge whining shells, hurl themselves belly-down, and twist across the ground, rolling this side, that side, then leaping, high, to keep foot free of wire-tangles and the wreckage of blasted comrades dropped on the blackened sand.

I really do not see . . .

Buzz. Buzz.

Did you catch it *then*?

No.

In that case I am going alone.

Oh, be reasonable. It is probably only the sunlight winking off the worn rim of an ornithologist's binoculars. Loins aching, crouched in his careful hide, hot to observe some rare behaviour, he will not thank you for blowing his cover.

Nonsense. It is certainly a semi-precious stone, or glow-worm.

Well, my head is aching. Look for yourself.

I will.

But wait. What if it is a man grown sick of his days and nights? Choosing a spot far from the interference of fellow humans he makes his bed on summer-dry undergrowth and lies on it, rubbing chest, arms, legs, trunk, and head with lighter-fuel, preparing to make a way with himself. But, a character much given to nerves, his chain-smoking habit has worn the nap off his flint and the lighter responds badly so that, frustrated, he sighs it needed but this! Then steels himself with a count of ten to press once more, but still no luck. And counts down again to the pressing point. No better.

Buzzz.

Until he hears you approach, ill at ease, clumsy, down that path the deer in the forest have beaten out with delicate slots through years of rut and grazing and, in a panic, he scrubs further counting and presses harder, quicker, till out of his lighter more than a mere spark holds and that flame-bright gorse grows flame indeed, and you in it, your waxed jacket melting upon you like the hero in the horse-man's shirt, and meanwhile I am forced to observe this terrible tragedy, whose memory will haunt me the rest of my days.

Well. I will not go down after all. It was probably a trick of the light.

If that. Let us get back to the car now dar-ling, and leave the flies to their work.

BUZZ BUZZ BUZZ BUZZ BUZZ.

What's that noise like a horn?
And in the deep of the woods
behind them ancient Silenus, in need

of a nymph to ravish.
  Enough to lament, that fact,
besides which he is always more than
half-sober these days, more than half-
sober.

HOLIDAY (QA)

What is the sure path?	This one.
Where does it go?	Away from here.
Is that enough?	That is enough.
What lies in wait?	Vertigo. Happiness.

What lies below?	Farms and forests.
What lies below?	Hills, valleys, meadows, grazing cattle, trampling flocks, the noise of bells.
What lies below?	Valley haze, dust from tracks, fields patched with wire, roads dewed with cars.
What lies beyond?	A cloud off a town that lies indistinct in its filth. A place with no horizons in it. My kennel.

What lies overhead?	The air, immobile.
What lies a mirror?	The mountain pool.
To what face?	The sky's. Mine.
What passes over?	A horse in cloud. The sun is

its eye, the wind its breath,
the universal fire its open
mouth.

(*brīhad*)

What like a baby?	The fire we made.
Why like it?	Fed, it gives delight.
How does it play?	We blow in its bosom.
Does it catch at the moon?	It shakes in its flames.

Did anyone dance?	Our batteries spent.
Did no one dance?	We are not a *tribe*.
Did anything dance?	Moths from the woods.
Did they dance well?	Tumble and scorch.

Do you want the world?	For this holy moment.
In what way holy?	Happy to die.
In what way happy?	My heart like a moth.
What if you bleed?	My wrists bleed milk.

Nadine Gordimer

HOMAGE

Read my lips.

Because I don't speak. You're sitting there, and when the train lurches you seem to bend forward to hear. But I don't speak.

If I could find them I could ask for the other half of the money I was going to get when I'd done it, but they're gone. I don't know where to look. I don't think they're here, any more, they're in some other country, they move all the time and that's how they find men like me. We leave home because of governments overthrown, a conscript on the wrong side; no work, no bread or oil in the shops, and when we cross a border we're put over another border, and another. What is your final destination? We don't know; we don't know where we can stay, where we won't be sent on somewhere else, from one tent camp to another in a country where you can't get papers.

I don't ever speak.

They find us there, in one of these places – they found me and they saved me, they can do anything, they got me in here with papers and a name they gave me; I buried my name, no one will ever dig it out of me. They told me what they wanted done and they paid me half the money right away. I ate and I had clothes to wear and I had a room in a hotel where people read the menu outside three different restaurants before deciding where to have their meal. There was free shampoo in the bathroom and the key to a private safe where liquor was kept instead of money.

They had prepared everything for me. They had followed

him for months and they knew when he went where, at what time – although he was such an important man, he would go out privately with his wife, without his state bodyguards, because he liked to pretend to be an ordinary person or he wanted to be an ordinary person. They knew he didn't understand that that was impossible for him; and that made it possible for them to pay me to do what they paid me to do.

I am nobody; no country counts me in its census, the name they gave me doesn't exist: nobody did what was done. He took time off, with his wife by the arm, to a restaurant with double doors to keep out the cold, the one they went to week after week, and afterwards, although I'd been told they always went home, they turned into a cinema. I waited. I had one beer in a bar, that's all, and I came back. People coming out of the cinema didn't show they recognised him because people in this country like to let their leaders be ordinary. He took his wife, like any ordinary citizen, to that corner where the entrance goes down to the subway trains and as he stood back to let her pass ahead of him I did it. I did it just as they paid me to, as they tested my marksmanship for, right in the back of the skull. As he fell and as I turned to run, I did it again, as they paid me to, to make sure.

She made the mistake of dropping on her knees to him before she looked up to see who had done it. All she could tell the police, the papers and the inquiry was that she saw the back of a man in dark clothing, a leather jacket, leaping up the flight of steps that leads from the side-street. This particular city is one of steep rises and dark alleys. She never saw my face. Years later now (I read in the papers) she keeps telling people how she never saw the face, she never saw the face of the one who did it, if only she had looked up seconds sooner – they would have been able to find me; the nobody who did it would have become me. She thinks all the time about the back of my head in the dark cap (it was not dark, really, it was a light green-and-brown check, an expensive cap I'd bought with the money, afterwards I threw it in the canal with a stone in it). She thinks of my neck, the bit of my neck she could have seen between the cap and the collar of the leather jacket (I couldn't throw that in the canal, I had it dyed). She thinks of the shine of the leather jacket across my shoulders under the puddle of light from a street-lamp that stands at the top of the flight, and my legs moving so fast I disappear while she screams.

The police arrested a drug-pusher they picked up in the alley at the top of the steps. She couldn't say whether or not it was him because she had no face to remember. The same with others the police raked in from the streets and from those with criminal records and political grievances; no face. So I had nothing to fear. All the time I was being pushed out of one country into another I was afraid, afraid of having no papers, afraid of being questioned, afraid of being hungry, but now I had nothing to be afraid of. I still have nothing to fear. I don't speak.

I search the papers for whatever is written about what was done; the inquiry doesn't close, the police, the people, this whole country, keep on searching. I read all the theories; sometimes, like now, in the subway train, I make out on the back of someone's newspaper a new one. An Iranian plot, because of this country's hostility towards some government there. A South African attempt to revenge this country's sanctions against some racist government there, at the time. I could tell who did it, but not why. When they paid me the first half of the money – just like that, right away! – they didn't tell me and I didn't ask. Why should I ask; what government, on any side, anywhere, would take me in. They were the only people to offer me anything.

And then I got only half what they promised. And there isn't much left after five years, five years next month. I've done some sort of work, now and then, so no one would be wondering where I got the money to pay the rent for my room and so on. Worked at the racecourse, and once or twice in night-clubs. Places where they don't register you with any labour office. What was I thinking I was going to do with the money if I had got it all, as they promised? Get away, somewhere else? When I think of going to some other country, like they did, taking out at the frontier the papers and the name of nobody they gave me, showing my face –

I don't talk.

I don't take up with anybody. Not even a woman. Those places I worked, I would get offers to do things, move stolen goods, handle drugs: people seemed to smell out that somehow I'd made myself available. But I am not! I am not here, in this city. This city has never seen my face, only the back of a man leaping up the steps that led to the alley near the subway station. It's said, I know, that you return to the scene of what you did. I never go near, I never walk past that subway station. I've never been back to those steps. When she screamed after me as I disappeared, I disappeared for ever.

I couldn't believe it when I read that they were not going to bury him in a cemetery. They put him in the bit of public garden in front of the church that's near the subway station. It's an ordinary-looking place with a few old trees dripping in the rain on gravel paths, right on a main street. There's an engraved stone and a low railing, that's all. And people come in their lunch-hour, people come while they're out shopping, people come up out of that subway, out of that cinema, and they tramp over the gravel to go and stand there, where he is. They put flowers down.

I've been there. I've seen. I don't keep away. It's a place like any other place, to me. Every time I go there, following the others over the crunch of feet on the path, I see even young people weeping, they put down their flowers and sometimes sheets of paper with what looks like lines of poems written there (I can't read this language well), and I see that the inquiry goes on, it will not end until they find the face, until the back of nobody turns about. All that will never happen. Now I do what the others do. It's the way to be safe, perfectly safe. Today I bought a cheap bunch of red roses held by an elastic band wound tight between their crushed leaves and wet thorns, and laid it there, before the engraved stone, behind the low railing, where my name is buried with him.

Peter Redgrove

CAT AND TREE

There is a fragrant and spiky small tree
In bud, into which the birds descend.
It is the cat's bird-machine.

He stands poised with one paw
Resting on the slender vibrant trunk, like a cellist
Testing the hall's atmosphere through his G-string before
He starts to play.

Birds descend and ascend, untroubled, pause
On a bough a while to contemplate and mute
Guano, they rise up having done so
With the cat like a black shadow at the trunk's foot.

There is a detonation from the docks, and the birds rise
And scatter like a black substance torn to fragments,
The cat merely lays his head back on his shoulder and
    watches
For the echoes to subside among the ship-machinery.

The echoing birds slip back one by one
Into his bird-machine; now they will scare less.
He pushes his stare forward and enters the slaughter-tree;
It is all cat now along every bough, as the spider
Lays a paw to her harmonium of gossamer.

A SHELL

The shell the skeleton of all the waves.
Lacking a sea view
I place it on the windowsill

Which watches the drizzle along the canals,
The chained doors of the Green Inn,
And the commercial district where there are no theatres.

On some magnetic points of the iron footbridge
I thought I could estimate by a certain note
The city river's depth;

During the demolitions
When the copper ceiling of the theatre fell
Bells sung in all the padlocked churches.

They took it away for a military bandstand
That green resonator. I return to my shell
As though it were my wife.

Was Lot's wife, bones and all, turned to salt?
She would stand there, a pillar, until the next shower.
The old buildings are showing their bones in this leached-
   down city.

I pick up my salt shell, and listen
To its hushing tune like the city's, listen
To city-air tossed here and there

In all its wave-shaped singing opus-chambers.

Louis de Bernières

LABELS

I WAS BROUGHT UP in the days when there was electric light but no television, and consequently people had to learn how to amuse themselves. It was the great heyday of hobbies. People made entire villages out of matchboxes, and battleships out of matches. They made balsa aeroplanes, embroidered cassocks with coats of arms and scenes of the martyrdom of saints, and pressed flowers. My grandfather knitted his own socks, made wooden toys, cultivated friendships with spiders in his garden shed, cheated at croquet, and learned how to produce his own shot-gun cartridges. My grandmother's hobby was flower-arranging and social climbing, and my mother played spirituals on the piano in between sewing new covers for the furniture and knitting woolly hats for the deserving poor. My uncle rolled his own cigars from tobacco grown and cured by himself. My other grandmother spent happy hours in the garden collecting slugs that she could drop down the grating outside the kitchen, and below a hoard of portly toads would eat them before hiding themselves once more beneath the accumulation of dead leaves.

My two sisters had a hobby called 'dressing up'. It consisted of emptying the trunks in the attic, and draping themselves in the extraordinary clothes inherited from previous generations. Then they would go out into the street, posing as indigent old ladies, and beg coins from passers-by. One of my sisters, I forget which one, actually managed to wheedle a florin from our own mother, who failed to recognise her. We spent the florin on jamboree bags, sherbet fountains, and those dangerous fireworks called 'jumping jacks'. We set them off all at once in a field of cows, and sat on the gate gleefully watching the ensuing stampede. It was only me who got spanked for it, however, since little girls in those days were not judged to be capable of such obviously boyish mischief.

As for me, I evolved through a series of pastimes, which began as a toddler. My first hobby was saying good morning. I had a little white floppy hat that I would raise to anyone at any time of day, in imitation of the good manners of my father, and I would solemnly intone 'good morning' in a lugubrious tone of voice that I had probably first admired in a vicar. After that I developed an interest in drains, and would squat before them, poking with a stick at the limp shreds of apple peel and cabbage that had failed to pass through the grate outside the kitchen. I noticed that in the autumn the leaves turned grey, and I discovered the miraculous binding quality of human hair when it is intermixed with sludge. From this I progressed naturally to a brief fascination with dog manure, and am perplexed to this day as to why it was that occasionally one came across a little pile that was pure white. Nowadays one never sees such faecal albinism. My wife recalls that as a child she had assumed that such deposits were made by white poodles.

As infancy blossomed into childhood, so my interests multiplied. I made catapults, tormented the cat, pretended to be a cowboy, made boxes with air-holes so that I could watch caterpillars become chrysalides, made a big collection of model biplanes and Dinky cars, amassed conkers, marbles, seagull feathers, and the squashy bags in the centre of golf balls. At one point I became interested in praying, and knelt quite often over the graves of our pet animals.

The morbidity of adolescence was to provide me with new joys, such as taxidermising dead animals and suffering relentless hours of torment from being agonisingly in love with several untouchable girls all at the same time. I read every Biggles book I could find, read Sir Walter Scott novels without realising that they were classics, memorised hundreds of filthy limericks and rugby songs that I can still recite faultlessly, and discovered that it was possible to have wet dreams whilst still wide awake.

Many of my friends pursued arcane hobbies, such as collecting cigarette cards and cheese wrappers, shrinking crisp packets in the oven, train and bus spotting, egg-blowing, origami, inspecting each other's endowments behind clumps of bamboo, collecting African stamps, and farming garden snails in a vivarium. One of my friends made a hobby of moles, and carved perfect representations of them in softwood with the aid of a scalpel. Another collected one hundred and fifty pairs of wings from small birds that he had shot with an air-rifle. He then suffered a crisis of conscience and joined the Royal Society for the Protection of Birds, becoming eventually one of the few people in this country to have spotted a Siberian warbler, which was unfortunately eaten by a sparrowhawk before the horrified eyes of thirteen twitchers concealed in one small hide.

Like everyone else I was reduced to extreme torpor and inactivity by the advent of television, but found that I was becoming increasingly depressed and irritable. After a couple of years I realised that I was suffering from the frustration of having no interests in life, and searched around for something to do.

I was in our corner-shop one day when I was most forcibly struck by the appealing eyes of a cat depicted on the label of a tin of catfood, and it occurred to me that a comprehensive collection of catfood labels might one day be of considerable interest to historians of industry, and that to be a connoisseur of catfood labels would surely be a sufficiently rare phenomenon for me to be able to become an eminent authority in a comparatively short time. Instantly I dismissed the idea from my mind as intrinsically absurd, and returned home.

An hour later however, I was mocking myself at the same time as I was buying the tin with the appealing picture of the cat. With the tin comfortingly weighing down the pocket of my jacket on one side, I returned home once more, and eagerly lowered it into a pan of hot water so that I could soak off the label. I wrecked it completely by trying to peel it off before the glue had properly melted, and had to go out to buy another tin. This time I waited for the paper to float free of the can, and carefully hung it up on a line that I had stretched from a hot water pipe in one corner of the kitchen over to a hook that I had screwed into the frame of the window. I went out to the stationers and bought a photograph album and some of those little corner pockets which are sticky on only one side. I walked restlessly about the house all evening, waiting for the label to dry, and then could not sleep all night for getting up every ten minutes to go and test it with my fingers. In the morning, my eyes itching with tiredness, I glued the label into my album, and wrote the date underneath in white ink. Afterwards I went out and bought a hair-dryer and two more cans of catfood.

I was to discover that different manufacturers have different methods of securing their labels. The easiest ones to get off are those which are glued with only one blob, relying on the rim of the can and their tight fit to keep them in place, and the worst ones are those which are stuck in place by means of large smears at every ninety degrees. On some of them the glue is so weak that one can peel it off immediately, without soaking, and others have to be immersed in white spirit. I made a comprehensive chart in order to determine at a glance the best methods of removing the labels.

I began to accumulate an embarrassment of delabelled tins, which grew unmanageable just as soon as I realised that one can obtain them in vast sizes, as well as in the smaller sizes that one commonly finds in supermarkets. I rebelled against the wasteful idea of simply throwing them away, and took to giving them away to friends who possessed cats. They were very suspicious at first, and were reluctant to give the food to their pets in case it turned out to be adulterated, or was in fact steamed pudding, or whatever. They soon came round to the idea, however, when the offerings were unspurned by their cats, as did the owners of the cat kennels, to whom I gave the industrial-sized cans. I did notice that many of these people were beginning to look at me askance, as though I were a little mad, and it is the truth that I stopped receiving invitations to dinner parties because my conversation had become monomaniac. I think the worst thing was when my wife left me, saying that she would not consider coming back until I had removed all the albums from her side of the bedroom. The house became a terrible tip because I had had no experience of doing the housework, and eventually I had to pay her to come back once a week in order to dust and tidy.

It occurred to me that the easiest way of obtaining labels would be to write to petfood companies and request samples, past and present, but I received no co-operation at all. My first reply was similar to all the others, and ran like this:

Dear Sir,
   Our manager asks me to thank you for your kind letter, and assures you that it is receiving his closest attention.
   With best wishes to you and your pussy, we remain, yours sincerely . . .

Having received this letter, I would hear nothing more.

It may surprise many people to know that the variety of catfood labels is virtually infinite. To begin with, every manufacturer changes the label fairly frequently in order to modify the targeting of the customer, and to attempt to gain an edge over other brands. Thus a brunette might be changed to a blonde to make a particular food more glamorous, and a Persian cat might be substituted for a ginger moggy in order to give an impression of high class. Shortly afterwards the woman might be changed to a beautiful Asian in order to appeal to the burgeoning immigrant market, and the cat be changed to a tabby to give it a no-nonsense, no-woofters-around-here, working-class appeal. The labels are often changed by the addition of 'special offer' announcements, or, most annoyingly, by 'free competitions' where the competition is on the back of the label so that one has to buy two cans the same in order to have both the obverse and the front of the sticker in one's album.

In addition, every supermarket has its own brand, and every manufacturer is constantly adding to the range, so that, whereas in the old days there was just Felix, Whiskas, Top

Cat, etc., each one now has flavours such as rabbit and tuna, quail, salmon, pigeon, truffles, and calf liver, each one with changing labels as detailed above. Everyone knows that the food is mostly made of whales slaughtered by the Japanese for 'scientific research', cereals, French horses, exhausted donkeys, and bits of the anatomy of animals that most people would prefer not to eat, but recently the producers have cottoned on to the fact that cat owners tend to buy the food that their cat likes the most, and consequently have introduced greater and greater quantities of finer meat, so that indeed one finds real pieces of liver and genuine lumps of rabbit.

It was when my collection began to go international that I hit the financial rocks. I had been working for several years as a bailiff, a job to which I was well suited on account of my great size and my ability to adopt an intimidating expression. I had managed to remain afloat by cutting expenses wherever possible; my house was falling apart, my garden was a wilderness, my car was ancient, I had bought no new clothes for five years, and I cut my own hair with the kitchen scissors. I once sat down with my albums and worked out that I had spent the equivalent of two years' salary on catfood. But I was not broke.

What brought everything to a crisis was a trip to France in pursuit of a debt defaulter. I stopped off in a Champion supermarket, and, whilst looking for a tin of cassoulet, I happened upon rows and rows of catfood with beautiful labels, many of them in black, with distinguished scrolly writing upon them. It was love at first sight, and I bought every single type I could find, not just there, but in every Mamouth and Leclerc supermarket that I passed. I broke the back axle on the way home, and my hoard of tins eventually arrived by courtesy of the Automobile Association's relay service.

Naturally it became worse and more disastrous by the month. I made frequent weekend trips to France, and returned burdened with cans of Luxochat, Poupouche and Minette Contente. Thereafter I took sick leave from work and discovered the treasure trove of Spain. Not for me the

Alhambra; it was Señorito Gatito, Minino, Micho Miau and Ronroneo.

I came home bursting with happiness and *joie de vivre*, planning to cover Germany, and found that my world had fallen apart. My skiving had been discovered, and I was fired from my job, at exactly the same time that I received final demands for the electricity, the gas, the telephone, and a reminder to pay my television licence. I sat amongst my albums and my pile of Spanish cans, and realised that I had allowed myself to drift into disaster. I beat myself about the head, first with my hands, and then with a rolled up newspaper. I raised my eyes to the heavens in exasperation, moaned, rocked upon my haunches, and smashed a dinner plate on the kitchen floor. Pulling myself together, I made an irrevocable decision to destroy my entire collection.

Out in the garden I built a sizeable bonfire out of garden waste and my old deck-chairs, and went indoors to collect the albums. I found myself flicking through them. I thought, 'Well, I might just keep that one, it's the only Chinese one I've got', and 'I'll not throw that one away, it's a Whiskas blue from ten years ago', or 'That was the last one I got before my wife left. It has sentimental value.' Needless to say, I didn't burn any of them; I just got on with soaking off the labels on the Spanish cans.

My unemployment benefit did not even begin to cover my personal expenses as well as the cost of acquiring new tins, and I was reduced to buying stale loaves from the baker, and butcher's bones with which to make broth. I had to slice the bread with a saw, and would attempt to extract the marrow from the bones with a large Victorian corkscrew. I became demented with hunger, and the weight fell off me at a rate equalled only by the precipitate loss of my hair from extreme worry. One day, in desperation, I opened one of my tins, sniffed the meat, and began to reason with myself.

'It's been sterilised,' I said to myself, 'and a vet told me that it's treated to a higher standard than human food. OK, so it's full of ground testicles, lips, udders, intestines and vulvas, but so are sausages, and you like them. And what about those pork pies that are full of white bits and taste of gunpowder? They don't taste of pork, that's for sure. Besides,' I continued, 'cats are notoriously fussy and dainty eaters, apart from when they eat raw birds complete with feathers, and so if a cat finds this acceptable and even importunes people for it, maybe it's pretty nice.'

I fetched a teaspoon, and dipped the very tip of it into the meat. I raised it to my nose and sniffed. I thought that in truth it smelt quite enticing. I forced myself to place the spoon in my mouth, conquered the urge to retch, and squashed the little lump against my palate. I chewed slowly, and then ran to the sink and spat it out, overwhelmed with disgust. I sat down, consumed with a kind of sorrowful self-hatred, and began to suffer that romantic longing for death that I had not felt since I was a teenager. My life passed before my eyes, and I had exactly the same kind of melancholy reflections about the futility and meaninglessness of existence as I had experienced after Susan Borrowdale refused to go to the cinema with me, and my sister came instead because she felt sorry for me.

But these cogitations were interrupted by a very pleasant aftertaste from my mouth, and by the fact that I was salivating copiously. I picked up the can at my feet, and sniffed it again. 'All it needs,' I said to myself, 'is a touch of garlic, a few herbs, and it would really make a very respectable terrine.'

I took it into the kitchen and emptied it out into a dish. I peeled three cloves of garlic and crushed them. I grated some fresh black pepper and some Herbes de Provence, and mashed the meat with the extra ingredients. I squashed it all into a bowl, levelled it off with a fork, decorated it with three bay leaves, and poured melted butter over it so that it would look like the real thing when it came out of the fridge.

It was absolutely delicious spread over thin toasted slices of stale bread; it was positively a spiritual experience. It was the gastronomical equivalent of making love for the first time to someone that one has pursued for years.

I suffered the indignity of being visited by the same firm of bailiffs for which I used to work, but my old mates were kind to me and took only things that I did not need very much, such as the grandfather clock and my ex-wife's Turkish carpet. They left me my fridge, my cooker, my collection of books on the manufacture of terrines and pâtés, my vast accumulation of garlic crushers, peppermills, herbs and French cast-iron cookware. I never could do things by halves, I always had to have complete collections.

I became extremely good at my new vocation. The more expensive catfoods made exquisite coarse pâtés and meat pies (my shortcrust pastry is quite excellent, and I never leave big gaps filled up with gelatine, like most pie-makers). The cheaper ones that have a lot of cereal generally do not taste very good unless they are considerably modified by the addition of, for example, diced mushroom and chicken livers fried in olive oil. Turkey livers are a little too strong and leave a slightly unpleasant aftertaste.

The fish-based catfoods are generally very hard to use. With the exception of the tuna and salmon, they always carry the unmistakable aroma of catfood, which is caused, I think, by the overuse of preservatives and flavour-enhancers. They are also conducive to lingering and intractable halitosis, as any owner of an affectionate cat will be able to confirm.

And so this is how catfood, which got me into so much trouble, also got me out of it. I began by supplying the local delicatessen, and was surprised to find that I was able to make over one hundred per cent profit. I redoubled my efforts, and learned to decorate my products with parsley and little slices of orange. I learned the discreet use of paprika, and even asafoetida. This spice smells of cat ordure, but is capable of replacing garlic in some recipes, and in that respect it is similar to Parmesan cheese, which, as everyone knows, smells of vomit but improves the taste of minced meat.

I also discovered that the addition of seven-star Greek brandy is an absolute winner, and this led me on to experiments with calvados, Irish whiskey, kirsch, armagnac, and all sorts of strange liquors from Eastern Europe and Scandinavia.

But what really made the difference was printing the labels in French, which enabled me to begin to supply all the really expensive establishments in London: *Terrine de Lapin à l'Ail* sounds far more sophisticated than 'Rabbit with Garlic', after all. I had some beautiful labels printed out, in black, with scrolly writing.

I have become very well-off, despite being a one-man operation working out of my own kitchen, and I am very contented. I have outlets in delicatessens and restaurants all over Britain, and one in Paris, and my products have even passed quality inspections by the Ministry of Agriculture and Foods. It might be of interest to people to know that my only complete failure was a duck pâté that was not made of catfood at all.

I go out quite often on trips across Europe, looking for superior brands of catfood with nice labels, and my ex-wife often comes with me, having moved back in as soon as I became successful. She has become most skilful at soaking off labels, and is a deft hand with an *hachoir*. The liver with chives was entirely her own invention, and she grows most of our herbs herself.

I recently received two letters which greatly amused me. One was from a woman in Bath who told me that my terrines are 'simply divine' and that her blue-point Persian pussycat 'absolutely adores them' as well.

The other was from a man who said that he was beginning a collection of my 'most aesthetically pleasing' labels, and did I have any copies of past designs that I could send to him? I wrote back as follows:

Dear Sir,
   Our manager thanks you for your letter and asks me to assure you that it is receiving his closest attention.

Naturally I never wrote back again, nor did I send him any labels. None the less I feel a little sorry for him, and anxious on his behalf; it's easy enough to turn catfood into something nice, but what do you do with hundreds of jars of pâté? With him in mind, I had a whole new range of labels printed in fresh designs, with details of a competition on the reverse.

Conor Cregan

OCHÓN

I AM DROWNING in a cold broth of words and memories.

My father was a big brute of a man who had joined the guards to escape the boat to England; a big brute of a distant man, with big brutish features and distance in his every move; a distant brute of a big man with the head of a block of Wicklow granite and hands the size of ploughshares, covered in warts the size of mountains and tufts of hair you could hide an army in; a granite-headed distant big brute, warted and hairy with teeth all gapped and twisted and stained like the land he came from, all bitter and biled like the people who'd spawned him; a biled brutish twisted gapped granite-headed warted hairy distant man with legs like the boughs of oak trees, dinged and bruised, buckled and bashed and bent. In short, he was like any other father of any other son of Éireann born in those dark days.

Those dark days, and dark indeed they were, dark depressed days, full of darkness and depression. I never saw the sun until I was ten, and then only for a moment, for my father, biled brutish twisted gapped granite-headed warted hairy distant man that he was, chose that time to speak his first words to me, his first drops of wisdom, for he was a man of few words and what words he spoke were indeed drops of wisdom with the value of gold; he chose to speak to me then, while I was enjoying the brief break in depression above my head and thanking God and His son and His mother and all the saints for allowing me the joy of sunshine for that instant of time, to speak to me in his all-powerful all-commanding deep bass-baritone voice that sounded like

420

the very depths of hell come up to meet you, to speak from the core of his genitals, the bowels of his being, words pregnant with meaning, fertilised with intent, fruitful as the half-acre of rural Ireland we kept for spuds and cabbages, the half-acre we knelt in every day of the year until the soil was part of us and we were part of it, and when it came time to pick the spuds and cabbages and eat them, it was like we were picking pieces of ourselves and eating them.

'To work,' he said.

And I felt the red heat of Satan across my face as my father clouted me with his mighty hand and pitched me headlong into a heap of steaming silage. To work. I pondered those words as he climbed on board his bicycle and headed for the barracks. For he never spoke to me again, except to curse me, before the day he passed into eternity. And that was far off then. To work.

My mother, God bless her, was a saint of a woman; a saint among women when women were saints; sainted and blessed, blessed and sainted. She had twenty-three children in twenty-three years and still remained a virgin; her body bore the sainted look of a fruit tree picked clean and the shape of a potato sack. Thirty years his junior, for my father was not a man of impulse, they were wed while he was on the run during the Tan War, in a small field by a fairy ring; wed at the dead of night with the rain coming down in buckets, tapping out a ghostly rhythm to the words of the priest. A lean girl, she was then, my mother, lean and pale, and she worked for the landlord in the big house.

The landlord! May his bones roast in the fires of hell for ever. And may the devil himself pull my brains out through my nose if I ever have a decent thought about him. The landlord, the curse of Cromwell. May the two of them suffer the sufferings suffered by my ancestors during all the years of oppression. Suffer them tenfold, and tenfold again, and tenfold times tenfold. May I never say their names without spitting; may the spirits of the famine forgive me for having to mention them now. The landlord, rack-renting rugby rapist that he was, took my mother on to work in his kitchen, took her on for sixpence and a jar of porter: her father, my grandfather, had a weakness for the porter, a weakness he prayed to God to set him free of, a weakness brought on by having to watch his family evicted from their sod hovel and their quarter-acre. So my mother was sold to the landlord – I spit – and my grandfather and his wife and his other eighteen children took to the road and disappeared into the mists of history.

And misty it was then. Misty dark depressing lost land, oft rained on, cloaked in sadness, heavy with oppression. And many walked stooped with the weight of oppression, bent double, buckled. My mother was such a one. Working all the hours God sent, and some more, in the kitchen of the landlord – I spit – chopping and boiling spuds and cabbage. Spuds and cabbage. Glory be to God for spuds and cabbage. Spuds and cabbage, the food of my nation. The food of my nation being tested and tasted by him – the landlord – I spit. Tested and tasted for his table; a table full of the tested and tasted things of my land; a land oppressed, misty and oppressed, weighed down and doubled up and lost in the mists of oppression.

What a night it was when the boys, and my father one of them, took the landlord out and beat him to death with hurleys; beat him so you wouldn't know him from the ground where he lay or the colour of the hills; beat him till he was flat and pulped; beat him till the last oppressing breath was driven from him to the eternal damnation awaiting it; beat him and beat him until the land was drunk on his blood. And then burned his great house to the ground, that great heresy of a home, blaspheming against our land, burnt down, wiped out, destroyed. And such a cry of release went out that night as could be heard by those yet to be born. I heard it, though many years were to pass before my incarnation. No small wonder my mother married a man of such courage. The General.

They still called him the General at the barracks, even though he'd only been a general for an hour, during the Civil War. An hour before the other lot dumped arms and the telegram arrived from Dublin, thanking him for his service and telling him they had no more use for him. A bitter way for a man to be treated, a bitter way which made him bitter, bitter as bog water, and hard. He beat my mother that day, beat her till there was no more beating in him, beat her like he was beating the landlord again; and she understood, understood like any wife would of a man who had done what he'd done, gave herself willingly to him to be punched and kicked and belted around the peat-smoked room in their little tenant cottage where generations of his family had lived and died, offered herself as any sainted woman would who knew men and what they needed, who knew this life for what it was, who knew the sanctity of suffering for a woman, and sought it, eagerly.

Eagerly did she seek it and teach her twenty-two daughters, my sisters, and pure honest daughters of Éireann they were, to seek it; to wait for him to consume gallons of poteen and porter – for he was a man of enormous appetites, unfulfilled appetites, hungry demons consuming him as he consumed porter and poteen – and offer themselves to the wrath of his belt or the hawthorn stick he kept in the corner; to offer themselves as Our Lady offered herself, handmaids of their lord, my father; a lord as lordly as any lord in Ireland, lording over his family like the chieftain he was, chieftain in his own land, chieftain of the half-acre, lord of the cottage. And with the anger of a lord, he would whip them and flay them till his hands were raw and he could no longer stand through exhaustion, and after, they would sit him down in his rocking chair and feed him broth and bread washed down with the blackest of black stewed tea, so black that even the loins of Beelzebub could not claim it for their own; and they would sit by him and read to him from the legends of old, old legends of young men and great deeds and women of beauty, such beauty as would burn the very eyes from your head.

And before he nodded off, he would say in a beaten voice: 'Women!'

Nor did I escape his fury when he saw fit to mete out punishment to me. Just punishment, may I say, punishment befitting the seriousness of my transgressions, for serious transgressions they were, and the most serious of all was self-abuse. The two most sinful words in the English language.

And English it would be, as only English could contain such words, only the language of the oppressor, Cromwell and the landlord – again I spit. Self-abuse. May I be struck down never to rise again if ever I practise such a terrible sin on our native soil again; if ever I stain my land with the evil seed of my lust. Lust! Another Saxon word. Endless, they are, endless words for the sins no son of Éireann would commit if his mind hadn't been polluted by the oppressor.

In our parish we were raised with a fearsome respect for the chastity of girls, and an even more fearsome fear of the consequences of disrespect. And should I hold that against them may the God that gave me life strike me from the face of my homeland with the agony I deserve. There were three of us lads in the parish school, three of us and the mounting lust of adolescence, three of us with a terrible respect for the lassies, three of us and sin. And sin was the strongest, the strongest by far; stronger than the desire to please God on the altar, than the desire to win county football honours, than the love we had for our native land. Yes, stronger even than that. And though we fought, aided by the savage strokes of Father Brogan's walking stick and the pictures of terrible torment he told us awaited the self-abuser in hell, unspeakable except in the confessional, through the medium of Latin, we were weak and self-abuse took place. Self-abuse of the temple, followed by tortuous guilt and pain and penance. We did penance. We did penance for our eternal souls, penance enough to cleanse the soul of Lucifer himself, and more, fierce merciless penance in the fields of our parish, the fields we tilled and loved, the fields we grew our spuds and cabbages in, the fields of our fathers, muddy stony fields of stone and mud, soaked with the rain of the grey skies, swept by the howling banshee winds of the mountains and the seas, swept soaked stony muddy fields, all stony and soaked and muddy and swept.

Beast that was in me, beast of the devil, full fanned the fires of lust; lust that possessed me, slave I was to it, slave to its carnality, slave to its pleasure. And the altar of that lust, that carnal fury, where we worshipped, all three of us lads, all three of us sons of Éireann, wanting desperately to serve our God and our land, the altar of our sinful mortality was the stone shed between the school and the barracks, the stone shed where Dev had hidden out for six months, the stone shed where the Virgin herself had appeared in all her glory, glorious woman that she is, the stone shed where Batt Molloy had murdered Planxty Quinn over a quarter-acre of prime and a hundredweight of spuds; murdered him terrible he did, and terrible it was and the end it brought for Molloy; swinging for an hour from the gibbet in Dublin, slow painful agony, cross in his hands, wriggling and writhing and writhing and wriggling at the end of the hangman's rope. Horrible, it was, and horrible it was told by my father who found Batt, drowned in drink and praying for forgiveness, and sent him to his doom.

And found us he did too, my father, big brutish man that he was, found us in the false ecstasy of self-abuse, seduced by Satan, preying on our weaknesses and frustrations, dank cold dark depressing day that it was, and us willing victims of the pleasures he offered, pleasures of the flesh that sinned against the soul, base animal pleasures, pleasures that tore us from our land and our God, damning us for all eternity. And beat us he did, my father, with the vengeance of God; beat us till our flesh was blue and our lungs were empty from screaming; beat us till the sun fell and rose five times, though with the clouds and the mist you couldn't see it; beat us with a horsewhip till the horsewhip broke into a hundred pieces; beat us with a shovel and a pick handle till they fell apart; beat us till his knuckles were skinned to the bone and the leather was worn from his huge peeler boots, boots that could kick the top off a mountain or split a man from his groin to his brain.

But even my father, brutish man that he was, could never deliver a blow as brutal as that delivered by the hand of God on our family when I was sixteen. As brutal a blow as was ever delivered on any home to any family in Ireland, a land of brutal blows, harsh and brutal and unforgiving. My mother, sainted woman that she was, dear suffering sainted woman, slipped on a stone and drowned in the icy waters of Lough Derg while on pilgrimage for our sins. Kneeling, she was, deep in prayer, lost in torment, for torment is a maze in which it is easy to become lost, kneeling for four days and nights, drenched by the rain and the mist, frozen by the wind, dizzy with the hunger, blood running from her knees to mix with the waters of the lough. Drowned and lost in those icy depths; and my father, rent with grief, tore the very shirt from his back and howled such a howl of pain as was never heard before or after in our parish or in any other parish in Ireland; and he raised his fists and cursed the God who'd made him, whose terrible plan he was a victim of, whose mind he never knew, cursed him in wild rage, not knowing the damnation he was bringing on himself, not caring. And my sisters fighting with him to shut him up, to pull him home, pleading with him to prostrate himself and beg God's forgiveness, to offer up every ounce of his being for his soul, not knowing his soul was slipping, slipping slowly in the rain and the wind and the mud, slipping into the darkness, dark darkness that it was, the darkest of dark darkness, black.

And black was the road to Dublin, black as pitch and full of holes. I wore away many a good pair of brogues bringing myself to that fair city. A year, it was, a year walking, a hard year, where I went four months without meeting another soul, carrying the curse of my father on me, big brutish curse that it was, the curse of a man whose son and heir has turned his back on him and his land to write poetry, the curse of a man left in the clutches of twenty-two daughters and none of them married for fear of sinning, the curse of a man smitten by drink, that faithless mistress, the curse of a man cursed by God, the curse of a man once a general. Once a general.

Long and sad were the poems I wrote, long and sad as the days I spent in Dublin, long poems with long words and long verses, sad poems blackened by the sadness within me, sadness for my home and my county and my family; and wander the streets I did, wander them alone, sad streets, lonely streets, with the only solace bottled and sold in glasses, bottled like the sadness within me and my poems, sold like the soul of my father. For a poor boy up from the country, Dublin is a web of temptation and sadness, and for a poor

boy wanting to write poetry, the drink is the quickest way
to get caught in that web. And get caught in it I did, drinking
till I hadn't penny enough to buy the dripping from a crust
of stale bread, drinking till I was thrown out on to the street,
left to live in doorways and sing songs about my home county
for a few leftovers. Dark was the depression which overcame
me then, and darker still when I remembered my home and
my county and my family.

And when I found work after two years, it was poor paid
work, for all work was poor paid in those days, paid poor
for poor it was the poor work we did. Poor work digging a
great gape of a hole in the city, a great gape of a hole, big as
any hole dug in any part of the world; and I was in that hole
five years digging it, without seeing the sun, up to my neck
in filth, all for a penny a month. But what a penny, and what
you could buy for that penny, though I never spent it all at
once for I was saving enough to be able to return home some
day. Home. Every son of Éireann's dream: to return to the
place from where he came. A noble dream, befitting a noble
race.

My dream, and what a dream it was, dreamt during those
long sad days in that gape of a hole. And in poems I wrote
of the dream, still hoping someone would put them to print
somewhere, someone who knew the worth of a poem, long
and sad that it was, the worth of a poem by a son of Éireann
lonely for his home parish. But the mention of self-abuse was
enough to have me damned, damned for writing such words,
damned for failing in my duty to my church. My church,
once my friend, was now my enemy, and what an enemy to
have, enemy that was once a friend, abuser of the self-abuser.
And hot-headed sinful beast that I was, with much of the big
brutishness of my father, I cursed the church and abused it
as I had once abused myself, with more ferocity than that
even, and wrote such words about it as should never again
be written by a son of Éireann about his land or his church.
Cruel vengeful words, sinful and full of the pride of youth,
savage as the beatings of my father, wicked as the mind of
Satan. And when we had fought, my church and I, and I had
lost as was only right, I had to give up my dream and use

what pennies I had to take the boat to England, land of the oppressor, cursed by my ancestors, devoid of soul, abandoned by God.

I was in England when I got word that my father was dying. Eaten away, he was, eaten away by the rancour within him. I packed a small bag, the smallest bag I had, with the smallest things I had, and took the boat home. Home to my native land, the land of my church, the church that had damned me, in the land that had spurned me, to the father that had cursed me. Dark land that it was, damning and spurning and cursing, cursed spurned damned land, all cursed and spurned and damned.

My father lay in his bed, my sisters sitting around him, talking, the priest saying the last rites over him, the matchmaker trying to tease the strength of the will from him; and him pale, deathly pale, yellowing at the eyes, ugly yellow there where his eyes looked up at the roof, struggling to get words from his twisted salivating mouth. There was a stench, the stench of death, I think, such a stench as would make you heave your dinners from a month before up on to the stone floor, vile stench, stinking, odious smell, choking smothering stink of a stench, bile-based and bitter.

'The end is near,' the priest said, looking at his watch.

I bent over my father.

Then, as if possessed, my father raised a hand from the bed and lifted it high, clouting eight of my sisters in the process and knocking them across the room like skittles, as if possessed by a demon, demonic in its possession, he raised that ploughshare of a hand, hairy and warty, raised it aloft and caught me by the head with the grip of a man possessed, caught me and pulled me to him, pulled me down to this twisted salivating mouth, and me desperately trying to make my peace with God for fear of what would happen, desperately regretting my life of poetry and self-abuse, desperately regretting my sins against the church and the land of my birth, terrified by the wrath of God and the wrath of my father and not able to distinguish between the two, being pulled down on that bed, petrified, bowels loosening by the second, smelling the awful smell of death around my father, down, down, deeper down.

'Son,' he whispered in my ear.

'Father,' I replied, held in his vice, feeling the warm liquid run down my leg.

'Son, it's terrified of dying I am, terrified. 'Tis an awful thing, death.'

'Yes.'

'I mean, an awful thing. Truly awful. And worse for a man with no soul. No soul, do you hear. No soul. Soulless. Glory be to Jesus, 'tis a fierce thing.'

'Is it, Father?'

His eyes looked around the room, at my sisters, at the priest, at the matchmaker.

'Maybe not.'

There was a noise in his lungs, a dreadful emptying noise, empty and dreadful, and he passed away to wherever he was going and whatever awaited him.

Jane Duran

THE GREAT PLAIN

It takes a fierce dog
to keep them to their imaginary
circle.

The sheep move forward
a blade of grass at a time –
their parked faces.
The snow mountains behind
applaud their births
and deaths.

Abandonment of place
makes their wool
grow deep.
Clouds shear the land.

It is so quiet
it could be Sunday.
The air rushes through their wool.
The ground is stone.
They have run out of field.

The shepherd makes a penitent
movement sideways.
The wind stops him here –
the great doors of this plain

you can throw yourself against
and call and call
and no one hears you.

David Kirkup

MELTDOWN AT CENTRAL STORAGE

ONLY A MIRACLE could explain the existence of ice on the island. A geological miracle that flew in the face of facts. Too numbing, too absolute, to be claimed by either church or state, its presence was taken for granted. There had always been a core of ice cosseted against the thermal fevers that raged through the earth's crust. Unfathomable and illogical, it was a remnant scrap from an age of ice, a stowaway hidden from the sun. Never healing, forever in flux, its frozen white blood regenerated endlessly through time. And miraculous too was Central Storage; a derelict folly of warehouses and cold stores that had grown over the glacier like a timber scab. A precarious and impossible city-state raised to harness the cold beneath it and reap its frigid harvest. A palace of thermometers and meat hooks without architect or plan, its deepest vaults carved into the ice and peopled only by cold store men.

Central Storage became a repository for life itself in frozen form. For every living creature outside its walls, another was stowed for a fee in its sheds. Nothing perished there, neither was anything born. The glut of dormant flesh amassed over the ice endured indefinitely. No one calculated the extent of the abundance; the temperature closed minds to the luxury of speculation. A credible inventory could not be made. The inner cold stores had collapsed long ago, their supports buckling under the weight of century-old stock, their contents irretrievable. The enormity of the hoard at Central Storage went unquestioned, the ledgers left to freeze

432

to their shelves and the business of long-term storage went on apace in its vast and restless hive.

As the old century gave way to the new, the dozen companies that had jostled for a share of the ice's profits were amalgamated. A grand entrance hall was built in snowy marble and a celebratory banquet held one summer night among its cold and gleaming pillars. Hired candelabra vied with the moon for brilliance. Cigar tips glowed like hot coals between the teeth of merchants and whalers and abattoir owners. Diamonds frosted the necks of their wives. An aching chill crept up through the floor and into their bones as they toasted the marriage of commerce and ice.

Beyond the great panelled doors all was order and industriousness. An army of storemen and porters laboured among sepulchral corridors whitewashed in ice. Frost grizzled their hair with silver and turned their clothes to ermine. They moved as soundlessly as wraiths over the sawdust-strewn floors, their breath hanging in chains through the air as they toiled. Great shanks of innumerable oxen, clad in muslin and heavy as standing stones, rumbled at the passing of their carts. Stilled weighing scales lay bathed in spectral light among a moraine of frozen carcasses. The numbing allegiance the men had sworn to the ice stole all colour from them. Each face was set hard as trampled snow.

Then the great thaw began.

The foreman was the first to notice a change. As he slid open the doors that led on to the ice the frozen white sea pushed him back with its terrible energy. The enveloping mist that rose from it night and day still hung in the air; but it was less thick, less concealing than it should have been. Spears of sunlight falling from the roof pierced it more deeply. It had lost its constancy. The foreman could see through it for the first time. In those first minutes were revealed secrets hidden from him by forty years of snow-blindness. He saw the lustrous ice itself, was able to stand at its edge unharmed and without fear of his eyes freezing open. Peering down he discovered the faintest colours stirring beneath the pellucid crust, saw greens and blues a thousand times diluted waking from watery dreams and gathering strength.

The temperature rose. The mercury in the thermometers crawled upwards like sap heralding a ruinous spring.

A chasm opened within days of the foreman's discovery, wide enough for a man to fall into and never crawl out again. Tormented by a slow and protracted thaw, the ice tore free its anchors and retracted its claws from the core of the world to begin a terrible contraction. It could no longer be tamed; a melting heart made it wild. Each fissure rending its hide leaked bile. All night its gasps echoed through the empty corridors of Central Storage to set the carcasses swinging on their rails and its cries prowled among the troubled dreams of sleeping islanders. But the thaw was merciless and the fangs it thrust at the vulturous heat soon turned to drool.

Nothing could be done; everything melted. Everything was lost in time.

Cursing their luck, the cold storage men turned their backs on the afflicted ice. Aware that the thaw would be complete within months, they filed down to the port to enlist on the first boats out of the island. They left for the polar trading posts, some north, some south, wrapped in their dirt-thickened furs. In the soft light each face was an expressionless mask, its mouth sewn tight with bitterness, its eyes revealing nothing. Only secretive men were given over to ice; one third of them broke the surface, the rest hung in the depths. Slush and dripping water disgusted them, meltwater made them see red. The *Dogfish* and the *Krakatoa* were the first to set sail with their new crews. Central Storage became a ghost town over night. Then a workforce of rats moved in through the drains, sensing the haul already unlocking with the relentless thaw. A cornucopia awaited them.

The melting ice was both an opening grave and a treasury, surrendering undreamt-of riches and unimaginable dross. It had enfolded in a bony grasp whatever had fallen or slipped or been thrown on to its surface, clutching for all time its frozen prey. Now those tendons turned to liquid and talons fell away, their frigid stranglehold on the past at an end.

As it thawed, the ice disgorged at will. Each day saw the

unleashing of another pocket of time with its own particular stench and drowned anatomy. The meltwater swirled with the ice's innards, each piece of flesh clouding its depth furred with corruption and delicate as a snowflake. The only paid work to be had was in manning the pumps and dredging the endless flotsam away. Cluttered in the boardroom above the hall, the Company turned its back on the unfolding calamity. Its coffer was now an ossuary. The directors were refined men. They had no stomach for an unseemly fight with scavengery. The thaw was a degradation and an affront to their senses that was best written off and forgotten. They washed their hands of the sorry affair. The townspeople were free to plunder while the buildings still stood. Gloved in frost, a thousand numb hands quarried frantically among the surrendering slush. It was a lucky dip; there was something for everyone. People kept whatever was valuable and flung the rest away.

Among the pillars of the central hall men waded knee-deep through marbled sludge to panhandle for treasure. Old women perched like herons on the stairs, eyes bright with concentration, their grappling hooks at the ready. Below them humming-birds, blown off course by antique winds, drifted like floating jewels among books awash with ink. Elver-fingered children crouched by the sluices, straining and sifting the mud through colanders and sieves, finding knives and toads and coins in abundance. Each made their own discovery, each had a tale to tell.

No one saw anything more beautiful than a child suspended fathoms deep in the ice; a boy hanging in deceptive levitation, his head falling back, his last breath spread about him in a trapped galaxy of bubbles. He was innocence suspended, a puppet with streaming hair like the tail of a comet. His mouth was an opening oyster, the pearl of an unformed word lay on his tongue. Around him sparrows with wings outstretched were frozen in their flight.

Those who saw him were drawn by invisible threads. It was their own past they saw entombed in glass, forever pupating, its face unblemished and whiter than snow. They yearned to wrap him in a blanket of warmth. But the ice held its prisoner in a jealous clinch; it would not melt for him. So people used ice-picks to claw down to his beckoning hand and began a moonlit tug of war with his blue-thimbled fingers, robbing them of their stiffness. Yet the ice defeated them. Neither stave nor crowbar nor axe could smash its teeth or prise its jaws apart. By the time the thaw released him he was spoiled beyond recognition. A boy of mud crying poisonous tears.

Driven through the ice, the timber crutches supporting the inner cold stores began to collapse. The foragers retreated and the meat was left where it hung. Life returned in secret beneath a writhing cloak of flies and canyons of long-dormant flesh struggled slowly awake. Carcasses found their pink and purple-hued complexions, branding-marks and bruises reappeared. Eyes opened and muscles flexed beneath a pinpricked mantle of phosphorus. A wanton putrefaction announced its presence. Hides leaked thick syrups and bellies distended with gas. The abandoned storerooms became palmhouses rich with orchid-bright sores and fallen petals of blood.

A pestilential stench then folded the town in its arms, sticking like tar to people's skin and hair. No one escaped its fetid embrace. Even the rain was tainted, besmirching the streets instead of washing them clean. Bonfires were lit to scorch the air and purge the wind of its terrible burden, but all to no avail. People pointed accusingly at the swollen brick face of Central Storage and retched in its carious breath, the scarves tied over their mouths and noses drenched with ineffectual perfumes.

The ambassadors left soon after, recalled by embarrassed governments intent on forging refrigeration pacts elsewhere, their new détentes carved in foreign ice. They departed in great state, with flashing medals on their chests and all the solemnity that protocol demanded. One by one, ambassadorial barques picked their way among the clanking bell buoys, the gilded dolphins at their prows nosing between the anchor chains of rusting hulks. No end of bowing and saluting could hide the fact that the island had been left to its fate.

Without commerce the port died and the waters that had once churned with tugs and dredgers were stilled. The whale boats and factory ships of the northern seas were all destined for other harbours, taking with them blizzards of gulls and the smoke from their blackened funnels. The crimson decks steaming with blood and the holds that spewed sour blubber were gone. Giant freezer vessels shuddering with the pulse of refrigerant no longer hid the sun and set the night ablaze with their lights. The cardinal's robes burnt scarlet against the oil-darkened waters as he waited on the quay to depart, the church's holy relics crated at his side. He blessed the town for the last time, genuflecting as the foghorns sounded their baleful farewell.

At last the great carpeted staircase of Central Storage became a rapid. The mosaic laid in the floor at its foot was washed clean away, the polar bears and penguins it pictured carried piecemeal down the front steps to choke the drains with a glittering shingle. Even the gilded company clock drowned in time, its arms propelled through a pulp of sodden numerals. Only the porphyry walruses guarding it with algae-green tusks remained to crash to the torrent below.

The bulwarked walls were finally breached. The sheds collapsed like matchsticks. Seething meltwater flooded the streets and engorged the sewers. The tide crashed through the cobbled lanes bearing a thundering flotilla of wreckage. Flies crested each wave. The town was no more than a sluice, its forges quenched and lights snuffed out. The curdled waters lapped against the hospital portico, fringing its doors with a scum of sodden dressings. Patients stared down from attic windows as rats, agile as gondoliers, rode the septic sea on surgical masks. The whole island was washed in filth.

Among the Company's board of directors there were those with ill-conceived notions of reversing the process at Central Storage. They dreamt of invoking science's myriad ingenuities, its improbable toolbox of miracles, to turn back the clock. When the board-in-exile met for the last time, they expressed their desire to re-throne the ice and bask again in its golden profit. But the pragmatists scowled, provoked beyond endurance by this clutching at straws on a busy morning. The earth's phenomena were naturally capricious, they thundered, and the damage was done. Nothing gained, nothing ventured was the prevailing opinion and the Company was wound up before lunch.

There was at last a levelling of the great floodwaters. They stole slowly back to the brim of their rocky chalice, a spent force. Meanwhile the sun slowly battened on a feast of abandoned lagoons. It had taken the ice a great act of will to melt and break the shackles of its own frigid order. Now all was exhaustion. The treasure dredged from its flooded socket was from the recent past. Hundreds of fathoms down mammoths hung in motionless orbit among veils of sediment. Escaping at last from their lungs, their breath took months to reach the surface then broke with the reek of history.

No one visits Central Storage any longer, apart from a curious few.

A. S. Byatt

A NEW BODY OF WRITING:
DARWIN AND RECENT BRITISH FICTION

I AM IN the habit of saying to journalists and academics abroad that I could make a list of at least forty really *good* British novelists working now, and can usually convert their looks of scepticism to nods of enthusiasm when I start explaining. I do think the British novel at the moment is full of truly inventive writing – new forms are being discovered, old forms are being subtly altered, there is a sense that anything is possible and, moreover, anything has a chance of being taken seriously. The earlier generation of novelists – Golding, Durrell, Burgess, Murdoch, Lessing, Spark, Naipaul, Penelope Fitzgerald, Anthony Powell, John Fowles, David Storey – were in fact remarkably eclectic formally. There is a wonderful mix of realism, romance, fable, satire, parody, play with form and philosophical intelligence. There is a version of literary history that says the British novel was moribund until invigorated by the 'writers from elsewhere' – Salman Rushdie, Timothy Mo, Christopher Hope, Kazuo Ishiguro – but I don't think this was so; the British novel was alive and humming, and there was a sense that discoveries were being made. Julian Barnes and Graham Swift write books that are in some sense deliberately small in scope and glancing rather than monumental – but they know their craft, and have something new to say.

I am writing this essay for *New Writing 4* because in 1993, with Salman Rushdie, Bill Buford of *Granta* and John Mitchison, an omnivorous bookseller, I judged the 'Twenty

Best of Young British Novelists'. Novelists, in my experience, don't much like reading a great deal of other people's fiction, and don't usually read it when it's new – but I thought I would do the judging out of curiosity to know what was going on – were there any good *young* writers, in what were they interested?

We had no trouble in finding twenty very varied and interesting young writers – and another five or six, at least, who might well have been on our arbitrary list. I will come to them later. First, I want to describe the interesting narrowness and badness of the bulk of what we read. We must have read about three hundred novels in all, of which the vast majority (leaving out a few sentimental echoes of the 20s, 30s and 50s) were concerned either with inept 'satire' on 'Thatcher's Britain' or, usually simultaneously, with the human body as an object of desire and butchery. We were in a world in which most of the action was penetration either by the penis or the knife or the needle, where everything dripped with blood or other fluids. Human concerns were confined to basics – 'relationships' in the narrow sense, greed, sado-masochism. There are a great many stories about butchery and cooking of human bodies – there were two of these in the last issue of *New Writing*, and several were submitted for this one. Some of this derives from the admiration of the younger generation for the brilliance of Martin Amis and the younger Ian McEwan. The way in which all this blood and pleasure in pain connects to the loathing of Mrs Thatcher felt by the aesthetic left is still waiting for its novelist – one less shrill, less *automatically* full of loathing, less knee-jerk than the majority of these writers. I myself feel that Mrs Thatcher has been demonised and there is an element of a witch-hunt about it all. Salman Rushdie discovered Anne Billson's novel, *Suckers*, a tale of a London of the 1980s secretly run by a conspiracy of vampires from Canary Wharf, red-mouthed, red-nailed and drinking Bloody Marys, which was a cool, poised metaphor for the general feel of the eighties distaste for their own fashions and preoccupations.

Although we had no trouble finding twenty, and more, good writers, we did have trouble finding good women writers. I once complained at the British Council's Walberberg seminar that the women's movement seemed to have reduced the ambition of women writers in Britain. Where once we had Lessing, Murdoch, Spark and Fitzgerald, who were the best of their generation, now women seemed to confine themselves to 'women's' subjects – gender, disadvantage – and even to start from an assumption that they were disadvantaged as writers, which in Britain has not been true since Eliot and the Brontës. I was criticised by the novelist Maggie Gee, who said that women started writing later, for a variety of reasons, and took longer to establish themselves. There is indeed a group of very good writers in their forties – too young for the 1983 Best of Young British Novelists competition, too old for the 1993 one, but writing excellent books: Hilary Mantel, Michèle Roberts, Jane Rogers, Pat Barker, Marina Warner, and Rose Tremain (who *was* selected in 1983).

One of the most pleasing things about our final list was its catholicity and its excitingly *mongrel* nature. Little Britain crosses Europe, Asia, Africa and America in splendidly inventive ways. Louis de Bernières writes about the Colombian drug barons in a mixture of South American magic realism and the grimmer and sharper comic tone of Evelyn Waugh. Kazuo Ishiguro writes parables about English butlers and English politics in the 1930s which Anthony Thwaite has compared to Japanese stories about the samurai and their retainers. Ben Okri writes a fluid prose about African spirits, Caryl Phillips writes substantial nineteenth-century prose about slavery, in the persona of a young, delicate, ignorant English female, Philip Kerr transports Raymond Chandler's style and incorruptible hero to Hitler's Berlin, Nicholas Shakespeare writes elegant English novels about South America and North Africa, and Hanif Kureishi has written a perfect sharp *English* comic suburban novel about the life of Asians in outer London. Tibor Fischer's *Under the Frog* is a surprising, comic, and moving account of a basketball team in the Hungary of the 1940s and 1950s. There is no lack of ambitious thought – Lawrence Norfolk's *Lemprière's Dictionary* weaves history, odd facts, myth, fantasy, into a labyrinthine account of the East India Company's financial manoeuvres in the eighteenth century, whilst Adam Lively's *Sing the Body Electric* is set in the future where the invention of a musical device that plays the movements of the brain raises questions of music and political control, freedom and mass violence that are new and gripping. Candia McWilliam has a wonderful baroque imagination of odd emotional structures, and Esther Freud records the sad effects of hippiedom on the next generation with wit and melancholy. Two books which just got left off our list were Adam Thorpe's much-admired *Ulverton* and Tim Pears's excellent first novel, *In the Place of Fallen Leaves*, perhaps, looking back, because both belong to what Malcolm Bradbury has called the 'new ruralism', and we were very urban judges. Salman Rushdie called Pears a García Márquez in Devon, and there is something new about his depiction of drought on an English farm, as well as something old, but still alive. He himself claims that the heat and dryness are a satire on Thatcher's Britain.

Connections can be seen between the badness of the bulk of bad novels and the virtues of the good ones. Jeanette Winterson's *Written on the Body*, a book which bears a considerable resemblance to Monique Wittig's *Le Corps Lesbien*, reduces love – and writing – to total obsession with the body of the beloved, inside and out. Alan Hollinghurst's elegant and elegiac *The Swimming-Pool Library* explores the 'innocent' world of pre-Aids gay sex, with an inventive and obsessive bodily narcissism. The undertow of this book is also bodily violence, beatings, earlier political betrayals, leading to violence and violation. D. J. Taylor's novel *Real Life* contrasts his hero's 1970s life as a sharp young executive in the world of pornographic films with his life in rural Norfolk, the stuff of the body of 'English' realism, and asks, with a mixture of parody and bodily matter-of-factness, 'What is real?' Much good writing runs alongside pornography, and I think this is for reasons deeper than the desire to *épater le bourgeois*, and sadder than the sixties dream of endless sexual freedom and possibility.

I think it is possible to connect the obsession with the rutting and dying body with the now almost obsessive recurrence of Darwin in modern fiction. In the 1960s Iris Murdoch created a series of characters who were writing ethical treatises on the Good but who did not believe in God. These philosophers were taunted by daemonic figures – mad priests, Jews from Auschwitz – who point out that if there is no God, there is no source or sanction for our morality. The 1960s novel was intensely religious – consider Golding's obsession with the numinous and with evil, consider Durrell's mysticism, consider Burgess's endlessly reenacted battle between Augustinian predestination and Pelagian freewill, consider Muriel Spark's Catholicism as an aesthetic imperative. The nineteenth-century novel described the disappearance of religious certainty, or attempted to reassert it (Dostoevsky), and if the nineteenth-century thinkers thought about what Darwin told us we were, it was always in terms of the religious vision we had lost. Now, I think, novelists are thinking about what it is to be a naked animal, evolved over unimaginable centuries, with a history constructed by beliefs which have lost their power. We look for our morality in works like Richard Dawkins's *The Selfish Gene* or E. O. Wilson's *On Human Nature*. And this leads both to historical fictions of a new seriousness and to the kind of flat, precise treatment of the human body, and human behaviour as meat, or specimens, or aesthetic objects.

Early Darwinian fictions were Graham Swift's *Waterland* with its seminal contrast between natural history and history, Peter Carey's *Oscar and Lucinda* with its interest in chance, gambling, and the unfortunate Philip Gosse who believed in the Creation. Lawrence Norfolk's herring's-eye view of the creation in this collection is a version of this preoccupation. Jenny Diski's new novel, *Monkey's Uncle*, concerns the breakdown of a woman who believes she is descended from Captain Robert Fitzroy of the *Beagle*, who committed suicide because he could not reconcile his religious views with his passenger's discoveries. She is troubled about her genetic heritage and in her madness visits an Alice-in-Wonderland underworld where Marx, Freud and Darwin sit and picnic by a lake whilst the heroine is entertained by an orang-outang. Graham Swift's *Ever After* is the story of a researcher who does not know his own paternity, is researching a Victorian who lost his faith because of Darwin, and loved his wife who is dead. Perhaps its most moving scene is a confrontation between the Victorian hero and his father-in-law, a clergyman whose faith is threatened by the younger man's Darwinian beliefs, whilst both are clad in netting and protective clothing standing beside the clergyman's beehives. The younger man's whole life has been changed by a meeting, or confrontation, with a fossilised ichthyosaurus at Lyme Regis, echoing both Fowles's *French Lieutenant's Woman* and Hardy's *A Pair of Blue Eyes*. Hilary Mantel's new novel, *A Change of Climate*, a perfectly controlled, chilling account of do-gooders and simple believers up against evil, also opens with a classic, but deeply felt account of the battle between a young man and his fundamentalist father. The young man collects fossils, but defers to his father's psychological violence and becomes a missionary. Early on he finds a fossil on a beach in Norfolk, a 'devil's claw' which is simultaneously a sinister form, and the remains of a living creature that was beautiful and interesting. Religion in this book is a killer, and yet, in the Murdoch sense, the source of decency too.

One of the most oddly moving scenes in contemporary fiction is the one at the end of Julian Barnes's *A History of the World in 10½ Chapters*, where the narrator wakes up, after death, in a kind of health farm where wishes are granted, and after a time realises that he wants to be *judged*, he thought he would be judged. Certainly, say the kindly assistants or officials, a lot of people seem to want that, and they arrange for him to meet a judge, who tells him, simply 'You're OK.' The whole world of this scene, the flatness, the boredom, the bodily pleasures, the sense of something missing, are an essential image of the world of many of these novels. Man is a religious creature, says the socio-biologist E. O. Wilson. No human society has not had a religion. Until now.

One could propose that the considerable amount of good historical writing going on in contemporary British fiction is part of a project of reassessing the past, our own ancestry, without the old framing certainties of Christianity or Marxism. Pat Barker's series of novels on the First World War, beginning with *Regeneration* and its powerful sequel, *The Eye in the Door*, are informed by a new kind of imaginative curiosity. Her hero is a neurologist and psychologist, and she probes the effects of war on body and mind, on sexuality and moral choice, with an energy deriving from a different curiosity. Jane Rogers's *Mr Wroe's Virgins* is a wonderful mixture of anthropological curiosity about the religious beliefs of a (real) nineteenth-century religious cult, and real human sympathy. Rose Tremain's *Restoration* deals with religion in the time of Charles II and Hilary Mantel's *A Place of Greater Safety* examines evil and belief in the time of the French Revolution. Or there is Penelope Fitzgerald suddenly recreating the Russia of the 1920s, as a background for a precise moral problem of English behaviour, and illuminating both. Or Elaine Feinstein in *Loving Brecht*, giving an imagined autobiographical account of what it was to be Brecht's mistress, in the high days of both Fascism and Marxism, convincing in its marginality and understatement. Abdulrazak Gurnah's brilliant and beautifully written new novel, *Paradise* is a study of slavery in an East African country before the coming of the colonialists – it combines images from the Koran, the Arabian Nights and Conrad with ease and passion in a perfect *English* prose. These historical examinations are an extension of the curiosity about the time before we lived, about the Second World War, in writers like Swift, McEwan, Christopher Hope and Louis de Bernières, who dedicates his book, *Captain Corelli's Mandolin*, on the Italian occupation of Greece, to his parents, who 'fought fascism and were not thanked'. I think we are interested in ancestors and inheritance because larger explanations have died and lost power. Malcolm Bradbury's *The History Man* seems to me to be still an underrated book, in its precise and comic account of the glittery fascination and danger of politico-historical-causative explanations and plots. Younger writers have fewer certainties (except that Thatcher is a demon) and are more quietly curious about origins. Their curiosity is framed by new knowledge about inheritance, about DNA and its works, by a new sense of the long history of the earth and the creatures on it.

The lack of certainties gives rise to the other side of the pattern I am trying to discern in modern writing – the satisfactory flatness, the deliberate limitation of many texts. The young Scottish writer, A. L. Kennedy, has said she admires Robert Carver for his sense of limitation, for his dealing with small precise human situations for themselves. Her own work has these virtues. The story by Philip Hensher in this collection for, and perhaps also Alasdair Gray's, have this quality of moving by reduction. Timothy Mo's *An Insular Possession* was a large political novel, rewriting the history of the Opium Wars. His later novel, *The Redundancy of Courage*, related to the war in East Timor, was flatter, it crossed the genre of the Forsyth thriller as Hollinghurst and Taylor cross pornography, and it told of suffering for no purpose, and precisely, of the redundancy of courage. It sticks in the mind as part of a new moral atmosphere.

Two final examples may sum up what I have been suggesting about the pervasiveness of Darwin and genetic explanations. Ian McEwan's *Black Dogs* is a book about the clash of religion and politics, typically in the parentless narrator's substitute parents, his parents-in-law, the father a Communist, the mother driven into a kind of religious mysticism by a horrific encounter with two malign black dogs. What is interesting from my point of view is the stance of the narrator, intensely curious about what drove his parents-in-law, even in the end coming to understand the apparently unimaginative life-choices of his own parents after the war, but centring his own moral life on his domestic happiness with his wife, and the need to understand his origins. He takes his father-in-law to the fall of the Berlin Wall, where they encounter muddle and incipient racist violence, and they discuss his father-in-law's entomological interests, and the battle he had with his wife over a dragon-fly he wanted to kill and collect. The wife, newly pregnant, feels the insect is 'life'; its death threatens her baby. The husband feels, 'Insect populations were enormous, even in a rare species. They were genetically clones of each other so it didn't make sense to talk of individuals, still less of their rights.' 'I was trying to explain Darwin to June and comfort her by saying that there simply was no place in the scheme of things for the kind of revenge she was talking about, and that nothing would happen to our baby . . .' And when the narrator has a *kind of* supernatural experience, a kind of warning from a ghost not to touch a cupboard door with a scorpion on it, the tender tone of the description of the insect is part of our modern sense of our place in the history of things.

'These creatures are ancient chelicerates who trace their ancestry back to Cambrian times, almost 600 million years ago, and it is a kind of innocence, a hopeless ignorance of modern post-Holocene conditions that brings them into the homes of the newfangled apes; you find them squatting on walls in exposed places, their claws and sting pathetic, out-dated defences against the obliterating swipe of a shoe. I took a heavy wooden spoon from the kitchen counter and killed this one with a single blow.'

Our Darwinian preoccupations touch our anxieties about the earth and what we are doing to it.

Finally Justin Cartwright's *Look at it This Way* (1990) deals supremely, because lightly and precisely and comically, with 'Thatcher's Britain'. It is a farce with a bite, in which a shifty and greedy merchant banker is eaten by a lion in Regent's Park, everyone sleeps with everyone, the 'hero' sub-sists on the illusion of making commercials about the 'real Britain' (cockney stereotypes and stately homes) for credit card companies, there is much discussion of meat and vio-lence, 'flat' descriptions of Thai boxing, and the only true love is that of the filmmaker for his eight-year-old daughter, who lives with his estranged mad wife in New York. He sees this in terms of DNA. 'Of course I know that vanity and self-regard are present in the love of one's children. Sometimes in the streets of London I see mothers hitting their children on the side of their head . . . These parents do this in public because they regard the child as part of their own self; they have an instinctive understanding of DNA. It is the obverse of the self-regard with which parents invest their children.' And he sees immortality, as well as love, in terms of DNA.

The novel is about London, phantasmagoria and the real city.

The illusion is that, like the bees, the citizens live without the knowledge of mortality. A great city is a tissue of immortality; it is the discarded skin of generations, it is countless strata of deception; for it is only in the illusion that it can exist. The bees hum the tune of immortality while they pursue the paths of mortality. They are immortal – another one will be along in a moment to replace the worn-out body of its predecessor. If you look at it this way, strictly in terms of cells and DNA, we are all immortal. We are only cells which shrivel and die but pop up again in new casings. In the documentary about camels it did not mention an Arab proverb: *Death is the black camel that kneels in every doorway.*

And on the next page, in quite another section, the hero goes to see Darwin's house, his beetle collection, and a painting by Stubbs of a lion stalking a horse, which turns out to be a copy, which perhaps once belonged to Josiah Wedgwood, Darwin's grandfather, who cooperated with Stubbs on an enamel of the same subject. This painting is a *leitmotif* in this novel – it stands for death, for the jungle, for long-toothed English lions, vanished British Empire, and English art, both now a little absurd, for illusion and reality. Combined with the beetles, the DNA and Darwin, this image is also part of the vitality and surprising re-formations of the British novel.

(This article is a considerably expanded version of an article first written for the *Daily Telegraph* following the selection of the Best of Young British Writers in 1993.)

BIOGRAPHICAL NOTES

Brian Aldiss recently published the well-received *Somewhere East of Life*, completing the Squire Quartet of novels, set within the framework of a changing Europe. This year, he has a collection of essays and articles, *The Detached Retina*, published by Liverpool University Press, and a collection of poems, *At the Caligula Hotel*, coming from Sinclair-Stevenson. Aldiss also acts in his own evening revue, *Science Fiction Blues*.

Patricia Beer was born and brought up in Devon where she now lives. She was educated at Exmouth Grammar School, Exeter University and St Hugh's College, Oxford, and taught at universities abroad and in Britain before becoming a full-time writer. Her *Collected Poems* came out in 1988. Her most recent volume is *Friend of Heraclitus*, which was a Poetry Book Society Choice and was short-listed for the T S Eliot Prize. She has also published a novel, two works of criticism and several anthologies. A book of memoirs is to appear in 1995. She broadcasts, and reviews regularly for the *London Review of Books*.

Louis de Bernières's first three novels are *The War of Don Emmanuel's Nether Parts* (Commonwealth Writers Prize, Best First Book Eurasia Region, 1991), *Señor Vivo and the Coca Lord* (Commonwealth Writers Prize, Best Book Eurasia Region, 1992) and *The Troublesome Offspring of Cardinal Guzman*. His most recent novel is *Captain Corelli's Mandolin*

(1994). The author, who lives in London, was selected as one of the Twenty Best of Young British Novelists 1993.

Elizabeth Berridge admits a preoccupation with aunts, and 'Poor Mary and the Book of Life' is an extract from a story to be included in a volume in preparation. She has published a short story collection, *Family Matters*, and seven novels, three of which were republished by Abacus/Sphere in 1986. *Across the Common* was awarded the *Yorkshire Post* Literary Prize and serialised on radio. She edited the early diary of Elizabeth Barrett Browning, *The Barretts at Hope End*, and has been a regular fiction reviewer for the *Daily Telegraph*. Her new novel, *The Shell House*, will be published later this year.

Conor Cregan was born in Dublin in 1962 and educated at University College, Dublin, where he took a degree in history. He subsequently worked in journalism in England and Australia, before taking up writing fiction full-time. Two of his novels, *Chrissie* and *The Poison Stream*, were published by the Poolbeg Press in Ireland, and his third, *With Extreme Prejudice*, was published by Hodder & Stoughton in 1994.

Helen Dunmore was born in Yorkshire. She has published six collections of poetry, of which the most recent are *Recovering a Body* (Bloodaxe, 1994) and *Secrets* (Bodley Head, 1994). Her novels for children, *Going to Egypt* (1992) and *In the Money* (1993), are published by Julia MacRae Books. Her adult novels are *Zennor in Darkness* (1993), which recently won the McKitterick Prize, and *Burning Bright* (1994), both from Viking Penguin. Her short stories have been widely published in magazines, and a collection is in preparation.

Jane Duran was born in Cuba in 1944 and brought up in the United States. She has lived in England since 1966. Her work has appeared in a number of magazines and anthologies. A pamphlet of her poems, *Boogie Woogie*, was published by Hearing Eye in 1991 and a selection of her work was included in *Poetry Introduction 8* (Faber and Faber, 1993). A first full collection, *Breathe Now, Breathe*, will be published by Enitharmon Press in 1995.

Janice Elliott was born in Derbyshire and brought up in wartime Nottingham, setting for her Southern Arts Award-winning novel, *Secret Places*, which was also made into a prize-winning film. She read English at Oxford, left the *Sunday Times* for full-time writing and now has twenty-four novels, a volume of short stories and five children's books to her credit. She and her husband now live in Cornwall, which inspired her novel, *The Sadness of Witches*. For many years she was a fiction reviewer for the *Sunday Telegraph*. She is a Fellow of the Royal Society of Literature. Her latest novel, *Figures in the Sand*, was published by Hodder & Stoughton/Sceptre in 1994.

D. J. Enright has taught in universities overseas and worked in publishing in England. Among his publications are several novels and books of criticism. His *Collected Poems* appeared in paperback in 1987, his *Selected Poems* in 1990 and his most recent book of poetry is *Old Men and Comets* (1993). He has compiled a number of anthologies, including *The Oxford Book of Death* (1983), *The Oxford Book of Friendship* (with David Rawlinson, 1991), and *The Oxford Book of the Supernatural* (1994). He lives in London.

Tibor Fischer was born in Stockport in 1959. His first novel, *Under the Frog*, was short-listed for the 1993 Booker Prize. His second, *The Thought Gang*, was published by Polygon in November 1994.

Penelope Fitzgerald was born in 1916 and spent her childhood in Sussex and Hampstead. She was educated at Somerville College, Oxford. Her first novel, *The Golden Child* (1977), was followed by *The Bookshop*, which was short-listed for the Booker Prize in 1978. She went on to win the Booker the following year with *Offshore*, based on her experiences of living on a houseboat on the Thames during the 1960s. Other novels include *Human Voices* (1980), based on her wartime experience at the BBC, *At Freddie's* (1985), *Innocence* (1978) and *The Beginning of Spring* (1988), also short-listed for the Booker Prize. Her most recent novel is *Gate of Angels* (1990).

Cliff Forshaw was born in Liverpool in 1953 and now lives in Brixton. He studied painting at Liverpool Art College before attending Warwick and Cambridge universities. More recently he researched Renaissance satirical and erotic verse at London University. He has lived in Italy, Spain, Mexico, New York and Germany and worked as teacher, translator, systems analyst and freelance writer. He has written radio scripts for the BBC World Service. His poems and verse translations have won a number of prizes and appeared widely here, as well as in the USA and India. His two collections are *Himalayan Fish* (Peacock Books, India, 1991) and *Esau's Children* (National Poetry Foundation, 1991). *The Dade County Book of the Dead* will appear in 1995. He also writes fiction and is currently finishing the second of three novels set in Latin America.

John Fuller was born in 1937. His latest collection of poems is *The Mechanical Body* (1991) and his most recent work of prose fiction is *The Worm and the Star* (1993), both published by Chatto & Windus.

Nadine Gordimer's novels include *The Conservationist, Burger's Daughter, July's People, A Sport of Nature, My Son's Story* and her latest, *None to Accompany Me*. Among her collections of short stories are *A Soldier's Embrace, Something Out There, Selected Stories* and *Jump*. Educated in South Africa, she has held honorary fellowships at universities including Harvard, Yale, Leuven and Oxford. In 1991 she was awarded the Nobel Prize for Literature. Among her other awards are the James Tait Black Memorial Prize, the Booker Prize (joint winner) and the CNA Literary Award.

Rebecca Gowers read English at Trinity College, Cambridge.

She works intermittently as a journalist, and is researching the life of a murderer, who gave her great-grandfather a poisoned cigar and attempted to push him into the Niagara Falls, before being hanged for shooting another young man in a nearby swamp.

Alasdair Gray was born in Glasgow in 1934, studied at Glasgow Art School and has since lived by painting, book design and writing. For the past eight years he has been working on *The Anthology of Prefaces*, a collection of introductions to great books in vernacular English arranged chronologically from Caedmon to Vonnegut, with historical, biographical and critical marginal commentaries. He expects to finish this work before the end of the twentieth century and meanwhile supports himself by the enjoyable exercise of writing popular fiction.

Stephen Gray was born in Cape Town in 1941 and educated at Cambridge and the Iowa Writers' Workshop. With David Philip he has published his *Selected Poems 1960–92*, and with Serif in London a novel, *War Child*. He lives in Johannesburg, South Africa, and contributes regularly to the *London Magazine*.

Lavinia Greenlaw was born in 1962 in London into a family of doctors and scientists, disciplines that she often writes about. She spent her teenage years in a village in Essex, then returned to London as a student. She read English at Kingston Polytechnic and went on to the London College of Printing before working in publishing as an editor for several years. She has had two pamphlets of poems published (*The Cost of Getting Lost in Space*, 1991, and *Love from a Foreign City*, 1992). Her first full-length collection, *Night Photograph*, was published by Faber in 1993 and was shortlisted for the Whitbread Poetry Prize and the Forward Prize.

Paul Henry was born in Aberystwyth, and grew up there and in two Breconshire villages. After graduating in English and Drama, he took up a variety of jobs and now works as a careers adviser in Cardiff. His songs, in Welsh and English, were broadcast on television and radio. He won a Gregory Award in 1989 and his first book, *Time Pieces* (Seren), was published in 1991. Recent poems have appeared in the *Independent*, the *Observer* and the *Times Literary Supplement*.

Philip Hensher was born in London, where he now lives. His first novel, *Other Lulus*, was published in 1994; his second, *Kitchen Venom*, is forthcoming.

Michael Hofmann was born in 1957 in Freiburg and came to England in 1961. He lives in London and teaches one term a year at the University of Florida in Gainesville. He has published three books of poems, most recently *Corona, Corona* (Faber, 1993), edited with James Lasdun *After Ovid: New Metamorphoses* (Faber, 1994) and translated a dozen works from the German: two novels, *The Film Explainer* by his late father Gert Hofmann, and *The Man Who Disappeared (America)* by Franz Kafka, are due out this year.

Christopher Hope was born in Johannesburg. He has published five novels: *A Separate Development* (winner of the 1981 David Higham Prize for Fiction), *Kruger's Alp* (winner of the 1985 Whitbread Prize for Fiction), *The Hottentot Room, My Chocolate Redeemer* and *Serenity House* (shortlisted for the 1992 Booker Prize); his sixth will be published by Macmillan later this year. Other books include *The Love Songs of Nathan J Swirsky, White Boy Running* and *Moscow! Moscow!*. He will be the co-editor of *New Writing 5*.

Glyn Hughes's first novel, *Where I Used to Play on the Green* (Gollancz, 1982/Penguin, 1984), won the Guardian Fiction Prize and the David Higham First Novel award. *The Antique Collector* (Simon and Schuster, 1990/Sceptre, 1991), was short-listed for the Whitbread Novel Prize. His other novels are *The Rape of the Rose* (Chatto, 1987/Penguin, 1989), *The Hawthorn Goddess* (Chatto, 1984/Penguin, 1985), which Nicholas Sackman used for the basis of his orchestral suite,

Hawthorn, commissioned for the 1993 Promenade Concerts, and *Roth* (Simon and Schuster, 1992/Sceptre, 1993). *Brontë* is due from Bantam at the end of 1995.

A. L. Kennedy was born and educated in Dundee and took a degree in Theatre Studies and Drama at Warwick University. She is the author of two short story collections, *Night Geometry and the Garscadden Trains* and *Now That You're Back,* and a novel, *Looking for the Possible Dance.* She has won two Scottish Arts Council awards, the Saltire Best First Book Award, the 1991 *Mail on Sunday*/John Llewellyn Rhys Prize, the 1993 *Scotsman* Fringe First and a 1994 Somerset Maugham Award. She is working on a second novel and dramas.

David Kirkup was born in 1959 in Newcastle upon Tyne and educated at Middlesex Univeristy and the University of East Anglia. He lives in South London and is currently completing his first novel.

Matthew Kneale was born in London in 1960 and studied history at Magdalen College, Oxford. He has travelled extensively exploring seventy countries, as well as living in Tokyo and Rome. His novels include *Whore Banquets,* which won a Somerset Maugham Award, and *Sweet Thames,* which won the *Mail on Sunday*/John Llewellyn Rhys Prize in 1993.

Stephen Knight was born in Swansea in 1960, read English at Oxford and spent a year at the Bristol Old Vic Theatre School. A selection of his poems was included in Faber's *Poetry Introduction 6,* and he received an Eric Gregory Award in 1987. He won the 1992 National Poetry Competition, and his first collection, *Flowering Limbs* (Bloodaxe Books, 1993), was a Poetry Book Society Choice. He is a freelance theatre director.

Hanif Kureishi was born and brought up in Kent. He read philosophy at King's College London, where he started to write plays. *My Beautiful Laundrette* received an Oscar nomination for Best Screenplay, and his other films are *Sammy and Rosie Get Laid* and *London Kills Me*, which he also directed. His novel, *The Buddha of Suburbia*, won the Whitbread First Novel Award and was recently televised by BBC Television. His new novel, *The Black Album*, will be published by Faber and Faber later this year. He lives in west London.

Candia McWilliam was born in Edinburgh in 1955, where she was educated until going to school in England at the age of thirteen. She has a son and daughter by her first marriage and a son by her present husband, with whom she lives in Oxford. Her first novel, *A Case of Knives*, appeared in 1988 and was followed by *A Little Stranger* (1989) and *Debatable Land* (1994). She was selected as one of the Twenty Best of Young British Novelists in 1993.

Paul Magrs (the *g* is silent) was born in 1969 and comes from Aycliffe in County Durham. His fiction is often set on council estates in the north and, while being working class, commits the crime of deviating from social realism. He is completing a PhD on Angela Carter and fiction at the *fin de siècle* at Lancaster University, where he also teaches Contemporary Literatures and Theory. 'Patient Iris' is his first published story.

E. A. Markham is Senior Lecturer in Creative Writing at Sheffield Hallam University. He has directed the Caribbean Theatre Workshop, been a media co-ordinator in Papua New Guinea and held writing posts in universities, colleges and schools. His books of verse include *Human Rites, Living in Disguise, Lambchops in PNG, Towards the End of the Century* and *Letter from Ulster & The Hugo Poems*. He has edited various literary magazines including *Artrage, Writing Ulster* and, at present, *Sheffield Thursday*, as well as *Hinterland* and *The Bloodaxe Book of Caribbean Verse*. He has published two collections of short stories, *Something Unusual* (1986) and *Ten Stories* (1994), and is at present editing *The Penguin Book of Caribbean Short Stories*.

Joan Michelson, an American resident in England since 1970, lectures at the University of Wolverhampton. She has published stories, poems and essays in both American and British literary magazines and anthologies, including *Spare Rib*, *Stand*, *Writing Women*, *New Poetry 3*, *New Writing 3* and *Panurge*.

Andrew Motion was born in 1952 and grew up in Essex, where his family have lived for several generations. He read English at University College, Oxford, and from 1976 to 1980 taught at the University of Hull where he came to know Philip Larkin, the subject of his most recent biography. He has published six volumes of poetry, including *Dangerous Play* (1984), *Natural Causes* (1987), *Love in a Life* (1991) and *The Price of Everything* (1994). His biography, *The Lamberts: George, Constant and Kit* was published in 1986 and his *Philip Larkin: A Writer's Life*, which won the Whitbread Prize for Biography, in 1993. He lives in London.

Joseph New was born in 1952 in South Shields. The same height and weight as the fossil man recently discovered in West Sussex, this late English Spenserian is married with two daughters. There is a book of his stories, *Little Tongues* (Thorn Press, 1991). He lives midway between Oxford, home of the brains, and Witney, home of the blankets. Without blankets, we could not sleep; without brains, read. Thus both towns are justified.

Lawrence Norfolk was born in London in 1963 but his family moved to Iraq before being evacuated in 1967. He graduated from King's College London, in 1986 and then studied for a PhD, taught, worked as a freelance writer on a number of reference books and reviewed poetry for the *Times Literary Supplement*. He is married and lives in Chicago. His first novel, *Lemprière's Dictionary*, was published in England in 1991 and in America in 1992; it has been sold into twenty-two translated editions.

Sean O'Brien was born in London in 1952 and grew up in

Hull. He read English at Cambridge. His collections are *The Indoor Park* (Bloodaxe, 1983), which won a Somerset Maugham Award, *The Frighteners* (Bloodaxe, 1987), which won the Cholmondeley Award, and *HMS Glasshouse* (Oxford University Press, 1991) for which he received the E. M. Forster Award from the American Academy for Arts and Letters. His work appears in the anthology *The New Poetry* (Bloodaxe, 1993). He has held writing fellowships at Dundee University and for Northern Arts, and is a regular reviewer. He lives in Newcastle upon Tyne.

Julia O'Faolain was born in London, brought up in Dublin and educated in Rome and Paris. She has worked as a teacher of languages and interpreting, and as a translator. Her earlier novels include *The Obedient Wife*, *No Country for Young Men* (short-listed for the Booker Prize) and, most recently, *The Judas Cloth*, and she is currently completing a collection of short stories, some of which have appeared in the *New Yorker* and *New Writing 3*.

Ruth Padel is a poet and scholar, and won prizes in the National Poetry Competitions of 1985 and 1992. Her second collection, *Angel* (1993, a Poetry Book Society Recommendation), explored images of madness through invented voices. Her poems have appeared widely in the UK and America. Her first prose book, *In and Out of the Mind* (1992), delved into ancient Greek images of the self. Her second, *Whom Gods Destroy* (due March 1995), compares madness in the ancient, Renaissance and modern worlds. She has read and lectured in many places in the USA, and in 1994 taught a course at Princeton University on opera and desire. She is currently writing a book on images of Ariadne.

Cate Parish was born in 1954, grew up in the USA and has lived in England since 1983. She now lives in Kent, where she works as a nursery teacher. She has had poems published previously in a number of periodicals and anthologies, including *Virago New Poets* and *As Girls Could Boast*.

Glenn Patterson is the author of two novels, *Burning Your Own* and *Fat Lad*. He is currently writer in residence at Queen's University Belfast. A new novel, *Black Night at Big Thunder Mountain*, will be published in July by Chatto & Windus.

Tim Pears was born in 1956. He grew up in Devon, left school at sixteen and has worked in a wide variety of jobs: farm and building labourer, mental hospital nurse, pianist's bodyguard, painter and decorator, college night porter, art gallery manager and others. He has published poetry and travel writing; his first novel, *In the Place of Fallen Leaves*, was published by Hamish Hamilton in 1993 (Black Swan, 1994), and won the Ruth Hadden Memorial Prize and the Hawthornden Prize. In 1993 he graduated from the Direction course at the National Film and Television School.

Peter Porter was born in Australia in 1929 and has lived in London since 1951. He has published thirteen collections of poetry and collaborated with the painter, Arthur Boyd, on four books of poems and pictures. He is also a reviewer of literature and music in journals and for the BBC. After his *Collected Poems* (Oxford University Press, 1983) his recent publications include *The Automatic Oracle* (1987), *Possible Worlds* (1989) and *The Chair of Babel* (1992). He will be the co-editor of *New Writing 5*.

Peter Reading was born in 1946 and trained as a painter at Liverpool College of Art. He has lived in Shropshire, where he worked at an agricultural feed-mill for over twenty years. He received the Cholmondeley Award for Poetry in 1978 and has published nineteen books, including *Diplopic*, which won the first Dylan Thomas Award in 1983, and *Stet* which won the 1986 Whitbread Prize for Poetry. In 1990 he was the recipient of a major literary fellowship from the Lannan Foundation, USA. His most recent publications are *Perduta Gente* (Secker & Warburg, 1989), *Evagatory* (Chatto & Windus, 1992) and *Last Poems* (Chatto & Windus, 1994).

Peter Redgrove was born in 1932. He is also a novelist, a playwright and co-author (with Penelope Shuttle) of *The Wise Wound*, a revolutionary study of the human fertility cycle. Besides his twenty-two books of verse, he has published nine works of prose fiction and a manifesto of contemporary romanticism, *The Black Goddess*. His radio drama, *Florent and the Tuxedo Millions*, won the Prix Italia. A study of his poetry, *The Lover, the Dreamer and the World* by Neil Roberts, was published in 1994, simultaneously with his latest poetry collection, *My Father's Trapdoors*.

Michèle Roberts was born in 1949 and is half-French. She has published seven novels, of which *Daughters of the House* (Virago) was short-listed for the 1992 Booker Prize and won the W H Smith Literary Award in 1993. Her most recent poetry collection is *All the Selves I Was* (Virago, 1995) and her most recent novel is *Flesh and Blood* (Virago, 1994). She has also written for the stage, film, television and radio.

Carol Rumens was born in south London in 1944. She has published nine volumes of poetry, including *Thinking of Skins* (Bloodaxe, 1993), and one novel, *Plato Park* (Chatto, 1988). She has edited several volumes of poetry, including *Making for the Open* (Chatto, 1987) and *New Women Poets* (Bloodaxe, 1990) and, most recently, *Brangle*, an anthology of work by new Northern Irish writers emerging from the creative-writing group she taught at Queen's University, Belfast, while Writer in Residence. 'Any City Death' is a chapter from a new novel-in-progress.

John Saul was born and grew up in Liverpool. After studying philosophy at Oxford, he taught for several years in London and was one of the founder members of a co-operative which produced the newspaper, *Issues in Race and Education*. Since 1985 his short fiction has been published extensively in the UK and in France, Italy and Germany. His stories have appeared in *The Best of the Fiction Magazine* (J M Dent) and in *Sex and the City* and *Border Lines*, both published by Serpent's Tail, who are shortly to publish a further anthology containing his work. His novel, *Heron and Quin*, was published by Aidan Ellis in 1990. He has spent much of his life in Europe and the Americas, and now lives in Hamburg, where he works for Greenpeace.

Helen Simpson's first collection of short stories, *Four Bare Legs in a Bed* (Heinemann, 1990), won the Sunday Times Young Writer of the Year Award and a Somerset Maugham Award. Her suspense novella, *Flesh and Grass* (Pandora, 1990), appeared with Ruth Rendell's *The Strawberry Tree* under the general title of *Unguarded Hours*. She was chosen as one of *Granta*'s Twenty Best of Young British Novelists in 1993. She has just finished a play, *Pinstripe*. Her second volume of stories will be published in 1995.

Muriel Spark, born and educated in Edinburgh, has been active in the field of creative writing since 1950 when she won a short-story competition in the *Observer*. Her first novel, *The Comforters*, appeared in 1957. Her subsequent novels and stories have brought her international fame. She has also written plays, poems, children's books and biographies of Mary Shelley, Emily Brontë and John Masefield. Among many other awards she has received the Italia Prize, the James Tait Black Memorial Prize, the FNAC Prix Etranger, the Saltire Prize and the Ingersoll T. S. Eliot Award. She was elected an honorary member of the American Academy of Arts and Letters in 1978 and to the Ordre des Arts et des Lettres in France in 1988. In 1993 she became a Dame of the British Empire. Among her best-known novels are *The Ballad of Peckham Rye*, *The Prime of Miss Jean Brodie*, *The Girls of Slender Means*, *The Mandelbaum Gate*, *The Abbess of Crewe* and *Loitering with Intent*.

Adam Thorpe was born in Paris in 1956 and brought up in India, Cameroon and England. He has had two collections of poetry published by Secker & Warburg: *Mornings in the Baltic* (1988) and *Meeting Montaigne* (1990). His first novel, *Ulverton* (1992), is a sequence spanning three centuries of a fictional English village. He lives in France with his wife and three children.

Charles Tomlinson was born in 1927. His paperback *Collected Poems* appeared in 1987 and *The Door in the Wall* in 1992. There are volumes of his work in Italian, Spanish and Portuguese, a large number of critical articles on it and four full-scale studies. In 1989 he received the Cittadella Premio Europeo for the *face-à-face* Italian edition of his poems. In 1993 he was given the *Hudson Review*'s Joseph Bennett Award in New York. Tomlinson is also a painter (*Eden: the Graphics of Charles Tomlinson*) and a literary critic (*Poetry and Metamorphosis*). He has translated widely from Spanish and Italian and edited the Penguin Octavio Paz. His *Selected Poems of Attilio Bertolucci* was published by Bloodaxe in 1993. A new collection, *Jubilation*, will appear in 1995 (Oxford University Press).

Jonathan Treitel was born in London in 1959 and trained as a physicist and philosopher. He has lived in San Francisco, New York, Paris, Jerusalem and Tokyo and has travelled in seventy countries. His stories have appeared in the *New Yorker*, on BBC Radio and in numerous British magazines and anthologies. He is also currently writing a collection of poems, a screenplay about Freud and angels, and a non-fiction book on the subject of time.

William Trevor was born in Mitchelstown, Co. Cork, in 1928 and spent his childhood in provincial Ireland. He attended a number of Irish schools and later Trinity College, Dublin. Among his books are *The Old Boys* (1964), winner of the Hawthornden Prize, *The Boarding House* (1965), *Mrs Eckdorf in O'Neill's Hotel* (1969), *Elizabeth Alone* (1973), *The Children of Dynmouth* (1976), winner of the Whitbread Award, *Fools of Fortune* (1983), winner of the Whitbread Award, *The Silence in the Garden* (1988), winner of the *Yorkshire Post* Book of the Year Award, and *Two Lives* (1991) which includes the Booker-shortlisted novella, *Reading Turgenev*, and *Felicia's Journey* (1994). His short stories have been published by Penguin in *Collected Stories*, together with stories not included in previous collections. He edited *The Oxford Book of Short Stories* (1989) and has also written plays for radio and television. In 1976 he received the Allied Irish Banks' Prize and in 1977 he was made an honorary CBE in recognition of his services to literature. In 1992 he received the *Sunday Times* award for literary excellence.

Patricia Tyrrell was educated in Norfolk and at Montgomery College, USA, and has worked as a nurse, civil servant, cook-housekeeper and flea-market stallholder. Her short stories have been widely published in magazines and anthologies and have won prizes in a number of competitions, including the international competitions held by *Stand Magazine* and Bridport Arts. She has also received an Ian St James Award. She lives in Cornwall and is currently finishing a novel.

Fay Weldon spent her childhood in New Zealand, went to a Scottish university, and now lives and works in London. Though writing mostly fiction – her novels, stories and stage-plays are translated into most world languages – she is also a journalist and critic, a member of the Royal Society of Literature, and a past Chairperson of the Booker Prize. Her most notable novel – *The Life and Loves of a She Devil* – became both a successful, and much repeated, TV serial, and a Hollywood film starring Roseanne Arnold and Meryl Streep. Her latest novel – *Splitting* – is soon to be published.

Susan Wicks was born in Kent in 1947 and studied French at the Universities of Hull and Sussex where she wrote a D.Phil. thesis on the fiction of André Gide. She has since lived in France, Ireland and the United States. Her first collection of poems, *Singing Underwater* (Faber, 1992), won the Aldeburgh Poetry Festival Prize and was a Poetry Book Society Recommendation. Her second, *Open Diagnosis*, was published in 1994. She was one of the Poetry Society's 'New

Generation Poets' in 1994 and lives in Kent with her husband and two daughters.

BOOKER

KEY LINKS IN THE FOOD CHAIN

WE BELIEVE
IN FOOD
FOR THOUGHT